PARANOIA

ALSO BY JOSEPH FINDER

FICTION

The Moscow Club

Extraordinary Powers

The Zero Hour

High Crimes

NONFICTION

Red Carpet: The Connection Between the Kremlin and America's Most Powerful Businessmen

PARANOIA

JOSEPH FINDER

ST. MARTIN'S PRESS NEW YORK

 For information, address St. Martin's Press, 175 Fifth Avenue, New York, N.Y. 10010.

www.stmartins.com

Grateful acknowledgment is made for permission to reprint the following material: "Band on the Run." Words and Music by McCartney. © 1974 Paul and Linda McCartney. Administered by MPL Communications, Inc. All Rights Reserved.

Book design by Nick Wunder

Library of Congress Cataloging-in-Publication Data

Finder, Joseph.
Paranoia / Joseph Finder—1st St. Martin's Press ed.
p. cm.
ISBN 0-312-31914-2
1. Business intelligence—Fiction. 2. Success in business—Fiction. 3. Corporate culture—Fiction. 4. Commercial crimes—Fiction. 5. Deception—Fiction. I. Title
PS3556.I458P37 2004
813'.54—dc22 2003058185

First Edition: January 2004

10 9 8 7 6 5 4 3 2 1

This one's for Henry: brother and consigliere
and, as always, for the two girls in my life:
my wife, Michele, and my daughter, Emma.

PART ONE
THE FIX

Fix: A CIA term, of Cold War origin, that refers to a person who is to be compromised or blackmailed so that he will do the Agency's bidding.

—*The Dictionary of Espionage*

1

Until the whole thing happened, I never believed the old line about how you should be careful what you wish for, because you might get it.

I believe it now.

I believe in all those cautionary proverbs now. I believe that pride goeth before a fall. I believe the apple doesn't fall far from the tree, that misfortune seldom comes alone, that all that glitters isn't gold, that lies walk on short legs. Man, you name it. I believe it.

I could try to tell you that what started it all was an act of generosity, but that wouldn't be quite accurate. It was more like an act of stupidity. Call it a cry for help. Maybe more like a raised middle finger. Whatever, it was my bad. I half thought I'd get away with it, half expected to be fired. I've got to say, when I look back on how it all began, I marvel at what an arrogant prick I was. I'm not going to deny that I got what I deserved. It just wasn't what I expected—but who'd ever expect something like this?

All I did was make a couple of phone calls. Impersonated the VP for Corporate Events and called the fancy outside caterer that did all of Wyatt Telecom's parties. I told them to just make it exactly like the bash they'd done the week before for the Top Salesman of the Year award. (Of course, I had no idea how lavish that was.) I gave them all the right disbursement numbers, authorized the transfer of funds in advance. The whole thing was surprisingly easy.

The owner of Meals of Splendor told me he'd never done a function on a company loading dock, that it presented "décor challenges," but I knew he wasn't going to turn away a big check from Wyatt Telecom.

Somehow I doubt Meals of Splendor had ever done a retirement party for an assistant foreman either.

I think that's what really pissed Wyatt off. Paying for Jonesie's retirement party—a *loading dock guy, for Christ's sake!*—was a violation of the natural order. If instead I'd used the money as a down payment on a Ferrari 360 Modena convertible, Nicholas Wyatt might have almost understood. He would have recognized my greed as evidence of our shared humanity, like a weakness for booze, or "broads," as he called women.

If I'd known how it would all end up, would I have done it all over again? Hell, no.

Still, I have to say, it was pretty cool. I was into the fact that Jonesie's party was being paid for out of a fund earmarked for, among other things, an "offsite" for the CEO and his senior vice presidents at the Guanahani resort on the island of St. Barthélemy.

I also loved seeing the loading dock guys finally getting a taste of how the execs lived. Most of the guys and their wives, whose idea of a splurge was the Shrimp Feast at the Red Lobster or Ribs On The Barbie at Outback Steakhouse, didn't know what to make of some of the weird food, the osetra caviar and saddle of veal Provençal, but they devoured the filet of beef en croûte, the rack of lamb, the roasted lobster with ravioli. The ice sculptures were a big hit. The Dom Perignon flowed, though not as fast as the Budweiser. (This I called right, since I used to hang out on the loading dock on Friday afternoons, smoking, when someone, usually Jonesie or Jimmy Connolly, the foreman, brought in an Igloo of cold ones to celebrate the end of another week.)

Jonesie, an old guy with one of those weathered, hangdog faces that make people like him instantly, was lit the whole night. His wife of forty-two years, Esther, at first seemed standoffish, but she turned out to be an amazing dancer. I'd hired an excellent Jamaican reggae group, and everyone got into it, even the guys you'd never expect to dance.

This was after the big tech meltdown, of course, and companies everywhere were laying people off and instituting "frugality" policies, meaning you had to pay for the lousy coffee, and no more free Cokes in the break room, and like that. Jonesie was slated to just stop work one Friday, spend a few hours at HR signing forms, and go home for the rest of his life, no party, no nothing. Meanwhile, the Wyatt Telecom E-staff was planning to head down to St. Bart's in their Learjets, boink their wives or girlfriends in their private villas, slather coconut oil on their love handles, and discuss companywide frugality policies over obscene buffet breakfasts of papayas and hummingbird tongues. Jonesie and his friends didn't really question too closely who was paying for it all. But it did give me some kind of twisted secret pleasure.

Until around one-thirty in the morning, when the sound of electric guitars and the screams of a couple of the younger guys, blotto out of their minds, must have attracted the curiosity of a security guard, a fairly new hire (the pay's lousy, turnover is unbelievable) who didn't know any of us and wasn't inclined to cut anyone any slack.

He was a pudgy guy with a flushed, sort of Porky Pig face, barely thirty. He just gripped his walkie-talkie as if it were a Glock and said, "What the hell?"

And my life as I knew it was over.

2

The voice mail was waiting for me when I got in to work, late as usual.

Even later than usual, actually. I felt queasy and my head thudded and my heart was going too fast from the giant cup of cheap coffee I'd gulped down on the subway. A wave of acid splashed over my stomach. I'd considered calling in sick, but that little voice of sanity in my head told me that after the events of last night the wiser thing to do was to show up at work and face the music.

Thing is, I fully expected to get fired—almost looked forward to it, the way you might both dread and look forward to having an aching tooth drilled. When I came out of the elevator and walked the half-mile through the lower forty of the cubicle farm to my workstation, I could see heads popping up, prairie-dog style, to catch a glimpse of me. I was a celebrity; the word was out. E-mail was no doubt flying.

My eyes were bloodshot, my hair was a mess, I looked like a walking JUST SAY NO public service spot.

The little LCD screen display on my IP phone said, "You have eleven voice mails." I put it on speaker and zipped through them. Just listening to the messages, frantic and sincere and wheedling, increased the pressure behind my eyeballs. I got out the Advil bottle from the bottom desk drawer and dry-swallowed two. That made six Advils already this morning, which exceeded the recommended maximum. So what could happen to me? Die from an ibuprofen overdose just moments before being fired?

I was a junior product line manager for routers in our Enterprise Division. You don't want the English translation, it's too mind-numbingly boring. I spent my days hearing phrases like "dynamic bandwidth circuit emulation service" and "integrated access device" and "ATM backbones" and "IP security tunneling protocol," and I swear I didn't know what half the shit meant.

A message from a guy in Sales named Griffin, calling me "big guy," boasting of how he'd just sold a couple dozen of the routers I was managing by assuring the customer that they'd have a particular feature—extra multicast protocols for live video streaming—that he knew damned well it didn't have. But it sure would be nice if the feature was added to the product, like maybe in the next two weeks, before the product was supposed to ship. Yeah, dream on.

A follow-up call five minutes later from Griffin's manager just "checking on the progress of the multicast protocol work we heard you're doing," as if I actually did the technical work myself.

And the clipped, important voice of a man named Arnold Meacham, who identified himself as Director of Corporate Security and asked me to please "come by" his office the moment I got in.

I had no idea who Arnold Meacham was, beyond his title. I'd never heard his name before. I didn't even know where Corporate Security was located.

It's funny: when I heard the message, my heart didn't start racing like you might expect. It actually slowed, as if my body knew the gig was up. There was actually something Zen going on, the inner serenity of realizing there's nothing you can do anyway. I almost luxuriated in the moment.

For a few minutes I stared at my cubicle walls, the nubby charcoal Avora fabric that looked like the wall-to-wall in my dad's apartment. I kept the panel walls free of any evidence of human habitation—no photos of the wife and kids (easy, since I didn't have any), no Dilbert cartoons, nothing clever or ironic that said I was here under protest, because I was way beyond that. I had one bookshelf, holding a routing protocol reference guide and four thick black binders containing the "feature library" for the MG-50K router. I would not miss this cubicle.

Besides, it wasn't like I was about to get shot; I'd *already* been shot, I figured. Now it was just a matter of disposing of the body and swabbing up the blood. I remember once in college reading about the guillotine in French history, and how one executioner, a medical doctor, tried this gruesome experiment (you get your kicks wherever you can, I guess). A few seconds after the head was lopped off he watched the eyes and lips twitch and spasm until the eyelids closed and everything stopped. Then he called out the dead man's name, and the eyes on the decapitated head popped open and stared right at the executioner. A few seconds more and the eyes closed, then the doctor called the man's name again, and the eyes came open again, staring. Cute. So thirty seconds after being separated from the body, the head's still reacting. This was how I felt. The blade had already dropped, and they're calling my name.

I picked up the phone and called Arnold Meacham's office, told his assistant that I was on my way, and asked how to get there.

My throat was dry, so I stopped at the break room to get one of the formerly-free-but-now-fifty-cent sodas. The break room was all the way back in the middle of the floor near the bank of elevators, and as I walked, in a weird sort of fugue state, a couple more colleagues caught sight of me and turned away quickly, embarrassed.

I surveyed the sweaty glass case of sodas, decided against my usual Diet Pepsi—I really didn't need more caffeine right now—and pulled out a Sprite. Just to be a rebel I didn't leave any money in the jar. Whoa, that'll show *them*. I popped it open and headed for the elevator.

I hated my job, truly despised it, so the thought of losing it wasn't exactly bumming me out. On the other hand, it wasn't as if I had a trust fund, and I sure did need the money. That was the whole point, wasn't it? I had moved back here essentially to help with my dad's medical care—my dad, who considered me a fuckup. In Manhattan, bartending, I made half the money but lived better. We're talking Manhattan! Here I was living in a ratty street-level studio apartment on Pearl Street that reeked of traffic exhaust, and whose windows rattled when the trucks rumbled by at five in the morning. Granted, I was able to go out a couple of nights a week with friends, but I usually ended up dipping into my checking account's credit line a week or so before my paycheck magically appeared on the fifteenth of the month.

Not that I was exactly busting my ass either. I coasted. I put in the minimum required hours, got in late and left early, but I got my work done. My performance review numbers weren't so good—I was a "core contributor," a two band, just one step up from "lowest contributor," when you should start packing your stuff.

I got into the elevator, looked down at what I was wearing—black jeans and a gray polo shirt, sneakers—and wished I'd put on a tie.

3

When you work at a big corporation, you never know what to believe. There's always a lot of tough, scary macho talk. They're always telling you about "killing the competition," putting a "stake in their heart." They tell you to "kill or be killed," "eat or be eaten," to "eat their lunch" and "eat your own dog food" and "eat your young."

You're a software engineer or a product manager or a sales associate, but after a while you start to think that somehow you got mixed up with one of those aboriginal tribes in Papua New Guinea that wear boar's tusks through their noses and gourds on their dicks. When the reality is that if you e-mail an off-color, politically incorrect joke to your buddy in IT, who then cc's it to a guy a few cubicles over, you can end up locked in a sweaty HR conference room for a grueling week of Diversity Training. Filch paper clips and you get slapped with the splintered ruler of life.

Thing is, of course, I'd done something a little more serious than raiding the office-supply cabinet.

They kept me waiting in an outer office for half an hour, forty-five minutes, but it seemed longer. There was nothing to read—just *Security Management*, stuff like that. The receptionist wore her ash-blond hair in a helmet, yellow smoker's circles under her eyes. She answered the phone, tapped away at a keyboard, glanced over at me furtively from time to time, the way you might try to catch a glimpse of a grisly car accident while you're trying to keep your eyes on the road.

I sat there so long my confidence began to waver. That might have been the point. The monthly paycheck thing was beginning to look like a good idea. Maybe defiance wasn't the best approach. Maybe I should eat shit. Maybe it was way past that.

Arnold Meacham didn't get up when the receptionist brought me in. He sat behind a giant black desk that looked like polished granite. He was around forty, thin and broad, a Gumby build, with a long square head, long thin nose, no lips. Graying brown hair that was receding. He wore a double-breasted blue blazer and a blue striped tie, like the president of a yacht club. He glared at me through oversized steel aviator glasses. You could tell he was totally humorless. In a chair to the right of his desk sat a woman a few years older than me who seemed to be taking notes. His office was big and spare, lots of framed diplomas on the wall. At one end, a half-opened door let onto a darkened conference room.

"So you're Adam Cassidy," he said. He had a prissy, precise way of speaking. "Party down, dude?" He pressed his lips into a smirk.

Oh, God. This was not going to go well. "What can I do for you?" I said. I tried to look perplexed, concerned.

"What can you *do* for me? How about start with telling the truth? *That's* what you can do for me." He had the slightest trace of a Southern accent.

Generally people like me. I'm pretty good at winning them over—the pissed-off math teacher, the enterprise customer whose order is six weeks overdue, you name it. But I could see at once this wasn't a Dale Carnegie moment. The odds of salvaging my odious job were dwindling by the second.

"Sure," I said. "The truth about what?"

He snorted with amusement. "How about last night's catered event?"

I paused, considered. "You're talking about the little retirement party?" I said. I didn't know how much they knew, since I'd been pretty careful about the money trail. I had to watch what I said. The woman with the notebook, a slight woman with frizzy red hair and big green eyes, was probably there as a witness. "It was a much-needed morale boost," I added. "Believe me, sir, it'll do wonders for departmental productivity."

His lipless mouth curled. " 'Morale boost.' Your fingerprints are all over the funding for that 'morale boost.' "

"Funding?"

"Oh, cut the crap, Cassidy."

"I'm not sure I'm understanding you, sir."

"Do you think I'm *stupid?*" Six feet of fake granite between him and me and I could feel droplets of his spittle.

"I'm guessing . . . no, sir." The trace of a smile appeared at the corner of my mouth. I couldn't help it: pride of workmanship. Big mistake.

Meacham's pasty face flushed. "You think it's funny, hacking into proprietary company databases to obtain confidential disbursement numbers? You think it's recreation, it's *clever?* It doesn't *count?*"

"No, sir—"

"You lying sack of shit, you *prick,* it's no better than stealing an old lady's purse on the fucking subway!"

I tried to look chastened, but I could see where this conversation was going and it seemed pointless.

"You stole *seventy-eight thousand dollars* from the Corporate Events account for a goddamned party for your buddies on the *loading dock?*"

I swallowed hard. Shit. Seventy-eight thousand dollars? I knew it was pretty high-end, but I had no idea how high-end.

"This guy in on it with you?"

"Who do you mean? I think maybe you're confused about—"

" 'Jonesie'? The old guy, the name on the cake?"

"Jonesie had nothing to do with it," I shot back.

Meacham leaned back, looking triumphant because he'd finally found a toehold.

"If you want to fire me, go ahead, but Jonesie was totally innocent."

"Fire you?" Meacham looked as if I'd said something in Serbo-Croatian. "You think I'm talking about *firing* you? You're a smart guy, you're good at computers and math, you can add, right? So maybe you can add up these numbers. Embezzling funds, that gets you five years of imprisonment and a two-hundred-fifty-thousand-dollar fine. Wire fraud and mail fraud, that's another five years in prison, but wait—if the fraud affects a financial institution—and lucky you, you fucked with our bank *and* the recipient bank, your lucky day, you little shit—that brings it up to thirty years in prison and a one-million-dollar fine. You tracking? What's that, thirty-five years in prison? And we haven't even got into forgery and computer crimes, gathering information in a protected computer to steal data, that'll get you anywhere from one year to twenty years in prison and more fines. So what have we got so far, forty, fifty, *fifty-five* years in prison? You're twenty-six now, you'll be, let's see, *eighty-one* when you get out."

Now I was sweating through my polo shirt, I felt cold and clammy. My legs were trembling. "But," I began, my voice hoarse, then cleared my throat. "Seventy-eight thousand dollars is a rounding error in a thirty-billion-dollar corporation."

"I suggest you shut your fucking mouth," Meacham said quietly. "We've consulted our lawyers, and they're confident they can get a charge of embezzlement in a court of law. Furthermore, you were clearly in a position to do more, and we believe that was just one installment in an ongoing scheme to defraud Wyatt Telecommunications, part of a pattern of multiple withdrawals and diversions. It's just the tip of the iceberg." For the first time he turned to the mousy woman taking notes. "We're off the record now." He turned back to me. "The U.S. Attorney was a college roommate of our house counsel, Mr. Cassidy, and we have every assurance he intends to throw the book at you. Plus, the district attorney's office, you may not have noticed, is on a white-collar crime campaign, and they're looking to make an example out of someone. They want a poster child, Cassidy."

I stared at him. My headache was back. I felt a trickle of sweat run down the inside of my shirt from my armpit to my waist.

"We've got both the state and the feds in our corner. We've *got* you, pure and simple. Now it's just a matter of how hard we're going to hit you, how much destruction we want to do. And don't imagine you're going to some country club, either. Cute young guy like you, you're going to be bent over the bunk someplace in Marion Federal Penitentiary. You're going to come out a toothless old man. And in case you're not current on our criminal justice system, there's no longer any parole at the federal level. Your life just changed as of this moment. You're fucked, pal." He looked at the woman with the notebook. "We're back on the record now. Let's hear what you have to say, and you'd better make it good."

I swallowed, but my saliva had stopped flowing. I saw flashes of white around the edges of my vision. He was dead serious.

In my high school and college years I got stopped fairly often for speeding, and I developed a reputation as a virtuoso at getting out of tickets. The trick is to make the cop feel your pain. It's psychological warfare. That's why they wear mirrored sunglasses, so you can't look into their eyes while you're pleading. They're human beings too, even cops. I used to keep a couple of law-enforcement textbooks on the front seat and tell them I was studying to be a police officer and I sure hoped this ticket wouldn't hurt my chances. Or I'd show them a prescription bottle and tell them I was in a rush because I needed to get mom her epilepsy medication as quickly as possible. Basically I learned that if you're going to start, you have to go all the way; you have to totally put your heart into it.

We were way beyond salvaging my job. I couldn't shake the image of that bunk at Marion Federal Penitentiary. I was scared shitless.

So I'm not proud of what I had to do, but you see, I had no choice. Either I reached deep inside and spun my very best tale for this security creep, or I was going to be someone's prison bitch.

I took a deep breath. "Look," I said, "I'm going to level with you."

"About time."

"Here's the thing. Jonesie—well, Jonesie has cancer."

Meacham smirked and leaned back in his chair, like, Entertain me.

I sighed, chewed the inside of my cheek like I was spilling something I really didn't want to. "Pancreatic cancer. Inoperable."

Meacham stared at me, stonefaced.

"He got the diagnosis three weeks ago. I mean, there's nothing they can do about it—the guy's dying. And so Jonesie, you know—well, you don't know him, but he's always putting on a brave front. He says to the oncologist, 'You mean I can stop flossing?' " I gave a sad smile. "That's Jonesie."

The note-taking woman stopped for a moment, actually looked stricken, then went back to her notes.

Meacham licked his lips. Was I getting to him? I couldn't really tell. I had to amp it up, really go for it.

"There's no reason you should know any of this," I went on. "I mean, Jonesie's not exactly an important guy around here. He's not a VP or anything, he's just a loading dock guy. But he's important to me, because . . ." I closed my eyes for a few seconds, inhaled deeply. "The thing is—I never wanted to tell anyone this, it was like our secret, but Jonesie's my father."

Meacham's chair slowly came forward. Now he was paying attention.

"Different last name and all—my mom changed my name to hers when she left him like twenty years ago, took me with her. I was a kid, I didn't know any better. But Dad, he . . ." I bit my lower lip. I had tears in my eyes now. "He kept on supporting us, worked two, sometimes three jobs. Never asked for anything. Mom didn't want him to see me at all, but on Christmas . . ." A sharp intake of breath, almost a hiccup. "Dad came by the house every Christmas, sometimes he'd ring the doorbell for an hour out in the freezing cold before Mom let him come in. Always had a present for me, some big expensive thing he couldn't afford. Later on, when Mom said she couldn't afford to send me to college, not on a nurse's salary, Dad started sending money. He—he said he wanted me to have the life he never had. Mom never gave him any respect, and she'd sort of poisoned me against him, you know? So I never even thanked the guy. I didn't even invite him to graduation, 'cause I knew Mom wouldn't feel comfortable with him around, but he showed up anyway, I saw him sort of hanging around, wearing some ugly old suit—I never saw him wear a suit or a tie before, he must have got it at the Salvation Army, because he really wanted to see me graduate from college, and he didn't want to embarrass me."

Meacham's eyes actually seemed to be getting moist. The woman had stopped taking notes, and was just watching me, blinking back tears.

I was on a roll. Meacham deserved my best, and he was getting it. "When I started working here at Wyatt, I never expected to find Dad working on the fucking *loading* dock. It was like the greatest accident. Mom died a couple of years ago, and here I am, connecting up with my father, this sweet wonderful guy who never ever asked anything from me, never demanded anything, working his fucking fingers to the bone, supporting a goddamned ungrateful son he never got to see. It's like fate, you know? And then when he gets this news, he's got inoperable pancreatic cancer, and he starts talking about killing himself before the cancer gets him, I mean . . ."

The note-taking woman reached for a Kleenex and blew her nose. She was glowering at Arnold Meacham now. Meacham winced.

I whispered, "I just had to show him what he meant to me—what he meant to all of us. I guess like it was my own sort of Make-a-Wish Foundation. I told him—I told him I'd hit the trifecta at the track, I didn't want him to know or to worry or anything. I mean, believe me, what I did was wrong, totally wrong. It was wrong in a hundred different ways, I'm not going to bullshit you. But maybe in just one small way it was right." The woman reached for another Kleenex and looked at Meacham as if he were the scum of the earth. Meacham was looking down, flushed and unable to meet my gaze. I was giving *myself* chills.

Then from the shadowed far end of the office I heard a door open and what sounded like clapping. Slow, loud clapping.

It was Nicholas Wyatt, the founder and CEO of Wyatt Telecommunications. He approached as he clapped, smiling broadly. "Brilliant performance," he said. "Absolutely brilliant."

I looked up, startled, then shook my head sorrowfully. Wyatt was a tall man, around six foot six, with a wrestler's build. He just got bigger and bigger as he got closer until, standing a few feet away from me, he seemed larger than life. Wyatt was known as a sharp dresser, and sure enough, he was wearing some kind of Armani-looking gray suit with a subtle pinstripe. He wasn't just powerful, he *looked* powerful.

"Mr. Cassidy, let me ask you a question."

I didn't know what to do, so I stood up, extended my hand to shake.

Wyatt didn't shake my hand. "What's Jonesie's first name?"

I hesitated, a beat too long. "Al," I finally said.

"Al? As in—what?"

"Al—Alan," I said. "Albert. Shit."

Meacham stared at me.

"Details, Cassidy," Wyatt said. "They'll fuck you over every time. But I have to say, you moved me—you really did. The part about the Salvation Army suit really got me right here." He tapped his chest with a fist. "Extraordinary."

I grinned sheepishly, really feeling like a tool. "The guy here said to make it good."

Wyatt smiled. "You're a supremely gifted young man, Cassidy. A goddamned Scheherazade. And I think we should have a talk."

4

Nicholas Wyatt was one scary dude. I had never met him before, but I'd seen him on TV, on CNBC, and on the corporate Web site, the video messages he'd recorded. I'd even caught a few glimpses of him, live, in my three years working for the company he founded. Up close he was even more intimidating. He had a deep tan, shoe polish–black hair that was gelled and combed straight back. His teeth were perfectly even and Vegas-white.

He was fifty-six but didn't look it, whatever fifty-six is supposed to look like. Anyway, he sure didn't look like my dad at fifty-six, a paunchy, balding old man even in his so-called prime. This was some other fifty-six.

I had no idea why he was here. What could the CEO of the company threaten me with that Meacham hadn't already pulled out? Death by a thousand paper cuts? Being eaten alive by wild boar?

Secretly I had this fleeting fantasy that he was going to high-five me, congratulate me for pulling off a good one, say he liked my spirit, my moxie. But that sad little daydream shriveled as quickly as it popped into my desperate mind. Nicholas Wyatt wasn't some basketball-playing priest. He was a vindictive son of a bitch.

I'd heard stories. I knew that if you had any brains you made a point of avoiding him. You kept your head down, tried not to attract his attention. He was famous for his rages, his tantrums and shouting matches. He was known to fire people on the spot, have Security pack up their desks, have them escorted out of the building. At his executive staff meetings he always picked one person to humiliate the whole time. You didn't go to him with bad news, and you didn't waste a split second of his time. If you were unlucky enough to have to make some PowerPoint presentation to him, you'd rehearse it and rehearse it until it was perfect, but if there was a single glitch in your presentation, he'd interrupt you, shouting, "I don't *believe* this!"

People said he'd mellowed a lot since the early years, but from what? He was viciously competitive, a weightlifter and triathlete. Guys who worked out in the company gym said he was always challenging the serious jocks to chin-up competitions. He never lost, and when the other guy gave up he'd taunt, "Want me to keep going?" They said he had the body of Arnold Schwarzenegger, like a brown condom stuffed with walnuts.

Not only was he insane about winning, for him it wasn't sweet unless he also got to ridicule the loser. At a companywide Christmas party he once wrote the name of his chief competitor, Trion Systems, on a wine bottle, and smashed it against the wall, to a lot of drunken cheering and catcalls.

He ran a high-testosterone shop. His top guys all dressed like he did, in seven-thousand-dollar suits by Armani or Prada or Brioni or Kiton or other designers I hadn't even heard of. And they put up with his shit because they were disgustingly well compensated for it. The joke about him that everybody's heard by now: What's the difference between God and Nicholas Wyatt? God doesn't think he's Nicholas Wyatt.

Nick Wyatt slept three hours a night, seemed to eat nothing but Power Bars for breakfast and lunch, was a nuclear reactor of nervous energy, perspired heavily. People called him "The Exterminator." He managed by fear and never forgot a slight. When an ex-friend of his got fired as CEO of some big tech company, he sent a wreath of black roses—his assistants always knew where to get black roses. The quote he's famous for, the one thing he repeated so often it should have been carved in granite above the main entrance, made into a screen saver on everyone's desktop, was "Of course I'm paranoid. I want everyone who works for me to be paranoid. Success *demands* paranoia."

I followed Wyatt down the hall from Corporate Security to his executive suite, and it was hard to keep up with him—he was a power-walker. I had to almost run. Behind me followed Meacham, swinging a black leather portfolio like a baton. As we approached the executive area, the walls went from white plasterboard to mahogany; the carpeting became soft and deep-pile. We were at his office, his lair.

His matched set of admins looked up and beamed at him as we caravaned through. One blonde, one black. He said, "Linda, Yvette," as if captioning them. I wasn't surprised they were both fashion-model beautiful—everything here was high-end, like the walls and the carpeting and the furniture. I wondered if their job description included nonclerical responsibilities, like blowjobs. That was the rumor, anyway.

Wyatt's office was vast. An entire Bosnian village could live there. Two of the walls were glass, floor to ceiling, and the views of the city were unbelievable. The other walls were fancy dark wood, covered with framed things, magazine covers with his mug on them, *Fortune, Forbes, Business Week.* I looked, goggle-eyed, as I half walked, half ran by. A photo of him and some other guys with the late Princess Diana. Him with both George Bushes.

He led us to a "conversation group" of tufted black leather chairs and sofa that looked like they belonged in MOMA. He sank down at one end of the enormous sofa.

My head was spinning. I was disoriented, in another world. I couldn't imagine why I was here, in Nicholas Wyatt's office. Maybe he'd been one of those boys who liked to pull the legs off insects one by one with tweezers, then burn them to death with a magnifying glass.

"So this is some pretty elaborate scam you pulled off," he said. "Very impressive."

I smiled, ducked my head modestly. Denial wasn't even an option. *Thank God,* I thought. It looked like we were going the high-five, moxie route.

"But no one kicks me in the balls and walks away, you should know that by now. I mean fucking *nobody.*"

He'd gotten out the tweezers and the magnifying glass.

"So what's your deal, you've been a PLM here for three years, your performance reviews suck, you haven't gotten a raise or a promotion the whole time you've been here; you're going through the motions, phoning it in. Not exactly an ambitious guy, are you?" He talked fast, which made me even more nervous.

I smiled again. "I guess not. I sort of have other priorities."

"Like?"

I hesitated. He'd got me. I shrugged.

"Everyone's got to be passionate about *something,* or they're not worth shit. You're obviously not passionate about your work, so what *are* you passionate about?"

I'm almost never speechless, but this time I couldn't think of anything clever to say. Meacham was watching me too, a nasty, sadistic little smile on his knife-blade face. I was thinking that I knew guys in the company, in my business unit, who were always scheming how to get thirty seconds with Wyatt, in an elevator or at a product launch or whatever. They'd even prepared an "elevator pitch." Here I was in the big guy's office and I was silent as a mannequin.

"You an actor or something in your spare time?"

I shook my head.

"Well, you're good, anyway. A regular Marlon fucking Brando. You may suck at marketing routers to enterprise customers, but you are a fucking *Olympic*-level bullshit artist."

"If that's a compliment, sir, thank you."

"I hear you do a damned good Nick Wyatt—that true? Let's see it."

I blushed, shook my head.

"Anyway, bottom line, you ripped me off and you seem to think you're going to get away with it."

I looked appalled. "No, sir, I *don't* think I'm going to 'get away with it.' "

"Spare me. I don't need another demonstration. You had me at hello." He flicked his hand like a Roman emperor, and Meacham handed him a folder. He glanced at it. "Your aptitude scores are in the top percentile. You were an engineering major in college, what kind?"

"Electrical."

"You wanted to be an engineer when you grew up?"

"My dad wanted me to major in something I could get a real job with. I wanted to play lead guitar with Pearl Jam."

"Any good?"

"No," I admitted.

He half-smiled. "You did college on the five-year-plan. What happened?"

"I got kicked out for a year."

"I appreciate your honesty. At least you're not trying that 'junior year abroad' shit. What happened?"

"I pulled a stupid prank. I had a bad semester, so I hacked into the college computer system and changed my transcript. My roommate's too."

"So it's an old trick." He looked at his watch, glanced at Meacham, then back at me. "I've got an idea for you, Adam." I didn't like the way he said my first name; it was creepy. "A very good idea. An extremely generous offer, in fact."

"Thank you, sir." I had no idea what he was talking about, but I knew it couldn't be good or generous.

"What I'm about to say to you I'm going to deny I ever said. In fact, I won't just deny it, I'll fucking sue you for defamation if you ever repeat it, are we clear? I will fucking crush you." Whatever he was talking about, he had the resources. He was a billionaire, like the third or fourth richest man in America, but he had once been number two before our share price collapsed. He wanted to be the richest—he was gunning for Bill Gates—but that didn't seem likely.

My heart thudded. "Sure."

"Are you clear on your situation? Behind door number one you've got the certainty—the fucking *certainty*—of at least twenty years in prison. So it's that, or else whatever's behind the curtain. You want to play Let's Make a Deal?"

I swallowed. "Sure."

"Let me tell you what's behind the curtain, Adam. It's a very nice future for a smart engineering major like you, only you have to play by the rules. My rules."

My face was prickly-hot.

"I want you to take on a special project for me."

I nodded.

"I want you to take a job at Trion."

"At . . . Trion Systems?" I didn't understand.

"In new product marketing. They've got a couple of openings in strategic places in the company."

"They'd never hire me."

"No, you're right, they'd never hire *you*. Not a lazy fuckup like you. But a

Wyatt superstar, a young hotshot who's on the verge of going supernova, they'd hire you in a nanosecond."

"I don't follow."

"Street-smart guy like you? You just lost a couple of IQ points. Come on, dipshit. The Lucid—that was your baby, right?"

He was talking about Wyatt Telecom's flagship product, this all-in-one PDA, sort of a Palm Pilot on steroids. An incredible toy. I had nothing to do with it. I didn't even own one.

"They'd never believe it," I said.

"Listen to me, Adam. I make my biggest business decisions on gut instinct, and my gut tells me you've got the brass balls and the smarts and the talent to do it. You in or out?"

"You want me to report back to you, is that it?"

His eyes bore down on me, steely. "More than that. I want you to get information."

"Like being a spy. A mole or whatever."

He turned his palms open, like, are you a moron or what? "Whatever you want to call it. There's some valuable, uh, *intellectual property* I want to get my hands on inside Trion, and their security is damned near impenetrable. Only a Trion insider can get what I want, and not just any insider. A major player. Either you recruit one, buy one, or you get one in the front door. Here we got a smart, personable young guy, comes highly recommended—I think we got a pretty decent shot."

"And what if I'm caught?"

"You won't be," Wyatt said.

"But if I am . . . ?"

"If you do the job right," Meacham said, "you won't be caught. And if somehow you screw up and you *are* caught—well, we'll be here to protect you."

Somehow I doubted that. "They'll be totally suspicious."

"Of what?" Wyatt said. "In this business people jump from company to company all the time. The top talent gets poached. Low-hanging fruit. You're fresh off a big win at Wyatt, you maybe don't have the juice you think you should, you're looking for more responsibility, a better opportunity, more money—the usual bullshit."

"They'll see right through me."

"Not if you do your job right," said Wyatt. "You're going to have to learn product marketing, you're going to have to be fucking brilliant, you're going to have to work harder than you've ever worked in your whole sorry life. Really bust your ass. Only a major player's going to get what I want. Try your phone-it-in shit at Trion, you'll either get shot or shoved aside, and then our little experiment is over. And you get door number one."

"I thought new product guys all have to have MBAs."

"Nah, Goddard thinks MBAs are bullshit—one of the few things we agree on. He doesn't have one. Thinks it's limiting. Speaking of limiting." He snapped his fingers, and Meacham handed him something, a small metal box, familiar looking. An Altoids box. He popped it open. Inside were a few white pills that looked like aspirin but weren't. Definitely familiar. "You're going to have to cut out this shit, this Ecstasy or whatever you call it." I kept the Altoids box on my coffee table at home; I wondered when and how they got it, but I was too dazed to be pissed off. He dropped the box into a little black leather trash can next to the couch. It made a *thunk* sound. "Same with pot, booze, all that shit. You're going to have to straighten up and fly right, guy."

That seemed like the least of my problems. "And what if I don't get hired?"

"Door number one." He gave an ugly smile. "And don't pack your golf shoes. Pack your K-Y."

"Even if I give it my best shot?"

"Your job is not to blow it. With the quals we're giving you, and with a coach like me, you won't have any excuse."

"What kind of money are we talking about?"

"What kind of *money?* The fuck do I know? Believe me, it'll be a hell of a lot more than you get here. Six figures anyway." I tried not to gulp visibly.

"Plus my salary here."

He turned his tight face over to me and gave me a dead stare. He didn't have any expression in his eyes. *Botox?* I wondered. "You're shitting me."

"I'm taking an enormous risk."

"Excuse me? *I'm* the one taking the risk. You're a total fucking black box, a big fat question mark."

"If you really thought so, you wouldn't ask me to do it."

He turned to Meacham. "I don't believe this shit."

Meacham looked like he'd swallowed a turd. "You little prick," he said. "I ought to pick up the phone right now—"

Wyatt held up an imperial hand. "That's okay. He's ballsy. I like ballsy. You get hired, you do your job right, you get to double-dip. But if you fuck up—"

"I know," I said. "Door number one. Let me think it over, get back to you tomorrow."

Wyatt's jaw dropped, his eyes blank. He paused, then said, all icy: "I'll give you till nine A.M. When the U.S. Attorney gets into his office."

"I advise you not to say a word about this to any of your buddies, your father, anybody," Meacham put in. "Or you won't know what hit you."

"I understand," I replied. "No need to threaten me."

"Oh, that's not a threat," said Nicholas Wyatt. "That's a promise."

5

There didn't seem to be any reason to go back to work, so I went home. It felt strange to be on the subway at one in the afternoon, with the old people and the students, the moms and kids. My head was still spinning, and I felt queasy.

My apartment was a good ten-minute walk from the subway stop. It was a bright day, ridiculously cheerful.

My shirt was still damp and gave off a funky sweat smell. A couple of young girls in overalls and multiple piercings were tugging a bunch of little kids around on a long rope. The kids squealed. Some black guys were playing basketball with their shirts off, on an asphalt playground behind a chain-link fence. The bricks on the sidewalk were uneven, and I almost tripped, then I felt that sickening slickness underfoot as I stepped in dog shit. Perfect symbolism.

The entrance to my apartment smelled strongly of urine, either from a cat or a bum. The mail hadn't come yet. My keys jingled as I unlocked the three locks on my apartment door. The old lady in the unit across the hall opened her door a crack, the length of her security chain, then slammed it; she was too short to reach the peephole. I gave her a friendly wave.

The room was dark even though the blinds were wide open. The air was stifling, smelled of stale cigarettes. Since the apartment was street level, I couldn't leave the windows open during the day to air it out.

My furnishings were pretty pathetic: the one room was dominated by a greenish tartan-plaid sleeper sofa, high-backed, beer-encrusted, gold threads woven throughout. It faced a Sanyo nineteen-inch TV that was missing the remote. A tall narrow unfinished-pine bookcase stood lonely in one corner. I sat down on the sofa, and a cloud of dust rose in the air. The steel bar underneath the cushion hurt my ass. I thought of Nicholas Wyatt's black leather sofa and wondered if he'd ever lived in such a dump. The story was that he came up from nothing, but I didn't believe it; I couldn't see him ever living in such a rat hole. I found the Bic lighter under the glass coffee table, lighted a cigarette, looked over at the pile of bills on the table. I didn't even open the envelopes anymore. I had two MasterCards and three Visas, and they all had whopping balances, and I could barely even make the minimum payments.

I had already made up my mind, of course.

6

"You get busted?"

Seth Marcus, my best buddy since junior high school, bartended three nights a week at a sort of yuppie dive called Alley Cat. During the days he was a paralegal at a downtown law firm. He said he needed the money, but I was convinced that secretly he was bartending in order to maintain some vestige of coolness, to keep from turning into the sort of corporate dweeb we both liked to make fun of.

"Busted for what?" How much had I told him? Did I tell him about the call from Meacham, the security director? I hoped not. Now I couldn't tell him a goddamned thing about the vise they'd got me in.

"Your big party." It was loud, I couldn't hear him well, and someone down at the other end of the bar was whistling, two fingers in his mouth, loud and shrill. "That guy whistling at *me?* Like I'm a fucking *dog?*" He ignored the whistler.

I shook my head.

"You got away with it, huh? You actually pulled it off, amazing. What can I get you to celebrate?"

"Brooklyn Brown?"

He shook his head. "Nah."

"Newcastle? Guinness?"

"How about a draft? They don't keep track of those."

I shrugged. "Sure."

He pulled me a draft, yellow and soapy: he was clearly new at this. It sloshed on the scarred wooden bar top. He was a tall, dark-haired, good-looking guy—a veritable chick magnet—with a ridiculous goatee and an earring. He was half-Jewish but wanted to be black. He played and sang in a band called Slither, which I'd heard a couple of times; they weren't very good, but he talked a lot about "signing a deal." He had a dozen scams going at once just so he wouldn't have to admit he was a working stiff.

Seth was the only guy I knew who was more cynical than me. That was probably why we were friends. That plus the fact that he didn't give me shit about my father, even though he used to play on the high school football team coached (and tyrannized) by Frank Cassidy. In seventh grade we were in the same homeroom, liked each other instantly because we were both singled out for ridicule by the math teacher, Mr. Pasquale. In ninth grade I left the public school and went to Bartholomew Browning & Knightley, the fancy prep school where my dad had just been hired as the football and hockey coach and I now got free tuition. For two years I rarely saw Seth, until Dad got fired for breaking two bones in a kid's right forearm and one bone in his left forearm. The kid's mother was head of the board of overseers of Bartholomew Browning. So the free tuition tap got shut off, and I went back to the public school. Dad got hired there too, after Bartholomew Browning.

We both worked at the same Gulf station in high school, until Seth got tired of the holdups and went to Dunkin' Donuts to make donuts on the overnight. For a couple of summers he and I worked cleaning windows for a company that did a lot of downtown skyscrapers, until we decided that dangling from ropes on the twenty-seventh floor sounded cooler than it actually was. Not only was it boring, but it was scary as hell, a lousy combination. Maybe some people consider hanging off the side of a building hundreds of feet up some kind of extreme sport, but to me it seemed more like a slow-motion suicide attempt.

The whistling grew louder. People were looking at the whistler, a chubby balding guy in a suit, and some people were giggling.

"I'm going to fucking lose it," Seth said.

"Don't," I said, but it was too late, he was already headed to the other end of the bar. I took out a cigarette and lighted it as I watched him lean over the bar, glowering at the whistler, looking like he was going to grab the guy's lapel but stopping short. He said something. There was some laughter from the whistler's general vicinity. Looking cool and relaxed, Seth headed back this way. He stopped to talk to a pair of beautiful women, a blonde and a brunette, and flashed them a smile.

"There. I don't believe you're still smoking," he said to me. "Fucking stupid, with your dad." He took a cigarette from my pack, lighted it, took a drag and set it down in the ashtray.

"Thank you for not thanking me for not smoking," I said. "So what's *your* excuse?"

He exhaled through his nostrils. "Dude, I like to multitask. Also, cancer doesn't run in my family. Just insanity."

"He doesn't have cancer."

"Emphysema. Whatever the fuck. How is the old man?"

"Fine." I shrugged. I didn't want to go there, and neither did Seth.

"Man, one of those babes wants a Cosmopolitan, the other wants a *frozen drink*. I hate that."

"Why?"

"Too labor-intensive, then they'll tip me a quarter. Women never tip, I've learned this. Jesus, you crack two Buds, you make a couple of bucks. Frozen drinks!" He shook his head. "Man."

He went off for a couple of minutes, banging things around, the blender screaming. Served the girls their drinks with one of his killer smiles. They weren't going to tip him a quarter. They both turned to look at me and smiled.

When he came back, he said, "What are you doing later?"

"Later?" It was already close to ten, and I had to meet with a Wyatt engineer at seven-thirty in the morning. A couple days training with him, some big shot on the Lucid project, then a couple more days with a new-products marketing manager, and regular sessions with an "executive coach." They'd lined up a vicious schedule. Boot camp for bootlickers, was how I thought of it. No more fucking off, getting in at nine or ten. But I couldn't tell Seth; I couldn't tell anyone.

"I'm done at one," he said. "Those two chicks asked if I wanted to go to Nightcrawler with them after. I told them I had a friend. They just checked you out, they're into it."

"Can't," I said.

"Huh?"

"Got to get to work early. On time, really."

Seth looked alarmed, disbelieving. "What? What's going on?"

"Work's getting serious. Early day tomorrow. Big project."

"This is a joke, right?"

"Unfortunately no. Don't you have to work in the morning too?"

"You becoming one of Them? One of the pod people?"

I grinned. "Time to grow up. No more kid stuff."

Seth looked disgusted. "Dude, it's *never* too late to have a happy childhood."

7

After ten grueling days of tutoring and indoctrination by engineers and product marketing types who'd been involved with the Lucid handheld, my head was stuffed with all kinds of useless information. I was given a tiny "office" in the executive suite that used to be a supply room, though I was almost never there. I showed up dutifully, didn't give anyone any trouble. I didn't know how long I'd be able to keep this up without flipping out, but the image of the prison bunk bed at Marion kept me motivated.

Then one morning I was summoned to an office two doors down the executive corridor from Nicholas Wyatt's. The name on the brass plate on the door said JUDITH BOLTON. The office was all white—white rug, white-upholstered furniture, white marble slab for a desk, even white flowers.

On a white leather sofa, Nicholas Wyatt sat next to an attractive, fortyish woman who was chatting away familiarly with him, touching his arm, laughing. Coppery red hair, long legs crossed at the knee, a slender body she obviously worked hard at, dressed in a navy suit. She had blue eyes, glossy heart-shaped lips, brows arched provocatively. She'd obviously once been a knockout, but she'd gotten a little hard.

I realized I'd seen her before, over the last week or so, at Wyatt's side, when he paid his quick visits to my training sessions with marketing guys and engineers. She always seemed to be whispering in his ear, watching me, but we were never introduced, and I'd always wondered who she was.

Without getting up from the couch, she extended a hand as I

approached—long fingers, red nail polish—and gave me a firm, no-nonsense shake.

"Judith Bolton."

"Adam Cassidy."

"You're late," she said.

"I got lost," I said, trying to lighten things up.

She shook her head, smiled, pursed her lips. "You have a problem with punctuality. I don't ever want you to be late again, are we clear?"

I smiled back, the same smile I give cops when they ask if I know how fast I was going. The lady was tough. "Absolutely." I sat down in a chair facing her.

Wyatt was watching the exchange with amusement. "Judith is one of my most valuable players," he said. "My 'executive coach.' My *consigliere,* and your Svengali. I suggest you listen to every fucking word she says. I do." He stood up, excused himself. She gave him a little wave as he left.

You wouldn't have recognized me anymore. I was a changed man. No more Bondomobile: now I drove a silver Audi A6, leased by the company. I had a new wardrobe, too. One of Wyatt's admins, the black one, who turned out to be a former model from the British West Indies, took me clothes shopping one afternoon at a very expensive place I had only seen from the outside, where she said she bought clothes for Nick Wyatt. She picked out some suits, shirts, ties, and shoes, and put it all on a company Amex card. She even bought what she called "hose," meaning socks. And this wasn't the Structure crap I usually wore, it was Armani, Ermenegildo Zegna. They had this aura: you could tell they were handstitched by Italian widows listening to Verdi.

The sideburns—"bugger's grips," she called them—had to go, she decided. Also no more of the scraggly bed-head look. She took me to a fancy salon, and I came out looking like a Ralph Lauren model, only not as fruity. I dreaded next time Seth and I got together; I knew I'd never hear the end of it.

A cover story was devised. My co-workers and managers in the Enterprise Division/Routers were informed that I had been "reassigned." Rumors circulated that I was being sent to Siberia because the manager of my division was tired of my attitude. Another rumor had it that one of Wyatt's senior VPs had admired a memo I'd written and "liked my attitude" and I was being given more responsibility, not less. No one knew the truth. All anyone knew was that one day I was suddenly gone from my cubicle.

If anyone had bothered to look closely at the org chart on the corporate Web site, they'd have noticed my title was now Director of Special Projects, Office of the CEO.

An electronic and paper trail was being created.

Judith turned back to me, continued as if Wyatt had never been there. "*If* you're hired by Trion, you're to arrive at your cube forty-five minutes early. Under no circumstances will you have a drink at lunch or after work. No happy hours, no cocktail parties, no 'hanging out' with 'friends' from work. No partying. If you have to attend a work-related party, drink club soda."

"You make it sound like I'm in AA."

"Getting drunk is a sign of weakness."

"Then I assume smoking's out of the question."

"Wrong," she said. "It's a filthy, disgusting habit, and it indicates a lack of self-control, but there are other considerations. Standing around in the smoking area is an excellent way to cross-pollinate, connect with people in different units, obtain useful intelligence. Now, about your handshake." She shook her head. "You blew it. Hiring decisions are made in the first five seconds—at the handshake. Anyone who tells you anything else is lying to you. You get the job with the handshake, and then the rest of the job interview you fight to keep it, to not lose it. Since I'm a woman, you went easy on me. Don't. Be firm, do it hard, and hold—"

I smiled impishly, cut in: "The last woman who told me that . . ." I noticed she'd frozen in midsentence. "Sorry."

Now, head cocked kittenishly to one side, she smiled. "Thanks." A pause. "Hold the shake a second or two longer. Look me in the eye, and smile. Aim your heart at me. Let's do it again."

I stood up, shook Judith Bolton's hand again.

"Better," she said. "You're a natural. People meet you and think, there's something about this guy I like, I don't know what it is. You've got the chops." She looked at me appraisingly. "You broke your nose once?"

I nodded.

"Let me guess: playing football."

"Hockey, actually."

"It's cute. Are you an athlete, Adam?"

"I was." I sat down again.

She leaned forward toward me, her chin resting in a cupped hand, checking me out. "I can tell. It's in the way you walk, the way you carry your body. I like it. But you're not synchronizing."

"Excuse me?"

"You've got to synchronize. *Mirror.* I'm leaning forward, so you do the same. I lean back, you lean back. I cross my legs, you cross your legs. Watch the tilt of my head, and mimic me. Even synchronize your *breathing* with mine. Just be subtle, don't be blatant about it. This is how you connect with people on a subconscious level, make them feel comfortable with you. *People like people who are like themselves.* Are we clear?"

I grinned disarmingly, or what I thought was disarmingly, anyway.

"And another thing." She leaned in even closer until her face was a few inches away from mine. She whispered, "You're wearing too much after-shave."

My face burned with embarrassment.

"Let me guess: Drakkar Noir." She didn't wait for my answer, because she knew she was right. "Very high school stud. Bet it made the cheerleaders weak at the knees."

Later, I learned who Judith Bolton was. She was a senior VP who'd been brought into Wyatt Telecom a few years earlier as a powerhouse consultant with McKinsey & Company to advise Nicholas Wyatt personally on sensitive personnel issues, "conflict resolution" in the uppermost echelons of the company, certain psy-ops aspects of deals, negotiations, and acquisitions. She had a Ph.D. in behavioral psychology, so she was called Dr. Bolton. Whether you called her an "executive coach" or a "leadership mastery strategist," she was kind of like Wyatt's private Olympic trainer. She advised him on who was executive material and who wasn't, who should be fired, who was plotting behind his back. She had an x-ray eye for disloyalty. No doubt he'd hired her away from McKinsey at some ridiculous salary. She was powerful enough and secure enough here to contradict him to his face, say shit to him he wouldn't take from anybody else.

"Now, our first assignment is to learn how to do a job interview," she said.

"I got hired here," I said, feebly.

"We're playing in a whole new league, Adam," she said, smiling. "You're a hotshot, and you have to interview like a hotshot, someone Trion's going to fall all over themselves to steal away from us. How do you like working at Wyatt?"

I looked at her, feeling stupid. "Well, I'm trying to leave there, aren't I?"

She rolled her eyes, inhaled sharply. "No. You keep it positive." She turned her head to one side and then did an amazing imitation of my voice: "I *love* it! It's totally *inspiring!* My co-workers are *great!*" The mimicry was so good, it weirded me out; it was like hearing your voice on an answering machine tape.

"So why am I interviewing at Trion?"

"*Opportunities*, Adam. There's *nothing* wrong with your job at Wyatt. You're *not* disgruntled. You're just taking the logical next step in your career, and there are more opportunities at Trion to do *even bigger, better things*. What's your greatest weakness, Adam?"

I thought for a second. "Nothing, really," I said. "Never admit to a weakness."

She scowled. "Oh, for Christ's sake. They'll think you're either delusional or stupid."

"It's a trick question."

"Of *course* it's a trick question. Job interviews are *minefields*, my friend. You *have* to 'admit' to weaknesses, but you must *never* tell them anything derogatory. So you confess to being *too faithful a husband, too loving a father*." She did the Adam-voice again: "Sometimes I get so comfortable with one software application that I don't explore others. Or: sometimes when little things bother me, I don't always speak up, because I figure most things tend to blow over. *You don't complain enough!* Or how about this: I tend to get *really absorbed in a project*, so I sometimes put in long hours, too long, because I love doing them, doing them right. Maybe I work on things more than is necessary. Get it? They'll be salivating, Adam."

I smiled, nodded. Man, oh man, what had I gotten myself into?

"What's the biggest mistake you ever made on the job?"

"Obviously I have to admit something," I said nervously.

"You're a fast study," she said dryly.

"Maybe I took on too much once, and I—"

"—And you fucked it up? So you don't know the depths of your own incompetence? I don't think so. You say, 'Oh, nothing really big. Once I was working on a big report for my boss and I forgot to back up, and my *computer crashed,* I lost everything. I had to stay up till three in the morning, completely re-create the work I'd lost. Boy, did *I* learn my lesson—always back up.' Get it? The biggest mistake you ever made was *not your fault,* plus you made everything right."

"I get it." My shirt collar felt too tight, and I wanted to get out of there.

"You're a natural, Adam," she said. "You're going to do just fine."

8

The night before my first interview at Trion I went over to see my dad. I did this at least once a week, sometimes more, depending on if he called and asked me to come over. He called a lot, partly because he was lonely (Mom had died six years earlier) and partly because he was paranoid from the steroids he took and convinced his caregivers were trying to kill him. So his calls were never friendly, never chatty; they were complaints, rants, accusations. Some of his painkillers were missing, he'd say, and he was convinced Caryn the nurse was pilfering them. The oxygen supplied by the oxygen company was of shitty quality. Rhonda the nurse kept tripping over his air hose and yanking the little tubes, the cannulas, out of his nose, nearly ripping his ears off.

To say that it was hard to retain people to take care of him was a comic understatement. Rarely did they last more than a few weeks. Francis X. Cassidy was a bad-tempered man, had been as long as I could remember, and had only grown angrier as he grew older and sicker. He'd always smoked a couple of packs a day and had a loud hacking cough, was always getting bronchitis. So it came as no surprise when he was diagnosed with emphysema. What did he expect? He hadn't been able to blow out the candles on his birthday cake for years. Now his emphysema was what they called end-stage, meaning that he could die in a couple of weeks, or months, or maybe ten years. No one knew.

Unfortunately, it fell to me, his only offspring, to arrange his care. He still lived in the first-floor-and-basement apartment in a triple-decker I'd grown up in, and he hadn't changed a thing since Mom died—the same harvest-gold refrigerator that never worked right, the couch that sagged on one side, the lace window curtains that had gone yellow with age. He hadn't saved any money, and his pension was pitiful; he barely had enough to cover his medical expenses. That meant part of my paycheck went to his rent, the home health aide's salary, whatever. I never expected any thanks, and never got any. Never in a million years would he ask me for money. We both sort of pretended that he was living off a trust fund or something.

When I arrived, he was sitting in his favorite Barcalounger, in front of the huge TV, his main occupation. It allowed him to complain about something in real time. Tubes in his nose (he got oxygen round the clock now), he was watching some infomercial on cable.

"Hey, Dad," I said.

He didn't look up for a minute or so—he was hypnotized by the infomercial, like it was the shower scene in *Psycho*. He'd gotten thin, though he still had a barrel chest, and his crew cut was white. When he looked up at me, he said, "The bitch is quitting, you know that?"

The "bitch" in question was his latest home healthcare aide, a pinched-faced, moody Irish woman in her fifties named Maureen with blazing fake red hair. She limped through the living room, as if on cue—she had a bad hip—with a plastic laundry basket heaped with neatly folded white T-shirts and boxer shorts, my dad's extensive wardrobe. The only surprise about her quitting was that it had taken her so long. He had a little Radio Shack wireless doorbell on the end table next to his Barcalounger that he'd press to call her whenever he needed something, which seemed to be constantly. His oxygen wasn't working, or the nose-tube thingies were drying out his nose, or he needed help getting to the bathroom to take a pee. Once in a while she'd take him out for "walks" in his motorized go-cart so he could cruise around the shopping mall and complain about "punks" and abuse her some more. He accused her of trying to poison him. It would drive a normal person crazy, and Maureen already seemed pretty high-strung.

"Why don't you tell him what you called me?" she said, setting the laundry down on the couch.

"Oh, for Christ's sake," he said. He spoke in short, clipped sentences, since he was always short of breath. "You've been putting antifreeze in my coffee. I can taste it. They call this eldercide, you know. Gray murders."

"If I wanted to kill you I'd use something better than antifreeze," she snapped back. Her Irish accent was still strong even after living here for twenty-some years. He inevitably accused his caretakers of trying to kill him. If they did, who could blame them? "He called me a—a word I won't even repeat."

"Jesus fucking Christ, I called her a cunt. That's a polite word for what she is. She assaulted me. I sit here hooked up to fucking air tubes, and this bitch is slapping me around."

"I grabbed a cigarette out of his hands," Maureen said. "He was trying to sneak a smoke when I was downstairs doing the laundry. As if I can't smell it throughout the house." She looked at me. One of her eyes wandered. "He's not allowed to smoke! I don't even know where he hides the cigarettes—he's hiding them somewhere, I *know* it!"

My father smiled triumphantly but said nothing.

"Anyway, what do I care?" she said bitterly. "This is my last day. I can't *take* it anymore."

The paid studio audience in the infomercial gasped and applauded wildly.

"Like I'm going to notice," Dad said. "She doesn't do shit. Look at the dust in this place. What the hell does the bitch *do?*"

Maureen picked up the laundry basket. "I should have left a month ago. I should never have taken this job." She left the room in her strange lame-pony canter.

"I should have fired her the minute I met her," he grumbled. "I could tell she was one of those gray-murderers." He breathed with pursed lips as if he were inhaling through a straw.

I didn't know what I was going to do now. The guy couldn't be alone—he couldn't get to the bathroom without help. He refused to go into a nursing home; he said he'd kill himself first.

I put my hand on his left hand, the one with an index finger hooked up to a glowing red indicator, the pulse oximeter, I think it was called. The digital numbers on the monitor read 88 percent. I said, "We'll get someone, Dad, don't worry about it."

He lifted his hand, flung mine away. "What the hell kind of nurse is she anyway?" he said. "She doesn't give a shit about anyone else." He went into a long coughing fit, hawked and spit into a balled-up handkerchief he pulled out from somewhere in his chair. "I don't know why the hell you don't move back in. The hell you got to do anyway? You got some go-nowhere job."

I shook my head, said gently, "I can't, Dad. I got student loans to pay off." I didn't want to mention that someone had to make money to pay for the help that was always quitting.

"Fat lot of good college did you," he said. "Huge waste of money, all it was. Spent your time carousing with all your fancy friends, I didn't need to spend twenty thousand bucks a year so you could fuck off. You coulda done that here."

I smiled to let him know I wasn't offended. I didn't know whether it was the steroids, the prednisone he took to keep his airways open, that was making him such an asshole, or just his natural sweet nature. "Your mother, rest in peace, spoiled you rotten. Made you into a big fat pussy." He sucked in some air. "You're wasting your life. When the fuck you gonna get a real job, anyway?"

Dad was skilled at pushing the right buttons. I let a wave of annoyance pass over me. You couldn't take the guy seriously, you'd go whacko. He had the temper of a junkyard dog. I always thought his anger was like rabies—he wasn't really in control, so you couldn't blame him. He'd never been able to control his temper. When I was a kid, small enough not to fight back, he'd whip off his leather belt at the slightest provocation, whomp the shit out of me. As soon as he finished the beating, he'd invariably mutter, "See what you made me do?"

"I'm working on that," I said.

"They can smell a loser a mile off, you know."

"Who?"

"These companies. Nobody wants a loser. Everyone wants winners. Go get me a Coke, would you?"

This was his mantra, and it came from his coaching days—that I was a "loser," that the only thing that counted was winning, that coming in second was losing. There was a time when that sort of talk used to piss me off. But I was used to it by now; I barely even heard it.

I went to the kitchen, thinking about what we were going to do now. He needed round-the-clock help, no question about that. But none of the agencies would send anyone anymore. At first we had real hospital nurses, doing outside shifts for money. When he'd chewed through those, we managed to find a series of marginally qualified people who'd done two weeks' training to get their nursing-assistant certificate. Then it was whoever the hell we could find through ads in the paper.

Maureen had organized the harvest-gold Kenmore refrigerator so that it could have belonged in a government lab. A row of Cokes stood, one behind the other, on a wire shelf that she'd adjusted so it was just the right height. Even the glasses in the cabinet, usually cloudy and smeared, sparkled. I filled two glasses with ice, poured the contents of a can into each. I'd have to sit Maureen down, apologize on Dad's behalf, beg and plead, bribe her if necessary. At least she could stay until I found a replacement. Maybe I could appeal to her sense of responsibility to the elderly, though I figured that had been pretty much eroded by Dad's bile. The truth was, I was desperate. If I blew the interviews tomorrow, I'd have all the time in the world, but I'd be behind bars somewhere in Illinois. That wouldn't help.

I came back out holding the glasses, the ice tinkling as I walked. The infomercial was still going. How long did these things go on for? Who watched them anyway? Besides my father, I mean.

"Dad, don't worry about anything," I said, but he'd passed out.

I stood before him for a few seconds, watching to see if he was still breathing. He was. His chin was on his chest, his head at a funny angle. The oxygen made a quiet whooshing sound. Somewhere in the basement Maureen was banging stuff around, probably mentally rehearsing her exit line. I set down the Cokes on his little end table, which was crowded with meds and remote controls.

Then I leaned over and kissed the old man's blotchy red forehead. "We'll get someone," I said quietly.

9

The headquarters of Trion Systems looked like a brushed-chrome Pentagon. Each of the five sides was a seven-story "wing." It had been designed by some famous architect. Underneath was a parking garage filled with BMWs and Range Rovers and a lot of VW bugs and you name it, but no reserved spaces, so far as I could see.

I gave my name to the B Wing "lobby ambassador," which was their fancy name for the receptionist. She printed out an ID sticker that said VISITOR. I pasted it onto the breast pocket of my gray Armani suit and waited in the lobby for a woman named Stephanie to come get me.

She was the assistant to the hiring VP, Tom Lundgren. I tried to zone out, meditate, relax. I reminded myself that I couldn't ask for a better setup. Trion was looking to fill a product marketing manager slot—a guy had left suddenly, and I'd been custom-tooled for the job, genetically engineered, digitally remastered. In the last few weeks a few selected headhunters had been told about this amazing young guy at Wyatt who was just ripe for the picking. Low-hanging fruit. The word was spread, casually, at an industry convention, on the grapevine. I began to get all sorts of calls from recruiters on my voice mail.

Plus I'd done my homework on Trion Systems. I'd learned it was a consumer-electronics giant founded in the early 1970s by the legendary Augustine Goddard, whose nickname was not Gus but Jock. He was almost a cult figure. He graduated from Cal Tech, served in the navy, went to work for

Fairchild Semiconductor and then Lockheed, and invented some kind of breakthrough technology for manufacturing color TV picture tubes. He was generally considered to be a genius, but unlike some of the tyrant geniuses who found huge multinational corporations, he apparently wasn't an asshole. People liked him, were fiercely loyal to him. He was kind of a distant, paternal presence. The rare glimpses of Jock Goddard were called "sightings," as if he were a UFO.

Even though Trion didn't make color TV tubes anymore, the Goddard tube had been licensed to Sony and Mitsubishi and all the other Japanese companies that make America's TVs. Later Trion moved into electronic communications—catapulted by the famous Goddard modem. These days Trion made cell phones and pagers, computer components, color laser printers, personal digital assistants, all that kind of stuff.

A wiry woman with frizzy brown hair emerged from a door into the lobby. "You must be Adam."

I gave her a nice firm handshake. "Nice to meet you."

"I'm Stephanie," she said. "I'm Tom Lundgren's assistant." She took me to the elevator and up to the sixth floor. We made small talk. I was trying to sound enthusiastic but not geeky, and she seemed distracted. The sixth floor was your typical cube farm, cubicles spread out as far as the eye could see, high as an elephant's eye. The route she led me down was a maze; I couldn't retrace my steps to the elevator bank if I dropped bread crumbs. Everything here was standard-issue corporate, except for the computer monitor I passed by whose screen saver was a 3-D image of Jock Goddard's head grinning and spinning like Linda Blair's in *The Exorcist.* Do that at Wyatt—with Nick Wyatt's head, I mean—and Wyatt's corporate goons would probably break your knees.

We came to a conference room with a plaque on the door that said STUDEBAKER.

"Studebaker, huh?" I said.

"Yeah, all the conference rooms are named after classic American cars. Mustang, Thunderbird, Corvette, Camaro. Jock loves American cars." She said Jock with a little twist, almost with quotation marks around it, seemingly indicating that she wasn't really on a first-name basis with the CEO but that's what everyone called him. "Can I get you something to drink?"

Judith Bolton had told me to always say yes, because people like doing favors, and everyone, even the admins, would be giving feedback on what they thought of me. "Coke, Pepsi, whatever," I said. I didn't want to sound too fussy. "Thanks."

I sat down at one side of the table, the side facing the door, not at the head of the table. A couple of minutes later a compact guy wearing khakis and a navy-blue golf shirt with the Trion logo on it came bounding into the room. Tom Lundgren: I recognized him instantly from the dossier that Dr. Bolton had prepared for me. The VP of the Personal Communications Sector business unit. Forty-three, five kids, an avid golfer. Right behind him followed Stephanie, holding a can of Coke and a bottle of Aquafina water.

He gave me a crusher handshake. "Adam, I'm Tom Lundgren."

"Nice to meet you."

"Nice to meet *you*. I hear great things about you."

I smiled, shrugged modestly. Lundgren wasn't even wearing a tie, I thought, and I looked like a funeral director. Judith Bolton warned me that might happen, but said it was better for me to overdress for the interviews than to go too casual. Sign of respect and all that.

He sat down next to me, turned to face me. Stephanie shut the door behind her quietly as she left.

"So working at Wyatt's pretty intense, I bet." He had thin, thin lips and a quick smile that clicked on and off. His face was chafed, reddened, like either he played too much golf or had rosacea or something. His right leg pistoned up and down. He was a bundle of nervous energy, a ganglion; he seemed overcaffeinated, and he made me talk fast. Then I remembered he was a Mormon and didn't drink caffeine. I'd hate to see him after a pot of coffee. He'd probably go into intergalactic orbit.

"Intense is how I like it," I said.

"Good to hear it. So do we." His smile clicked on, then off. "I think there's more type A people here than anywhere else. Everyone's got a faster clock speed." He unscrewed the top of his water bottle and took a sip. "I always say Trion's a great place to work—when you're on vacation. You can return e-mails, voice mails, get all kinds of stuff done, but man, you pay a price for taking off time. You come back, your voice mailbox is full, you get crushed like a grape."

I nodded, smiled conspiratorially. Even marketing guys at high-tech corporations like to talk like engineers, so I gave some back. "Sounds familiar," I said. "You only have so many cycles, you've got to decide what to spend your cycles on." I was mirroring his body language, almost aping him, but he didn't seem to notice.

"Absolutely. Now, we're not really in a hiring mode these days—no one is. But one of our new-product managers got transferred suddenly."

I nodded again.

"The Lucid is genius—really saved Wyatt's bacon in an otherwise dismal quarter. That's your baby, huh?"

"My team, anyway. I was just part of the team. Wasn't running the show."

He seemed to like that. "Well, you were a pretty key player, from what I've heard."

"I don't know about that. I work hard and I love what I do, and I found myself in the right place at the right time."

"You're too modest."

"Maybe." I smiled. He got it, really gobbled up the fake modesty and the directness.

"How'd you do it? What's the secret?"

I blew out a puff of air through pursed lips, as if recalling running a marathon. I shook my head. "No secret. Teamwork. Driving consensus, motivating people."

"Be specific."

"The basic idea started as a Palm-killer, to be honest." I was talking about Wyatt's wireless PDA, the one that buried the Palm Pilot. "At the early concept-planning sessions, we got together a cross-functional group—engineering, marketing, our internal ID folks, an external ID firm." ID is the jargon for industrial design. I was jamming; I knew this answer by heart. "We looked at the market research, what the flaws were in the Trion product, in Palm, Handspring, Blackberry."

"And what was the flaw in our product?"

"Speed. The wireless sucks, but you know that." This was a carefully planned dig: Judith had downloaded for me some candid remarks Lundgren had made at industry conferences, in which he confessed as much. He was blisteringly critical of Trion's efforts whenever they fell short. My bluntness was a calculated risk on Judith's part. Based on her assessment of his management style, she'd concluded he despised toadyism, grooved on straight talk.

"Correct," he said. He flashed a millisecond of a smile.

"Anyway, we went through a whole range of scenarios. What would a soccer mom really want, a company exec, a construction foreman. We talked feature set, form factor, all that. The discussions were pretty free-form. My big thing was elegance of design married to simplicity."

"I wonder if maybe you erred too much on the side of design, sacrificing functionality," Lundgren put in.

"How do you mean?"

"Lack of a flash slot. The only serious weakness in the product, far as I can see."

A big fat pitch, and I swung at it. "I absolutely agree." Hey, I was totally prepped with stories of "my" successes, and pseudofailures I managed so well they might as well have been battlefield victories. "A big screwup. That was definitely the biggest feature that got jettisoned—it was in the original product definition, but it grew the form factor outside of the bounds we wanted, so it got scrapped midway through the cycle." Take *that*.

"Doing anything about it in the next generation?"

I shook my head. "Sorry, I can't say. That's proprietary to Wyatt Telecom. This isn't just a legal nicety, it's a moral thing with me—when you give your word, it's got to mean something. If that's a problem . . ."

He gave what looked like a genuine, appreciative smile. Slam dunk. "Not a problem at all. I respect that. Anyone who leaks proprietary information from their last employer would do the same to me."

I noted the words "last employer": Lundgren had already signed on, he'd just given it away.

He pulled out his pager and quickly checked it. He'd gotten several pages while we were talking, on the silent vibrate mode. "I don't need to take any more of your time, Adam. I want you to meet Nora."

10

Nora Sommers was blond, around fifty, with wide-set staring eyes. She had the carnivore look of a wild pack animal. Maybe I was biased by her dossier, which described her as ruthless, tyrannical. She was a director, the team leader of the Maestro project, a sort of scaled-down Blackberry knockoff that was circling the drain. She was notorious for calling seven A.M. staff meetings. No one wanted to be on her team, which was why they were having a hard time filling the job internally.

"So Nick Wyatt must be no fun to work for, huh?" she began.

I didn't need Judith Bolton to tell me you're never supposed to complain about your previous employer. "Actually," I said, "he's demanding, but he brought out the best in me. He's a perfectionist. I have nothing but admiration for him."

She nodded wisely, smiled as if I'd selected the right multiple-choice answer. "Keeps the drive alive, hmm?"

What did she expect me to say, the truth about Nick Wyatt? That he's a boor and an asshole? I don't think so. I riffed a bit longer: "Working at Wyatt is like getting ten years of experience in one year—instead of one year of experience ten times."

"Nice answer," she said. "I like my marketing people to try to snow me. It's a key component of the skill-set. If you can snow me, you can snow the *Journal.*"

Danger, Will Robinson. I wasn't going there. I could see the teeth of that jaw trap. So I just looked at her blankly.

"Well," she went on, "the word has certainly spread about you. What was the hardest battle you had to wage on the Lucid project?"

I rehashed the story I'd just given Tom Lundgren, but she sounded underwhelmed. "Doesn't sound like much of a battle to me," she countered. "I'd call that a trade-off."

"Maybe you had to be there," I said. Lame. I scrolled through my mental CD-ROM of anecdotes about the development of the Lucid. "Also, there was a pretty big tussle over the design of the joy pad. That's a five-way directional pad with the speaker built into it."

"I'm familiar with it. What was the controversy?"

"Well, our ID people really keyed in on that as a focal point of the product—it really drew your eye to it. But I was getting major pushback on that from the engineers, who said it was near impossible, way too tricky; they wanted to separate the speaker from the directional pad. The ID guys were convinced that if you separated them, the design would get cluttered, asymmetric. That was tense. So I had to put my foot down. I said this was cornerstone. The design not only made a visual statement, but it also made a major technology statement—told the market we could do something our competitors couldn't."

She was lasering in on me with her wide-set eyes like I was a crippled chicken. "Engineers," she said with a shudder. "They can really be impossible. No business sense at all."

The metal teeth of the jaw trap were glistening with blood. "Actually, I never have problems with engineers," I said. "I think they're really the heart of the enterprise. I never confront them; I *inspire* them, or try, anyway. Thought leadership and mindshare, those are the keys. That's one of the things that most appeals to me about Trion—engineers reign supreme here, which is as it should be. It's a real culture of innovation."

All right, so I was pretty much parroting an interview Jock Goddard once gave to *Fast Company*, but I thought it worked. Trion's engineers were famous for loving Goddard, because he was one of them. They considered it a cool place to work, since so much of Trion's funding went into R&D.

She was speechless for a second. Then she said, "At the end of the day, innovation is mission-critical." Jesus, I thought I was bad, but this woman spoke business cliché as a second language. It was as if she'd learned it from a Berlitz book.

"Absolutely," I agreed.

"So tell me, Adam—what's your greatest weakness?"

I smiled, nodded, and mentally uttered a prayer of gratitude to Judith Bolton.

Score.

Man, it all seemed almost too easy.

11

I got the news from Nick Wyatt himself. When I was shown into his office by Yvette, I found him on his Precor elliptical trainer in a corner of his office. He was wearing a sweat-soaked tank top and red gym shorts and looked buff. I wondered if he did steroids. He had a wireless phone headset on and was barking orders.

More than a week had gone by since the Trion interviews, and nothing but radio silence. I knew they'd gone well, and I had no doubt that my references were spectacular, but who knows, anything could happen.

I figured, wrongly, that once I'd done my interviews I'd be given time off from KGB school, but no such luck. The training went on, including what they called "tradecraft"—how to steal stuff without getting caught, copy documents and computer files, how to search the Trion databases, how to contact them if something came up that couldn't wait for a scheduled rendezvous. Meacham and another veteran of Wyatt's corporate security staff, who'd spent two decades in the FBI, taught me how to contact them by e-mail, using an "anonymizer," a remailer based in Finland that buries your real name and address; how to encrypt my e-mail with this super-strong 1,024-bit software developed, against U.S. law, somewhere offshore. They taught me about traditional spy stuff like dead drops and signals, how to let them know I had documents to pass to them. They taught me how to make copies of the ID badges most corporations use these days, the ones that unlock a door when you wave them at a sensor. Some of this stuff was pretty cool. I was beginning to feel like a real spy. At the time, anyway, I was into it. I didn't know any better.

But after a few days of waiting and waiting for some word from Trion, I was scared shitless. Meacham and Wyatt had been pretty clear about what would happen if I didn't land the job.

Nick Wyatt didn't even look at me.

"Congratulations," he said. "I got the word from the headhunter. You just got parole."

"I got an offer?"

"A hundred seventy-five thousand to start, stock options, the whole deal. You're being hired in as an individual contributor at the manager level but without any direct reports, grade ten."

I was relieved, and amazed by the amount. That was about three times what I was making now. Adding in my Wyatt salary took me to two hundred and thirty-five thousand. Jesus.

"Sweet," I said. "Now what do we do, negotiate?"

"The fuck you talking about? They interviewed eight other guys for the job. Who knows who's got a favorite candidate, a crony, whatever. Don't risk it, not yet. Get in the door, show 'em your stuff."

"My stuff—"

"Show 'em how amazing you are. You've already whetted their appetites with a few hors d'oeuvres. Now you blow 'em away. If you can't blow 'em away after graduating our little charm school here, and with me and Judith whispering in your ear, then you're an even bigger fucking loser than I thought."

"Right." I realized I was mentally rehearsing this sick fantasy of telling Wyatt off as I walked out the door to go work for Trion, until I remembered that not only was Wyatt still my boss, he pretty much had me by the balls.

Wyatt stepped off the machine, drenched with sweat, grabbed a white towel off the handlebars, and blotted his face, his arms, his armpits. He stood so close to me I could smell the musk of his perspiration, his sour breath. "Now, listen carefully," he said with an unmistakable note of menace. "About sixteen months ago Trion's board of directors approved an extraordinary expenditure of almost five hundred million dollars to fund some kind of skunkworks."

"A what?"

He snorted. "A top-secret in-house project. Anyway, it's highly unusual for a board to approve an expenditure that large without a lot of information. In this case they approved it blind, based solely on assurances from the CEO. Goddard's the founder, so they trust him. Also, he assured them the technology they were developing, whatever the hell it is, was a monumental breakthrough. I mean huge, paradigm-shifting, a quantum leap. Disruptive beyond disruptive. He assured them that it's the biggest thing since the transistor, and anyone who's not a part of this gets left behind."

"What is it?"

"If I knew, you wouldn't be here, idiot. My sources assure me that it's going to transform the telecommunications industry, turn everything upside down. And I don't intend to get left behind, you follow me?"

I didn't, but I nodded.

"I've invested far too much in this firm to let it go the way of the mastodon and the dodo. So your assignment, my friend, is to find out everything you can about this skunkworks, what it's up to, what they're developing. I don't care whether they're developing some fucking electronic pogo stick, point is, I'm not taking any chances. Clear?"

"How?"

"That's your job." He turned, walked across the vast expanse of office toward an exit I hadn't noticed before. He opened the door, revealing a gleaming marble bathroom with a shower. I stood there awkwardly, not sure whether I was supposed to wait for him, or leave, or what.

"You'll get the call later on this morning," Wyatt said without turning around. "Act surprised."

PART TWO

BACKSTOPPING

Backstopping: An array of bogus cover identifications issued to an operative that will stand up to fairly rigorous investigation.

—*The Dictionary of Espionage*

12

I'd placed an ad in three local papers looking for a home healthcare aide for my dad. The ad made it clear anyone was welcome, the requirements weren't exactly strict. I doubted there was anyone left out there—I'd already been to the well too many times.

Exactly seven responses came in. Three of them were from people who somehow misunderstood the ad, were themselves looking to hire someone. Another two phone messages were in foreign accents so thick I couldn't even be sure they were trying to speak English. One was from a perfectly reasonable-sounding, pleasant-voiced man who said his name was Antwoine Leonard.

Not that I had much free time, but I arranged to meet this guy Antwoine for coffee. I wasn't going to have him meet my father until he had to—I wanted to hire him first, before he could see what he was going to have to deal with, so he couldn't back out so easily.

Antwoine turned out to be a huge, scary-looking black dude with prison tats and dreadlocks. My guess was right: just as soon as he could, he told me he'd just got out of prison for auto theft, and it wasn't his first stint in the slammer. He gave me the name of his parole officer as a reference. I liked the fact that he was so open about it, didn't try to hide it. In fact, I just liked the guy. He had a gentle voice, a surprisingly sweet smile, a low-key manner. Granted, I was desperate, but I also figured that if anyone could handle my dad, he could, and I hired him on the spot.

"Listen, Antwoine," I said as I got up to leave. "About the prison thing?"

"It's a problem for you, isn't it?" He looked at me directly.

"No, it's not that. I like you being so straight with me about it."

He shrugged. "Yeah, well—"

"I just think you don't need to be so totally honest with my dad."

The night before I started at Trion, I got to bed early. Seth had left a phone message inviting me to go out with him and some friends of ours, since he wasn't working that night, but I said no.

The alarm clock went off at five-thirty, and it was like something was wrong with the clock: it was still nighttime. When I remembered, I felt a jolt of adrenaline, a weird combination of terror and excitement. I was going into the big game, this was it, practice time was over. I showered and shaved with a brand-new blade, went slow so I didn't cut myself. I'd actually laid out my clothes before I went to sleep, picked out my suit and tie, gave my shoes a glossy shine. I figured I'd better show up on the first day in a suit no matter how out-of-it I looked; I could always take off the jacket and tie.

It was bizarre—for the first time in my life I was making a six-figure salary, even though I hadn't actually gotten any of the paychecks yet, and I was still living in the rat hole. Well, that would change soon enough.

When I got into the silver Audi A6, which still had that new-car smell, I felt more high-end, and to celebrate my new station in life I stopped at a Starbucks and got a triple grande latte. Almost four dollars for a goddamned cup of coffee, but hey, I was making the big bucks now. I cranked up the volume on Rage Against the Machine all the way to the Trion campus so that by the time I got there Zack de la Rocha was screaming "Bullet in the Head" and I was screaming, "No escape from the mass mind rape!" along with him, wearing my perfect corporate Zegna suit and tie and Cole-Haan shoes. I was pumped.

Amazingly, there were a fair number of cars in the underground garage, even at seven-thirty. I parked two levels down.

The lobby ambassador in B Wing couldn't find my name on any list of visitors or new employees. I was a nobody. I asked her to call Stephanie, Tom

Lundgren's admin, but Stephanie wasn't in yet. Finally she reached someone in HR, who told her to send me up to the third floor of E Wing, a long walk.

For the next two hours I sat in the Human Resources reception area with a clipboard, filling out form after form: W-4, W-9, credit union account, insurance, automatic deposit to my bank account, stock options, retirement accounts, nondisclosure agreements. . . . They took my picture and gave me an ID badge and a couple of other little plastic cards that attached to my badge holder. They said things like TRION—CHANGE YOUR WORLD and OPEN COMMUNICATION and FUN and FRUGALITY. It was kind of Soviet, but it didn't really bother me.

One of the HR people took me on a quickie tour of Trion, which was pretty impressive. A great fitness center, ATM cash machines, a place to drop off your laundry and dry cleaning, break rooms with free sodas, bottles of water, popcorn, cappuccino machines.

In the break rooms they had big glossy color posters up that showed a group of square-shouldered men and women (Asian, black, white) posed triumphantly on top of planet Earth under the words DRINK RESPONSIBLY! DRINK FRUGALLY! "The typical Trion employee consumes five beverages a day," it said. "Simply by taking one less cold beverage per day, Trion could save $2.4 million a year!"

You could get your car washed and detailed; you could get discount tickets to movies, concerts, and baseball games; they had a baby gift program ("one gift per household, per occurrence"). I noticed that the elevator in D Wing didn't stop on the fifth floor—"Special Projects," she explained. "No access." I tried not to register any particular interest. I wondered if this was the "skunkworks" Wyatt was so interested in.

Finally, Stephanie came by to take me up to the sixth floor of B Wing. Tom was on the phone but waved me in. His office was lined with photos of his kids—five boys, I noticed—individually and in groups, and drawings they'd done, stuff like that. The books on the shelf behind him were all the usual suspects—*Who Moved My Cheese?*; *First, Break All the Rules*; *How to Be a CEO*. His legs were pistoning away like crazy, and his face looked like it had been scrubbed raw with a Brillo pad. "Steph," he said, "can you ask Nora to come by?"

A few minutes later he slammed down the phone and sprang to his feet, shook my hand. His wedding band was wide and shiny.

"Hey, Adam, welcome to the team!" he said. "Man, am I glad we bagged you! Sit down, sit down." I did. "We need you, buddy. Bad. We're all stretched thin here, really raked. We're covering twenty-three products, we've lost some key staff, and we're stretched way thin. The gal you're replacing got transferred. You're going to be joining Nora's team, working on the refresh of the Maestro line which, as you'll find out, is running into some heavy weather. There are some serious fires to put out, and—here she is!"

Nora Sommers was standing at the doorway, one hand on the doorjamb, posing like a diva. She extended the other hand coyly. "Hi, Adam, welcome! *So* glad you're with us."

"Nice to be here."

"It was not an easy hire, I'll tell you frankly. We had a lot of really strong candidates. But as they say, cream rises to the top. Well, shall we get right to it?"

Her voice, which had almost had a girlish lilt to it, seemed to deepen instantly as soon as we walked away from Tom Lundgren's office. She spoke faster, almost spitting out her words. "Your cubicle's right over here," she said, jabbing the air with her index finger. "We use Web phones here—I assume you know how?"

"No worries."

"Computer, phone—you should be all set. Anything else, just call Facility Services. All right, Adam, I should warn you, we don't hold hands around here. It's a pretty steep learning curve, but I have no doubt you're up to it. We throw you right in the pool, sink or swim." She looked at me challengingly.

"I'd rather swim," I said with a sly smile.

"Good to hear it," she said. "I like your attitude."

13

I had a bad feeling about Nora. She was the type who'd put cement boots on me, bundle me into the trunk of a Cadillac, and throw me in the East River. Sink or swim, tell me about it.

She left me at my new cube to finish reading orientation stuff, learn code names for all the projects. Every high-tech company gives their products code names; Trion's were types of storms—Tornado, Typhoon, Tsunami, and so on. Maestro was codenamed Vortex. It was confusing, all the different names, and on top of it I was trying to get the lay of the land for Wyatt. Around noon, when I was starting to get really hungry, a stocky guy in his forties, graying black hair in a ponytail, wearing a vintage Hawaiian shirt and round black heavy-framed glasses, appeared at my cube.

"You must be the latest victim," he said. "The fresh meat hurled into the lion cage."

"And you all seem so friendly," I said. "I'm Adam Cassidy."

"I know. I'm Noah Mordden. Trion Distinguished Engineer. It's your first day, you don't know who to trust, who to align yourself with. Who wants to play with you, and who wants you to fall flat on your face. Well, I'm here to answer all your questions. How would you like to grab some lunch in the subsidized employee cafeteria?"

Strange guy, but I was intrigued. As we walked to the elevator, he said, "So, they gave you the job no one else wanted, huh?"

"That right?" Oh, great.

"Nora wanted to fill the slot internally, but no one qualified wanted to work for her. Alana, the woman whose job you're filling, actually begged to get out from under her thumb, so they moved her somewhere else in-house. Word on the street is, Maestro's on the bubble." I could barely hear him; he was muttering quietly as he strode toward the elevator bank. "They're always quick to pull the plug when something's failing. Around here, you catch a cold and they're measuring you for a coffin."

I nodded. "The product's redundant."

"A piece of crap. Also doomed. Trion's also coming out with an all-in-one cell phone that has the exact same wireless text-messaging packet, so what's the point? Put the thing out of its misery. Plus, it doesn't help that Nora's a bitch on wheels."

"Is she?"

"If you didn't figure that out within ten seconds of meeting her, you're not as bright as your advance billing. But do not underestimate her: she's got a black belt in corporate politics, and she has her lieutenants, so beware."

"Thank you."

"Goddard's into classic American cars, so she's into them too. Owns a couple of restored muscle cars, though I've never seen her drive any of them. I think the point is for Jock Goddard to know she's cut from the same cloth. She's slick, that Nora."

The elevator was crowded with other employees going down to the third-floor cafeteria. A lot of them wore Trion-logo golf or polo shirts. The elevator stopped on every floor. Someone behind me joked, "Looks like we got the local." I think someone cracks that joke in every single corporate elevator around the world every single day.

The cafeteria, or employee dining room as it was called, was immense, buzzing with the electricity of hundreds, maybe thousands, of Trion employees. It was like a food court in a fancy shopping mall—a sushi bar, with two sushi chefs; a gourmet choose-your-own-topping pizza counter; a burrito bar; Chinese food; steaks and burgers; an amazing salad bar; even a vegetarian/vegan counter.

"Jesus," I said.

"Give the people bread and circuses," Noah said. "Juvenal. Keep the peasants well fed and they won't notice their enslavement."

"I guess."

"Contented cows give better milk."

"Whatever works," I said, looking around. "So much for frugality, huh?"

"Ah. Take a look at the vending machines in the break rooms—twenty-five cents for peanut satay chicken, but a buck for a Klondike bar. Fluids and caffeinated substances are free. Last year the CFO, a man named Paul Camilletti, tried to eliminate the weekly beer bashes, but then managers started spending their own pocket money to buy beer, and someone circulated an e-mail that set out a business case for keeping the beer bashes. Beer costs X per year, whereas it costs Y to hire and train new employees, so given the morale-boosting and employee-retaining costs, the return on investment, ya de ya de ya, you get it. Camilletti, who's all about making the numbers, gave in. Still, his frugality campaign rules the day."

"Same way at Wyatt," I said.

"Even on overseas flights, employees are required to fly economy. Camilletti himself stays at Motel 6 when he travels in the U.S. Trion doesn't have a corporate jet—I mean, let's be clear, Jock Goddard's wife bought one for him for his birthday, so we don't have to feel sorry for him."

I got a burger and Diet Pepsi and he got some kind of mysterious Asian stir-fry thing. It was ridiculously cheap. We looked around the room, holding our trays, but Mordden didn't find anyone he wanted to sit with, so we sat at a table by ourselves. I had that first-day-of-school feeling, when you don't know anyone. It reminded me of when I started Bartholomew Browning.

"Goddard doesn't stay at Motel 6s too, does he?"

"I doubt it. But he's not too in-your-face about his money. He won't take limos. He drives his own car—though granted he has a dozen or so, all antiques he's restored himself. Also, he gives his top fifty execs the luxury car of their choice, and they all make a shitload of money—really obscene. Goddard's smart—he knows you've got to pay the top talent well in order to retain them."

"What about you Distinguished Engineers?"

"Oh, I've made an obscene amount of money here myself. I could in theory tell everyone to go fuck themselves and still have trust funds for my kids, if I had any kids."

"But you're still working."

He sighed. "When I struck gold, just a few years after I started here, I quit and sailed around the world, packing only my clothes and several heavy suitcases containing the Western canon."

"The western cannon?"

He smiled. "The greatest hits of Western literature."

"Like Louis L'Amour?"

"More like Herodotus, Thucydides, Sophocles, Shakespeare, Cervantes, Montaigne, Kafka, Freud, Dante, Milton, Burke—"

"Man, I slept through that class in college," I said.

He smiled again. Obviously he thought I was a moron.

"Anyway," he said, "once I'd read everything, I realized that I'm constitutionally unable not to work, and I returned to Trion. Have you read Étienne de la Boétie's *Discourse on Voluntary Servitude*?"

"Will that be on the final?"

"The only power tyrants have is that relinquished by their victims."

"That and the power to hand out free Pepsis," I said, tipping my can toward him. "So you're an engineer."

He gave a polite smile that was more of a grimace. "Not just any engineer, take note, but, as I said, a Distinguished Engineer. That means I have a low employee number and I can pretty much do whatever I want. If that means being a thorn in Nora Sommers's side, so be it. Now, as for the cast of characters on the marketing side of your business unit. Let's see, you've already met the toxic Nora. And Tom Lundgren, your exalted VP, who's basically a straight shooter who lives for the church, his family, and golf. And Phil Bohjalian, old as Methuselah and just about as technologically up-to-date, who started at Lockheed Martin when it was called something else and computers were as big as houses and ran on IBM punch cards. His days are surely numbered. And—lo and behold, it's Elvis himself, venturing into our midst!"

I turned to where he was looking. Standing by the salad bar was a white-haired, stoop-shouldered guy with a heavily lined face, heavy white eyebrows, large ears, and a sort of pixieish expression. He was wearing a black turtleneck. You could sense the energy in the room change, rippling around him in waves, as people turned to look, whispered, everyone trying to be blasé and subtle.

Augustine Goddard, Trion's founder and chief executive officer, in the flesh.

He looked older than in the pictures I'd seen. A much younger and taller guy was standing next to him, saying something. The younger guy, around forty, was lean and really fit, black hair run through with gray. Italian-looking, movie-star handsome like an action hero who was aging really well, but with deeply pitted cheeks. Except for the bad skin, he reminded me of Al Pacino in the first couple of *Godfather* movies. He was wearing a great charcoal-gray suit.

"That Camilletti?" I asked.

"Cutthroat Camilletti," Mordden said, digging into his stir-fry with chopsticks. "Our chief financial officer. The czar of frugality. They're together a lot, those two." He spoke through a mouthful of food. "You see his face, those *acne vulgaris* scars? Rumor has it they say 'eat shit and die' in Braille. Anyway, Goddard considers Camilletti the second coming of Jesus Christ, the man who's going to slash operating costs, increase profit margins, launch Trion stock back into the stratosphere. Some say Camilletti is Jock Goddard's id, the bad Jock. His Iago. The devil on his shoulder. I say he's the bad cop who lets Jock be the good cop."

I finished my burger. The CEO and his CFO were in line, paying for their salads, I noticed. Couldn't they just walk out without paying? Or butt to the front of the line or something?

"It's also very Camilletti to get lunch in the employee dining room," Mordden continued, "to demonstrate to the masses his commitment to slashing costs. He doesn't cut costs, he 'slashes' them. No executive dining room at Trion. No personal executive chef. No catered lunches brought in, not for them, oh no. Break bread with the peasants." He took a swallow of Dr Pepper. "Where were we in my little *Playbill*, my Who's Who in the Cast? Ah, yes. There's Chad Pierson, Nora's golden-haired boy and protégé, boy wonder and professional suckup. MBA from Tuck, moved from B school right into product marketing at Trion, recently did a stint in Marketing Boot Camp, and no doubt he's going to consider you a threat to be eliminated. And there's Audrey Bethune, the only black woman in . . ."

Noah fell silent suddenly, poked more stir-fry into his mouth. I saw a handsome blond guy around my age gliding quickly up to our table, a shark through water. Button-down blue shirt, preppy-looking, a jock. One of those white-blond guys you see in multipage magazine ad spreads, consorting with other specimens of the master race at a cocktail party on the lawn of their baronial estate.

Noah Mordden took a hasty swig of his Dr Pepper and stood up. He had brown stir-fry stains on the front of his Aloha shirt. "Pardon me," he said uncomfortably. "I have a one-on-one." He left his dishes spread out on the table and bolted just as the white-blond guy got there, hand outstretched.

"Hey, man, how you doing?" the guy said. "Chad Pierson."

I went to shake his hand, but he did one of those hip-hop too-cool-to-shake-hands-the-normal-way hand-slide things. His fingernails looked manicured. "Man," he said, "I've heard so much about you, you stud!"

"All bullshit," I said. "Marketing, you know."

He laughed conspiratorially. "Nah, you're supposed to be the *man*. I'm hangin' with you, learn a trick or two."

"I'm going to need all the help I can get. They tell me it's sink-or-swim around here, and it definitely looks like the deep end."

"So, Mordden give you his cynical egghead shit?"

I smiled neutrally. "Gave me his take."

"All negative. He thinks he's in some kind of soap opera, some Machiavelli-type deal. Maybe *he* is, but I wouldn't pay him much attention."

I realized that I'd just sat with the unpopular kid on the first day of school, but that just made me want to defend Mordden. "I like him," I said.

"He's an engineer. They're all weird. You play hoops?"

"Some, sure."

"Every Tuesday and Thursday lunchtime in the gym there's always a pick-up game, we gotta get you on the court. Plus maybe you and me can go out for a drink some time, catch a game, whatever."

"Sounds great," I said.

"Anyone tell you about the Corporate Games beer bash yet?"

"Not yet."

"I guess that's not exactly Mordden's thing. Anyway, it's a blast." He was hyper, torquing his body from side to side like a basketball player looking for a lane to make a monster dunk. "So, bud, you're going to be at the two o'clock, right?"

"Wouldn't miss it."

"Cool. Nice having you on the team, bud. We're gonna do some damage, you and me." He gave me a big smile.

14

Chad Pierson was standing at a whiteboard, writing up a meeting agenda with red and blue markers, when I walked into Corvette. This was a conference room like every other conference room I'd ever seen—the big table (only high-tech-designer black instead of walnut), the Polycom speakerphone console sitting in the middle of the table like a geometric black widow spider, a basket of fruit and ice bucket of soft drinks and juice boxes.

He gave me a quick wink as I sat down on one of the long sides of the table. There were a couple of other people already there. Nora Sommers was sitting at the head of the table, wearing black reading glasses on a chain around her neck, reading through a file and occasionally muttering something to Chad, her scribe. She didn't seem to notice me.

Next to me sat a gray-haired guy in a blue Trion polo shirt tapping away on a Maestro, probably doing e-mail. He was thin but had a potbelly, skinny arms and knobby elbows poking out of his short-sleeved shirt, a fringe of gray hair and unexpectedly long gray sideburns, big red ears. He wore bifocals. If he'd had a different kind of shirt on, he'd probably be wearing a plastic shirt-pocket protector. He looked like an old-style nerd engineer from the Hewlett-Packard-calculator days. His teeth were small and brown, like he chewed tobacco.

This had to be Phil Bohjalian, the old-timer, though from the way Mordden talked about him, I half expected him to be using a quill and parchment. He kept sneaking nervous, furtive glances at me.

Noah Mordden slipped quietly into the room, didn't acknowledge me or anyone else for that matter, and opened his notebook computer at the far end of the conference table. More people filed in, laughing and talking. There were maybe a dozen people in the room now. Chad finished at the white-board and put his stuff down in the empty seat next to me. He clapped a hand on my shoulder. "Glad you're with us," he said.

Nora Sommers cleared her throat, stood up, walked over to the white-board. "Well, why don't we get started? All right, I'd like to introduce our newest team member, to those of you who haven't yet had the privilege of meeting him. Adam Cassidy, welcome."

She fluttered her red fingernails at me, and all heads turned. I smiled modestly, ducked my head.

"We were very fortunate in being able to steal Adam away from Wyatt, where he was one of the key players on Lucid. We're hoping he'll apply some of his magic to Maestro." She smiled beatifically.

Chad spoke up, looking from side to side as if he were sharing a secret. "This bad boy's a genius, I've talked to him, so everything you've heard is true." He turned to me, his baby-blues wide, and shook my hand.

Nora went on, "As we all know far too well, we're getting some serious pushback on Maestro. The knives are out throughout Trion, and I don't have to name names." There was some low chortling. "We have a rather large, looming deadline—a presentation before Mr. Goddard himself, where we will make the case for maintaining the Maestro product line. This is far more than a functional staff update, more than a checkpoint meeting. This is life or death. Our enemies want to put us in the electric chair; we're pleading for a stay of execution. Are we clear about that?"

She looked around menacingly, saw obedient nods. Then she turned around and slashed through the first item in the agenda with a purple marker, a little too violently. Whipping back around, she handed a sheaf of stapled papers to Chad, who began passing them around to his right and left. They looked like some kind of specs, a product definition or product protocol or whatever, but the name of the product, presumably on the top sheet, had been removed.

"Now," she said, "I'd like us to do an exercise—a demonstration, if you will. Some of you may recognize this product protocol, and if so, keep it to yourselves. As we work to refresh the Maestro, I want us all to think outside the box for a couple of moments, and I'd like to ask our newest star to look this over and give us his thoughts."

She was looking right at me.

I touched my chest and said stupidly, "Me?"

She smiled. "You."

"My . . . thoughts?"

"That's right. Go/no-go. Greenlight this project or no. You, Adam, are the gatekeeper on this proposed product. Tell us what you think. Do we go for it, or not?"

My stomach dropped. My heart started thudding. I tried to control my breathing, but I could feel my face flushing as I thumbed through it. It was all but inscrutable. I really didn't know what the hell it was for. I could hear little nervous noises in the silence—Nora clicking the top of the Expo marker off and on, twisting it with a scrunchy noise. Someone was playing with the little plastic flex-straw on his Minute Maid apple juice box, pushing it in and pulling it out, making it squeak.

I nodded slowly, wisely as I scanned it, trying not to look like a deer caught in the headlights, which was how I felt. There was some gobbledygook there about "market segment analysis" and "rough estimate of size of market opportunity." Man oh man. The nerve-wracking music from *Jeopardy* was playing in my head.

Scrunch, scrunch. Squeak, squeak.

"Well, Adam? Go or no-go?"

I nodded again, trying to look fascinated and amused at the same time. "I like it," I said. "It's clever."

"Hmm," she said. There was some low chuckling. Something was up. Wrong answer, I guessed, but I could hardly change it now.

"Look," I said, "based solely on the product definition, of course, it's hard to say much more than—"

"That's all we have to go on at this point," she interrupted. "Right? Go or no-go?"

I riffed. "I've always believed in being bold," I said. "I'm intrigued. I like the form factor, the handwriting recognition specs. . . . Given the usage model, the market opportunity, I'd certainly pursue this further, at least to the next checkpoint."

"Aha," she said. One side of her mouth turned up in an evil smile. "And to think our friends in Cupertino didn't even need Adam's wisdom to green-light this stink bomb. Adam, these are the specs for the Apple Newton. One of the biggest bombs Cupertino ever dropped. Cost them over five hundred million dollars to develop, and *then,* when it came out, they lost sixty million bucks a *year* on it." More chuckles. "But it sure gave *Doonesbury* and Jay Leno plenty of material back in 1993."

People were looking away from me. Chad was biting the inside of his cheek, looking grave. Mordden seemed to be in another world. I wanted to rip Nora Sommers's face off, but I did the good-loser thing.

Nora looked around the table, from one face to the next, her eyebrows arched. "There's a lesson here. You've always got to drill down, look beyond the marketing hype, get under the hood. And believe me, when we present to Jock Goddard in two weeks, he's going to be getting under the hood. Let's keep that at top of mind."

Polite smiles all around: everyone knew Goddard was a gearhead, a car nut.

"All right," she said. "I think I've made my point. Let's move on."

Yeah, I thought. Let's move on. Welcome to Trion. You've made your point. I felt a hollowness in the pit of my stomach.

What the hell had I gotten myself into?

15

The meeting between my dad and Antwoine Leonard did not go smoothly. Well, actually, it was a total, unmitigated disaster. Put it this way: Antwoine encountered significant pushback. No synergy. Not a strategic fit.

I arrived at Dad's apartment right after I finished my first day at Trion. I parked the Audi down the block, because I knew Dad was always looking out of his window, when he wasn't watching his thirty-six-inch TV screen, and I didn't want to get grief from him about my new car. Even if I told him I'd gotten a big raise or something, he'd find a way to put some nasty spin on it.

I got there just in time to see Maureen wheeling a big black nylon suitcase up to a cab. She was tight-lipped, wearing her "dressy" outfit, a lime green pantsuit with a riot of tropical flowers and fruits all over it, and a perfectly white pair of sneakers. I managed to intercept her just as she was yelling at the driver to put her suitcase in the trunk and handed her a final check (including a generous bonus for pain and suffering), thanked her profusely for her loyal service, and even tried to give her a ceremonial peck on the cheek, but she turned her head away. Then she slammed the door, and the cab took off.

Poor woman. I never liked her, but I couldn't help but feel sorry for the torture my father had put her through.

Dad was watching Dan Rather, really mostly yelling at Rather, when I arrived. He despised all the network anchormen equally, and you didn't want to get him started on the "losers" on cable. The only cable shows he liked were the ones where opinionated right-wing hosts bait their guests, try to piss them off, froth at the mouth. That was his kind of sport these days.

He was wearing one of those sleeveless white undershirts that are sometimes called "wifebeaters." They always gave me the willies. I had bad associations with them—whenever he "disciplined" me as a kid, he seemed to be wearing one. I could still remember, clear as a snapshot, the time when, eight years old, I accidentally spilled Kool-Aid on his Barcalounger, and he took the strap to me, standing over me—stained ribbed undershirt, red sweating face—roaring, "See what you made me do?" Not the most pleasant memory.

"When's this new guy getting here?" he said. "He's already late, isn't he?"

"Not yet." Maureen refused to spend a minute showing him the ropes, so unfortunately there'd be no overlap.

"What're you all dressed up for? You look like an undertaker—you're making me nervous."

"I told you, I started a new job today."

He turned back to Rather, shaking his head in disgust. "You got fired, didn't you?"

"From Wyatt? No, I left."

"You tried to coast like you always do, and they fired you. I know how these things work. They can smell a loser a mile off." He took a couple of heavy breaths. "Your mother always spoiled you. Like hockey—you coulda gone pro if you applied yourself."

"I wasn't that good, Dad."

"Easy to say that, isn't it? Makes it easier if you just say that. That's where I really fucked you up—I put you through that high-priced college so you could spend all your time partying with your fancy friends." He was only partly right, of course: I did work-study to put myself through college. But let him remember what he wanted to remember. He turned to look at me, his eyes bloodshot, beady. "So where are all your fancy friends now, huh?"

"I'm okay, Dad," I said. He was on one of his jags, but fortunately the doorbell rang, and I almost ran to answer it.

Antwoine was right on time. He was dressed in pale blue hospital scrubs, which made him look like an orderly or a male nurse. I wondered where he picked them up, since he'd never worked in a hospital, as far as I knew.

"Who's that?" Dad shouted hoarsely.

"It's Antwoine," I said.

"*Antwoine?* What the hell kinda name is Antwoine? You hired some French faggot?" But Dad had already turned to see Antwoine standing at the front door, and his face had gone purple. He was squinting, his mouth open in horror. "Jesus—Christ!" he said, puffing hard.

"How's it going?" Antwoine said, giving me a bone-crushing handshake. "So this must be the famous Francis Cassidy," he said, approaching the Barcalounger. "I'm Antwoine Leonard. Pleasure to meet you, sir." He spoke in a deep, pleasant baritone.

Dad kept staring, puffing in and out. Finally he said, "Adam, I wanna talk to you, right now."

"Sure, Dad."

"No—you tell *An-twoine* or whatever the hell his name is to get outta here, let you and me talk."

Antwoine looked at me, puzzled, wondering what he should do.

"Why don't you bring your stuff to your room?" I said. "It's the second door on the right. You can start unpacking."

He carried two nylon duffel bags down the hall. Dad didn't even wait for him to get out of the room before he said, "Number one, I don't want a *man* taking care of me, you understand? Find me a woman. Number two, I don't want a *black* man here. They're unreliable. What were you thinking? You were gonna leave me alone with Leroy? I mean, look at your *homeboy* here, the tattoos, the braids. I don't want that in my house. Is this so damned much to ask?" He was puffing harder than ever. "How can you bring a black guy in here, after all the trouble I have with those goddamned kids from the projects breaking into my apartment?"

"Yeah, and they always turn right around when they figure out there's nothing here worth stealing." I kept my voice down, but I was pissed. "Number one, Dad, we don't really have a choice here, because the agencies won't even *deal* with us anymore, because you've made so many people quit, okay? Number two, I can't stay with you, because I've got a day job, remember? And number three, you haven't even given the guy a chance."

Antwoine came back down the hall toward us. He approached my father, almost menacingly close, but he spoke in a soft, gentle voice. "Mr. Cassidy, you want me to leave, I'll leave. Hell, I'll leave right now, I don't got no problem with that. I don't stay where I'm not wanted. I don't need a job *that* bad. As long as my parole officer knows I made a serious attempt to get a job, I'm cool."

Dad was staring at the TV, an ad for Depends, a vein twitching under his left eye. I'd seen that face before, usually when he was chewing someone out, and it could scare the shit out of you. He used to make his football players run till someone puked, and if anyone refused to keep going, they got the Face. But he'd used it so many times on me that it had lost its power. Now he pivoted around and turned it on Antwoine, who'd no doubt seen a hell of a lot worse in the joint.

"Did you say *parole officer?*"

"You heard me right."

"You're a fucking *convict?*"

"*Ex*-con."

"The *hell* you trying to do to me?" he said, staring at me. "You trying to kill me before the disease does? Look at me, I can't hardly move, and you put me alone in the house with a fucking *convict?*"

Antwoine didn't even seem to be annoyed. "Like your son says, you ain't got nothing worth stealing, even if I wanted to," he said calmly, through sleepy eyes. "At least give me a little credit, if I wanted to pull off some kinda scam, I wouldn't take a job *here*."

"You hear *that?*" Dad puffed, enraged. "You hear *that?*"

"Plus, if I'm going to stay, we gotta come to agreement on a couple of things, you and me." Antwoine sniffed the air. "I can smell the smokes, and you're going to have to cut that shit out right now. That's the shit that got you here." He reached out one huge hand and tapped the arm of the Barca-lounger. A compartment popped open, which I'd never seen before, and a red-and-white pack of Marlboros popped up like a jack-in-the-box. "Thought so. That's where my dad always hid his."

"Hey!" my dad yelled. "I don't believe this!"

"And you're gonna start a workout routine. Your muscles are wasting away. Your problem isn't your lungs, it's your muscles."

"Are you out of your fuckin' mind?" Dad said.

"You got the respirtary disease, you gotta exercise. Can't do anything about the lungs, those are gone, but the muscles we can do something about.

We're gonna start with some leg lifts in your chair, get your leg muscles working again, and then we're going to walk for one minute. My old man had the emphysema, and me and my brother—"

"You tell this big—tattooed nigger," Dad said between puffs, "to get his stuff—out of that room—and get the hell out of my house!"

I almost lost it. I'd just had a supremely lousy day, and my temper was short, and for months and months I'd been busting my ass trying to find someone who'd put up with the old guy, replacing each one as he made them leave, a whole long parade, a huge waste of time. And here he was, summarily dismissing the latest who, granted, may not have been an ideal candidate, but was the only one we had. I wanted to let into him, let fly, but I couldn't. I couldn't scream at my father, this pathetic dying old man with end-stage emphysema. So I held it in, at the risk of exploding.

Before I could say anything, Antwoine turned to me. "I believe your son hired me, so he's the only one who can fire me."

I shook my head. "No such luck, Antwoine. You're not getting out of here—not so easy. Why don't you get started?"

16

I needed to blow off steam. It was everything—the way Nora Sommers had rubbed my face in it, being unable to tell her to go fuck herself, the impossibility of my surviving at Trion long enough to steal even a coffee mug, the general feeling of being in way over my head. And then, the cherry on the cake: my dad. Keeping the anger in, stopping myself from telling him off—*you fucking ungrateful bigot, die already!*—was corroding my insides.

So I just showed up at Alley Cat, knowing that Seth would be working that night. I just wanted to sit at the bar and get shitfaced on free booze.

"Hey, homey," Seth said, delighted to see me, "your first day at the new place, huh?"

"Yeah."

"That bad, huh?"

"I don't want to talk about it."

"Seriously bad. Wow." He poured me a Scotch like I was some old drunk, a regular. "*Love* the haircut, dude. Don't tell me you got drunk and woke up with that haircut."

I ignored him. The Scotch went immediately to my head. I hadn't eaten any supper, and I was tired. It felt great.

"How bad could it be, bud? It's your first day, they like show you where the bathroom is, right?" He looked up at the basketball game on TV, then back at me.

I told him about Nora Sommers and her cute little Apple Newton trick.

"What a bitch, huh? What'd she come down on you so hard for? What'd she expect—you're new, you don't know anything, right?"

I shook my head. "No, she— " Suddenly I realized that I'd left out a key part of the story, the part about my allegedly being a superstar at Wyatt Telecom. Shit. The anecdote only made sense if you knew the dragon lady was trying to take me down a peg. My brain was fried. Trying to extricate myself from this minor slip seemed an insurmountable goal, like climbing Mount Everest or swimming across the Atlantic. Already I'd gotten caught in a lie. I felt gooey inside and very tired. Fortunately someone caught Seth's eye, signaled to him. "Sorry, man, it's half-price hamburger night," he announced as he went to fetch someone a couple of beers.

I found myself thinking about the people I'd met today, the "cast of characters" as the bizarro Noah Mordden had referred to them, who were now parading through my head, getting more and more grotesque. I wanted to debrief with somebody, but I couldn't. Mostly I wanted to *download*, talk about Chad and Phil Whatever, the old-timer. I wanted to tell someone about Trion and what it was like and about my sighting of Jock Goddard in the cafeteria. But I couldn't, because I didn't trust myself to remember where the Great Wall ran, which part no one was supposed to know about.

The Scotch buzz began to fade, and this humming low note of anxiety, a pedal note, was slowly growing louder, gradually getting higher-pitched, like microphone feedback, high and ear-splitting. By the time Seth came back, he'd forgotten what we were talking about. Seth, like most guys, tends to focus more on his own stuff than on anyone else's. Saved by male narcissism.

"God, women love bartenders," he said. "Why is that?"

"I don't know, Seth. Maybe it's you." I tipped my empty glass toward him.

"No doubt. No doubt." He glugged another few ounces of Scotch in there, refreshed the ice. In a low, confiding voice, barely audible over the din of whooping voices and the blaring ballgame, he said, "My manager says he doesn't like my pour. Keeps making me use a pour tester, practice all the time. Plus he's always testing me now. 'Pour for me! Too much! You're giving away the store!' "

"I think your pour's perfectly fine," I said.

"I'm really supposed to write up a ticket, you know."

"Go ahead. I'm making the big bucks now."

"Na-ah, they let us comp four drinks a night, don't worry about it. So, you think you've got it bad at work. My boss at the firm is always giving me shit if I'm like ten minutes late."

I shook my head.

"I mean, Shapiro doesn't know how to use the copier. He doesn't know how to send a fax. He doesn't even know how to do a Lexis-Nexis search. He'd be totally sunk without me."

"Maybe he wants someone else to do the shitwork."

Seth didn't seem to hear me. "So did I tell you about my latest scam?"

"Tell me."

"Get this—jingles!"

"Huh?"

"*Jingles!* There—like that!" He pointed up at the TV, some cheesy low-production-value ad for a mattress company with a stupid, annoying song they were always playing. "I met this guy at the law firm who works for an ad agency, he told me all about it. Told me he could get me an audition with one of those jingle companies like Megamusic or Crushing or Rocket. He said the easiest way to break in is by writing one of them."

"You can't even read music, Seth."

"Neither can Stevie Wonder. Look, a lot of the really talented guys can't read music. I mean, how long does it take to learn a thirty-second piece of music? This girl who does all those JCPenney ads, he said she can barely read music, but she's got the *voice!*"

A woman next to me at the bar called out to Seth, "What kind of wine do you have?"

"Red, white, and pink," he said. "What can I get you?"

She said white, and he poured some into a water glass.

He circled back to me. "The big bucks is in the singing, though. I just got to put a reel together, a CD, and pretty soon I'll be on the A list—it's all who you know. You following me? No work, mucho bucks!"

"Sounds great," I said with not enough enthusiasm.

"You're not into this?"

"No, it sounds great, it really does," I said, mustering a little more enthusiasm. "Great scam." In the last couple of years, Seth and I talked a lot about scamming by, about how to do the least work possible. He loved hearing my stories of how I used to goof off at Wyatt, how I used to spend hours on the Internet looking at *The Onion* or Web sites like BoredAtWork.com or ILove-Bacon.com or FuckedCompany.com. I especially liked the sites that had a "manager" button you could click when your manager passed by, that killed the funny stuff and put back up whatever boring Excel spreadsheet you were working on. We both took pride in how little work we could get away with. That's why Seth loved being a paralegal—because it allowed him to be marginal, mostly unsupervised, cynical, and uncommitted to the working world.

I got up to take a leak and on the way back bought a pack of Camel straights from the vending machine.

"Again with this shit?" Seth said when he spied me tearing the plastic off the cigarette pack.

"Yeah, yeah," I said in a leave-me-alone tone.

"Don't come to me for help wheeling your oxygen tank around." He pulled a chilled martini glass out of the freezer, poured in a little vermouth. "Watch this." He tossed the vermouth out, over his shoulder, then poured in some Bombay Sapphire. "Now *that's* a perfect martini."

I took a long swig of the Scotch as he went to ring up the martini and deliver it, enjoyed the burn at the back of my throat. Now it was really starting to kick in. I felt a little unsteady on the bar stool. I was drinking like your proverbial coal miner with a paycheck in his pocket. Nora Sommers and Chad Pierson and all the others had begun to recede, to shrink, to take on a harmless, antic, cartoon-character aura. So I had a shitty first day, what was so unusual about that? Everyone felt a little out-of-their-element on the first day in a new job. I was *good*, I had to keep this in mind. If I weren't so good, Wyatt would never have chosen me for his mission. Obviously he and his *consigliere* Judith wouldn't be wasting their time on me if they didn't think I could pull it off. They'd have just fired me and tossed me into the legal system to fend for myself. I'd be bent over that bunk in Marion.

I began to feel a pleasant, alcohol-fueled surge of confidence bordering on megalomania. I'd been parachuted into Nazi Germany, with little more than K rations and a shortwave radio, and the success of the allies was riding entirely on me, nothing less than the fate of Western civilization.

"I saw Elliot Krause today downtown," Seth said.

I looked at him, uncomprehending.

"Elliot Krause? Remember? Elliot Port-O-San?"

My reaction time had slowed; it took me a few seconds, but then I burst out laughing. I hadn't heard Elliot Krause's name in years.

"He's a partner in some law firm, of course."

"Specializing in . . . environmental law, right?" I said, choking with laughter, spitting out a mouthful of Scotch.

"Do you remember his face?"

"Forget his face, remember his *pants*?"

This was why I liked spending time with Seth. We talked in Morse code; we got each other's references, all the inside jokes. Our shared history gave us a secret language, the way twins talk to each other when they're babies. One summer in high school when Seth was working at a snooty tennis club doing grounds maintenance during a big international tennis match, he let me sneak in without paying. They'd brought in some of those rented "portable restroom facilities" for the influx of spectators—Handy Houses or Port-O-Sans or Johnny On the Job, whatever cute name they had, I don't remember—those things that look like big old refrigerators. By the second or third day they'd gotten full, the Handy House crew hadn't bothered to come by and pump them out, and they reeked.

There was this preppy kid named Elliot Krause we both hated, partly because he'd stolen Seth's girlfriend, and partly because he looked down on us as working-class kids. He showed up at the tournament, dressed in a faggoty tennis sweater and white duck pants, Seth's girlfriend on his arm, and he made the mistake of going into one of the Handy Houses to relieve himself. Seth, who was spearing trash at the moment, saw this and gave me an evil smile. He ran over to the booth, jammed the wooden handle of his trash-picker-upper thing through the latch, and me and a friend of ours, Flash Flaherty, started rocking the Porta Potti back and forth. You could hear Elliot inside shouting, "Hey! Hey! What the hell's going on?" and you could hear the sloshing of the unspeakable contents, and finally we got the thing flipped over, with Elliot trapped inside. I don't want to think about what the poor guy was floating in. Seth lost his job but he insisted that it was worth it—he'd have paid good money just for the privilege of seeing Elliot Krause emerge in his no-longer-white tennis whites, retching, covered in shit.

By this point, recalling Elliot Krause putting his shit-splashed glasses back on his shit-covered face as he stumbled out of the Handy House, I was laughing so hard I lost my balance and sprawled onto the floor. For a couple of seconds I lay there, unable to get up. People crowded around me, giant heads leaning in, asking if I was okay. I was definitely looped. Everything had gotten smeary. For some reason I flashed on an image of my father and Antwoine Leonard, and the thought struck me as screamingly hilarious, and I couldn't stop laughing.

I felt someone grab me by the shoulder, someone else grab me by the elbow. Seth and another guy were helping me out of the bar. Everyone seemed to be watching me.

"Sorry, man," I said, feeling a wave of embarrassment wash over me. "Thanks. My car's right here."

"You're not driving, bud."

"It's right *here*," I insisted feebly.

"That's not your car. That's an Audi or something."

"It's mine," I said firmly, punctuating the statement with a vigorous nod. "Audi—A6, I think."

"What happened to Bondo?"

I shook my head. "New car."

"Man, this new job, they paying you a lot more?"

"Yeah," I said, then I added, my words slurred, "not that much more."

He whistled for a cab, and he and the other guy hustled me into it. "You remember where you live?" Seth said.

"Come on," I said. "Of course I remember."

"You want a coffee for the ride home, sober you up a little?"

"Nah," I said. "I got to get to sleep. Work tomorrow."

Seth laughed. "I don't envy you, man," he said.

17

In the middle of the night my cell phone rang, ear-splittingly loud, only it wasn't the middle of the night. I could see a shaft of light behind the shades. The clock said five-thirty—A.M.? P.M.? I was so disoriented I had no idea. I grabbed the phone, wished I hadn't left it on.

"Yeah?"

"You're still asleep?" a voice said, incredulous.

"Who is this?"

"You left the Audi in a tow zone." Arnold Meacham, I realized at once: Wyatt's security Nazi. "It's not *your* car, it's leased by Wyatt Telecommunications, and the least you can do is take decent care of it—not leave it lying around like a discarded *condom*."

It came back to me: last night, getting wasted at Alley Cat, somehow getting home, forgetting to set the alarm . . . Trion!

"Oh, shit," I said, jolting upright, my stomach doing a flip. My head throbbed, felt enormous, like one of those aliens on *Star Trek*.

"We set out the rules quite clearly," Meacham said. "No more carousing. No partying. You're expected to function at peak capacity." Was he talking faster and louder than normal? He sure seemed to be. I could barely keep up.

"I know," I croaked lamely.

"This is not an auspicious start."

"It was real—real busy yesterday. My first day, and my father—"

"I really don't give a shit. We have an explicit agreement, which you're expected to abide by. And what have you turned up on the skunkworks?"

"Skunkworks?" I flung my legs around to the floor, sat on the edge of the bed, massaged my temples with my free hand.

"Classified, codeword projects. What the hell do you think you're there for?"

"No, it's too early," I said. "Too soon, I mean." Slowly my brain was starting to function. "I was escorted everywhere yesterday. There wasn't a minute when I was left alone. It would have been far too risky for me to do anything sneaky. You don't want me blowing this assignment on the first day."

Meacham was silent for a few seconds. "Fair enough," he said. "But you should have an opportunity quite soon, and I expect you to take advantage of it. I want a report by close of business *today*, are we clear?"

18

By lunchtime I began to feel less like the walking wounded, and I decided to go up to the gym—the "fitness center," excuse me—to get in a quick workout. The fitness center was on the roof of E Wing, in a sort of bubble, with tennis courts, all sorts of cardio equipment, treadmills and StairMasters and elliptical trainers all outfitted with individual TV/video screens. The locker room had a steam room and sauna and was as spacious as any high-end sports club I'd ever seen.

I'd changed and was about to hit the machines and the weights when Chad Pierson sauntered into the locker room.

"There he is," Chad said. "How's it going, big guy?" He opened a locker near mine. "You here for B-ball?"

"Actually, I was going to—"

"There's probably a game on, you wanna play?"

I hesitated a second. "Sure."

There was no one else on the basketball court, so we waited around for a couple of minutes, dribbling and taking shots. Finally, Chad said, "How about a little one-on-one?"

"Sure."

"To eleven. Winners out?"

"Okay."

"Listen, how 'bout we put a little wager on the game, huh? I'm not really a competitive guy—maybe that'll juice it up a little."

Yeah, right, I thought. *You're* not competitive. "Like a six-pack or something?"

"Come on, man. A C-note. Hundred bucks."

A *C-note?* What, were we in Vegas with the Rat Pack? Reluctantly, I said, "Okay, sure, whatever."

A mistake. Chad was good, played aggressively, and I was hungover. He went to the top of the three-point line, shot, and sank it. Then, looking pleased with himself, he made a pistol with his finger and thumb, blew the smoke off the barrel, and said, "Smokin'!"

Backing me in, he hit a few fadeaway jumpers and immediately took the lead. From time to time he'd do this little Alonzo Mourning move where he waggled both hands back and forth like a sharpshooter slinging his guns around at a shootout. It was supremely annoying. "Looks like you didn't bring your A game, huh?" he said. His expression seemed benevolent, even concerned, but his eyes gleamed with condescension.

"Guess not," I said. I was trying to be a nice guy, enjoy the game, not go after him like a dick, but he was beginning to piss me off. When I drove, I wasn't in sync, didn't have a feel yet. I missed a few shots, and he blocked a couple. But then I scored a few points off him, and before long it was six to three. I began to notice he kept driving right.

He pumped his fist, did his stupid finger-pistol thing. He drove right, hit another jumper. "Money!" he crowed.

It was at that point that I sort of hit a mental toggle switch and let the competitive juices flow. Chad kept driving to the right and shooting right, I noticed. It was obvious he couldn't go left, didn't have a decent left hand. So I started taking away his right, forcing him left, then I hit a layup.

I'd guessed right. He had no left hand. He missed shots going left, and a couple of times I easily picked off the ball as his dribble crossed over. I got in front of him, then suddenly jumped back and to the right, forcing him to switch directions quickly. Mostly, as I got into the rhythm of the game, I'd been driving, so Chad must have figured I didn't have a jump shot. He looked stunned when my jump shot started dropping.

"You've been holding out on me," he said through gritted teeth. "You *do* have a jump shot—but I'm going to shut it down."

I started playing with his mind a little. I faked going for a jump shot, forcing him up in the air, then blew right by him. This worked so well that I tried it again; Chad was so unnerved that it worked even better the second time. Pretty soon the score was even.

I was getting under his skin. I'd do a little stutter step, just a little movement, fake to the left, and he'd jump left, giving me space to drive right. With each score you could see he was getting more and more rattled.

I drove in and shot a layup, then hit my fadeaway. I was ahead now, and Chad was getting red-faced, short of breath. No more cocky repartee.

I was ahead, ten to nine, when I drove hard and then suddenly stopped short. Chad reeled back and fell on his ass. I took my time, got my feet set, and put up my shot—all net. I made a little pistol with my thumb and forefinger, blew off the smoke, and, with a nice big smile, said, "Smokin'."

Half backing up, half collapsing against the padded gym wall, Chad gasped, "Well, you surprised me, big guy. You've got more game than I thought." He took a deep gulp of air. "This was good. Lot of fun. But I'm going to kick your ass next time, buddy—I know your game now." He grinned, like he was only kidding, reached out and put a clammy, sweaty hand on my shoulder. "I owe you a Benjamin."

"Forget about it. I don't like playing for money anyway."

"No, really. I insist. Buy yourself a new tie or something."

"No way, Chad. Won't take it."

"I owe you—"

"You don't owe me anything, man." I thought for a moment. There's nothing people love to part with more than advice. "Except maybe a Nora tip or two."

His eyes lit up; I was playing on his field now. "Aw, she does that to all the newbies. It's her own form of hazing, doesn't mean anything more than that. It's nothing personal, believe me—I got the same treatment when I started here."

I noticed the unstated, *And now look at me*. He was careful not to criticize Nora; he knew to be wary of me, not to open up. "I'm a big boy," I said. "I can take it."

"I'm saying you won't have to, bud. She made her point—just stay on your toes—and now she'll move on. She wouldn't have done that if she didn't consider you a high-po." High-potential, he meant. "She likes you. She wouldn't have fought to get you on her team if she didn't."

"Okay." I couldn't tell if he was holding out on me or not.

"I mean, if you wanna . . . like, this afternoon's meeting—Tom Lundgren's going to be there, reviewing the product specs, right? And we've been spinning our wheels for weeks already, stuck in some dumbass debate over whether to add GoldDust functionality." He rolled his eyes. "Like, give me a break. Don't even get Nora started on that crap. Anyway, it's probably a good idea if you have *some* opinion on GoldDust—you don't have to agree with Nora that it's complete and total bullshit and a huge waste of money. The important thing is to just have an opinion on it. She likes informed debate."

GoldDust, I knew, was the latest big thing in electronic consumer products. It was some engineering industry committee's fancy marketing name for low-power, short-range wireless transmission technology that's supposed to let you connect your Palm or Blackberry or Lucid to a phone or a laptop or a printer, whatever. Anything within twenty feet or so. Your computer can talk to your printer, everything talks to everything else, and no unsightly cables to trip over. It was going to free us all from our chains, from wires and cables and tethers. Of course, what the industry geeks who invented GoldDust didn't figure on was the explosion in WiFi, 802.11 wireless. Hey, even before Wyatt put me through the Bataan Death March, I had to know about WiFi. GoldDust I learned about from Wyatt's engineers, who ridiculed it up and down.

"Yeah, there was always someone at Wyatt trying to push that on us, but we held the line."

He shook his head. "Engineers want to pack everything into everything, no matter what it costs. What do they care if it pushes our price point up over five hundred bucks? Anyway, that'll come up for sure—I'll bet you can really whale on it."

"All I know is what I read, you know?"

"I'll tee it up for you at the meeting, you can whomp it. Earn a couple of strategic brownie points with the boss, can't hurt, right?"

Chad was like tracing paper: he was translucent; you could see his motives. He was a snake and I knew I could never trust him, but he was obviously trying to establish an alliance with me, probably on the theory that it was better for him to be aligned with the hot new talent, be my buddy, than to appear to be threatened by me, which of course he was.

"All right, man, thanks," I said.

"Least I can do."

By the time I got back to my cube there was half an hour before the meeting, so I got on the Internet and did some quick-and-dirty research on GoldDust so at least I could sound like I knew what I was talking about. I was whipping through dozens of Web sites of varying quality, some industry-promo types, and some (like GoldDustGeek.com) run by geeks obsessed with this shit, when I noticed someone standing over my shoulder, watching me. It was Phil Bohjalian.

"Eager beaver, huh?" he said. He introduced himself. "Only your second day, and look at you." He shook his head in wonderment. "Don't work too hard, you'll burn out. Plus you'll make us all look bad." He made a sort of chortle, like this was a line out of *The Producers* or something, and he exited stage left.

19

The Maestro marketing group met once again in Corvette, everyone sitting pretty much in the same place, as if we had assigned seats.

But this time Tom Lundgren was in the room, sitting in a chair against the wall in the back, not at the conference table. Then, just before Nora called the meeting to order, in walked Paul Camilletti, Trion's CFO, looking spiffy, like a matinee idol out of *Love Italian Style*, wearing a nubby dark-gray houndstooth jacket over a black mock turtleneck. He took a seat next to Tom Lundgren, and you could feel the entire room go still, electrically charged, as if someone had flipped a power switch.

Even Nora looked a little rattled. "Well," she said, "why don't we get started? I'm pleased to welcome Paul Camilletti, our chief financial officer—welcome, Paul."

He ducked his head, the kind of acknowledgment that said, *Don't pay any attention to me—I'm just going to sit here incognito, anonymous, like an elephant in the room.*

"Who else is with us today? Who's teleconning in?"

A voice came over the intercom speaker: "Ken Hsiao, Singapore."

Then: "Mike Matera, Brussels."

"All right," she said, "so the gang's all here." She looked excited, jazzed, but it was hard to tell how much of that was a show of enthusiasm she was putting on for Tom Lundgren and Paul Camilletti. "This seems as good a time as any to take a look at forecasts, drill down, get a sense of where we stand. None of us wants to hear that old cliché, 'dying brand,' am I right? Maestro is no dying brand. We are not going to torpedo the brand equity that Trion has built up in this product line just for the sake of novelty. I think we're all on board on that."

"Nora, this is Ken in Singapore."

"Yes, Ken?"

"Uh, we're feeling some pressure here, I have to say, from Palm and Sony and Blackberry, especially in the Enterprise space. Advance orders for Maestro Gold in Asia Pacific are looking a little soft."

"Thank you, Ken," she said hastily, cutting him off. "Kimberly, what's your sense of the channel community?"

Kimberly Ziegler, wan and nervous-looking with a head of wild curls and horn-rimmed glasses, looked up. "My take is quite different from Ken's, I have to say."

"Really? In what way?"

"I'm seeing product differentiation that's benefiting us, actually. We've got a better price point than either Blackberry or Sony's advanced text-paging devices. It's true there's a little wear-and-tear on the brand, but the upgrade in the processor and the flash memory are really going to add value. So I think we're hanging in there, especially in the vertical markets."

Suckup, I thought.

"Excellent," Nora beamed. "Good to hear. I'd also be quite interested to hear whatever feedback that's come in on GoldDust—" She saw Chad holding his index finger in the air. "Yes, Chad?"

"I thought maybe Adam might have a thought or two about GoldDust."

She turned to me. "Terrific, let's hear it," she said as if I'd just volunteered to sit down and play the piano.

"GoldDust?" I said with a knowing smirk. "Like, how 1999 is that? The Betamax of wireless. It's up there with New Coke, cold fusion, XFL football, and the Yugo."

There were some appreciative titters. Nora was watching me closely.

I went on, "The compatibility problems are so massive, we don't even want to go there—I mean, the way GoldDust-enabled devices work only with devices from the same manufacturer, the lack of any standardized code. Philips keeps saying they're going to come out with a new, standardized version of GoldDust—yeah, right, maybe when we're all speaking Esperanto."

Some more laughter, though I noticed in passing that maybe half the people in the room were stone-faced. Tom Lundgren was looking at me with a funny crooked smile, his right leg jackhammering.

I was really grooving now, getting into it. "I mean, the transfer rate is, what, less than one megabit per second? Really pathetic. Less than a tenth of WiFi. This is horse-and-buggy stuff. And let's not even talk about how easy it is to intercept—no security whatsoever."

"Right on," someone said in a low voice, though I didn't catch who it was. Mordden was downright beaming. Phil Bohjalian was watching me through narrowed eyes, his expression cryptic, unreadable. Then I looked over and saw Nora. Her face was flushing. I mean, you could see a wave of red rising from her neck to her wide-set eyes.

"Are you finished?" she snapped.

I felt queasy all of a sudden. This was not the reaction I expected. What, had I gone on too long? "Sure," I said warily.

An Indian-looking guy sitting across from me said, "Why are we revisiting this? I thought you made a final decision on this last week, Nora. You seemed to feel very strongly that the added functionality was worth the cost. So why are you marketing people going back to this old debate? Isn't the matter settled?"

Chad, who'd been studying the table, said, "Hey, come on, guys, give the newbie a break, huh? You can't expect him to know everything—the guy doesn't even know where the cappuccino machine is yet, come on."

"I think we don't need to waste any more time here," said Nora. "The matter's decided. We're adding GoldDust." She gave me a look of the darkest fury.

When the meeting ended, a stomach-churning twenty minutes later, and people began filing out of the room, Mordden gave my shoulder a quick, furtive pat, which should have told me everything. I'd fucked up, big time. People were giving me all sorts of curious looks.

"Uh, Nora," said Paul Camilletti, holding up a finger, "you mind staying behind a sec? I want to go over a few things."

As I walked out, Chad came up to me and spoke in a low voice. "Sounds like she didn't take it well," he said, "but that was really valuable input, guy."

Yeah right, motherfucker.

20

Maybe fifteen minutes after the meeting broke up, Mordden stopped by my cubicle.

"Well, I'm impressed," he said.

"Really," I said without much enthusiasm.

"Absolutely. You've got more spine than I'd have given you credit for. Taking on your manager, the dread Nora, on her pet project. . . ." He shook his head. "Talk about creative tension. But you should be made aware of the consequences of your actions. Nora does not forget slights. Bear in mind that the most ruthless of the guards in the Nazi concentration camps were women."

"Thanks for the advice," I said.

"You should be on the alert for subtle signs of Nora's displeasure. For instance, empty boxes stacked up next to your cubicle. Or suddenly being unable to log on to your computer. Or HR demanding your badge back. But fear not, they'll give you a strong recommendation, and Trion outplacement services are provided *gratis*."

"I see. Thanks."

I noticed that I had a voice mail. When Mordden left, I picked up the phone.

It was a message from Nora Sommers, asking me—no, *ordering* me—to come to her office at once.

She was tapping away at her keyboard when I got there. She gave a quick, sidelong, lizardlike glance and went back to her computer. She ignored me like that for a good two minutes. I stood there awkwardly. Her face had started flushing again—I felt sort of bad that her own skin gave her away so easily.

Finally she looked up again, wheeled around in her chair to face me. Her eyes glistened, but not with sadness. Something different, something almost feral.

"Listen, Nora," I said gently. "I want to apologize for my—"

She spoke so quietly I could barely hear her. "I suggest *you* listen, Adam. You've done quite enough talking today."

"I was an idiot—" I began.

"And to make such a remark in the presence of Camilletti, Mister Bottom Line, Mister Profit Margin. . . . I've got some serious damage control to do with him, thanks to you."

"I should have kept my mouth—"

"You try to undermine me," she said, "you don't know what you've taken on."

"If I'd known—" I tried to get in.

"Don't even go there. Phil Bohjalian told me he passed by your cube and saw you feverishly doing research on GoldDust before the meeting, before your 'casual,' 'offhand' dismissal of this vital technology. Let me assure you of this, Mr. Cassidy. You may think you're some hot shit because of your track record at Wyatt, but I wouldn't get too comfortable here at Trion. If you don't get on the bus, you're going to get run over. And mark my words: I'm going to be behind the wheel."

I stood there for a few seconds while she bore down on me with those wide-set predator eyes. I looked down at the floor, then back up again. "I blew it big-time," I said, "and I really owe you a huge apology. Obviously I misjudged the situation, and I probably brought with me my old Wyatt Telecom biases, but that's no excuse. It won't happen again."

"There won't be an opportunity for it to happen again," she said quietly. She was tougher than any jackbooted state trooper who'd ever flagged me over to the side of the road.

"I understand," I said. "And if anyone had told me the decision had been made, I certainly would have kept my big mouth shut. I guess I was going on the assumption that folks here at Trion had heard about Sony, that's all. My bad."

"Sony?" she said. "What do you mean, 'heard about Sony?' "

Wyatt's competitive-intelligence people had sold him this tidbit, which he'd given me to use at a strategic moment. I figured that saving my ass counted as a strategic moment. "You know, just that they're scrapping their plans to incorporate GoldDust in all their new handhelds."

"Why?" she asked suspiciously.

"The latest release of Microsoft Office isn't going to support it. Sony figures if they incorporate GoldDust, they lose out on millions of dollars of enterprise sales, so they're going with BlackHawk, the local-wireless protocol that Office *will* support."

"It will?"

"Absolutely."

"And you're sure about this? Your sources are completely reliable?"

"Completely, one hundred percent. I'd stake my life on it."

"You'd stake your career on it as well?" Her eyes drilled into me.

"I think I just did."

"Very interesting," she said. "*Extremely* interesting, Adam. Thank you."

21

I stayed late that evening.

By seven-thirty, eight, the place was empty. Even the diehard workaholics worked from home at night, logging back on to the Trion network, so there was no need to stay late at the office anymore. By nine o'clock, there was no one in sight. The overhead fluorescent lights stayed on, faintly flickering. The floor-to-ceiling windows looked black from some angles; from other angles you could see the city spread out before you, lights twinkling, headlights streaking by noiselessly.

I sat at my cubicle and started poking around the Trion internal Web site.

If Wyatt wanted to know who'd been hired in to some kind of "skunk-works" that had been started some time in the last two years, I figured I should try to find out who Trion had *hired* in the last two years or so. That was as good a start as any. There were all sorts of ways to search the employee database, but the problem was, I didn't really know exactly who or what I was looking for.

After a while, I figured it out: the employee number. Every Trion employee gets a number. A lower number means you were hired earlier on. So after looking at a bunch of different, random employee bios, I began to see the range of numbers of people who'd started working here two years ago. Luckily (for my purposes anyway), Trion had been in a real slow period, so there weren't that many. I came up with a list of a few hundred new hires—

new being within the last two years—and downloaded all the names and their bios to a CD. So that was a start at least.

Trion had its own, proprietary instant-messaging service called InstaMail. It worked just like Yahoo Messenger or America Online's Instant Messenger—you could keep a "buddy list" that told you when colleagues were online and when they weren't. I noticed that Nora Sommers was logged in. She wasn't here, but she was online, which meant she was working from home.

Which was good, because that meant I could now attempt to break into her office without the risk of her showing up unannounced.

The thought of doing it made my guts clench like a fist, but I knew I had no choice. Arnold Meacham wanted tangible results, like yesterday. Nora Sommers, I knew, was on several Trion new product–marketing committees. Maybe she'd have information on any new products or new technology Trion was secretly developing. At the very least it was worth a close look.

The most likely place where she'd keep this information would be on her computer, in her office.

The plaque on the door said N. SOMMERS. I summoned up the nerve to try the doorknob. It was locked. That didn't entirely surprise me, since she kept sensitive HR records there. I could see right through the plate glass into her darkened office, all of ten feet by ten feet. There was not much in it, and it was, of course, fanatically neat.

I knew there had to be a key somewhere in her admin's desk. Strictly speaking, her administrative assistant—a large, broad-beamed, tough woman of around thirty named Lisa McAuliffe—wasn't only *hers*. Nominally, Lisa worked for all of Nora's unit, including me. Only VPs got their own admins; that was Trion policy. But that was just a formality. I'd already figured out that Lisa McAuliffe worked for Nora and resented anybody who got in the way.

Lisa wore her hair really short, almost in a crew cut, and wore overalls or painters' pants. You wouldn't think Nora, who always dressed fashionably and femme, would have an admin like Lisa McAuliffe. But Lisa was fiercely loyal to Nora; she reserved her few smiles for Nora and scared the bejesus out of everyone else.

Lisa was a cat person. Her cubicle was cluttered with dozens of cat things: Garfield dolls, Catbert figurines, that sort of thing. I looked around, saw no one, and began to pull open her desk drawers. After a few minutes I found the key ring hidden on the soil of her fluorescent light–compatible plant, inside a plastic paper clip holder. I took a deep breath, took the key ring—it must have had twenty keys on it—and began trying the keys, one by one. The sixth key opened Nora's door.

I flipped on the lights, sat down at Nora's desk, and powered up her computer.

In case anyone happened to come by unexpectedly, I was prepared. Arnold Meacham had pumped me full of strategies—go on the offensive, ask *them* questions—but what were the odds that a cleaning person, who spoke Portuguese or Spanish and no English, was going to figure out that I was in somebody else's office? So I focused on the task at hand.

The task at hand, unfortunately, wasn't so easy. USER NAME/PASSWORD blinked on the screen. Shit. Password-protected: I should have expected it. I typed in NSOMMERS; that was standard. Then I typed NSOMMERS in the password space. Seventy percent of people, I'd been taught, make their password the same as their user name.

But not Nora.

I had a feeling that Nora wasn't the sort of person who wrote down her passwords on a Post-it note in a desk drawer or something, but I had to make sure. I checked the usual places—under the mouse pad, under the keyboard, in back of the computer, in the desk drawers, but nothing. So I'd have to wing it.

I tried just SOMMERS; I tried her birth date, tried the first and last seven digits of her Social Security number, her employee number. A whole range of combinations. DENIED. After the tenth try, I stopped. Each attempt was logged, I had to assume. Ten attempts was already too many. People generally didn't fumble more than two or three times.

This was not good.

But there were other ways to crack the password. I'd gone through hours of training on that, and they'd supplied me with some equipment that was almost idiotproof. I wasn't a computer hacker or anything, but I was decent at computers—enough to get into a world of trouble back at Wyatt, right?—and the stuff they gave me was ridiculously easy to install.

Basically, it was a device called a "keystroke logger." These things secretly record every keystroke a computer's user makes.

They can be software, like computer programs, or actual hardware devices. But you had to be careful about installing the software versions, because you never knew how closely the corporation's network systems were being monitored; they might be able to detect it. So Arnold Meacham urged me to use the equipment.

He'd given me an assortment of little toys. One was a tiny cable connector that got plugged in between a computer keyboard and the PC. You'd never notice it. It had a chip embedded in it that recorded and stored up to two million keystrokes. You just came back later and took it off the target's computer, and you had a record of everything the person had typed in.

In a total of about ten seconds, I unplugged Nora's keyboard, attached it to the little Keyghost thing, and then plugged that into her computer. She'd never see it, and in a couple of days I'd come back and get it.

But I wasn't going to leave her office empty-handed. I looked through some of the stuff on her desk. Not much here. I found a draft of an e-mail to the Maestro team, which she hadn't yet sent. "My most recent market research," she wrote, "indicates that, though GoldDust is undoubtedly superior, Microsoft Office will instead be supporting BlackHawk wireless technology. Though this may be a disruption to our fine engineers, I'm sure we all agree it's best not to swim against the Microsoft tide. . . ."

Fast work, Nora, I thought. I hoped to hell Wyatt was right.

There were also the file cabinets to go through. Even in a high-tech place like Trion, important files almost always exist on paper, whether originals or hard-copy backups. This is the great truth of the so-called paperless office: the more we all use computers, the more reams of copy paper we seem to go through. I opened the first cabinet I came to, which turned out to be not a file cabinet at all but an enclosed bookcase. Why were some books kept in here, out of sight, I wondered? Then I looked closely at the titles and I whooped out loud.

She had rows and rows of books with titles like *Women Who Run with the Wolves* and *Hardball for Women* and *Play Like a Man, Win Like a Woman.* Titles like *Why Good Girls Don't Get Ahead . . . but Gutsy Girls Do* and *Seven Secrets of Successful Women* and *The Eleven Commandments of Wildly Successful Women.*

Nora, Nora, I found myself thinking. You *go,* girl.

Four of her file cabinets were unlocked, and I went for those first, thumbed through the stultifyingly dull contents: ops reviews, product specs, product development files, financial. . . . She documented seemingly everything, probably printed out a copy of every e-mail she sent or received. The good stuff, I knew, had to be in the locked cabinets. Why else would they be locked?

Pretty quickly I located the small file-cabinet key on Lisa's key ring. In the locked drawers I found a lot of HR files on her subordinates, which might have made for interesting reading if I had the time. Her personal financial records indicated that she'd been at Trion a long time, a lot of her options had vested, and she traded actively, so her net worth was in seven figures. I found my file, which was thin and contained nothing scary. Nothing of interest.

Then I looked closer and came across a few pieces of paper, printouts of e-mails Nora had received from someone high up at Trion. From what I could tell, the woman named Alana Jennings, who'd had my job before me, had abruptly been transferred somewhere else inside the company. And Nora was pissed—so pissed, in fact, that she escalated her complaint all the way up the food chain to the senior vice president level, a pretty bold move:

SUBJ: Re: Reassignment of Alana Jennings
DATE: Tuesday, April 8, 8:42:19 AM
FROM: GAllred
TO: NSommers

Nora,
I am in receipt of your several e-mails protesting the transfer of ALANA JENNINGS to another division of the company. I understand your upset, since Alana is your highest-ranked employee as well as a valued player on your team.
Regretfully, however, your objections have been overruled on the highest authority. Alana's skill set is urgently needed in Project AURORA.
Let me assure you that you will not lose your head count. You have been granted a backfill requisition, so that you

may fill Alana's position with any interested and qualified employee within the company.

Please let me know if I can do anything further to help.

Best,

Greg Allred

Senior VP, Advanced Research Business Unit

Trion Systems

Helping You Change the Future

And then, two days later, another e-mail:

SUBJ: Re: Re: Reassignment of Alana Jennings

DATE: Thursday, April 10, 2:13:07 PM

FROM: GAllred

TO: NSommers

Nora,

Regarding AURORA, my deepest apologies, but I am not at liberty to disclose the exact nature of this project except to say that it is mission-critical to the future of Trion. Since AURORA is a classified R&D project of the utmost sensitivity, I would respectfully ask you not to pursue the matter further.

That said, I appreciate your difficulty in filling Alana's position internally with someone appropriately qualified. Therefore I am happy to tell you that you are, in this instance, permitted to disregard the general companywide ban on hiring from outside. This slot may be designated a "silver bullet" position, enabling you to hire from outside Trion. I trust and hope this will allay your concerns.

Don't hesitate to call or write with any questions.

Best,

Greg Allred
Senior VP, Advanced Research Business Unit
Trion Systems
Helping You Change the Future

Whoa. Suddenly things were starting to make a little sense. I'd been hired to replace this Alana woman, who'd been moved into something called Project AURORA.

Project AURORA was clearly a top-secret undertaking—a skunkworks. I'd found it.

It didn't seem like a good idea to pull out the e-mails and take them out to the copy machine, so I took a yellow legal pad from a tall stack in Nora's supply closet and began taking notes.

I don't know how long I'd been sitting there on the carpeted floor of her office, writing, but it must have been a good four or five minutes. And suddenly I became aware of something in my peripheral vision. I glanced up, saw a security guard standing in the open doorway watching me.

Trion didn't do rent-a-cops; they had their own security personnel, who wore navy blazers and white shirts and looked sort of like policemen, or church ushers. This guy was a tall, beefy black man with gray hair and a lot of moles, like freckles, on his cheeks. He had large, heavy-lidded, basset-hound eyes and wore wire-rimmed glasses. He was standing there, watching me.

For all the time I'd spent mentally rehearsing what I'd say if I was caught, I went blank.

"I see what you got there," the guard said. He wasn't looking at me; he was staring right toward Nora's desk. At the computer—the Keyghost? No, God, please, *no*.

"Excuse me?" I said.

"I see what you got there. Hell, yeah. I *know* it."

I freaked, heart racing. Jesus Christ almighty, I thought: I'm hosed.

22

He blinked, kept staring. Had he seen me install the device? And then I was suddenly seized by another, equally sickening thought: had he noticed Nora's name on the door? Wouldn't he wonder why a man was in a woman's office, thumbing through her files?

I glanced over at the name plaque on the open door, right behind the guard. It said N. SOMMERS. N. SOMMERS could be anyone, male *or* female. Then again, for all I knew he'd been patrolling the halls forever, and he and Nora went way back.

The guard was still standing in the doorway, blocking the exit. What the hell was I supposed to do now? I could try to bolt, but I'd first have to get by the man, which meant I'd have to take a dive at him, tackle him to the ground, get him out of the way. He was big, but old, probably not fast; it might work. So what were we talking about here, assault and battery? On an old guy? *Christ.*

I thought quickly. Should I say I was new? I ran though a series of explanations in my head: I was Nora Sommers's new assistant. I was her direct report—well, I *was*—working late at her behest. What the hell did this guy know? He was a goddamned *security guy.*

He took a few steps into the office, shook his head. "Man, I thought I'd seen everything."

"Look, we've got a huge project due tomorrow morning—" I started to say, indignantly.

"You got a Bullitt there. That's a genuine Bullitt."

Then I saw what he was staring at, moving toward. It was a large color photograph in a silver frame hanging on the wall. A picture of a beautifully restored, vintage muscle car. He was moving toward it in a daze, as if he were approaching the Ark of the Covenant. "Shit, man, that's a genuine 1968 Mustang GT three-ninety," he breathed like he'd just seen the face of God.

The adrenaline kicked in and the relief seeped out of my pores. Jesus.

"Yep," I said proudly. "Very good."

"Man, look at that 'Stang. That pony a factory GT?"

What the hell did I know? I couldn't tell a Mustang from a Dodge Dart. For all I knew that could have been a picture of an AMC Gremlin. "Sure," I said.

"Lotta fakes out there, you know. You ever check under the rear seat, see if it got those extra metal plates, those reinforcements for the dual exhaust?"

"Oh yeah," I said airily. I stood up, extended my hand. "Nick Sommers."

His handshake was dry, his hand large, engulfing mine. "Luther Stafford," he said. "I haven't seen you 'round here before."

"Yeah, I'm never here at night. This damned project—it's always, 'We need it at nine A.M., big rush,' hurry up and wait." I tried to sound casual. "Glad to see I'm not the only one working late."

But he wouldn't drop the car. "Man, I don't think I've ever seen a fastback pony in Highland Green. Outside the movies, I mean. That looks like the exact same one Steve McQueen used to chase the evil black Dodge Charger off the road and into the gas station. Hubcaps flying all over the place." He gave a low, mellow, cigarette-and-whiskey chuckle. "*Bullitt*. My favorite movie. I must've seen it a thousand times."

"Yep," I said. "Same one."

He moved in closer. Suddenly I realized that there was a huge gold statuette on the shelf right next to the silver-framed photo. Engraved on the statuette's base, in huge black letters, was WOMAN OF THE YEAR, 1999. PRESENTED TO NORA SOMMERS. Quickly I walked over behind the desk, blocking the security guard's view of the award with my body, as if I too were inspecting the photograph closely.

"Got the rear spoiler and everything," he went on. "Dual exhaust tips, right?"

"Oh, yeah."

"With the rolled edges and everything?"

"Absolutely."

He shook his head again. "Man. You restore it yourself?"

"Nah, I wish I had the time."

He laughed again, a low, rumbling laugh. "I know what you mean."

"Got it from a guy who'd been keeping it in his barn."

"Three-twenty horsepower on that pony?"

"Right," I said, like I knew.

"Look at the turn-signal hood on that baby. I once had a '68 hardtop but I had to get rid of it. My wife made me, after we had the first kid. I've been lusting after it ever since. But I won't even look at that new GT Bullitt Mustang, no sir."

I shook my head. "No way." I didn't know what the hell he was talking about. Was everyone in this company obsessed with cars?

"Correct me if I'm wrong, but it looks like you got GR-seventy–size tires on fifteen-by-seven American Torque Thrust rims, that right?"

Jesus, could we move off this topic? "Truth is, Luther, I don't know shit about Mustangs. I don't even deserve to own one. My wife just got it for me for my birthday. 'Course, it's going to be *me* paying off the loan for the next seventy-five years."

He chuckled a little more. "I hear you. I've been there." I noticed him looking down at the desk, and then I realized what he was looking at.

It was a big manila envelope with Nora's name on it in big, bold capital letters in red Sharpie marker. NORA SOMMERS. I looked around the desk for something to slide over it, to cover it up, just in case he hadn't yet read the name, but Nora kept her desk immaculate. Trying to act casual, I yanked at a page of the legal pad and ripped it out quietly, let it drop to the surface of the desk and slid it over the envelope with my left hand. Real cool, Adam. The yellow paper had a few notes on it in my handwriting, but nothing that would make any sense to anyone.

"Who's *Nora* Sommers?" he said.

"Ah, that's my wife."

"Nick and Nora, huh?" he chortled.

"Yeah, we get that all the time." I smiled broadly. "It's why I married her. Well, I'd better get back to the files, or I'm going to be here all night. Nice to meet you, Luther."

"Same here, Nick."

By the time the security guy left I was so nervous I couldn't do much more than finish copying the e-mails, then turn off the light and relock Nora's office door. As I turned to return the key ring to Lisa McAuliffe's cubicle, I noticed someone walking not too far away. Luther again, I figured. What did the guy want, more Mustang talk? All I wanted was to drop off the keys unseen, and I was out of here.

But it wasn't Luther; it was a paunchy guy with horn-rim glasses and a ponytail.

The last person I expected to see in the office at ten o'clock at night, but then again, engineers worked strange hours.

Noah Mordden.

Had he seen me locking up Nora's office, or maybe even *in* it? Or was his eyesight not that good? Maybe he wasn't even paying attention; maybe he was in his own world—but what was he *doing* here?

He didn't say anything, didn't acknowledge me. I wasn't even sure he noticed me at all. But I was the only other person in the vicinity, and he wasn't blind.

He turned into the next aisle down and left a folder in someone's cubicle. Fake-casually, I strolled past Lisa's cubicle and deposited the key ring in the plant, right in the soil where I'd found it, one swift movement, then I kept moving.

I was halfway to the elevators when I heard, "Cassidy."

I turned back.

"And I thought only engineers were nocturnal creatures."

"Just trying to get caught up," I said lamely.

"*I* see," he said. The way he said it sent a chill up my spine. Then he asked, "In what?"

"Sorry?"

"What are you caught up in?"

"I'm not sure I understand," I said, my heart pounding.

"Try to remember that."

"Come again?"

But Mordden was already on his way to the elevator, and he didn't answer.

PART THREE

PLUMBING

Plumbing: Tradecraft jargon for various support assets such as safehouses, dead drops, et al. of a clandestine intelligence agency.

—*The International Dictionary of Espionage*

23

By the time I got home, I was a wreck, even worse than before. I wasn't cut out for this line of work. I wanted to go out and get smashed again, but I had to get to bed, get some sleep.

My apartment seemed even smaller and more squalid than ever. I was making a six-figure salary, so I should have been able to afford one of those apartments in the new tall buildings on the wharf. There was no reason for me to stay in this hellhole except that it was *my* hellhole, my reminder of the low-life underachieving bum I really was, not the well-dressed, slick poseur I'd become. Plus I didn't have the time to look for a new place.

I hit the light switch by the door and the room stayed dark. Damn. That meant the bulb in the big ugly lamp by the sofa, the main light source in the room, had burned out. I always kept the lamp switched on so I could turn it on and off at the door. Now I had to stumble through the dark apartment to the little closet where I kept the spare bulbs and stuff. Fortunately I knew every inch of the tiny apartment, literally with my eyes closed. I felt around in the corrugated cardboard box for a new bulb, hoping it was a hundred-watt and not a twenty-five or something, and then navigated through the room to the sofa table, unscrewed the thing that keeps the shade on, unscrewed the bulb, put in the new one. Still no light came on. Shit: a fitting end to a lousy day. I found the little switch on the lamp's base and turned it, and the room lit up.

I was halfway to the bathroom when the thought hit me: How'd the lamp get switched off? I never turned it off there—never. Was I losing my mind?

Had someone been in the apartment?

It was a creepy feeling, some flicker of paranoia. Someone *had* been here. How else could the lamp have been switched off at its base?

I had no roommates, no girlfriend, and no one else had the key. The sleazy management company that ran the building for the sleazy absentee slumlord never accessed the units. Not even if you begged them to send someone over to fix the radiators. No one was *ever* in here but me.

Looking over at the phone directly beneath the lamp, this old black Panasonic telephone/answering-machine combo whose answering machine part I never used anymore, now that I had voice mail through the phone company, I saw something else was off. The black phone cord lay across the phone's keypad, on top of it, instead of coiled to one side of the phone the way it always was. Granted, these were dumb little details, but you do notice these things when you live alone. I tried to remember when I'd last made a phone call, where I'd been, what I'd been doing. Was I so distracted that I hung up the phone wrong? But I was sure the phone hadn't been like this when I left this morning.

Someone had *definitely* been in here.

I looked back at the phone/answering-machine thing and realized something else was wrong, and this wasn't even subtle. The answering machine that I never used had one of those dual-tape systems, one microcassette for the outgoing message, another to record incoming messages.

But the cassette that recorded incoming messages was gone. *Someone had removed it.*

Someone, presumably, who wanted a copy of my phone messages.

Or—the idea suddenly hit me—who wanted to make sure I hadn't used the answering machine to *record* any phone calls I'd received. That had to be it. I got up, started searching for the only other tape recorder I had, a small microcassette thing I'd bought in college for some reason I no longer remembered. I vaguely remembered seeing it in my bottom desk drawer some weeks ago when I'd been searching for a cigarette lighter. Pulling open the desk drawer, I rummaged through it, but it wasn't there. Nor was it in any of the other desk drawers. The more I looked, the more certain I was that I'd seen the tape recorder in the bottom drawer. When I looked again, I found the AC power adapter that went with it, confirming my suspicion. That recorder was gone too.

Now I was certain: whoever had searched my apartment had been looking for any tape recordings I might have made. The question was, who had searched my apartment? If it was Wyatt and Meacham's people, that was totally infuriating, outrageous.

But what if it wasn't them? What if it was *Trion?* That was so scary I didn't even want to think about it. I remembered Mordden's blank-faced question: *What are you caught up in?*

24

Nick Wyatt's house was in the poshest suburb, a place everyone's heard of, so rich that they make jokes about it. It was easily the biggest, fanciest, most outrageously high-end place in a town known for big, fancy, and outrageously high-end estates. No doubt it was important to Wyatt to live in the house that everyone talked about, that *Architectural Digest* put on its cover, that the local journalists were always trying to find excuses to get into and write about. They loved doing awestruck, jaw-dropping takes on this Silicon San Simeon. They loved the Japanese thing—the fake Zen serenity and spareness and simplicity clashing so grotesquely with Wyatt's fleet of Bentley convertibles and his totally un-Zen stridency.

In Wyatt Telecommunications's PR department one guy's entire job was handling Nick Wyatt's personal publicity, planting items in *People* and *USA Today* or wherever. From time to time he put out stories about the Wyatt estate, which was how I knew it had cost fifty million dollars, that it was way bigger and fancier than Bill Gates's lake house near Seattle, that it was a replica of a fourteenth-century Japanese palace that Wyatt had had built in Osaka and shipped in pieces to the U.S. It was surrounded by forty acres of Japanese gardens full of rare species of flowers, rock gardens, a man-made waterfall, a man-made pond, antique wooden bridges flown in from Japan. Even the irregularly cut stones paving the driveway had been shipped from Japan.

Of course I didn't see any of this as I drove up the endless stone driveway. I saw a stone guardhouse and a tall iron gate that swung open automatically, seemingly miles of bamboo, a carport with six different-colored Bentley convertibles like a roll of Lifesavers (no American muscle cars for this guy), and a huge low-slung wooden house surrounded by a tall stone wall.

I'd gotten the order to report for this meeting from Meacham by secure e-mail—a message to my Hushmail account from "Arthur," sent through the Finnish anonymizer, the remailer that made it untraceable. There was a whole vocabulary of code language that made it look like a confirmation of an order I'd placed with some online merchant, but actually told me when and where and so on.

Meacham had given me precise instructions on where and how to drive. I had to drive to a Denny's parking lot and wait for a dark blue Lincoln, which I then followed to Wyatt's house. I guess the point was to make sure *I* wasn't being followed there. They were being a little paranoid about it, I thought, but who was I to argue? After all, I was the guy on the hot seat.

As soon as I got out of the car, the Lincoln pulled away. A Filipino man answered the door, told me to take off my shoes. He led me into a waiting room furnished with shoji screens, tatami mats, a low black lacquered table, a low futon-looking squarish white couch. Not very comfortable. I thumbed through the magazines arrayed artistically on the black coffee table—*The Robb Report*, *Architectural Digest* (including, naturally, the issue with Wyatt's house on the cover), a catalog from Sotheby's.

Finally, the houseman or whatever you call him reappeared and nodded at me. I followed him down a long hallway and walked toward another almost-empty room where I could see Wyatt seated at the head of a long, low black dining table.

As we approached the entrance to the dining room I suddenly heard a high-pitched alarm go off, incredibly loud. I looked around in bewilderment but before I could figure out what was going on I was grabbed by the Filipino man and another guy who appeared out of nowhere, and the two of them wrestled me to the ground. I said, "What the fuck?" and struggled a little, but these guys were as powerful as sumo wrestlers. The second guy then held me while the Filipino patted me down. What were they looking for, weapons? The Filipino guy found my iPod MP3 music player, yanked it out of my workbag. He looked at it, said something in whatever they speak in the Philippines, handed it to the other guy, who looked at it, turned it over, said something gruff and indecipherable.

I sat up. "This how you welcome all Mr. Wyatt's guests?" I said. The houseman took the iPod and, entering the dining room, handed it to Wyatt, who was watching the action. Wyatt handed it right back to the Filipino without even looking at it.

I got to my feet. "Your guys never seen one of those before? Or is outside music not allowed in here?"

"They're just being thorough," Wyatt said. He was wearing a tight black long-sleeved shirt that looked like it was made of linen, and probably cost more than I made in a month, even now at Trion. He seemed to be more tanned than normal. He must sleep in a tanning bed, I thought.

"Afraid I might be packing?" I said.

"I'm not 'afraid' of anything, Cassidy. I like everyone to play by the rules. If you're smart and don't try to get tricky, everything will go fine. Don't even think about trying to take out an 'insurance policy,' because we're way ahead of you." Funny, the idea had never occurred to me until he mentioned it.

"I don't follow."

"I'm saying that if you plan to do something foolish like try to tape-record our meetings or any phone calls you get from me or anyone else associated with me, things will not go well for you. You don't need insurance, Adam. *I'm* your insurance."

A beautiful Japanese woman in a kimono appeared with a tray and handed him a rolled hot towel with silver tongs. He wiped his hands and handed it back to her. Up close you could tell that he'd had a facelift. The skin was too tight, gave his eyes an almost Eskimo cast.

"Your home phone isn't secure," he continued. "Neither is your home voice mail or computer or your cell phone. You're to initiate contact with us only in case of emergency, except in response to a request from us. All other times you'll be contacted by secure, encrypted e-mail. Now, may I see what you have?"

I gave him the CD of all recent Trion hires I'd downloaded from the Web site, and a couple of sheets of paper, covered with typed notes. While he was reading through my notes, the Japanese woman came back with another tray and began to set before Wyatt an array of tiny, perfect, sculptural pieces of sushi and sashimi on lacquered mahogany boxes, with little mounds of white rice and pale-green wasabi and pink slices of pickled ginger. Wyatt didn't look up; he was too absorbed in the notes I'd brought him. After a few minutes he picked up a small black phone on the table, which I hadn't noticed before, and said something in a low voice. I thought I heard the word "fax."

Finally he looked at me. "Good job," he said. "Very interesting."

Another woman appeared, a prim middle-aged woman, lined face, gray hair, reading glasses on a chain around her neck. She smiled, took the sheaf of papers from him, left without saying a word. Did he keep a secretary on call all night?

Wyatt picked up a pair of chopsticks and lifted a morsel of raw fish to his mouth, chewed thoughtfully while he stared at me. "Do you understand the superiority of the Japanese diet?" he said.

I shrugged. "I like tempura and stuff."

He scoffed, shook his head. "I'm not talking about tempura. Why do you think Japan leads the world in life expectancy? A low-fat, high-protein diet, rich in plant foods, high in antioxidants. They eat forty times more soy than we do. For centuries they refused to eat four-legged creatures."

"Okay," I said, thinking: And your point *is* . . . ?

He took another mouthful of fish. "You really ought to get serious about enhancing the quality of your life. You're, what, twenty-five?"

"Twenty-six."

"You've got decades ahead of you. Take care of your body. The smoking, the drinking, the Big Macs and all that crap—that shit's got to stop. I sleep three hours a night. Don't need more than that. Are you having fun, Adam?"

"No."

"Good. You're not there to have fun. Are you comfortable at Trion in your new role?"

"I'm learning the ins and outs. My boss is a serious bitch—"

"I'm not talking about your cover. I'm talking about your *real* job—the penetration."

"Comfortable? No, not yet."

"It's pretty high-stakes. I feel your pain. You still see your old friends?"

"Sure."

"I don't expect you to dump them. That might raise suspicions. But you better make goddamned sure you keep your mouth shut, or you'll be in a world of shit."

"Understood."

"I assume I don't need to remind you of the consequences of failure."

"I don't need to be reminded."

"Good. Your job's difficult, but failure is far worse."

"Actually, I sort of like being at Trion." I was being truthful, but I also knew he'd take it as a jab.

He looked up, smirked as he chewed. "I'm delighted to hear that."

"My team is making a presentation before Augustine Goddard pretty soon."

"Good old Jock Goddard, huh. Well, you'll see quickly he's a pretentious, sententious old gasbag. I think he actually believes all the ass-kissing profiles, that 'conscience of high-tech' bullshit you always see in *Fortune*. Really believes his shit doesn't stink."

I nodded; what was I supposed to say? I didn't know Goddard, so I couldn't agree or disagree, but Wyatt's envy was pretty transparent.

"When are you presenting to the old fart?"

"Couple weeks."

"Maybe I can be of some assistance."

"I'll take whatever help I can get."

The phone rang, and he picked it right up. "Yes?" He listened for a minute. "All right," he said, then hung up. "You hit something. In a week or two you'll be receiving a complete backgrounder on this Alana Jennings."

"Sure, like I got on Lundgren and Sommers."

"No, this is of another magnitude of detail."

"Why?"

"Because you'll want to follow up. She's your way in. And now that you have a code name, I want the names of everyone connected in any way with AURORA. Everyone, from project director all the way down to janitor."

"How?" As soon as I said it, I regretted it.

"Figure it out. That's your job, man. And I want it tomorrow."

"Tomorrow?"

"That's right."

"All right," I said, with just a little defiance creeping into my voice. "But then you'll have what you need, right? And we'll be done."

"Oh, no," he said. He smiled, flashing his big white chompers. "This is only the beginning, guy. We've barely scratched the surface."

25

By now I was working insane hours, and I was constantly zonked. In addition to my normal work hours at Trion, I was spending long hours, late into the night, every night, doing Internet research or going over the competitive-intelligence files that Meacham and Wyatt sent over, the ones that made me sound so smart. A couple of times, on the long, traffic-constipated drive home, I almost fell asleep at the wheel. I'd suddenly open my eyes, jolt awake, stop myself at the last second from veering into the lane of oncoming traffic or slamming into the car in front of me. After lunch I'd usually start to fade, and it took massive infusions of caffeine to keep me from folding my arms and passing out in my cubicle. I would fantasize about going home early and getting under the covers in my dark hovel and falling deep asleep in the middle of the afternoon. I was living on coffee and Diet Pepsi and Red Bull. You could see dark circles under my eyes. At least workaholics get some kind of sick buzz out of it; I was just whipped, like a flogged horse in some Russian novel.

But running on fumes wasn't even my biggest problem. The thing was, I was losing track of what my "real" job was and what my "cover" job was. I was so busy just getting by from meeting to meeting, trying to stay on top of things enough that Nora wouldn't smell blood in the water and go after me, that I barely had time to skulk around and gather information on AURORA.

Every once in a while I'd see Mordden, at Maestro meetings or in the employee dining room, and he'd stop to chat. But he never mentioned that night when he either did or didn't see me coming out of Nora's office. Maybe he hadn't seen me in her office. Or maybe he had and he was for some reason not saying anything about it.

And then every couple of nights I'd get an e-mail from "Arthur" asking me where I was with the investigation, how things were going, what the hell was taking me so long.

I stayed late almost every night, and I was hardly ever at home. Seth left a bunch of phone messages for me and after a week or so gave up. Most of my other friends had given up on me, too. I'd try to squeeze in half an hour here or there to drop by Dad's apartment and check in on him, but whenever I'd show up, he was so pissed off at me for avoiding him that he barely looked at me. A sort of truce had settled in between Dad and Antwoine, some kind of a Cold War. At least Atwoine wasn't threatening to quit. Yet.

One night I got back into Nora's office and removed the little key logger thing, quickly and uneventfully. My Mustang-loving-guard friend usually came by on his rounds at between ten o'clock and ten-twenty, so I did it before he showed up. It took less than a minute, and Noah Mordden was nowhere in sight.

That tiny cable now stored hundreds of thousands of Nora's keystrokes, including all her passwords. It was just a matter of plugging the device into my computer and downloading the text. But I didn't dare do it right there at my cubicle. Who knew what kind of detection programs they had running on the Trion network? Not a risk worth taking.

Instead, I logged on to the corporate Web site. In the search box I typed in AURORA, but nothing came up. Surprise, surprise. But I had another thought, and I typed in Alana Jennings's name and pulled up her page. There was no photo there—most people had their pictures up, though some didn't—but there was some basic information like her telephone extension, her job title (Marketing Director, Disruptive Technologies Research Unit), her department number, which was the same as her mailstop.

This little number, I knew, was extremely useful information. At Trion, just like at Wyatt, you were given the same department number as everyone else who worked in your part of the company. All I had to do was to punch that number into the corporate database and I had a list of everyone who worked directly with Alana Jennings—which meant that they all worked in the AURORA Project.

That didn't mean I had the *complete* list of AURORA employees, who might be in separate departments on the same floor, but at least I had a good chunk of them: forty-seven names. I printed out each person's Web page and slipped the sheets into a folder in my workbag. That, I figured, should keep Wyatt's people happy for a while.

When I got home that night, around ten, intending to sit down at my computer and download all the keystrokes from Nora's computer, something else grabbed my attention. Sitting in the middle of my "kitchen" table—a Formica-topped thing I'd bought at a used furniture place for forty-five bucks—was a crisp-looking, thick, sealed manila envelope.

It hadn't been there in the morning. Once again, someone from Wyatt had slipped into my apartment, almost as if they were trying to make the point that they could get in anywhere. Okay, point made. Maybe they figured this was the safest way to get something to me without being observed. But to me it seemed almost like a threat.

The envelope contained a fat dossier on Alana Jennings, just as Nick Wyatt had promised. I opened it, saw a whole bunch of photos of the woman, and suddenly lost interest in Nora Sommers's keystrokes. This Alana Jennings was, not to put too fine a point on it, a real hottie.

I sat down in my reading chair and pored over the file.

It was obvious that a lot of time and effort and money had gone into it. P.I.s had followed her around, taken close note of her comings and goings, her habits, the errands she ran. There were photos of her entering the Trion building, at a restaurant with a couple of female friends, at some kind of tennis club, working out at one of those all-women health clubs, getting out of her blue Mazda Miata. She had glossy black hair and blue eyes, a slim body (that was fairly evident from the Lycra workout togs). Sometimes she wore heavy-framed black glasses, the kind that beautiful women wear to signal that they're smart and serious and yet so beautiful that they can wear ugly glasses. They actually made her look sexier. Maybe that was the point.

After an hour of reading the file, I knew more about her than I ever knew about any girlfriend. She wasn't just beautiful, she was rich—a double threat. She'd grown up in Darien, Connecticut, went to Miss Porter's School in Farmington, and then went to Yale, where she'd majored in English, specializing in American literature. She also took some classes in computer science and electrical engineering. According to her college transcript she got mostly As and A minuses and was elected to Phi Beta Kappa in her junior year. Okay, so she was smart, too; make that a triple threat.

Meacham's staff had pulled up all kinds of financial background on her and her family. She had a trust fund of several million dollars, but her father, a CEO of a small manufacturing company in Stamford, had a portfolio worth a whole lot more than that. She had two younger sisters, one still in college, at Wesleyan, the other working at Sotheby's in Manhattan.

Since she called her parents almost every day, it was a fair guess that she was close with them. (A year's worth of phone bills were included, but fortunately someone had predigested them for me, summarized who she called most often.) She was single, didn't seem to be seeing anyone regularly, and owned her own condo in a very upper-crust town not far from Trion headquarters.

She shopped for groceries every Sunday at a whole-foods supermarket and seemed to be a vegetarian, because she never bought meat or even chicken or fish. She ate like a bird, a bird from the tropical rainforest—lots of fruits, berries, nuts. She didn't do bars or happy hours, but she did get the occasional delivery from a liquor store in her neighborhood, so she had at least one vice. Her house vodka seemed to be Grey Goose; her house gin was Tanqueray Malacca. She went out to restaurants once or twice a week, and not Denny's or Applebee's or Hooters; she seemed to like high-end, "chef-y" places with names like Chakra and Alto and Buzz and Om. Also she went to Thai restaurants a lot.

She went out to movies at least once a week, and usually bought her tickets ahead of time on Fandango; she occasionally saw your typical chick flick but mostly foreign films. Apparently this was a woman who'd rather watch *The Tree of Wooden Clogs* than *Porky's*. Oh, well. She bought a lot of books online, from Amazon and Barnes and Noble, mostly trendy serious fiction, some Latin American stuff, and a fair number of books about movies. Also, recently, some books on Buddhism and Eastern wisdom and crap like that. She'd also bought some movies on DVD, including the whole *Godfather* boxed set as well as some forties noir classics like *Double Indemnity*. In fact, she'd bought *Double Indemnity* twice, once in video a few years earlier, and once, more recently, on DVD. Obviously she'd only gotten a DVD player within the last two years; and obviously that old Fred MacMurray/Barbara Stanwyck flick was a favorite of hers. She seemed to have bought every record ever made by Ani DiFranco and Alanis Morissette.

I stored these facts away. I was beginning to get a picture of Alana Jennings. And I was beginning to come up with a plan.

26

Saturday afternoon, dressed in tennis whites (which I'd bought that morning—normally I play tennis in ragged cutoffs and a T-shirt) and wearing a ridiculously expensive Italian diver's watch I'd recently splurged on, I arrived at a very hoity-toity, very exclusive place called the Tennis and Racquet Club. Alana Jennings was a member, and according to the dossier she played here most Saturdays. I confirmed her court time by calling the day before, saying I was supposed to play her tomorrow and forgot the time, couldn't reach her, when was that again? Easy. She had a four-thirty doubles game.

Half an hour before her scheduled game I had a meeting with the club's membership director to get a quick tour of the place. That took a little doing, because it was a private club; you couldn't just walk in off the street. I had Arnold Meacham ask Wyatt to arrange to have some rich guy, a club member—a friend of a friend of a friend, a couple of degrees removed from Wyatt—contact the club about sponsoring me. The guy was on the membership committee, and his name obviously pulled some weight at the club, because the membership director, Josh, seemed thrilled to take me around. He even gave me a guest pass for the day so I could check out the courts (clay, indoor and out), maybe pick up a game.

The place was a sprawling Shingle Style mansion that looked like one of those Newport "cottages." It sat in the middle of an emerald-green sea of perfectly manicured lawn. I finally shook Josh at the café by pretending to wave at someone I knew. He offered to arrange a game for me, but I told him I was cool, I knew people here, I'd be fine.

A couple of minutes later I saw her. You couldn't miss this babe. She was wearing a Fred Perry shirt and she had (for some reason the surveillance photos didn't really show this) bodacious ta-tas. Her blue eyes were dazzling. She came into the cafe with another woman around her age, and both of them ordered Pellegrinos. I found a table close to hers, but not too close, and behind her, out of her line of sight. The point was to observe, watch, listen, and most of all not be seen. If she noticed me, I'd have a major problem next time I tried to loiter nearby. It's not like I'm Brad Pitt, but I'm not exactly butt-ugly either; women do tend to notice me. I'd have to be careful.

I couldn't tell if the woman Alana Jennings was with was a neighbor or a college friend or what, but they clearly weren't talking business. It was a fair guess that they didn't work together on the AURORA team. This was unfortunate—I wasn't going to overhear anything juicy.

But then her cell phone rang. "This is Alana," she said. She had a velvety-smooth, private-school voice, cultured without being too affected.

"You did?" she said. "Well, it sounds like you've solved it."

My ears pricked up.

"Keith, you've just slashed the time to fab in half, that's *incredible*."

She was definitely talking business. I moved a little closer toward her so I could hear more clearly. There was a lot of laughter and the clinking of dishes and the *thop thop* of tennis balls, which was making it hard to hear much of what she was saying. Someone squeezed by my table, a big guy with a huge gut that jostled my Coke glass. He was laughing loudly, obliterating Alana's conversation. *Move,* asshole.

He waddled by, and I heard another snatch of her conversation. She was now talking in a hushed voice, and only random bits floated my way. I heard her say: ". . . Well, that's the sixty-four-*billion*-dollar question, isn't it? I wish I knew." Then, a little louder: "Thanks for letting me know—great stuff." A little beep tone, and she ended the call. "Work," she said apologetically to the other woman. "Sorry. I wish I could keep this thing off, but these days I'm supposed to be on call 'round the clock. There's Drew!" A tall, studly guy came up to her—early thirties, bronzed, the broad and flat body of a rower—and gave her a kiss on the cheek. I noticed he didn't kiss the other woman.

"Hey, babe," he said.

Great, I thought. So Wyatt's goons didn't pick up on the fact that she was seeing someone after all.

"Hey, Drew," she said. "Where's George?"

"He didn't call you?" Drew said. "That space shot. He forgot he's got his daughter for the weekend."

"So we don't have a fourth?" the other woman said.

"We can pick someone up," said Drew. "I can't believe he didn't call you. What a wuss."

A lightbulb went on over my head. Jettisoning suddenly my carefully worked-out plan of anonymous observation, I made a bold split-second decision. I stood up and said, "Excuse me."

They looked over at me.

"You guys need a fourth?" I said.

I introduced myself by my real name, told them I was checking the place out, didn't mention Trion. They seemed relieved I was there. I think they assumed from my Yonex titanium pro racquet that I was really good, though I assured them I was just okay, that I hadn't played in a long time. Basically true.

We had one of the outdoor courts. It was sunny and warm and a little windy. The teams were Alana and Drew versus me and the other woman, whose name was Jody. Jody and Alana were about evenly matched, but Alana was by far the more graceful player. She wasn't particularly aggressive, but she had a nice backhand slice, she always returned serves, always got the ball, no wasted movements. Her serve was simple and accurate: she almost always got it in. Her game was as natural as breathing.

Unfortunately, I'd underestimated Pretty Boy. He was a serious player. I started out shaky, pretty rusty, and I double-faulted my first serve, to Jody's visible annoyance. Soon, though, my game came back. Meanwhile, Drew was playing like he was at Wimbledon. The more my game returned, the more aggressive he got, until it was ridiculous. He started poaching at the net, crossing over the court to get shots that were meant for Alana, really hogging the ball. You could see her grimace at him. I began to sense some kind of history between the two of them—some serious tension here.

There was this whole other thing going here—the battle of the Alpha Males. Drew started serving right at me, hitting them really hard, sometimes too long. Though his serves were viciously fast, he didn't have much control, and so he and Alana started losing. Also, I got onto him after a while, anticipating that he was going to poach, disguising my shots, hitting the ball behind him. Pretty Boy had pressed that same old competition button in me. I wanted to put him in his place. Me want other caveman's woman. Pretty soon I was working up a sweat. I realized I was working way too hard at it, being too aggressive for this mostly social game; it didn't look right. So I dialed back and played a more patient point, keeping the ball in play, letting Drew make his mistakes.

Drew came up to the net and shook my hand at the end. Then he patted me on the back. "You're a good fundamental player," he said in this fake-chummy way.

"You too," I said.

He shrugged. "I had to cover a lot of court."

Alana heard that, and her blue eyes flashed with annoyance. She turned to me. "Do you have time for a drink?"

It was just Alana and me, on the "porch," as they called it—this mammoth wooden deck overlooking the courts. Jody had excused herself, sensing through some kind of female windtalking that Alana didn't want a group, saying that she had to get going. Then Drew saw what was happening, and he excused himself too, though not as graciously.

The waitress came around, and Alana told me to go first, she hadn't decided what she wanted. I asked for a Tanqueray Malacca G & T. She gave me a startled glance, just a split second, before she regained her composure.

"I'll second that," Alana said.

"Let me go check and see if we have that," the waitress, a horsy blond high-school student, said. A few minutes later she came back with the drinks.

We talked for a while, about the club, the members ("snotty," she said), the courts ("best ones around by *far*"), but she was too sophisticated to do the whole boring what-do-*you*-do? thing. She didn't mention Trion, so neither did I. I began to dread that part of the conversation, wasn't sure how I'd smooth over the bizarre coincidence that we both worked at Trion, and hey, *you* used to have *my* very exact job! I couldn't believe I'd volunteered to join their game, vaulted myself right into her orbit instead of keeping a low profile. It was a good thing we'd never seen each other at work. I wondered whether the AURORA people used a separate entrance. Still, the gin went to my head pretty quickly, and it was this beautiful sunny day, and the conversation really flowed.

"I'm sorry about Drew being so out of control," she said.

"He's good."

"He can be an asshole. You were a threat. Must be a male thing. Combat with racquets."

I smiled. "It's like that Ani DiFranco line, you know? ' 'Cause every tool is a weapon if you hold it right.' "

Her eyes lit up. "Exactly! Are you into Ani?"

I shrugged. " 'Science chases money, and money chases its tail—' "

" 'And the best minds of my generation can't make bail,' " she finished. "Not many men are into Ani."

"I'm a sensitive guy, I guess," I deadpanned.

"I *guess*. We should go out some time," she said.

Was I hearing right? Had she just asked *me* out?

"Good idea," I said. "So, do you like Thai food?"

27

I got to my dad's apartment so exhilarated from my mini-date with Alana Jennings that I felt like I was wearing a suit of armor. Nothing he did or said could get to me now.

As I climbed the splintery wooden-deck front steps I could hear them arguing—my dad's high-pitched, nasal squawk, sounding more and more like a bird, and Antwoine's rumbling reply, deep and resonant. I found them in the first-floor bathroom, which was filled with steam billowing out of a vaporizer. Dad was lying facedown on a bench, a bunch of pillows under his head and chest propping him up. Antwoine, his pale-blue scrubs soaking wet, was thumping on Dad's naked back with his huge hands. He looked up when I opened the door.

"Yo, Adam."

"This son of a bitch is trying to kill me," Dad screeched.

"This is how you loosen the phlegm in the lungs," Antwoine said. "That shit get all gunked up in there 'cause of all the damaged cilias." He went back to it, making a hollow thump. Dad's back was sickly pale, paper-white, droopy and saggy. It seemed to have no muscle tone. I remembered what my father's back used to look like, when I was a kid: ropy, sinewy, almost frightening. This was old-man skin, and I wished I hadn't seen it.

"The bastard lied to me," Dad said, his voice muffled by the pillows. "He told me I was just going to breathe in steam. He didn't say he was going to crack my goddamned *ribs*. Jesus Christ, I'm on *steroids*, my bones are fragile, you goddamned nigger!"

"Hey, Dad," I yelled, "enough!"

"I'm not your *prison bitch*, nigger!" he said.

Antwoine showed no reaction. He kept clapping on Dad's back, steadily, rhythmically.

"Dad," I said, "this man is a whole lot bigger and stronger than you. I don't think it's a good idea to alienate him."

Antwoine looked up at me with sleepy, amused eyes. "Hey, man, I had to deal with Aryan Nation every day I was jammed up. Believe me, a mouthy old cripple's no big deal."

I winced.

"You *god*damned son of a *bitch!*" Dad shrieked. I noticed he didn't use the N-word.

Later Dad was parked in front of the TV, hooked up to the bubbler, the tube in his nose.

"This arrangement is not working out," he said, scowling at the TV. "Have you seen the kind of rabbit-food shit he tries to give me?"

"It's called fruits and vegetables," Antwoine said. He was sitting in the chair a few feet away. "I know what he likes—I can see what's in the pantry. Dinty Moore beef stew in the big can, Vienna sausages, and liverwurst. Well, not as long as I'm here. You need the healthy stuff, Frank, build up your immunity. You catch a cold, you end up with pneumonia, in the hospital, and then what am I going to do? You're not going to need me when you're in the hospital."

"Christ."

"Plus no more Cokes, that shit is over. You need fluids, thin your mucus, nothing with the caffeine in it. You need potassium, you need calcium 'cause of the steroids." He was jabbing his index finger into his palm like he was a trainer for the world heavyweight champion.

"Make whatever rabbit-food crap you want, I won't eat it," Dad said.

"Then you're just killing yourself. Takes you ten times more energy to breathe than a normal guy, so you need to eat, build up your strength, your muscle mass, all that. You expire on my watch, I'm not taking the rap."

"Like you really give a shit," Dad said.

"You think I'm here to help you die?"

"Looks that way to me."

"If I wanted to kill you, why would I do it the slow way?" Antwoine said. "Unless you think this is fun for me. Like maybe I *enjoy* this shit."

"This is a blast, isn't it?" I said.

"Hey, wouldja check out the watch on that man?" Antwoine suddenly said. I'd forgotten to take off the Panerai. Maybe subconsciously I thought it wouldn't even register with him or my dad. "Let me see that." He came up to me, inspected it, marveling. "Man, that's gotta be a five-thousand-dollar watch." He was pretty close. I was embarrassed—it was more than he made in two months. "That one of those Italian diving watches?"

"Yep," I said hastily.

"Oh, you gotta be shittin' me," Dad said, his voice like a rusty hinge. "I don't fucking *believe* this." Now he was staring at my watch too. "You spent five thousand dollars on a goddamned *watch?* What a loser! Do you have any idea how I used to bust my hump for five thousand bucks when I was putting you through school? You spent that on a fucking *watch?*"

"It's my money, Dad." Then I added, feebly, "It's an investment."

"Oh, for Christ's sakes, you think I'm an *idiot? An investment?*"

"Dad, look, I just got a huge promotion. I'm working at Trion Systems for, like, twice the salary I was getting at Wyatt, okay?"

He looked at me shrewdly. "What kinda money they paying you, you can throw away five *thousand*—Jesus, I can't even say it."

"They're paying me a lot, Dad. And if I want to throw my money away, I'll throw it away. I've earned it."

"You've earned it," he repeated with thick sarcasm. "Any time you want to pay me back for"—he took a breath—"I don't know *how* many tens of thousands of dollars I dumped on you, be my guest."

I came this close to telling him then how much money I threw his way, but I pulled back just in time. The momentary victory wouldn't be worth it. Instead I told myself over and over, this is not your dad. It's an evil cartoon version of Dad, animated by Hanna-Barbera, distorted out of recognition by prednisone and a dozen other mind-altering substances. But of course I knew that wasn't quite true, that this really was the same old asshole, just with the dial turned up a couple of notches.

"You're living in a fantasy world," Dad went on, then took a loud breath. "You think just 'cause you buy the two-thousand-dollar suits and the five-hundred-dollar shoes and the five-thousand-dollar watches you're going to become one of *them*, don't you?" He took a breath. "Well, let me tell you something. You're wearing a fucking Halloween costume, that's all. You're dressing up. I tell you this 'cause you're my son and no one else is going to give it to you straight. You're nothing more than an ape in a fucking tuxedo."

"What's that supposed to mean?" I mumbled. I noticed Antwoine tactfully walking out of the room. My face went all red.

He's a sick man, I told myself. He has end-stage emphysema. He's dying. He doesn't know what he's saying.

"You think you're ever gonna be one of them? Boy, you'd like to think that, wouldn't you? You think they're gonna take you in and let you join their private clubs and screw their daughters and play fucking *polo* with them." He sucked in a tiny lungful of air. "But *they* know who you are, son, and where you come from. Maybe they'll let you play in their sandbox for a while, but as soon as you start to forget who you really are, someone's going to fucking remind you."

I couldn't restrain myself any longer. He was driving me crazy. "It doesn't work that way in the business world, Dad," I said patiently. "It's not like a club. It's about making money. If you help them make money, you fulfill a need. I'm where I am because they need me."

"Oh, they *need* you," Dad repeated, drawing out the word, nodding. "That's a good one. They need you like a guy taking a shit needs a piece of toilet paper, you unnerstand me? Then when they're done wiping away their shit, they flush. Lemme tell you, all they care about is winners, and they know you're a loser and they're not going to let you forget it."

I rolled my eyes, shook my head, didn't say anything. A vein throbbed at my temple.

A breath. "And you're too stupid and full of yourself to know it. You're living in a goddamned fantasy world, just like your mother. She always thought she was too good for me, but she wasn't shit. She was dreaming. And you ain't shit. You went to a fancy prep school for a couple of years, and you got a high-priced do-nothing college degree, but you still ain't shit."

He took a deep breath, and his voice seemed to soften a little. "I tell you this because I don't want you to be fucked over the way they fucked me over, son. Like that fucking candy-ass prep school, the way all the rich parents looked down on me, like I wasn't one of them. Well, guess what. Took me a while to figure it out, but they were right. I wasn't one of them. Neither are you, and the sooner you figure it out, the better off you'll be."

"Better off, like you," I said. It just slipped out.

He stared at me, his eyes beady. "At least I know who I am," he said. "You don't fucking know who you are."

28

The next morning was Sunday, my only chance to sleep late, so of course Arnold Meacham insisted on meeting me early. I'd replied to his daily e-mail using the name "Donnie," which told him I had something to deliver. He e-mailed right back, told me to be at the parking lot of a particular Home Depot at nine A.M. sharp.

There were a lot of people here already—not everyone slept late on Sunday—buying lumber and tile and power tools and bags of grass seed and fertilizer. I waited in the Audi for a good half hour.

Then a black BMW 745i pulled into the space next to mine, looking a little out of place among the pickup trucks and SUVs. Arnold Meacham was wearing a baby-blue cardigan sweater and looked like he was on his way to play golf somewhere. He signaled for me to get into his car, which I did, and I handed him a CD and a file folder.

"And what do we have here?" he asked.

"List of AURORA Project employees," I said.

"All of them?"

"I don't know. At least some."

"Why not all?"

"It's forty-seven names there," I said. "It's a decent start."

"We need the complete list."

I sighed. "I'll see what I can do." I paused for a second, torn between not wanting to tell the guy anything I didn't have to—the more I told him, the more he'd push me—and wanting to brag about how much progress I'd been making. "I have my boss's passwords," I finally said.

"Which boss? Lundgren?"

"Nora Sommers."

He nodded. "You use the software?"

"No, the Keyghost."

"What'll you do with them?"

"Search her archived e-mail. Maybe go into her MeetingMaker and find out who she meets with."

"That's penny-ante shit," Meacham said. "I think it's time to penetrate AURORA."

"Too risky right now," I said, shaking my head.

"Why?"

A guy rolled a shopping cart stacked with green bags of Scott's starter fertilizer by Meacham's window. Four or five little kids ran around behind him. Meacham looked over, electrically rolled up his window, turned back to me. "Why?" he repeated.

"The badge access is separate."

"For Christ's sake, follow someone in, steal a badge, whatever. Do I need to put you back in basic training?"

"They log all entries, and every entrance has a turnstile, so you can't just sneak in."

"What about the cleaning crew?"

"There's also closed-circuit TV cameras trained on every entry point. It's not so easy. You don't want me to get caught, not now."

He seemed to back down. "Jesus, the place is well defended."

"You could probably learn a trick or two."

"Fuck you," he snapped. "What about HR files?"

"HR's pretty well protected too," I said.

"Not like AURORA. That ought to be relatively easy. Get us the personnel files on everyone you can who's associated in any way with AURORA. At least the people on this list." He held up the CD.

"I can try for it next week."

"Do it tonight. Sunday night's a good time to do it."

"I've got a big day tomorrow. We're making a presentation to Goddard."

He looked disgusted. "What, you're too busy with your cover job? I hope you haven't forgotten who you really work for."

"I've got to be up to speed. It's important."

"All the more reason why you'd be in the office working tonight," he said, and he turned the key in the ignition.

29

Early that evening I drove to Trion headquarters. The parking garage was almost entirely empty, the only people there probably security, the people who manned the twenty-four-hour ops centers, and the random work-crazed employee, like I was pretending to be. I didn't recognize the lobby ambassador, a Hispanic woman who didn't look happy to be there. She barely looked at me as I let myself in, but I made a point of saying hi, looking harried or sheepish or something. I went up to my cubicle and did a little real work, some spreadsheets on Maestro sales in the region of the world they call EMEA, for Europe/Middle East/Asia. The trend lines weren't good, but Nora wanted me to massage the numbers to bring out whatever encouraging data points I could.

Most of the floor was dark. I even had to switch on the lights in my area. It was unnerving.

Meacham and Wyatt wanted the personnel files on everyone in AURORA. They wanted to find out each person's employment history, which would tell them what companies they were all hired from and what they did at their last jobs. It was a good way to suss out what AURORA was all about.

But it wasn't as if I could just saunter into Human Resources, pull open some file cabinets, and pluck out whatever files I wanted. The HR department at Trion, unlike most other parts of the company, actually took security precautions. For one thing, their computers weren't accessible through the main corporate database; it was a whole separate network. I guess that made sense—personnel records contained all sorts of private information like people's performance appraisals, the value of their 401(k)s and stock options, all that. Maybe HR was afraid that the rank-and-file would find out how much more the top Trion execs got paid than everyone else and there'd be riots down in the cube farms.

HR was located on the third floor of E Wing, a long hike from New Product Marketing. There were a lot of locked doors along the way, but my badge would probably open each one of them.

Then I remembered that somewhere it was recorded who entered which checkpoints and at what time. The information was stored, which didn't necessarily mean that anybody looked at it or did anything about it. But if there were ever trouble later, it wouldn't look good that on a Sunday night for some reason I walked from New Products to Personnel, leaving digital bread crumbs along the way.

So I left the building, just took the elevator down and took one of the back entrances. The thing about these security systems was that they only kept track of entrances, not exits. When you walked out, you didn't use your badge. This might have been some fire-department code thing, I didn't know. But that meant that I could leave the building without anyone knowing I'd left.

It was dark outside by now. The Trion building was lit up, its brushed-chrome skin gleaming, the glass windows a midnight blue. It was relatively quiet out here at night, just the *shush* of the occasional car passing by on the highway.

I walked around to E Wing, where a lot of the administrative functions seemed to be housed—Central Purchasing, Systems Management, that sort of thing—and saw someone coming out of a service entrance.

"Hey, can you hold the door?" I shouted. I waved my Trion badge at the guy, who looked like he was on the cleaning crew or something. "Damned badge isn't working right."

The man held the door open for me, didn't give me a glance, and I walked right in. Nothing recorded. As far as the central system was concerned, I was still upstairs at my cubicle.

I took the stairs to the third floor. The door to the third floor was unlocked. This, too, was a fire department law of some kind: in buildings above a certain height you had to be able to go from floor to floor by the stairs, in case of emergency. Probably some floors had a badge-reader station just inside the stair exit. But the third floor didn't. I walked right into the reception area outside Human Resources.

The waiting area had just the right kind of HR look—a lot of dignified mahogany, to say we're serious and this is about your career, and colorful, welcoming, cushy-looking chairs. Which told you that whenever you came to HR you were going to sit there on your butt for an ungodly long time.

I looked around for closed-circuit TV cameras and didn't see any. Not that I was expecting any; this wasn't a bank—or the skunkworks—but I just wanted to make sure. Or as sure as I could be, anyway.

The lights were on low, which made the place look even more stately. Or spooky, I couldn't decide.

For a few seconds I stood there, thinking. There weren't any cleaning people around to let me in; they probably came late at night or early in the morning. That would have been the best way in. Instead, I'd have to try the same old my-badge-won't-work trick, which had gotten me this far. I went back downstairs and headed into the lobby through the back way, where a female lobby ambassador with big brassy red hair was watching a rerun of *The Bachelor* on one of the security monitors.

"And I thought I was the only one who had to work on Sunday," I said to her. She looked up, laughed politely, turned back to her show. I looked like I belonged, I had a badge clipped to my belt, and I was coming from the inside, so I was supposed to be there, right? She wasn't the talkative type, but that was a good thing—she just wanted to be left alone to watch *The Bachelor*. She'd do anything to get rid of me.

"Hey, listen," I said, "sorry to bother you, but do you have that machine to fix badges? It's not like I *want* to get into my office or anything, but I have to or I'm out of a job, and the damned badge-reader won't let me in. It's like it *knows* I should be home watching football, you know?"

She smiled. She probably wasn't used to Trion employees even noticing her. "I know what you mean," she said. "But sorry, the lady who does that won't be in till tomorrow."

"Oh, man. How am I supposed to get in? I can't wait till tomorrow. I'm totally screwed."

She nodded, picked up her phone. "Stan," she said, "can you help us out here?"

Stan, the security guard, showed up a couple minutes later. He was a small, wiry, swarthy guy in his fifties with an obvious toupee that was jet black while the fringe of real hair all around it was going gray. I could never understand why you would bother to wear a hairpiece if you weren't going to update it once in a while to make it look halfway convincing. We took the elevator up to the third floor. I gave him some complicated blather about how HR was on a hierarchically separate badging system, but he wasn't too interested. He wanted to talk sports, and that I could do, no problem. He was bummed out about the Denver Broncos, and I pretended I was too. When we got to HR, he took out his badge, which probably let him in anywhere he worked in this part of the building. He waved it at the card reader. "Don't work too hard," he said.

"Thanks, brother," I said.

He turned to look at me. "You better get that badge fixed," he said.

And I was in.

30

Once you got past the reception area, HR looked like every other damned office at Trion, the same generic cube-farm layout. Only the emergency lights were on, not the overhead fluorescents. From what I could see walking around, all of the cubicles were empty, as were all the offices. It didn't take long to figure out where the records were kept. In the center of the floor was a huge grid made up of long aisles of beige horizontal files.

I'd thought about trying to do my espionage totally online, but that wouldn't work without an HR password. While I was here, though, I figured I'd leave one of those key logger devices. Later on I could come back and get it. Wyatt Telecom was paying for these little toys, not me. I found a cubicle and installed the thing.

For now, though, I had to root around through the file drawers, find the AURORA people. And I'd have to move fast—the longer I stayed here, the greater the chance I'd be caught.

The question was, how were they organized? Alphabetically, by name? In order of employee number? The more I looked over the file drawer labels, the more discouraged I got. What, did I think I was just going to waltz in and slide open a door and pluck out a few choice files? There were rows of drawers titled BENEFITS ADMINISTRATION and PENSION/ANNUITY/RETIREMENT and SICK, ANNUAL AND OTHER LEAVE RECORDS; drawers labeled CLAIMS, WORKMEN'S COMPENSATION and CLAIMS, LITIGATED; one area called IMMIGRATION AND NATURALIZATION RECORDS . . . and on and on. Mind-numbing.

For some reason some sappy golden-oldie song was playing in my head—"Band on the Run," by Paul McCartney in his unfortunate Wings period. A song I really detest, worse even than anything by Celine Dion. The tune is annoying but catchy, like pinkeye, and the words make no sense. "A bell was ringing in the village square for the *rabbits on the run!*" Um, okay.

I tried one of the file drawers, and of course it was locked; they all were. Each file cabinet had a lock at the top, and they had to be all keyed alike. I looked for an admin's desk, and meanwhile that damned song was circling around in my head. . . . *"The county judge . . . held a grudge"* . . . as I looked for an admin's desk, and sure enough, a key to the files was there, on a ring in an unlocked top center drawer. Boy, Meacham was right; the key's always easy to find.

I went for the alphabetized employee files.

Choosing one name from the AURORA list—Yonah Oren—I looked under O. Nothing there. I looked for another name—Sanjay Kumar—and found nothing there either. I tried Peter Daut: nothing. Strange. Just to be thorough, I checked under those names in the INSURANCE POLICIES, ACCIDENT drawers. Nothing. Same with the pension files. In fact, nothing in any of the files, so far as I could see.

"The jailer man and Sailor Sam. . . ." This was like Chinese water torture—what did those insipid lyrics mean anyway? Did anyone know?

What was strange was that in the places where the records *should* have been, there sometimes seemed to be little gaps, little loose places, as if the files had been removed. Or was I just imagining this? Just when I was about to give up, I took one more circuit around the rows of file cabinets, and then I noticed an alcove—a separate, open room next to the grid of file drawers. A sign posted on the entrance to the alcove said:

CLASSIFIED PERSONNEL RECORDS—
ACCESS ONLY BY DIRECT AUTHORIZATION
OF JAMES SPERLING OR LUCY CELANO.

I entered the alcove and was relieved to see that things were simple here: the drawers were organized by department number. James Sperling was the director of HR, and Lucy Celano, I knew, was his administrative assistant. It took me a couple of minutes to find Lucy Celano's desk, and maybe thirty seconds to find her key ring (bottom right drawer).

Then I returned to the restricted file cabinets and found the drawer that held the department numbers, including the AURORA project. I unlocked the cabinet, and pulled it open. It made a kind of metallic *thunk* sound, as if some caster at the back of the drawer had somehow dropped. I wondered how often anyone actually went into these drawers. Did they work with online records mostly, keeping the hard copies just for legal and audit reasons?

And then I saw something truly bizarre: *all* of the files for the AURORA department were gone. I mean, there was a gap of a foot and a half, maybe two feet, between the number before and the number after. The drawer was half empty.

The AURORA files had been removed.

For a second it felt as if my heart had stopped. I felt light-headed.

Out of the corner of my eye, I saw a bright light start to flash. It was one of those xenon emergency strobe lights mounted high on the wall, near the ceiling, just outside the file alcove. What the hell was that for? And a few seconds later there came the unbelievably loud, throaty *hoo-ah, hoo-ah* of a siren.

Somehow I'd triggered an intrusion-detection system, no doubt protecting the classified files.

The siren was so loud you could probably hear it throughout the whole wing.

31

Any second Security would be here. Maybe the only reason they hadn't shown up yet was that it was a weekend and there were fewer of them around.

I raced to the door, slammed my side against the crash bar, and the door didn't move. The impact hurt like hell.

I tried again; the door was bolted shut. Oh, Jesus. I tried another door, and that too was locked from inside.

Now I realized what that funny metallic thunking sound had been a minute or two earlier—by opening the file drawer I must have set off some kind of mechanism that auto-locked all the exit doors in the area. I ran to the other side of the floor, where there was another set of exit doors, but they wouldn't open either. Even the emergency fire-escape door to a small back stairwell was locked, and that *had* to be against code.

I was trapped like a rat in a maze. Security would be here any second now, and they'd search the place.

My mind raced. Could I try to pull something over on them? Stan, the security guard, had let me in—maybe I could convince him I'd just accidentally stepped into the wrong area, pulled open the wrong drawer. He seemed to like me, that might work. But then, what if he actually did his job right, asked to look at my badge, saw that I didn't belong anywhere remotely near here?

No, I couldn't chance it. I had no choice, I had to hide.

I was stuck inside here.

"Stuck inside these four walls," Wings wailed sickeningly at me. *Christ!*

The xenon strobe was pulsing, blindingly bright, and the alarm was going *hoo-ah, hoo-ah,* as if this were a nuclear reactor during a core melt.

But *where* could I hide? I figured the first thing I should do was create some sort of a diversion, some plausible, innocent explanation for why the alarm had gone off. Shit, there was no time!

If I was caught here, it was over. Everything. I wouldn't just lose my job at Trion. Far worse. It was a disaster, a total nightmare.

I grabbed the nearest metal trash can. It was empty, so I grabbed a piece of paper off a nearby desk, crumpled it up, took my lighter and lit it. Running back toward the classified-records alcove, I set it against the wall. Then I took out a cigarette from my pack and tossed it into the can too. The paper burned, flamed out, sending up a big cloud of smoke. Maybe, if part of the cigarette were found, they'd blame the old smoldering butt. Maybe.

I heard loud footsteps, voices that seemed to be coming from the back stairwell.

No, please, God. It's all over. It's all over.

I saw what looked like a closet door. It was unlocked. Behind was a supply closet, not very wide, but maybe twelve feet deep, crowded with tall rows of shelves stacked with reams of paper and the like.

I didn't dare put the light on, so it was hard to see, but I could make out a space between two shelves in the rear where I might be able to squeeze myself in.

Just as I pulled the door shut behind me I heard another door open, and then muffled shouts.

I froze. The alarm kept whooping. People were running back and forth, shouting louder, closer.

"Over here!" someone bellowed.

My heart was thundering. I held my breath. When I moved even slightly, the shelf in back of me squeaked. I shifted, and my shoulder brushed against a box, making a rustling sound. I doubted anyone passing by could hear the small noises I was making, not with all that racket out there, the shouting and the sirens and all. But I forced myself to remain totally still.

"—fucking *cigarette!*" I heard, to my relief.

"—extinguisher!—" someone replied.

For a long, long time—it could have been ten minutes, it could have been half an hour, I had no idea, I couldn't move my arm to check my wristwatch—I stood there squirming uncomfortably, hot and sweaty, in a state of suspended animation, my feet going numb because of the funny position I was in.

I waited for the closet door to swing open, the light to cascade in, the jig to be up.

I didn't know what the hell I could say then. Nothing, really. I would be caught, and I had no idea how I could possibly explain my way out of it. I'd be *lucky* just to be fired. I'd likely face legal action at Trion—there was simply no good explanation for my being here. I didn't want to *think* about what Wyatt would do to me.

And for all my trouble, what had I turned up here? Nothing. All the AURORA records were gone anyway.

I could hear some kind of hosing, squirting sound, obviously a fire extinguisher going off, and by now the shouts had diminished. I wondered whether Security had called in-house firefighters, or the local fire department. And whether the wastebasket fire had explained away the alarm. Or would they keep searching the place?

So I stood there, my feet turning into tingling blocks of ice while sweat ran down my face, and my shoulders and back seized up with cramps.

And I waited.

Once in a while I heard voices, but they seemed calmer, more matter-of-fact. Footsteps, but no longer frantic.

After an endless stretch of time, everything went quiet. I tried to raise my left arm to check the time, but my arm had fallen asleep. I wriggled it, moved my right arm around to pinch at the dead left one until I was able to move it up toward my face and check the illuminated dial. It was a few minutes after ten, though I'd been in there so long I was sure it was after midnight.

Slowly I extricated myself from my contortionist's position, moved noiselessly toward the door of the closet. There I stood for a few moments, listening intently. I couldn't hear a sound. It seemed a safe bet that they'd gone—they'd put out the fire, satisfied themselves that there hadn't been a break-in after all. Human beings, especially security guards who must on some level resent all those computers that have all but put them out of a job, don't trust machines anyway. They'd be quick to blame it on some alarm-system glitch. Maybe, if I were really lucky, no one would wonder why the *intrusion*-detection alarm had gone off before the *smoke* alarm had.

Then I took a breath and slowly opened the door.

I looked to either side and straight ahead, and the area seemed to be empty. No one there. I took a few steps, paused, looked around again.

No one.

The place smelled pretty strongly of smoke, and also some kind of chemical, probably from the fire extinguisher stuff.

Quietly, I made my way along the wall, away from any outside windows or glass-paneled doors, until I reached one of the sets of exit doors. Not the main reception doors, and not the rear stairwell doors through which the security guys had entered.

And they were locked.

Still locked.

Christ, no.

They hadn't deactivated the auto-lock. Moving a little more quickly now, the adrenaline surging again, I went to the reception-area doors and pushed against the crash bars, and those too were locked.

I was still locked inside.

Now what?

I had no choice. There was no way to unlock the doors from inside, at least no way that I'd been taught. And I couldn't exactly call Security for help, especially not after what had just happened.

No. I'd just have to stay inside here until someone let me out. Which might not be until the morning, when the cleaning crew came in. Or worse, when the first HR staff arrived. And then I'd have some serious explaining to do.

I was also exhausted. I found a cubicle far from any door or window, and sat down. I was totally fried. I needed sleep badly. So I folded my arms and, like a frazzled student at the college library, passed right out.

32

Around five in the morning I was awakened by a clattering noise. I bolted upright. The cleaning crew had arrived, wheeling big yellow plastic buckets and mops and the kind of vacuum cleaners you strap to your shoulder. There were two men and a woman, speaking rapidly to each other in Portuguese. I knew a little: a lot of our neighbors growing up were Brazilians.

I'd drooled a little puddle of saliva onto whoever's desk this was. I mopped it up with my sleeve, then got up and sauntered over to the exit doors, which they'd propped open with a rubber doorstop.

"*Bom dia, como vai?*" I said. I shook my head, looking embarrassed, glanced ostentatiously at my watch.

"*Bem, obrigado e o senhor?*" the woman replied. She grinned, exposing a couple of gold teeth. She seemed to get it—poor office guy, working all night, or maybe in here ridiculously early, she didn't know or care.

One of the men was looking at the scorched metal waste can and saying something to the other guy. Like, what the hell happened here?

"*Cançado,*" I said to the lady: I'm tired, that's how I am. "*Bom, até logo.*" See you later.

"*Até logo, senhor,*" the woman said as I walked out the door.

I thought for a second about driving home, changing clothes, turning right back around. But that was more than I could handle, so instead I left E Wing—by now people were starting to come in—and re-entered B Wing and went up to my cubicle. Okay, so if anyone checked the entrance records, they'd see that I'd come in to the building Sunday night around seven, then came back around five-thirty in the morning on Monday. Eager beaver. I just hoped I didn't run into anyone I knew, looking the way I did, like I'd slept in my clothes, which of course I had. Fortunately I didn't see anyone. I grabbed a Diet Vanilla Coke from the break room and took a deep swig. It tasted nasty this early in the morning, so I made a pot of coffee in the Bunn-O-Matic, and went to the men's room to wash up. My shirt was a little wrinkled, but overall I looked presentable, even if I felt like shit. Today was a big day, and I had to be at my best.

An hour before the big meeting with Augustine Goddard, we gathered in Packard, one of the bigger conference rooms, for a dress rehearsal. Nora was wearing a beautiful blue suit and she looked like she'd had her hair done specially for the occasion. She was totally on edge; she crackled with nervous energy. She was smiling, her eyes wide.

She and Chad were rehearsing in the room while the rest of us gathered. Chad was playing Jock. They were doing this back-and-forth like an old married couple going through the paces of a long-familiar argument, when suddenly Chad's cell phone rang. He had one of those Motorola flip phones, which I was convinced he favored so he could end a call by snapping it shut.

"This is Chad," he said. His tone abruptly warmed. "Hey, Tony." He held an index finger in the air to tell Nora to wait, and he went off into a corner of the room.

"Chad," Nora called after him with annoyance. He turned back, nodded at her, held up his finger again. A minute or so later I heard him snap the phone closed, and then he came up to Nora, speaking fast in a low voice. We were all watching, listening in; they were in the center ring.

"That's a buddy of mine in the controller's office," he said quietly, grimfaced. "The decision on Maestro has already been made."

"How do you know?" Nora said.

"The controller just put through the order to do a one-time write-off of fifty million bucks for Maestro. The decision's been made at the top. This meeting with Goddard is just a formality."

Nora flushed deep crimson and turned away. She walked over to the window and looked out, and for a full minute she didn't say anything.

33

The Executive Briefing Center was on the seventh floor of A Wing, just down the hall from Goddard's office. We trooped over there in a group, the mood pretty low. Nora said she'd join us in a few minutes.

"Dead men walking!" Chad sang out to me as we walked. "Dead men walking!"

I nodded. Mordden glanced at Chad walking beside me, and he kept his distance, no doubt thinking all kinds of evil thoughts about me, trying to figure out why I wasn't giving Chad the cold shoulder, what I was up to. He hadn't been stopping by my cubicle as often since the night I'd sneaked into Nora's office. It was hard to tell if he was acting strangely, since strange was his default mode. Also, I didn't want to succumb to the situational paranoia—was he looking at me funny, that sort of thing. But I couldn't help wondering whether I had blown the whole mission with one single act of carelessness, whether Mordden was going to cause me serious trouble.

"Now, seating's crucial, big guy," Chad muttered to me. "Goddard always takes the center seat on the side of the table near the door. If you want to be invisible, you sit on his right. If you want him to pay attention to you, either sit to his left or directly across the table from him."

"Do I *want* him to pay attention to me?"

"I can't answer that. He *is* the boss."

"Have you been in a lot of meetings with him?"

"Not that many," he shrugged. "A couple."

I made a mental note to sit anywhere Chad recommended against, like to Goddard's right. Fool me once, shame on you, and all that.

The EBC was a truly impressive sight. There was a huge wooden conference table made of some kind of tropical-looking wood that took up most of the room. One entire end of the room was a screen for presentations. There were heavy acoustic blinds that you could tell were supposed to slide down electrically from the ceiling, probably not only to block out light but to keep anyone outside from hearing what went on inside the room. Built into the table were speakerphones and little screens in front of each chair that slid up when a button was pushed somewhere.

There was a lot of whispering, nervous laughter, muttered wisecracks. I was sort of looking forward to seeing the famous Jock Goddard up close and personal, even if I never got to shake his hand. I didn't have to speak or make any part of the presentation, but I was a little nervous anyway.

By five minutes before ten, Nora still hadn't shown up. Had she jumped out of a window? Was she calling around, trying to lobby, making a last-ditch effort to save her precious product, pulling whatever strings she had?

"Think she got lost?" Phil joked.

Two minutes before ten, Nora entered the room, looking calm, radiant, somehow more attractive. She looked like she'd put on fresh makeup, lipliner and all that stuff. Maybe she'd even been meditating or something, because she looked transformed.

Then, at exactly ten o'clock, Jock Goddard and Paul Camilletti entered the room, and everyone went quiet. "Cutthroat" Camilletti, in a black blazer and an olive silk T-shirt, had slicked his hair back and looked like Gordon Gekko in *Wall Street*. He took a seat way off at a corner of the immense table. Goddard, in his customary black mock turtleneck under a tweedy brown sport coat, walked up to Nora and whispered something that made her laugh. He put his hand on her shoulder; she put her hand on top of his hand for a few seconds. She was acting girlish, sort of flirtatious; it was a side of Nora I'd never seen before.

Goddard then sat down right at the head of the table, facing the screen. Thanks, Chad. I was across the table and to his right. I could see him just fine and I sure didn't *feel* invisible. He had round shoulders, a little stooped. His white hair, parted on one side, was unruly. His eyebrows were bushy, white, each one looked like a snow-capped mountaintop. His forehead was deeply creased, and he had an impish look in his eyes.

There were an awkward few seconds of silence, and he looked around the big table. "You all look so nervous," he said. "Relax! I don't bite." His voice was pleasant and sort of crackly, a mellow baritone. He glanced at Nora, winked. "Not often, anyway." She laughed; a couple of other people chuckled politely. I smiled, mostly to say, I appreciate that you're trying to put us all at ease.

"Only when you're threatened," she said. He smiled, his lips forming a V. "Jock, do you mind if I start off here?"

"Please."

"Jock, we've all been working so incredibly hard on the refresh of Maestro that I think sometimes it's just hard to get outside ourselves, get any real perspective. I've spent the last thirty-six hours thinking about pretty much nothing else. And it's clear to me that there are several important ways in which we can update, improve Maestro, make it more appealing, increase market share, maybe even significantly."

Goddard nodded, made a steeple with his fingers, looked down at his notes.

She tapped the laminated bound presentation notebook. "We've come up with a strategy, quite a good one, adding twelve new functionalities, bringing Maestro up to date. But I have to tell you quite honestly that if I were sitting where you're sitting, I'd pull the plug."

Goddard turned suddenly to look at her, his great white eyebrows aloft. We all stared at her, shocked. I couldn't believe I was hearing this. She was burning her entire team.

"Jock," she went on, "if there's one thing you've taught me, it's that sometimes a true leader has to sacrifice the thing he loves most. It kills me to say it. But I simply can't ignore the facts. Maestro was great for its time. But its time has come—and gone. It's Goddard's Rule—if your product doesn't have the potential to be number one or number two in the market, you get out."

Goddard was silent for a few moments. He looked surprised, impressed, and after a few seconds he nodded with a shrewd I-like-what-I-see smile. "Are we—is everyone in agreement on this?" he drawled.

Gradually people started nodding their heads, jumping on the moving train as it pulled out of the station. Chad was nodding, biting his lip the way Bill Clinton used to; Mordden was nodding vigorously, like he was finally able to express his true opinion. The other engineers grunted, "Yes" and "I agree."

"I must say, I'm surprised to hear this," Goddard said. "This is certainly not what I expected to hear this morning. I was expecting the Battle of Gettysburg. I'm impressed."

"What's good for any of us as individuals in the short term," Nora added, "isn't necessarily what's best for Trion."

I couldn't believe the way Nora was leading this immolation, but I had to admire her cunning, her Machiavellian skill.

"Well," Goddard said, "before we pull the trigger, hang on for a minute. You—I didn't see you nodding."

He seemed to be looking directly at me.

I glanced around, then back at him. He was definitely looking at me.

"You," he said. "Young man, I didn't see you nodding your head with the rest."

"He's new," Nora put in hastily. "Just started."

"What's your name, young man?"

"Adam," I said. "Adam Cassidy." My heart started hammering. Oh, shit. It was like being called on in school. I felt like a second-grader.

"You got some kind of problem with the decision we're making here, uh, Adam?" said Goddard.

"Huh? No."

"So you're in agreement on pulling the plug."

I shrugged.

"You are, you're not—what?"

"I certainly see where Nora's coming from," I said.

"And if you were sitting where I'm sitting?" Goddard prompted.

I took a deep breath. "If I were sitting where you're sitting, I wouldn't pull the plug."

"No?"

"And I wouldn't add those twelve new features, either."

"You wouldn't?"

"No. Just one."

"And what might that be?"

I caught a quick glimpse of Nora's face, and it was beet red. She was staring at me as if an alien were bursting out of my chest. I turned back toward Goddard. "A secure-data protocol."

Goddard's brows sunk all the way down. "Secure data? Why the hell would that attract consumers?"

Chad cleared his throat and said, "Come on, Adam, look at the market research. Secure data's like what? Number seventy-five on the list of features consumers are looking for." He smirked. "Unless you think the average consumer is Austin Powers, International Man of Mystery."

There was some snickering from the far reaches of the table.

I smiled good-naturedly. "No, Chad, you're right—the average consumer has no interest in secure data. But I'm not talking about the average consumer. I'm talking about the military."

"The military." Goddard cocked one eyebrow.

"Adam—" Nora interrupted in a flat, warning sort of voice.

Goddard fluttered a hand toward Nora. "No, I want to hear this. The military, you say?"

I took a deep breath, tried not to look as panicked as I felt. "Look, the army, the air force, the Canadians, the British—the whole defense establishment in the U.S., the U.K., and Canada—recently overhauled their global communications system, right?" I pulled out some clippings from *Defense News, Federal Computer Week*—magazines I always happen to have hanging around the apartment, of course—and held them up. I could feel my hand shaking a little and hoped no one else noticed. Wyatt had prepared me for this, and I hoped I had the details right. "It's called the Defense Message System, the DMS—the secure messaging system for millions of defense personnel around the world. It's all done via desktop PCs, and the Pentagon is desperate to go wireless. Imagine what a difference that could make—secure wireless remote access to classified data and communications, with authentication of senders and receivers, end-to-end secure encryption, data protection, message integrity. Nobody owns this market!"

Goddard tilted his head, listening intently.

"And Maestro's the perfect product for this space. It's small, sturdy—practically indestructible—and totally reliable. This way, we turn a negative into a positive: the fact that Maestro is dated, legacy technology, is a *plus* for the military, since it's totally compatible with their five-year-old wireless transfer protocols. All we need to add is secure data. The cost is minimal, and the potential market is huge—I mean, *huge!*"

Goddard was staring at me, though I couldn't tell if he was impressed or he thought I'd lost my mind.

I went on: "So instead of trying to tart up this old, frankly inferior product, we remarket it. Throw on a hardened plastic shell, pop in secure encryption, and we're golden. We'll *own* this niche market, if we move fast. Forget about writing off fifty mil—now we're talking about hundreds of millions in added revenue per year."

"Jesus," Camilletti said from his end of the table. He was scrawling notes on a pad.

Goddard started nodding, slowly at first, then more vigorously. "Most intriguing," he said. He turned toward Nora. "What's his name again—Elijah?"

"Adam," Nora said crisply.

"Thank you, Adam," he said. "That's not bad at all."

Don't thank me, I thought; thank Nick Wyatt.

And then I caught Nora looking at me with an expression of pure and undisguised hatred.

34

The official word came down by e-mail before lunch: Goddard had ordered a stay of execution for Maestro. The Maestro team was ordered to crash a proposal for minor retooling and repackaging to meet the military's requirements. Meanwhile, Trion's Government Affairs staff would start negotiating a contract with the Pentagon's Defense Information Systems Agency Department of Acquisition and Logistics.

Translation: slam dunk. Not only had the old product been taken off life support, but it had gotten a heart transplant and a massive blood transfusion.

And the shit had hit the fan.

I was in the men's room, standing in front of the urinal and unzipping my fly, when Chad came sauntering in. Chad, I'd noticed, seemed to have a sixth sense that I was pee-shy. He was always following me into the men's room to talk work or sports and effectively shut off my spigot. This time he came right up to the next urinal, his face all lit up like he was thrilled to see me. I could hear him unzip. My bladder clamped down. I went back to staring at the tile grout above the urinal.

"Hey," he said. "Nice job, big guy. *That's* the way to 'manage up'!" He shook his head slowly, made a sort of spitting sound. His urine splashed noisily against the little lozenge at the bottom of the urinal. "Christ." He oozed sarcasm. He'd crossed some invisible line—he wasn't even pretending anymore.

I thought, Could you please go now so I can relieve myself? "I saved the product," I pointed out.

"Yeah, and you burned Nora in the process. Was it worth it, just so you could score some points with the CEO, get yourself a little face time? That's not how it works around here, bud. You just made a huge fucking mistake." He shook dry, zipped up, and walked out of the rest room without washing his hands.

A voice mail from Nora was waiting for me when I returned to my cubicle.

"Nora," I said as I entered her office.

"Adam," she said softly. "Sit down, please." She was smiling, a sad, gentle smile. This was ominous.

"Nora, can I say—"

"Adam, as you know, one of the things we pride ourselves on at Trion is always striving to fit the employee to the job—to make sure our most high-potential people are given responsibilities that best suit them." She smiled again, and her eyes glittered. "That's why I've just put through an employee transfer request form and asked Tom to expedite it."

"Transfer?"

"We're all awfully impressed with your talents, your resourcefulness, the depth of your knowledge. This morning's meeting illustrated that just so well. We feel that someone of your caliber could do a world of good at our RTP facility. The supply-chain management unit down there could really use a strong team player like you."

"RTP?"

"Our Research Triangle Park satellite office. In Raleigh-Durham, North Carolina."

"North *Carolina?*" Was I hearing her right? "You're talking about transferring me down to North Carolina?"

"Adam, you make it sound like it's Siberia. Have you ever been to Raleigh-Durham? It's really such a lovely area."

"I—but I can't move, I've got responsibilities here, I've got—"

"Employee Relocation will coordinate the whole thing for you. They cover all your moving expenses—everything within reason, of course. I've already started the ball rolling with HR. Any move can be a little disruptive, obviously, but they make it surprisingly painless." Her smile broadened. "You're going to love it there, and they're going to love *you!*"

"Nora," I said, "Goddard asked me for my honest thoughts, and I'm a big fan of everything you've done with the Maestro line, I wasn't going to deny it. The last thing I intended to do was to piss you off."

"Piss me off?" she said. "Adam, on the contrary—I was grateful for your input. I only wish you'd shared your thoughts with me *before* the meeting. But that's water under the bridge. We're on to bigger and better things. And so are *you!*"

The transfer was to take place within the next three weeks. I was completely freaked out. The North Carolina site was for strictly back-office stuff. A million miles away from R&D. I'd be useless to Wyatt there. And he'd blame me for screwing up. I could practically hear the guillotine blade rushing down on its tracks.

It's funny: not until I walked out of her office did I think about my dad, and then it really hit me. I *couldn't* move. I couldn't leave the old man here. Yet how could I refuse to go where Nora was sending me? Short of escalating—going over her head, or at least trying to, which would surely backfire on me—what choice did I have? If I refused to go to North Carolina, I'd have to resign from Trion, and then all hell would break loose.

It felt as if the whole building were revolving slowly; I had to sit down, had to think. As I passed by Noah Mordden's office he waggled his finger at me to summon me in.

"Ah, Cassidy," he said. "Trion's very own Julien Sorel. Do be nice to the Madame de Renal."

"Excuse me?" I said. I didn't know what the hell he was talking about.

In his signature Aloha shirt and his big round black glasses he was looking more and more like a caricature of himself. His IP phone rang, but naturally it wasn't any ordinary ring tone. It was a sound file clipped from David Bowie's "Suffragette City": "Oh *wham* bam thank you *ma'am!*"

"I suspect you impressed Goddard," he said. "But at the same time, you must also take care not to unduly antagonize your immediate superior. Forget Stendahl. You might want to read Sun Tzu." He scowled. "The ass you save could be your own."

Mordden's office was decorated with all sorts of strange things. There was a chessboard painstakingly laid out in midgame, an H.P. Lovecraft poster, a large doll with curly blond hair. I pointed to the chessboard questioningly.

"Tal-Botvinnik, 1960," he said, as if that meant anything to me. "One of the great chess moves of all time. In any case, my point is, one does not besiege walled cities if it can be avoided. Moreover, and this is wisdom not from Sun Tzu but from the Roman emperor Domitian, if you strike at a king, you must kill him. Instead, you waged an attack on Nora without arranging air support in advance."

"I didn't intend to wage an attack."

"Whatever you intended to accomplish, it was a serious miscalculation, my friend. She will surely destroy you. Remember, Adam. Power corrupts. PowerPoint corrupts absolutely."

"She's transferring me to Research Triangle."

He cocked an eyebrow. "Could have been much worse, you know. Have you ever been to Jackson, Mississippi?"

I had, and I liked the place, but I was bummed and didn't feel like engaging in a long conversation with this strange dude. He made me nervous. I pointed to the ugly doll on the shelf and said, "That yours?"

"Love Me Lucille," he said. "A huge flop and one that, I'm proud to say, was my initiative."

"You engineered . . . *dolls?*"

He reached over and squeezed the doll's hand, and it came to life, its scary-realistic eyes opening and then actually squinting with the animation of a human being. Its cupid's bow mouth opened and turned down into a frightening scowl.

"You've never seen a doll do that."

"And I don't think I ever want to again," I said.

Mordden allowed a glint of a smile. "Lucille has a full range of human facial expressions. She's fully robotic, and actually quite impressive. She whines, she gets fussy and annoying, just like a real baby. She requires burping. She gurgles, coos, even tinkles in her diaper. She exhibits alarming signs of colic. She does everything but get diaper rash. She has speech-localization, which means she looks at whoever's talking to her. You teach her to speak."

"I didn't know you did dolls."

"Hey, I can do anything I want here. I'm a Trion Distinguished Engineer. I invented it for my little niece, who refused to play with it. She thought it was creepy."

"It *is* kind of homely," I said.

"The sculpt was bad." He turned to the doll and spoke slowly. "Lucille? Say hello to our CEO."

Lucille turned her head slowly to Mordden. I could hear a faint mechanical whir. She blinked, scowled again, and began speaking in the deep voice of James Earl Jones, her lips forming the words: "Eat my shorts, Goddard."

"*Jesus*," I blurted out.

Lucille turned slowly to me, blinked again, and smiled sweetly.

"The technological guts inside this butt-ugly troll were way ahead of its time," Mordden said. "I developed a full multithreaded operating system that runs on an eight-bit processor. State-of-the-art artificial intelligence on some really tightly compiled code. The architecture's quite clever. Three separate ASICs in her fat tummy, which I designed."

An ASIC, I knew, was geek-speak for a fancy custom-designed computer chip that does a bunch of different things.

"Lucille?" Mordden said, and the doll turned to look at him, blinking. "Fuck you, Lucille." Lucille's eyes slowly squinted, her mouth turned down, and she emitted an anguished-sounding *wa-a-h*. A single tear rolled down her cheek. He pulled up her frilly pink pajama top, exposing a small rectangular LCD screen. "Mommy and Daddy can program her and see the settings on this little proprietary Trion LCD here. One of the ASICs drives this LCD, another drives the motors, another drives the speech."

"Incredible," I said. "All this for a doll."

"Correct. And then the toy company we partnered with fucked up the launch. Let this be a lesson to you. The packaging was terrible. They didn't ship until the last week in November, which is about eight weeks too late—Mommy and Daddy have already made up their Christmas lists by then. Moreover, the price point sucked—in this economy, Mommy and Daddy don't like spending over a hundred bucks for a fucking toy. Of course, the marketing geniuses in Trion Consumer and Educational thought I'd invented the next Beanie Baby, so we stockpiled several hundred thousand of these custom chips, manufactured for us in China at enormous expense and good for nothing else. Which means Trion got stuck with almost half a million ugly dolls that no one wanted, along with three hundred thousand extra doll parts waiting to be assembled, sitting to this day in a warehouse in Van Nuys."

"Ouch."

"It's okay. Nobody can touch me. I've got kryptonite."

He didn't explain what he meant, but this was Mordden, borderline crazy, so I didn't pursue it. I returned to my cubicle, where I found that I had several voice messages. When I played the second one, I recognized the voice with a jolt even before he identified himself.

"Mr. Cassidy," the scratchy voice said, "I really. . . . Oh, this is Jock Goddard. I was very much taken by your remarks at the meeting today, and I wonder if you might be able to stop by my office. Do you think you could call my assistant Flo and set something up?"

PART FOUR

COMPROMISE

Compromise: The detection of an agent, a safe house, or an intelligence technique by someone from the other side.

—*The Dictionary of Espionage*

35

Jock Goddard's office was no bigger than Tom Lundgren's or Nora Sommers's. This realization blew me away. The goddamned CEO's office was maybe a few feet bigger than my own pathetic cubicle. I walked right by it once, sure I was in the wrong place. But the name was there—AUGUSTINE GODDARD—on a brass plaque on his door, and he was in fact standing right outside his office, talking to his admin. He had on one of his black mock turtlenecks, no jacket, and wore a pair of black reading glasses. The woman he was talking to, who I assumed was Florence, was a large black woman in a magnificent silver-gray suit. She had skunk stripes of gray running through her hair on either side of her head and looked formidable.

They both looked up as I approached. She had no idea who I was, and it took Goddard a minute, but then he recognized me—it was the day after the big meeting—and said, "Oh, Mr. Cassidy, great, thanks for coming. Can I get you something to drink?"

"I'm all set, thanks," I said. I remembered Dr. Bolton's advice, then said, "Well, maybe some water." Up close he seemed even smaller, more stoop-shouldered. His famous pixie face, the thin lips, the twinkling eyes—it looked exactly like the Halloween masks of Jock Goddard that one of the business units had had made for last year's companywide Halloween party. I'd seen one hanging from a pushpin on someone's cubicle wall. Everyone in the unit wore one and did some kind of skit or something.

Flo handed him a manila file—I could see it was my HR file—and he told her to hold all calls and showed me into his office. I had no idea what he wanted, so my guilty conscience went into full swing. I mean, here I'd been skulking around the guy's corporation, doing spy-versus-spy stuff. I'd been careful, sure, but there'd been a couple of goofs.

Still, could it really be anything bad? The CEO never swings the axe himself, he always has his henchmen do it. But I couldn't help but wonder. I was ridiculously nervous, and I wasn't doing much of a job of hiding it.

He opened a small refrigerator concealed in a cabinet and handed me a bottle of Aquafina. Then he sat down behind his desk and immediately leaned back in his high leather chair. I took one of two chairs on the other side of the desk. I looked around, saw a photograph of an unglamorous-looking woman who I assumed was his wife, since she was around the same age. She was white-haired, plain, and amazingly wrinkled (Mordden had called her the shar-pei) and she wore a Barbara Bush–style three-strand pearl necklace, probably to conceal the wattles under her chin. I wondered if Nick Wyatt, so consumed with bilious envy toward Jock Goddard, had any idea who Augustine Goddard came home to every night. Wyatt's bimbos were changed, or rotated, every couple of nights and they all had tits like a centerfold; that was a job requirement.

One entire shelf was taken up with old-fashioned tin models of cars, convertibles with big tail fins and swooping lines, a few old Divco milk trucks. They were models from the forties and fifties, probably when Jock Goddard was a kid, a young man.

He saw me looking at them and said, "What do you drive?"

"Drive?" For a moment I didn't get what he was talking about. "Oh, an Audi A6."

"Audi," he repeated as if it were a foreign word. Okay, so maybe it is. "You like it?"

"It's okay."

"I would have thought you'd drive a Porsche 911, or at least a Boxster, or something of that sort. Fella like you."

"I'm not really a gearhead," I said. It was a calculated response, I'll admit, deliberately contrarian. Wyatt's *consigliere*, Judith Bolton, had even devoted part of a session to talking about cars so I could fit in with the Trion corporate culture. But my gut now told me that one-on-one I wasn't going to pull it off. Better to avoid the subject entirely.

"I thought everyone at Trion was into cars," Goddard said. I could see he was being arch. He was making a jab at the slavishness of his cult following. I liked that.

"The ambitious ones, anyway," I said, grinning.

"Well, you know, cars are my only extravagance, and there's a reason for that. Back in the early seventies, after Trion went public and I started making more money than I knew what to do with, I went out one day and bought a boat, a sixty-one-footer. I was so damned pleased with this boat until I saw a seventy-footer in the marina. Nine damned feet longer. And I felt this twinge, you understand. My competitive instincts were aroused. Suddenly I'm feeling—oh, I know it's childish, but I can't help it, I need to get me a bigger boat. So you know what I did?"

"Bought a bigger boat."

"Nope. Could have bought a bigger boat no sweat, but then there'd always be some other jackass with a bigger boat. Then who's really the jackass? Me. Can't win that way."

I nodded.

"So I sold the damned thing. I mean the next day. Only thing keeping that craft afloat was fiberglass and jealousy." He chuckled. "That's why this small office. I figured if the boss's office is the same as every other manager's, at least we're not going to have much office-envy in the company. People are always going to compete to see whose is bigger—let 'em focus on something else. So, Elijah, you're a new hire."

"It's Adam, actually."

"Damn, I keep doing that. I'm sorry. Adam, Adam. Got it." He leaned forward in his chair, put on his reading glasses, and scanned my HR file. "We hired you away from Wyatt, where you saved the Lucid."

"I didn't 'save' the Lucid, sir."

"No need for false modesty here."

"I'm not being modest. I'm being accurate."

He smiled as if I amused him. "How does Trion compare to Wyatt? Oh, forget I asked that. I wouldn't want you to answer it anyway."

"That's okay, I'm happy to answer it," I said, all forthrightness. "I like it here. It's exciting. I like the people." I thought for a split second, realizing how kiss-ass this sounded, such complete bullshit. "Well, most of them."

His pixie eyes crinkled. "You took the first salary package we offered you," he said. "Young fellow with your credentials, your track record, you could have negotiated for a good bit more."

I shrugged. "The opportunity interested me."

"Maybe, but it tells me you were eager to get the hell out of there."

This was making me nervous, and anyway, I knew Goddard would want me to be discreet. "Trion's more my kind of place, I think."

"You getting the opportunity you hoped for?"

"Sure."

"Paul, my CFO, mentioned to me your intervention on GoldDust. You've obviously got sources."

"I stay in touch with friends."

"Adam, I like your idea for retooling the Maestro, but I worry about the ramp-up time of adding the secure encryption protocol. The Pentagon's going to want working prototypes yesterday."

"Not a problem," I said. The details were still fresh in my head like I'd crammed for an organic chemistry final. "Kasten Chase has already developed the RASP secure access data security protocol. They've got their Fortezza crypto card, Palladium secure modem—the hardware and software solutions have already been developed. It might add two months to incorporate into the Maestro. Long before we're awarded the contract, we'd be good to go."

Goddard shook his head, looked befuddled. "The whole goddamned market has changed. Everything is e-this and i-that, and all the technology's converging. It's the age of all-in-one. Consumers don't want a TV and a VCR and a fax and computer and stereo and phone and you-name-it." He looked at me out of the corner of his eye. He was obviously floating the idea to see what I thought. "Convergence is the future. Don't you think?"

I looked skeptical, took a deep breath and said, "The long answer is . . . No."

After a few seconds of silence, he smiled. I'd done my homework. I'd read a transcript of some informal remarks Goddard had made at one of those future-of-technology conferences, in Palo Alto a year ago. He'd gone on a rant against "creeping featurism," as he called it, and I'd committed it to memory, figuring I could pull it out at a Trion meeting some time.

"How come?"

"That's just featuritis. Loading on the chrome at the expense of ease of use, simplicity, elegance. I think we're all getting fed up with having to press thirty-six buttons in sequence on twenty-two remote controls just to watch the evening news. I think it already pisses a lot of people off to have the CHECK ENGINE light go on in your car, and you can't just pop the hood and check it out—you've got to take it in to some specialty mechanic with a diagnostic computer and an engineering degree from MIT."

"Even if you're a gearhead," Goddard said with a sardonic smile.

"Even if. Plus, this whole convergence thing is a myth anyway, a buzzword that's dangerous if you take it seriously. Bad for business. Canon's fax-phone was a flop—a mediocre fax and an even lousier phone. You don't see the washing machine converging with the dryer, or the microwave converging with the gas oven. I don't want a combination microwave-refrigerator-electric range-television if I just want something to keep my Cokes cold. Fifty years after the computer was invented, it's converged with—what? Nothing. The way I see it, this convergence bullshit is just the jackalope all over again."

"The what?"

"The jackalope—a mythical creation of some nutty taxidermist, made up out of a jackrabbit and an antelope. You see 'em on postcards all over the West."

"You don't mince words, do you?"

"Not when I'm convinced I'm right, sir."

He put down the HR file, leaned back in his chair again. "What about the ten-thousand-foot view?"

"Sir?"

"Trion as a whole. Any other strong opinions?"

"Some, sure."

"Let's hear 'em."

Wyatt was always commissioning competitive analyses of Trion, and I'd committed them to memory. "Well, Trion Medical Systems is a pretty robust portfolio, real best-in-class technologies in magnetic resonance, nuclear medicine, and ultrasound, but a little weak in the service stuff like patient information management and asset management."

He smiled, nodded. "Agreed. Go on."

"Trion's Business Solutions unit obviously sucks—I don't have to tell *you* that—but you've got most of the pieces in place there for some serious market penetration, especially in IP-based and circuit-switched voice and ethernet data services. Yeah, I know fiber optic's in the toilet right now, but broadband services are the future, so we've gotta hang tough. The Aerospace division has had a rough couple of years, but it's still a terrific portfolio of embedded computing products."

"But what about Consumer Electronics?"

"Obviously it's our core competency, which is why I moved here. I mean, our high-end DVD players beat Sony's hands down. Cordless phones are strong, always have been. Our mobile phones are killer—we rule the market. We've got the marquee name—we're able to charge up to thirty percent more for our products, just because they say Trion on the label. But there are just way too many soft spots."

"Such as?"

"Well, it's crazy that we don't have a real Blackberry-killer. Wireless communications devices should be our playground. Instead, it's like we're just ceding the ground to RIM and Handspring and Palm. We need some serious hip-top wireless devices."

"We're working on that. We've got a pretty interesting product in the pipeline."

"Good to hear," I said. "I do think we're really missing the boat on technology and products for transmitting digital music and video over the Internet. We really should focus on R&D there, maybe partnering. *Huge* potential for revenue generation."

"I think you're right."

"And, forgive me for saying it, but I think it's sort of pathetic that we don't have a serious kid-targeted product line. Look at Sony—their PlayStation game console can make the difference between red ink and black ink some years. The demand for computers and home electronics seems to slump every couple of years, right? We're fighting electronics makers in South Korea and Taiwan, we're waging price wars over LCD monitors and digital video decks and cell phones—this is a fact of life. So we should be selling to kids—'cause children don't care about recessions. Sony's got their PlayStations, Microsoft's got its Xbox, Nintendo has GameCube, but what do we have for television video games? Diddly squat. It's a *major* weakness in a consumer-oriented product line."

I'd noticed he was sitting upright again, looking at me with a cryptic smile on his crinkly face. "How would you feel about priming the retooling of the Maestro?"

"Nora owns that. I wouldn't feel comfortable about it, frankly."

"You'd report to her."

"I'm not sure she'd like that."

His grin got crooked. "She'd get over it. Nora knows what side her bread's buttered on."

"Obviously I won't fight you on it, sir, but I think it might be bad for morale."

"Well, then, how would you like to come work for me?"

"Don't I already?"

"I mean here, on the seventh floor. Special assistant to the chairman for new-product strategy. Dotted line responsibility to the Advanced Technology unit. I'd give you an office, just down the hall. But no bigger than mine, you understand. Interested?"

I couldn't believe what I was hearing. I felt like bursting from excitement and nerves.

"Well, sure. Reporting directly to you?"

"That's right. So, do we have a deal?"

I gave a slow smile. In for a penny, I thought, and all that. "I think more responsibility calls for more money, sir, don't you?"

He laughed. "Oh, does it?"

"I'd like the additional fifty thousand I should have asked for when I started here. And I'd like forty thousand more in stock options."

He laughed again, a robust, almost Santa Claus–y ho-ho. "You've got balls, young man."

"Thank you."

"I'll tell you what. I'm not going to give you fifty thousand more. I don't believe in incrementalism. I'm going to *double* your salary. *Plus* your forty thousand options. That way you'll feel all sorts of pressure to bust your ass for me."

To keep from gasping, I bit the inside of my lip. *Jesus.*

"Where do you live?" he asked.

I told him.

He shook his head. "Not quite appropriate for someone of your level. Also, the hours you're going to be working, I don't want you driving forty-five minutes in the morning and another forty-five minutes at night. You're going to be working late nights, so I want you living close by. Why don't you get yourself one of those condos in the Harbor Suites? You can afford it now. We've got a lady who works with the Trion E-staff, specializes in corporate housing. She'll set you up with something nice."

I swallowed. "Sounds okay," I said, trying to suppress the little nervous chuckle.

"Now, I know you've said you're not a gearhead, but this Audi . . . I'm sure it's perfectly nice, but why don't you get yourself something fun? I think a man should love his car. Give it a chance, why don't you? I mean, don't go overboard or anything, but something *fun*. Flo can make the arrangements."

Was he saying they were going to give me a *car*? Good God.

He stood up. "So, are you on board?" He stuck out his hand.

I shook. "I'm not an idiot," I said good-naturedly.

"No, that's obvious. Well, welcome to the team, Adam. I look forward to working with you."

I stumbled out of his office and toward the bank of elevators, my head in a cloud. I could barely walk right.

And then I caught myself, remembered why I was here, what my real job was—how I'd gotten here, into Goddard's office, even. I'd just been promoted way, way above my ability.

Not that I even knew what my ability *was* anymore.

36

I didn't have to break the news to anyone: the miracle of e-mail and instant messaging had already taken care of that for me. By the time I got back to my cube, the word was all over the department. Obviously Goddard was a man of immediate action.

No sooner had I reached the men's room for a much-needed pee than Chad burst in and unzipped at the urinal next to me. "So, are the rumors true, dude?"

I looked impatiently at the wall tile. I really needed to go. "Which rumors?"

"I take it congratulations are in order."

"Oh, that. No, congratulations would be premature. But thanks, anyway." I stared at the little automatic-flush thing that was attached to the American Standard urinal. I wondered who invented that, whether they got rich and their family made cute jokes about the family fortune being in the toilet. I wanted Chad to just leave already.

"I underestimated you," he said, letting loose a powerful stream. Meanwhile my own internal Colorado River was threatening the Hoover Dam.

"Oh, yeah?"

"Oh, yeah. I knew you were good, but I didn't know how good. I didn't give you credit."

"I'm lucky," I said. "Or maybe I just have a big mouth, and for some reason Goddard likes that."

"No, I don't think so. You've got some kind of Vulcan mind-meld going with the old guy. You, like, know all the right buttons to push. I'll bet you two don't even need to talk. That's how good you are. I'm impressed, big guy. I don't know how you did it, but I'm seriously impressed."

He zipped up, clapped me on the shoulder.

"Let me in on the secret, will ya?" he said, but he didn't wait for a reply.

When I got back to my cubicle, Noah Mordden was standing at my cubicle inspecting the books on top of the file cabinet. He was holding a gift-wrapped package, which looked like a book.

"Cassidy," he said. "Our too-cool-for-school Widmerpool."

"Excuse me?" Man, was the guy into cryptic references.

"I want you to have this," he said.

I thanked him and unwrapped the package. It was a book, an old one that smelled of mildew. *Sun Tzu on The Art of War* was stamped on the cloth front cover.

"It's the 1910 Lionel Giles translation," he said. "The best, I think. Not a first edition, which is impossible to come by, but an early printing at least."

I was touched. "When did you have time to buy this?"

"Last week, online, actually. I didn't intend it to be a departure gift, but there you are. At least now you'll have no excuse."

"Thank you," I said. "I'll read it."

"Please do. I suspect you'll need it all the more. Recall the Japanese *kotowaza*, 'the nail that sticks up gets hammered down.' You're fortunate that you're being moved out of Nora's orbit, but there are great perils in rising too quickly in any organization. Hawks may soar, but chipmunks don't get sucked into jet engines."

I nodded. "I'll keep that in mind," I said.

"Ambition is a useful quality, but you must always cover your tracks," he said.

He was definitely hinting at something—he *had* to have seen me coming out of Nora's office—and it scared the shit out of me. He was toying with me, sadistically, like a cat with a mouse.

Nora summoned me to her office by e-mail, and I braced myself for a shitstorm. "Adam," she called out as I approached. "I just heard the news."

She was smiling. "Sit down, sit down. I am *so* happy for you. And maybe

I shouldn't reveal this, but I'm *delighted* that they took my enthusiasm about you seriously. Because, you know, they don't always listen."

"I know."

"But I assured them, if you do this, you won't be sorry. Adam's got the right stuff, I told them, he's going to go the extra mile. You've got my word on it. I *know* him."

Yeah, I thought, you think you know me. You have no idea.

"I could see you were concerned about relocating, so I made a few calls," she said. "I'm so happy things are turning out right for you."

I didn't reply. I was too busy thinking about what Wyatt would say when he heard.

37

"Holy shit," Nicholas Wyatt said.

For a split second his polished, self-contained, deep-tanned shell of arrogance had cracked open. He gave me a look that almost seemed to border on respect. Almost. Anyway, this was a whole new Wyatt, and I enjoyed seeing it.

"You are fucking kidding me." He continued staring. "This better not be a joke." Finally he looked away, and it was a relief. "This is un-fucking-believable."

We were sitting on his private plane, but it wasn't moving anywhere. We were waiting for his latest bimbo girlfriend to show up so the two of them could take off for the Big Island of Hawaii, where he had a house in the Hualalai resort. It was me, Wyatt, and Arnold Meacham. I'd never been in a private jet before, and this one was sweet, a Gulfstream G-IV, interior cabin twelve feet wide, sixty-something feet long. I'd never seen all this empty space in an airplane. You could practically play football in here. No more than ten seats, a separate conference room, two huge bathrooms with showers.

Believe me, I wasn't flying to the Big Island. This was just a tease. Meacham and I would get off before the plane went anywhere. Wyatt was wearing some kind of black silk shirt. I hoped he got skin cancer.

Meacham smiled at Wyatt and said quietly, "Brilliant idea, Nick."

"I gotta give credit to Judith," Wyatt said. "She came up with the idea in the first place." He shook his head slowly. "But I doubt even she could have seen this coming." He picked up his cell, hit two keys.

"Judith," he said. "Our boy is now working directly for Mister Big himself. The Big Kahuna. Special executive assistant to the CEO." He paused, smiled at Meacham. "I kid you not." Another pause. "Judith, sweetheart, I want you to do a crash course with our young man here." Pause. "Right, well, obviously this is top priority. I want Adam to know that guy inside and out. I want him to be the best fucking special assistant the guy's ever hired. Right." And he ended the call with a beep. Looking back at me, he said, "You just saved your own ass, my friend. Arnie?"

Meacham looked like he'd been waiting for this cue. "We ran all the AURORA names you gave us," he said darkly. "Not a single fucking one of them popped up with anything."

"What does that mean?" I asked. God, did I hate the guy.

"No Social Security numbers, no nothing. Don't fuck with us, buddy."

"What are you talking about? I downloaded them directly from the Trion directory on the Web site."

"Yeah, well, they're not real names, asshole. The admin names are real, but the research-division names are obviously cover names. That's how deep they're buried—they don't even list their real names on the Web site. Never heard of such a thing."

"That doesn't sound right," I said, shaking my head.

"Are you being straight with us?" Meacham said. "Because if you aren't, so help me, we will fucking crush you." He looked at Wyatt. "He totally fucked up the personnel records—got diddly-squat."

"The records were *gone*, Arnold," I shot back. "Removed. They're being super-careful."

"What do you have on the broad?" Wyatt broke in.

I smiled. "I'm seeing 'the broad' next week."

"Like boyfriend-girlfriend stuff?"

I shrugged. "The woman's interested in me. She's on AURORA. She's a direct link into the skunkworks."

To my surprise, Wyatt just nodded. "Nice."

Meacham seemed to sense which way the wind was blowing now. He'd been stuck on how I'd blown the HR operation, and how the AURORA names on the Trion Web site were for some reason fake, but his boss was focusing on what was going *right*, on the amazing turn of events, and

Meacham didn't want to be out of lockstep. "You're going to have access to Goddard's office now," he said. "There's any number of devices you can plant."

"This is so fucking incredible," Wyatt said.

"I don't think we need to be paying him his old Wyatt salary," Meacham said. "Not with what he's making at Trion now. Christ, this goddamned kite's making more than *me*."

Wyatt seemed amused. "Nah, we made a deal."

"What'd you call me?" I asked Meacham.

"There's a security risk in having us transfer corporate funds into an account for this kid, no matter how many shells it goes through," Meacham said to Wyatt.

"You called me a 'kite,' " I persisted. "What's that supposed to mean?"

"I thought it's untraceable," Wyatt said to Meacham.

"What's a 'kite'?" I said. I was a dog with a bone; I wasn't letting this drop, no matter how much I annoyed Meacham.

Meacham wasn't even listening, but Wyatt looked at me and muttered, "It's corporate-spy talk. A kite's a 'special consultant' who goes out there and gathers the intel by whatever means necessary, does the work."

"Kite?" I said.

"You fly a kite, and if it gets caught in a tree, you just cut the string," Wyatt said. "Plausible deniability, you ever hear of that?"

"Cut the string," I repeated dully. On one level I wouldn't mind that at all, because that string was really a leash. But I knew when they talked about cutting the string, they meant leaving me high and dry.

"If things go bad," Wyatt said. "Just don't let things go bad, and no one has to cut the string. Now, where the hell is this bitch? If she's not here in two minutes, I'm taking off without her."

38

So I did something then that was totally insane but felt great. I went out and got myself a ninety-thousand-dollar Porsche.

There was a time when I would have celebrated some great piece of news by getting hammered, maybe splurging on champagne or a couple of CDs. But this was a whole new league. I liked the idea of cutting my Wyatt apron strings by exchanging the Audi for a Porsche, lease courtesy of Trion.

Ever been in a Porsche dealership? It's not like buying a Honda Accord, okay? You don't just walk in off the street and ask for a test drive. You have to go through a lot of foreplay. You've got to fill out a form, they want to talk about why you're here, what do you do, what's your sign.

Also, there's so many options you could go out of your mind. You want bi-xenon headlights? Arctic Silver instrument panel? You want leather or *supple* leather? You want Sport Design wheels or Sport Classic II wheels or Turbo-Look I wheels?

What I wanted was a Porsche, and I didn't want to wait four to six months for it to be custom built in Stuttgart-Zuffenhausen. I wanted to drive it off the lot. I wanted it *now*. They had only two 911 Carrera coupes on the lot, one in Guards Red and one in metallic Basalt Black. It came down to the stitching on the leather. The red car had black leather that felt like leatherette and, worst of all, had red stitching on it, which looked cowboy-western and gross. Whereas the Basalt Black model had a terrific Natural Brown supple leather interior, with a leather gearshift and steering wheel. I came right back from the test drive and said let's do it. Maybe he'd sized me up as the kind of guy who was just looking, or wouldn't in the end be able to pull the trigger, but I did it, and he assured me I was making a smart move. He even offered to have someone return the leased Audi to the Audi dealership—totally zipless.

It was like flying a jet; when you floored it, it even *sounded* like a 767. Three hundred twenty horsepower, zero to sixty in five-point-zero seconds, unbelievably powerful. It throbbed and roared. I popped in my latest favorite burned CD and blasted the Clash, Pearl Jam, and Guns N' Roses while redlining it to work. It made me feel like everything was happening right.

Even before I moved into my new office, Goddard wanted me to find a new place to live, more convenient to the Trion building. I wasn't exactly going to argue; it was long past time.

His people made it easy for me to abandon the dump I'd lived in for so long and move into a new apartment on the twenty-ninth floor of the south tower of the Harbor Suites. Each of the two towers had like a hundred and fifty condos, on thirty-eight floors, ranging from studios to three-bedrooms. The towers were built on top of the swankiest hotel in the area, whose restaurant was top-rated in Zagat's.

The apartment looked like something out of an *In Style* photo shoot. It was around two thousand square feet, with twelve-foot ceilings, hardwood parquet and stone floors. There was a "master suite" and a "library" that could also be used as a spare bedroom, a formal dining room, and a giant living room.

There were floor-to-ceiling windows with the most staggering views I'd ever seen. The living room itself looked over the city, spread out below, in one direction, and over the water in another.

The eat-in kitchen looked like a showroom display at a high-end kitchen-design firm, with all the right names: Sub-Zero refrigerator, Miele dishwasher, Viking duel-fuel oven/range, cabinets by Poggenpohl, granite countertops, even a built-in wine "grotto."

Not that I'd ever need the kitchen. If you wanted "in-room dining," all you had to do was pick up the wall phone in the kitchen and press a button, and you could get a room service meal from the hotel, even have a cook from the hotel restaurant come up on short notice and make dinner for you and your guests.

There was an immense, state-of-the-art health club, a hundred thousand square feet, where a lot of rich people who didn't live here worked out or played squash or did Taoist yoga, followed by saunas and protein smoothies at the café.

You didn't even park your own car. You drove it up to the front of the building, and the valet would whisk it away somewhere and park it for you, and you called down to get it back.

The elevators zoomed at such supersonic speed that your ears popped. They had mahogany walls and marble floors and were about the same size as my old apartment.

The security here was a whole hell of a lot better too. Wyatt's goons wouldn't be able to break in here so easily and search my stuff. I liked that.

None of the Harbor Suites apartments cost less than a million, and this baby was over two million, but it was all free—furnishings included—courtesy of Trion Systems, as a perk.

Moving in was painless, since I kept almost nothing from my old apartment. Goodwill and the Salvation Army came and took away the big ugly plaid couch, the Formica kitchen table, the box spring and mattress, all the assorted junk, even the cruddy old desk. Crap fell out of the couch as they dragged it away—Zig-Zag papers, roaches, assorted druggie paraphernalia. I kept my computer, my clothes, and my mother's black cast-iron frying pan (for sentimental reasons—not that I ever used it). I packed all my stuff into the Porsche, which tells you how little there was, because there's almost zero luggage space in a Porsche. All the furniture I ordered from that fancy furniture store Domicile (the agent's suggestion)—big, puffy, overstuffed couches you could get swallowed up in, matching chairs, a dining table and chairs that looked like they came out of Versailles, a huge bed with iron railing, Persian area rugs. Super-expensive Dux mattress. Everything. A shitload of money, but hey—I wasn't paying for any of it.

In fact, Domicile was delivering all the furniture when the doorman, Carlos, called up to me to tell me that I had a visitor downstairs, a Mister Seth Marcus. I told him to send Seth right up.

The front door was already open for the delivery people, but Seth rang the doorbell and stood there in the hall. He was wearing a Sonic Youth T-shirt and ripped Diesel jeans. His normally lively, even manic, brown eyes looked dead. He was subdued—I couldn't tell if he was intimidated, or jealous, or pissed off that I'd disappeared from his radar screen, or some combination of all three.

"Hey, man," he said. "I tracked you down."

"Hey, man," I said, and gave him a hug. "Welcome to my humble abode." I didn't know what else to say. For some reason I was embarrassed. I didn't want him to see the place.

He stayed where he was in the hall. "You weren't going to tell me you were moving?"

"It kind of happened suddenly," I said. "I was going to call you."

He pulled a bottle of cheap New York State champagne from his canvas bicycle-courier bag, handed it to me. "I'm here to celebrate. I figured you were too good for a case of beer anymore."

"Excellent!" I said, taking the bottle and ignoring the dig. "Come on in."

"You dog. This is great," he said in a flat, unenthusiastic voice. "Huge, huh?"

"Two thousand square feet. Check it out." I gave him the tour. He said funny-cutting stuff like "If that's a library, don't you need to have books?" and "Now all you need to furnish the bedroom is a babe." He said my apartment was "sick" and "ill," which was his pseudogangsta way of saying he liked it.

He helped me take the plastic wrap and tape off one of the enormous couches so we could sit on it. The couch had been placed in the middle of the living room, sort of floating there, facing the ocean.

"Nice," he said, sinking in. He looked like he wanted to put his feet up on something, but they hadn't brought in the coffee table yet, which was a good thing, because I didn't want him putting his mud-crusted Doc Martens on it.

"You getting manicures now?" he said suspiciously.

"Once in a while," I admitted in a small voice. I couldn't believe he noticed a little detail like my fingernails. Jesus. "Gotta look like an executive, you know."

"What's with the haircut? Seriously."

"What about it?"

"Don't you think it's, I don't know, sort of fruity?"

"Fruity?"

"Like all fancy looking. You putting shit in your hair, like gel or mousse or something?"

"A little gel," I said defensively. "What about it?"

He squinted, shook his head. "You got cologne on?"

I wanted to change the subject. "I thought you worked tonight," I said.

"Oh, you mean the bartending gig? Nah, I quit that. It turned out to be totally bogus."

"Seemed like a cool place."

"Not if you work there, man. They treat you like you're a fucking *waiter.*"

I almost burst out laughing.

"I got a much better gig," he said. "I'm on the 'mobile energy team' for Red Bull. They give you this cool car to drive around in, and you basically hand out samples and talk to people and shit. Hours are totally flexible. I can do it after the paralegal gig."

"Sounds perfect."

"Totally. Gives me plenty of free time to work on my corporate anthem."

"Corporate anthem?"

"Every big company's got one—like, cheesy rock or rap or something." He sang, badly: "*Trion!—Change your world!* Like that. If Trion doesn't have one, maybe you could put in a word for me with the right guy. I bet I'd get royalties every time you guys sing it at a corporate picnic or whatever."

"I'll look into it," I said. "Hey, I don't have any glasses. I'm expecting a delivery, but it hasn't come yet. They say the glass is mouth-blown in Italy—wonder if you can still smell the garlic."

"Don't worry about it. The champagne's probably shit anyway."

"You still working at the law firm too?"

He looked embarrassed. "It's my only steady paycheck."

"Hey, that's important."

"Believe me, man, I do as little as possible. I do just enough to keep Shapiro off my back—faxes, copies, searches, whatever—and I still have plenty of time to surf the Web."

"Cool."

"I get like twenty bucks an hour for playing Web games and burning music CDs and pretending to work."

"Great," I said. "You're really getting one over on them." It was pathetic, actually.

"You got it."

And then I don't know why I came out with it, but I said, "So, who do you think you're cheating the most, them or yourself?"

Seth looked at me funny. "What are you talking about?"

"I mean, you fuck around at work, you scam by, doing as little as possible—you ever ask yourself what you're doing it for? Like, what's the point?"

Seth's eyes narrowed in hostility. "What's up with you?"

"At some point you got to commit to something, you know?"

He paused. "Whatever. Hey, you want to get out of here, go somewhere? This is sort of too grown-up for me, it's giving me hives."

"Sure." I'd been debating calling down to the hotel to send up a cook to make us dinner, because I thought Seth might be impressed, but then I came to my senses. It would not have been a good idea. It would have sent Seth over the edge. Relieved, I called down to the valet and asked them to bring my car around.

It was waiting for me by the time we got down there.

"That's *yours?*" he gasped. "No fucking way."

"Way," I said.

His cynical, aloof composure had finally cracked. "This baby must cost like a hundred grand!"

"Less than that," I said. "Way less. Anyway, the company leases it for me."

He approached the Porsche slowly, awestricken, the way the apes approached the monolith in *2001: A Space Odyssey*, and he stroked the gleaming Basalt Black door.

"All right, buddy," he demanded, "what's your scam? I want a piece of this."

"Not a scam," I said uncomfortably as we got in. "I sort of fell into this."

"Oh, come on, man. This is *me* you're talking to—Seth. Remember me? Are you selling drugs or something? Because if you are, you better cut me in."

I laughed hollowly. As we roared away, I saw a stupid-looking car parked on the street that had to be his. A huge blue-silver-and-red can of Red Bull was mounted on top of a dinky car. A joke.

"That yours?"

"Yep. Cool, huh?" He didn't sound so enthusiastic.

"Nice," I said. It was ridiculous.

"You know what it cost me? Nada. I just gotta drive it around."

"Good deal."

He leaned back in the supple leather seat. "Sweet ride," he said. He took a deep breath of the new-car smell. "Man, this is great. I think I want your life. Wanna trade?"

39

It was totally out of the question, of course, for me to meet again with Dr. Judith Bolton at Wyatt headquarters, where I might be seen coming or going. But now that I was hunting with the big cats, I needed an in-depth session. Wyatt insisted, and I didn't disagree.

So I met her at a Marriott the next Saturday, in a suite set up for business meetings. They'd e-mailed me the room number to go to. She was already there when I arrived, her laptop hooked up to a video monitor. It's funny, the lady still made me nervous. On the way I stopped for another hundred-dollar haircut, and I wore decent clothes, not my usual weekend junk.

I'd forgotten how intense she was—the ice-blue eyes, the coppery red hair, the glossy red lips and red nail polish—and how hard-looking at the same time. I gave her a firm handshake.

"You're right on time," she said, smiling.

I shrugged, half-smiled back to say I got it but I wasn't really amused.

"You look good. Success seems to agree with you."

We sat at a fancy conference table that looked like it belonged in someone's dining room—mine, maybe—and she asked me how it was going. I filled her in, the good stuff and the bad, including about Chad and Nora.

"You're going to have enemies," she said. "That's to be expected. But these are threats—you've left a cigarette butt smoldering in the woods, and if you don't put them out you may have a forest fire on your hands."

"How do I put them out?"

"We'll talk about that. But right now I want to focus on Jock Goddard. And if you take away nothing else today, I want you to remember this: he's *pathologically honest*."

I couldn't help smiling. This from the chief consigliere to Nick Wyatt, a guy so crooked he'd cheat on a prostate exam.

Her eyes flashed in annoyance, and she leaned in toward me. "I'm not making a joke. He's singled you out not just because he likes your mind, your ideas—which of course aren't your ideas at all—but because he finds your honesty refreshing. You speak your mind. He likes that."

"That's 'pathological'?"

"Honest is practically a fetish with him. The blunter you are, the less calculating you seem, the better you'll play." I wondered briefly if Judith saw the irony in what she was doing—counseling me in how to pull the wool over Jock Goddard's eyes by feigning honesty. One hundred percent synthetic honesty, no natural fibers. "If he starts to detect anything shifty or obsequious or calculating in your manner—if he thinks you're trying to suck up or game him—he'll cool on you fast. And once you lose that trust, you may never regain it."

"Got it," I said impatiently. "So from now on, no gaming the guy."

"Sweetheart, what planet are you living on?" she shot back. "Of *course* we game the old geezer. That's lesson two in the art of 'managing up,' come on. You'll mess with his head, but you have to be supremely artful about it. Nothing obvious, nothing he'll sniff out. The way dogs can smell fear, Goddard can smell bullshit. So you've got to come across as the ultimate straight shooter. You tell him the bad news other people try to sugarcoat. You show him a plan he likes—then you be the one to point out the flaws. Integrity's a pretty scarce commodity in our world—once you figure out how to fake it, you'll be on the good ship *Lollipop*."

"Where I want to be," I said dryly.

She had no time for my sarcasm. "People always *say* that nobody likes a suckup, but the truth is, the vast majority of senior managers *adore* suckups, even when they know they're being sucked up to. It makes them feel powerful, reassures them, bolsters their fragile egos. Jock Goddard, on the other hand, has no need for it. Believe me, he thinks quite highly of himself already. He's not blinded by need, by vanity. He's not a Mussolini who needs to be surrounded by yes-men." Like anyone we know? I wanted to say. "Look who he surrounds himself with—bright, quick-witted people who can be abrasive and outspoken."

I nodded. "You're saying he doesn't like flattery."

"No, I'm not saying that. Everyone likes flattery. But it's got to feel real to him. A little story: Napoleon once went hunting in the Bois de Boulogne with Talleyrand, who desperately wanted to impress the great general. The woods were teeming with rabbits, and Napoleon was delighted when he killed fifty of them. But when he found out later that these weren't wild rabbits—that Talleyrand had sent one of his servants to the market to buy dozens of rabbits and then set them loose in the woods—well, Napoleon was enraged. He never trusted Talleyrand again."

"I'll keep that in mind next time Goddard invites me rabbit hunting."

"The point *is*," she snapped, "that when you flatter, do so *indirectly*."

"Well, I'm not running with rabbits, Judith. More like wolves."

"There you go. Know much about wolves?"

I sighed. "Bring it on."

"It's all laid bare. There's always an Alpha male, of course, but what's interesting to keep in mind is that the hierarchy's always being tested. It's highly unstable. Sometimes you'll see the Alpha male wolf drop a fresh piece of meat on the ground right in front of the others and then move away a couple of feet and just *watch*. He's outright *daring* the other ones to even sniff at it."

"And if they do, they're supper."

"Wrong. The Alpha usually doesn't have to do anything more than glare. Maybe posture a bit. Raise his tail and ears, snarl, make himself look big and fierce. And if a fight does break out, the Alpha will attack the least vulnerable parts of the transgressor's body. He doesn't want to seriously maim a member of his own pack, and certainly not kill anyone. You see, the Alpha wolf *needs* the others. Wolves are small animals, and no individual wolf is going to bring down a moose, a deer, a caribou, without help from a pack. Point is, they're *always testing*."

"Meaning that I'm always going to be tested." Yeah, I didn't need an MBA to work for Goddard. I needed a veterinary degree.

She gave me a sidelong glance. "The point, Adam, is that the testing is always subtle. But at the same time, the leader of a wolf pack wants strength on his team. That's why occasional displays of aggression are acceptable—they demonstrate the stamina, the strength, the vitality of the entire pack. This is the importance of honesty, of *strategic candor*. When you flatter, do it subtly and indirectly, and make sure that Goddard thinks he can always get the unvarnished truth from you. Jock Goddard realizes what a lot of other CEOs don't—that candor from his aides is vital if he's going to know what's going on inside his company. Because if he's out of touch with what's really happening, he's history. And let me tell you something else you need to know. In every male mentor-protégé relationship there's a father-son element, but I suspect it's even more germane in this case. You likely remind him of his son, Elijah."

Goddard had called me that a couple of times by mistake, I recalled. "My age?"

"Would have been. He died a couple of years ago at the age of twenty-one. Some people think that since the tragedy Goddard has never been the same, that he got a little too soft. The point is, just as you may come to idealize Goddard as the father you wish you had"—she smiled, she *knew* about my Dad somehow—"you may well remind him of the son he wishes *he* still had. You should be aware of this, because it's something you may be able to use. And it's something to watch out for—he may cut you some undeserved slack at times, yet at other times he may be unreasonably demanding."

She turned to her laptop and tapped at a few keys. "Now, I want your undivided attention. We're going to watch some television interviews Goddard has given over the years—an early one from *Wall Street Week with Louis Rukeyser*, several from CNBC, one he did with Katie Couric on *The Today Show*."

A video image of a much younger Jock Goddard, though still impish, pixielike—was frozen on the screen. Judith whirled around in her chair to face me. "Adam, this is an extraordinary opportunity you've been handed. But it's also a far more dangerous situation than you've been in at Trion, because you'll be far more constrained, far less able to move about the company unnoticed or just 'hang out' with regular people and network with them. Paradoxically, your intelligence-gathering assignment has just become *hugely* more difficult. You're going to need all the ammunition you can collect. So before we finish today, I want you to know this fellow *inside and out*, are you with me?"

"I'm with you."

"Good," she said, and gave me her scary little smile. "I *know* you are." Then she lowered her voice almost to a whisper. "Listen, Adam, I have to tell you—for your own sake—that Nick is getting very impatient for results. You've been at Trion for how many weeks?—and he has yet to know what's going on in the skunkworks."

"There's a limit," I began, "to how aggressive—"

"Adam," she said quietly, but with an unmistakable note of menace. "This is *not* someone you want to fuck with."

40

Alana Jennings lived in a duplex apartment in a redbrick town house not far from Trion headquarters. I recognized it immediately from the photograph.

You know how when you just start going out with a girl and you notice everything, where she lives and how she dresses and her perfume, and everything seems so different and new? Well, the strange thing was how I knew so much about her, more than some husbands know about their wives, and yet I'd spent no more than an hour or two with her.

I pulled up to the town house in my Porsche—isn't that part of what Porsches are for, to impress chicks?—and climbed the steps and rang the doorbell. Her voice chirped over the speaker, said she'd be right down.

She was wearing a white embroidered peasant blouse and black leggings and her hair was up, and she wasn't wearing the scary black glasses. I wondered whether peasants ever actually wore peasant blouses, and whether there really were peasants in the world anymore, and if there were, whether they thought of themselves as peasants. She looked too spectacularly beautiful. She smelled great, different from most of the girls I usually went out with. A floral fragrance called Fleurissimo; I remembered reading that she'd pick it up at a place called the House of Creed whenever she went to Paris.

"Hey," I said.

"Hi, Adam." She had glossy red lipstick on and was carrying a tiny square black handbag over one shoulder.

"My car's right here," I said, trying to be subtle about the brand-new shiny black Porsche ticking away right in front of us. She gave it an appraising glance but didn't say anything. She was probably putting it together in her mind with my Zegna jacket and pants and open-collar black casual shirt, maybe the five-thousand-dollar Italian navy watch too. And thinking I was either a show-off or trying too hard. She wore a peasant blouse; I wore Ermenegildo Zegna. Perfect. She was pretending to be poor, and I was trying to look rich and probably overdoing it.

I opened the passenger's side door for her. I'd moved the seat back before I got here so there'd be plenty of legroom. Inside, the air was heavy with the aroma of new leather. There was a Trion parking sticker on the left rear side of the car, which she hadn't yet noticed. She wouldn't see it from inside the car either, but soon enough she would, when we were getting out at the restaurant, and that was just as well. She was going to find out soon enough, one way or another, that I worked at Trion too, and that I'd been hired to fill the job she used to have. It was going to be a little weird, the coincidence, given that we hadn't met at work, and the sooner it came up the better. In fact, I was ready with a dumb line of patter. Like: "You're kidding me. You do? So do I! How bizarre!"

There were a few moments of awkward silence as I drove toward her favorite Thai restaurant. She glanced up at the speedometer, then back at the road. "You should probably watch it around here," she said. "This is a speed trap. The cops are just waiting for you to go over fifty, and they really sock you."

I smiled, nodded, then remembered a riff from one of her favorite movies, *Double Indemnity*, which I'd rented the night before. "How fast was I going, officer?" I said in that sort of flat-affect film-noir Fred MacMurray voice.

She got it immediately. Smart girl. She grinned. "I'd say around ninety." She had the vampish Barbara Stanwyck voice down perfectly.

"Suppose you get down off your motorcycle and give me a ticket."

"Suppose I let you off with a warning this time," she came back, playing the game, her eyes alive with mischief.

I faltered for only a few seconds until the line came to me. "Suppose it doesn't take."

"Suppose I have to whack you over the knuckles."

I smiled. She was good, and she was into it. "Suppose I bust out crying and put my head on your shoulder."

"Suppose you try putting it on my husband's shoulder."

"That tears it," I said. End of scene. Cut, print, that's a take.

She laughed delightedly. "How do you *know* that?"

"Too much wasted time watching old black-and-white movies."

"Me too! And *Double Indemnity* is probably my favorite."

"It's right up there with *Sunset Boulevard*." Another favorite of hers.

"Exactly! 'I *am* big. It's the pictures that got small.' "

I wanted to quit while I was ahead, because I'd pretty much exhausted my supply of memorized noir trivia. I moved the conversation into tennis, which was safe. I pulled up in front of the restaurant, and her eyes lit up again. "You know about this place? It's the best!"

"For Thai food, it's the only place, as far as I'm concerned." A valet parked the car—I couldn't believe I was handing the keys to my brand-new Porsche to an eighteen-year-old kid who was probably going to take it out on a joyride when business got slow—and so she never saw the Trion sticker.

It was actually a great date for a while. That *Double Indemnity* stuff seemed to have set her at ease, made her feel that she was with a kindred spirit. Plus a guy who was into Ani DiFranco, what more could she ask for? Maybe a little depth—women always seemed to like depth in a guy, or at least the occasional fleeting moment of self-reflection, but I was all over that.

We ordered green papaya salad and vegetarian spring rolls. I considered telling her I was a vegetarian, like she was, but then I decided that would be too much, and besides, I didn't know if I could stand to keep up the ruse for more than one meal. So I ordered Masaman curry chicken and she ordered a vegetarian curry without coconut milk—I remembered reading that she was allergic to shrimp—and we both drank Thai beer.

We moved from tennis to the Tennis and Racquet Club, but I quickly steered us away from those dangerous shoals, which would raise the question of how and why I was there that day, and then to golf, and then to summer vacations. She used "summer" as a verb. She figured out pretty quickly that we came from different sides of the tracks, but that was okay. She wasn't going to marry me or introduce me to her father, and I didn't want to have to fake my family background too, which would be a lot of work. And besides, it didn't seem necessary—she seemed to be into me anyway. I told her some stories about working at the tennis club, and doing the night shift at the gas station. Actually, she must have felt a little uncomfortable about her privileged upbringing, because she told a little white lie about how her parents forced her to spend part of her summers doing scutwork "at the company where my dad works," neglecting to mention that her dad was the CEO. Also, I happened to know she had never worked at her father's company. Her summers were spent on a dude ranch in Wyoming, on safari in Tanzania, living with a couple of other women in an apartment paid for by Daddy in the Sixth in Paris, interning at the Peggy Guggenheim on the Grand Canal in Venice. She wasn't pumping gas.

When she mentioned the company where her father "worked," I braced myself for the inevitable subject of what-do-you-do, where-do-you-work. But it never happened, until much later. I was surprised when she brought it up in a strange way, kind of making a game of it. She sighed. "Well, I suppose now we have to talk about our jobs, right?"

"Well . . ."

"So we can talk endlessly about what we do during the day, right? I'm in high-tech, okay? And you—wait, I know, don't tell me."

My stomach tightened.

"You're a chicken farmer."

I laughed. "How'd you guess?"

"Yep. A chicken farmer who drives a Porsche and wears Fendi."

"Zegna, actually."

"Whatever. I'm sorry, you're a guy, so work is probably all you want to talk about."

"Actually, no." I modulated my voice into a tone of bashful sincerity. "I really prefer to live in the present moment, to be as mindful as I can. You know, there's this Vietnamese Buddhist monk who lives in France, named Thich Nhat Nanh, and he says—"

"Oh, my God," she said, "this is so uncanny! I can't believe you know Thich Nhat Nanh!"

I hadn't actually read anything this monk had written, but after I saw how many books of his she'd ordered from Amazon I did look him up on a couple of Buddhist Web sites.

"Sure," I said as if everyone had read the complete works of Thich Nhat Nanh. " 'The miracle is not to walk on water, the miracle is to walk on the green earth.' " I was pretty sure I had that right, but just then my cell phone vibrated in my jacket pocket. "Excuse me," I said, taking it out and glancing at the caller ID.

"One quick second," I apologized, and answered the phone.

"Adam," came Antwoine's deep voice. "You better get over here. It's your dad."

41

Our dinners were barely half eaten. I drove her home, apologizing profusely all the while. She could not have been more sympathetic. She even offered to come to the hospital with me, but I couldn't expose her to my father, not this early on: that would be too gruesome.

Once I'd dropped her off, I took the Porsche up to eighty miles an hour and made it to the hospital in fifteen minutes—luckily, without being pulled over. I raced into the emergency room in an altered state of consciousness: hyper-alert, scared, with tunnel vision. I just wanted to get to Dad and see him before he died. Every damned second I had to wait at the ER desk, I was convinced, might be the moment Dad died, and I'd never get a chance to say good-bye. I pretty much shouted out his name at the triage nurse, and when she told me where he was, I took off running. I remember thinking that if he was already dead she'd have said something to that effect, so he must still be alive.

I saw Antwoine first, standing outside the green curtains. His face was for some reason scratched and bloodied, and he looked scared.

"What's up?" I called out. "Where is he?"

Antwoine pointed to the green curtains, behind which I could hear voices. "All of a sudden his breathing got all labored. Then he started turning kind of dark in the face, kind of bluish. His fingers started getting blue. That's when I called the ambulance." He sounded defensive.

"Is he—?"

"Yeah, he's alive. Man, for an old cripple he's got a lot of fight left in him."

"He did that to you?" I asked, indicating his face.

Antwoine nodded, smiling sheepishly. "He refused to get into the ambulance. He said he was fine. I spent like half an hour fighting with him, when I should have just picked him up and threw him in the car. I hope I didn't wait too long to call the ambulance."

A small, dark-skinned young guy in green scrubs came up to me. "Are you his son?"

"Yeah?" I said.

"I'm Dr. Patel," the man said. He was maybe my age, a resident or an intern or whatever.

"Oh. Hi." I paused. "Um, is he going to make it?"

"Looks like it. Your father has a cold, that's all. But he doesn't have any respiratory reserve. So a minor cold, for him, is life-threatening."

"Can I see him?"

"Of course," he said, stepping to the curtain and pulling it back. A nurse was hooking up an IV bag to Dad's arm. He had a clear plastic mask on over his mouth and nose, and he stared at me. He looked basically the same, just smaller, his face paler than normal. He was connected to a bunch of monitors.

He reached down and pulled the mask off his face. "Look at all this fuss," he said. His voice was weak.

"How're you doing, Mr. Cassidy?" Dr. Patel said.

"Oh, great," Dad said, heavy on the sarcasm. "Can't you tell?"

"I think you're doing better than your caregiver."

Antwoine was sidling up to take a look. Dad looked suddenly guilty. "Oh, that. Sorry about your face, there, Antwoine."

Antwoine, who must have realized this was as elaborate an apology as he was ever going to get from my father, looked relieved. "I learned my lesson. Next time I fight back harder."

Dad smiled like a heavyweight champ.

"This gentleman saved your life," Dr. Patel said.

"Did he," Dad said.

"He sure did."

Dad shifted his head slightly to stare at Antwoine. "What'd you have to go and do that for?" he said.

"Didn't want to have to look for another job so quick," Antwoine said right back.

Dr. Patel spoke softly to me. "His chest X ray was normal, for him, and his white count is eight point five, which is also normal. His blood gasses came back indicating he was in impending respiratory failure, but he appears to be stable now. We've got him on a course of IV antibiotics, some oxygen, and IV steroids."

"What's the mask?" I said. "Oxygen?"

"It's a nebulizer. Albuteral and Atrovent, which are bronchodilators." He leaned over my father and put the mask back in place. "You're a real fighter, Mr. Cassidy."

Dad just blinked.

"*That's* an understatement," Antwoine said, laughing huskily.

"Excuse us." Dr. Patel pulled back the curtain and took a few steps. I followed him, while Antwoine hung back with Dad.

"Does he still smoke?" Dr. Patel asked sharply.

I shrugged.

"There are nicotine stains on his fingers. That's completely insane, you know."

"I know."

"He's killing himself."

"He's dying one way or the other."

"Well, he's hastening the process."

"Maybe he wants to," I said.

42

I started my first official day of working for Jock Goddard having been up all night.

I'd gone from the hospital to my new apartment around four in the morning, considered trying to grab an hour of sleep, then rejected the idea because I knew I'd oversleep. That might not be the best way to start off with Goddard. So I took a shower, shaved, and spent some time on the Internet reading about Trion's competitors, poring over News.com and Slashdot for the latest tech news. I dressed, in a lightweight black pullover (the closest thing I had to one of Jock Goddard's trademark black mock turtlenecks), a pair of dress khakis, and a brown houndstooth jacket, one of the few "casual" items of clothing Wyatt's exotic admin had picked out for me. Now I looked like a full-fledged member of Goddard's inner posse. Then I called down to the valet and asked them to have my Porsche brought around.

The doorman who seemed to be on in the early morning and evening, when I most often came and went, was a Hispanic guy in his mid-forties named Carlos Avila. He had a strange, strangled voice as if he'd swallowed a sharp object and couldn't get it all the way down. He liked me—mostly, I think, because I didn't ignore him like everybody else who lived there.

"Workin' hard, Carlos?" I said as I passed by. Normally this was the line he used on me, when I came home ridiculously late, looking wiped out.

"Hardly workin', Mr. Cassidy," he said with a grin and turned back to the TV news.

I drove it a couple of blocks away to the Starbucks, which was just opening, and bought a triple grande latte, and while I was waiting for the Seattle-grunge-wannabe multiple-piercing-victim kid to steam a quart of two-percent milk, I picked up a *Wall Street Journal*, and my stomach seized up.

There, right on the front page, was an article about Trion. Or, as they put it, "Trion's woes." There was an engraved-looking, stippled drawing of Goddard, looking inappropriately chipper, as if he were totally out of it, didn't get it. One of the smaller headlines said, "Are Founder Augustine Goddard's Days Numbered?" I had to read that twice. My brain wasn't functioning at peak capacity, and I needed my triple grande latte, which the grunge kid seemed to be struggling over. The article was a hard-hitting and smart piece of reporting by a *Journal* regular named William Bulkeley, who obviously had good contacts at Trion. The gist of it seemed to be that Trion's stock price was slipping, its products were long in the tooth, the company ("generally deemed the leader in telecommunications-based consumer electronics") was in trouble, and Jock Goddard, Trion's founder, seemed to be out of touch. His heart wasn't in it anymore. There was a whole riff about the "long tradition" of founders of high-technology companies who got replaced when their company reached a certain size. It asked whether he was the wrong person to preside over the period of stability that followed a period of explosive growth. There was a lot of stuff in there about Goddard's philanthropy, his charitable efforts, his hobby of collecting and repairing vintage American cars, how he'd completely rebuilt his prize 1949 Buick Roadmaster convertible. Goddard, the article said, seemed to be headed for a fall.

Great, I thought. If Goddard falls, guess who falls with him.

Then I remembered: Wait a second, Goddard's not my real employer. He's the *target*. My real employer is Nick Wyatt. It was easy to forget where my true loyalties were supposed to lie, with the excitement of the first day and all.

Finally my latte was ready, and I stirred in a couple of Turbinado sugar packets, took a big gulp, which scalded the back of my throat, and pressed on the plastic top. I sat down at a table to finish the rest of the article. The journalist seemed to have the goods on Goddard. Trion people were talking to him. The knives were out for the old guy.

On the drive in, I tried to listen to an Ani DiFranco CD I'd picked up at

Tower as part of my Alana research project, but after a few cuts I ejected the thing. I couldn't stand it. A couple of songs weren't songs at all but just spoken pieces. If I wanted that, I'd listen to Jay-Z or Eminem. No thanks.

I thought about the *Journal* piece and tried to come up with a spin in case anyone asked me about it. Should I say it was a piece of crap planted by one of our competitors to undermine us? Should I say the reporter had missed the real story (whatever that was)? Or that he'd raised some good questions that had to be dealt with? I decided to go with a modified version of this last one—that whatever the truth of the allegations, what counted was what our shareholders thought, and they almost all read the *Wall Street Journal*, so we'd have to take the piece seriously, truth or not.

And privately I wondered who Goddard's enemies were who might be stirring up trouble—whether Jock Goddard really was in trouble, and I was boarding a sinking ship. Or, to be accurate about it, whether Nick Wyatt had *put* me on a sinking ship. I thought: The guy *must* be in bad shape—he hired me, didn't he?

I took a sip of coffee, and the lid wasn't quite on tight, and the warm milky brown liquid doused my lap. It looked like I'd had an "accident." What a way to start the new job. I should have taken it as a warning.

43

On my way out of the lobby men's room, where I did my best to blot up the coffee spill, leaving my khakis damp and wrinkled, I passed the small newsstand in the lobby of A Wing, the main building, which sold the local papers plus *USA Today*, the *New York Times*, the salmon-colored *Financial Times*, and the *Journal*. The normally towering pile of *Wall Street Journals* was already half gone and it was barely seven in the morning. Obviously everyone at Trion was reading it. I figured copies of the piece from the *Journal*'s Web site were in everyone's e-mail by now. I said hi to the lobby ambassador and took the elevator to the seventh floor.

Goddard's chief admin, Flo, had already e-mailed me the details of my new office. That's right, not cubicle, but a real office, the same size as Jock Goddard's (and, for that matter, the same size as Nora's and Tom Lundgren's). It was down the hall from Goddard's office, which was dark like all the other offices on the executive corridor. Mine, however, was lit up.

Sitting at her desk outside my office was my new administrative assistant, Jocelyn Chang, a fortyish, imperious-looking Chinese-American woman in an immaculate blue suit. She had perfectly arched eyebrows, short black hair, and a tiny bow-shaped mouth decorated with wet-looking peach-colored lipstick. She was labeling a sorter for correspondence. As I approached, she looked up with pursed lips and stuck out her hand. "You must be Mr. Cassidy."

"Adam," I said. I didn't know, was that my first mistake? Was I supposed to maintain a distance, be formal? It seemed ridiculous and unnecessary. After all, almost everyone here seemed to call the CEO "Jock." And I was about half her age.

"I'm Jocelyn," she said. She had some kind of a flat, nasal Boston-area accent, which I hadn't expected. "Nice to meet you."

"You too. Flo said you've been here forever, which I'm glad to hear." Oops. Women don't like being told that.

"Fifteen years," she said warily. "The last three for Michael Gilmore, your immediate predecessor. He was reassigned a couple of weeks ago, so I've been floating."

"Fifteen years. Excellent. I'll need all the help I can get."

She nodded, no smile, nothing. Then she seemed to notice the *Journal* under my arm. "You're not going to mention that to Mr. Goddard, are you?"

"Actually, I was going to ask you to have it mounted and framed as a gift to him. For his office."

She gave me a long, terrified stare. Then a slow smile. "That's a joke," she said. "Right?"

"Right."

"Sorry. Mr. Gilmore wasn't really known for his sense of humor."

"That's okay. I'm not either."

She nodded, not sure how to react. "Right." She glanced at her watch. "You've got a seven-thirty with Mr. Goddard."

"He's not in yet."

She looked at her watch again. "He will be. In fact, I'll bet he just got in. He keeps a very regular schedule. Oh, hold on." She handed me a very fancy-looking document, easily a hundred pages long, bound in some kind of blue leatherette, that said BAIN & COMPANY on the front. "Flo said Mr. Goddard wanted you to read this before the meeting."

"The meeting . . . in two and a half minutes."

She shrugged.

Was this my first test? There was no way I could read even a page of this incomprehensible gibberish before the meeting, and I sure wasn't going to be late. Bain & Company is a high-priced global management-consulting firm that takes guys around my age, guys that know even less than I do, and works them until they're drooling idiots, making them visit companies and write reports and bill hundreds of thousands of dollars for their bogus wisdom. This one was stamped TRION SECRET. I skimmed it quickly, and all the clichés and buzzwords jumped right out at me—"streamlined knowledge management," "competitive advantage," "operations excellence," "cost inefficiencies," "diseconomies of scale," "minimizing non–value-adding work," blah blah blah—and I knew I didn't even have to read the thing to know what was up.

Layoffs. Head-harvesting on the cubicle farm.

Groovy, I thought. Welcome to life at the top.

44

Goddard was already sitting at a round table in his back office with Paul Camilletti and another guy when Flo escorted me in. The third guy was in his mid- to late fifties, bald with a gray fringe, wearing an unfashionable gray plaid suit, shirt, and tie right out of a shopping mall men's store, a big bulky class ring on his right hand. I recognized him: Jim Colvin, Trion's chief operations officer.

The room was the same size as Goddard's front office, ten by ten, and with only four guys here and the big round table it felt crowded. I wondered why we weren't meeting in some conference room, someplace a little bigger, more fitting for such high-powered executives. I said hi, smiled nervously, sat in a chair near Goddard, and put down my Bain document and the Trion mug of coffee Flo had given me. I took out a yellow pad and pen and got ready to take notes. Goddard and Camilletti were in shirtsleeves, no jackets—and no black turtlenecks. Goddard looked even older and more tired than last time I'd seen him. He had on a pair of black half-glasses on a string around his neck. Spread out on the table were several copies of the *Wall Street Journal* article, one of them marked up with yellow and green highlighter.

Camilletti scowled at me as I sat down. "Who's this?" he said. Not exactly 'Nice to have you aboard.'

"You remember Mr. Cassidy, don't you?"

"No."

"From the Maestro meeting? The military thing?"

"Your new assistant," he said without enthusiasm. "Right. Welcome to damage control central, Cassidy."

"Jim, this is Adam Cassidy," Goddard said. "Adam, Jim Colvin, our COO."

Colvin nodded. "Adam."

"We were just talking about this darned *Journal* piece," Goddard said, "and how to handle it."

"Well," I said sagely, "it's just one article. It'll blow over in a couple of days, no doubt."

"Bullshit," Camilletti snapped, glaring at me with an expression so scary I thought I was going to turn to stone. "It's the *Journal*. It's front-page. Everyone reads it. Board members, institutional investors, analysts, everyone. This is a friggin' train wreck."

"It's not good," I agreed. I told myself to keep my mouth shut from now on.

Goddard exhaled noisily.

"The worst thing to do is to over-rotate," Colvin said. "We don't want to send up panic smoke signals to the industry." I liked "over-rotate." Jim Colvin was obviously a golfer.

"I want to get Investor Relations in here now, Corporate Communications, and draft a response, a letter to the editor," Camilletti said.

"Forget the *Journal*," Goddard said. "I think I'd like to offer a face-to-face exclusive to the *New York Times*. An opportunity to address issues of broad concern to the whole industry, I'll say. They'll get it."

"Whatever," said Camilletti. "In any case, let's not protest too loudly. We don't want to force the *Journal* to do a follow-up, stir up the mud even more."

"Sounds to me like the *Journal* reporter must have talked to insiders here," I said, forgetting the part about keeping my mouth shut. "Do we have any idea who might have leaked?"

"I did get a voice mail from the reporter a couple of days ago, but I was out of the country," Goddard said. "So I'm 'unavailable for comment.' "

"The guy may have called me—I don't know, I can check my voice mail—but I surely didn't return his call," said Camilletti.

"I can't imagine anyone at Trion would knowingly have any part in this," Goddard said.

"One of our competitors," Camilletti said. "Wyatt, maybe."

No one looked at me. I wondered if the other two knew I came from Wyatt.

Camilletti went on, "There's a lot of stuff here quoting some of our resellers—British Tel, Vodafone, DoCoMo—about how the new cell phones aren't moving. The dogs aren't eating the dog food. So how does a reporter with a New York byline even *know* to call DoCoMo in Japan? It's got to be Motorola or Wyatt or Nokia who dropped a dime."

"Anyway," Goddard said, "it's all water under the bridge. My job isn't to manage the media, it's to manage the darned company. And this asinine piece, however skewed and unfair it might be—well, how terrible is it, really? Apart from the grim-reaper headline, what's in here that's all that new? We used to hit our numbers on the dot each quarter, never missed, maybe beat 'em by a penny or two. We were Wall Street's darling. Okay, revenue growth is flat, but good Lord, the entire industry is suffering! I can't help but detect a little Schadenfreude in this piece. Mighty Homer has nodded."

"Homer?" said Colvin, confused.

"But all this tripe about how we may be facing our first quarterly loss in fifteen years," said Goddard, "that's pure invention—"

Camilletti shook his head. "No," he said quietly. "It's even worse than that."

"What are you talking about?" Goddard said. "I just came from our sales conference in Japan, where everything was hunky-dory!"

"Last night when I got the e-mail alert about this article," Camilletti said, "I fired off e-mails to the VP/Finance for Europe and for Asia/Pacific telling them I wanted to see all the revenue numbers as of this week, the QTD sales revenue numbers broken down by customer."

"And?" prompted Goddard.

"Covington in Brussels just got back to me an hour ago, Brody in Singapore in the middle of the night, and the numbers look like crap. The sell-in was strong, but the sell-through has been terrible. Between Asia/Pacific and EMEA, that's sixty percent of our revenue, and we're falling off a cliff.

The fact is, Jock, we're going to miss this quarter, and miss big. It's a flat-out disaster."

Goddard glanced at me. "You're obviously hearing some privileged, non-public information, Adam, let's be clear about that, not a word—"

"Of course."

"We've got," Goddard began, faltered, then said, "for God's sake, we've got AURORA—"

"The revenue from AURORA is several quarters off," said Camilletti. "We've got to manage for *now*. For current operations. And let me tell you, when these numbers come out, the stock's going to take a *huge* hit," Camilletti went on. He spoke in a low voice. "Our revenues for the fourth quarter are going to be off by *twenty-five percent*. We're going to have to take a significant charge for excess inventory."

Camilletti paused, gave Goddard a significant look. "I'm estimating a pretax loss of close to half a *billion* dollars."

Goddard winced. "My God."

Camilletti went on, "I happen to know that CS First Boston is *already* about to downgrade us from 'overweight' to 'market weight.' That's from a 'buy' to a 'hold.' And that's *before* any of this comes out."

"Good Lord," Goddard said, groaning and shaking his head. "It's so absurd, given what we *know* we have in the pipeline."

"That's why we need to take another look at this," Camilletti said, jabbing his copy of the blue Bain document with his index finger.

Goddard's fingers drummed on the Bain study. His fingers, I noticed, were chubby, the back of his hands liver-spotted. "And quite the handsomely bound report it is, too," he said. "You never told me what it cost us."

"You don't want to know," Camilletti said.

"I don't, do I?" He grimaced, as if he'd made his point. "Paul, I swore I would never do this. I gave my word."

"Christ, Jock, if this is about your ego, your vanity—"

"This is about keeping my word. It's also about my credibility."

"Well, you should never have made such a promise. Never say never. In any case, you were talking in a different economy—prehistoric times. The Mesozoic Era, for God's sake. Rocketship Trion, growing at warp speed. We're one of the few high-tech companies that *hasn't* gone through layoffs yet."

"Adam," Goddard said, turning to me and looking over his glasses, "have you had a chance to plow through all this gobbledygook?"

I shook my head. "Just got it a few minutes ago. I've skimmed it."

"I want you to look closely at the projections for consumer electronics. Page eighty-something. You have some familiarity with that."

"Right now?" I asked.

"Right now. And tell me if they look realistic to you."

"Jock," said Jim Colvin, "it's just about impossible to get honest projections from any of the division heads. They're all protecting their head count, guarding their turf."

"That's why Adam's here," Goddard replied. "He doesn't have turf to protect."

I frantically thumbed through the Bain report, trying to look like I knew what I was doing.

"Paul," Goddard said, "we've gone through all this before. You're going to tell me we have to slash eight thousand jobs if we want to be lean and mean."

"No, Jock, if we want to remain *solvent*. And it's more like ten thousand jobs."

"Right. So tell me something. Nowhere in this darned treatise does it say that a company that downsizes or rightsizes or whatever the hell you want to call it is ever better off in the long run. All you hear about is the short term." Camilletti looked like he was about to respond, but Goddard kept going. "Oh, I know, everyone does it. It's a knee-jerk response. Business stinks? Get rid of some people. Throw the ballast overboard. But do layoffs ever really lead to a *sustained* increase in share price, or market share? Hell, Paul, you know as well as I do that as soon as the skies clear up again we just end up hiring most of 'em back. Is it really worth all the goddamned *turmoil?*"

"Jock," Jim Colvin said, "it's what they call the Eighty-Twenty Rule—twenty percent of the people do eighty percent of the work. We're just cutting the fat."

"The 'fat' is dedicated Trion employees," Goddard shot back. "To whom we issue those little culture badges that talk about loyalty and dedication. Well, it's a two-way street, isn't it? We expect loyalty from them, but they don't get it back from us? Far as I'm concerned, you go down this road, you lose more than head count. You lose a fundamental sense of trust. If our employees have upheld their half of the contract, how come we don't have to? It's a damned breach of trust."

"Jock," Colvin said, "the fact is, you've made a lot of Trion employees very rich in the last ten years."

Meanwhile I was racing through the charts of projected earnings, trying to compare them to the numbers I'd seen over the last couple of weeks.

"This is no time to be high-minded, Jock," Camilletti said. "We don't have that luxury."

"Oh, I'm not being high-minded," Goddard said, drumming his fingers some more on the tabletop. "I'm being brutally practical. I don't have a problem with getting rid of the slackers, the coasters, the rest-'n-vesters. Screw 'em. But layoffs on this scale just lead to increased absenteeism, sick leaves, people standing around the water cooler asking each other about the latest rumor. Paralysis. Put it in a way you can understand, Paul, that's called a decrease in productivity."

"Jock—" Colvin began.

"*I'll* give you an eighty-twenty rule," Goddard said. "If we do this, eighty percent of my remaining employees are going to be able to focus no more than about twenty percent of their mental abilities on their work. Adam, how do the forecasts look to you?"

"Mr. Goddard—"

"I fired the last guy who called me that."

I smiled. "Jock. Look, I'm not going to dance around here. I don't *know* most of the numbers, and I'm not going to shoot from the hip. Not on something this important. But I do know the Maestro numbers, and I can tell you these look overly optimistic, frankly. Until we start shipping to the Pentagon—assuming we land that deal—these numbers are way high."

"Meaning the situation could be even worse than our hundred-thousand-dollar consultants tell us."

"Yes, sir. At least, if the Maestro numbers are any indication."

He nodded.

Camilletti said, "Jock, let me put it to you in human terms. My father was a goddamned schoolteacher, okay? Sent six kids through college on a schoolteacher's salary, don't ask me how, but he did. Now he and my mom are living off his measly life's savings, most of which is tied up in Trion stock, because I told him this was a great company. This is not a lot of money, by our standards, but he's already lost twenty-six percent of his nest egg, and he's about to lose a whole hell of a lot more. Forget about Fidelity and TIAA-CREF. The vast majority of our shareholders are Tony Camillettis, and what are we supposed to tell *them?*"

I had the distinct feeling that Camilletti was making this up, that in reality his investment-banker father lived in a gated community in Boca and played a lot of golf, but Goddard's eyes seemed to glisten.

"Adam," Goddard said, "*you* see my point, don't you?"

For a moment I felt like a deer frozen in the headlights. It was obvious what Goddard wanted to hear from me. But after a few seconds I shook my head. "To me," I said slowly, "it looks like if you don't do it now, you'll probably have to cut even more jobs a year from now. So I have to say I'm with Mr.—with Paul."

Camilletti reached out a hand and patted me on the shoulder. I recoiled a little. I didn't want it to look like I was choosing sides—against my boss. Not a good way to start off the new job.

"What sort of terms are you proposing?" Goddard said with a sigh.

Camilletti smiled. "Four weeks of severance pay."

"No matter how long they've been with us? No. Two weeks of severance pay for every year they've been with us, plus an additional two weeks for every year beyond ten years."

"That's *insane*, Jock! In some cases, we'll be paying out a year's severance pay, maybe more."

"That's not severance," muttered Jim Colvin, "that's welfare."

Goddard shrugged. "Either we lay off on those terms, or we don't lay off at all." He gave me a mournful look. "Adam, if you ever go out to dinner with Paul, don't let him choose the wine." Then he turned back to his CFO. "You want the layoffs effective June 1, is that right?"

Camilletti nodded warily.

"Somewhere in the back of my mind," Goddard said, "I have this vague recollection that we signed a one-year severance contract with the CableSign division we acquired last year that expires on May thirty-first. Day before."

Camilletti shrugged.

"Well, Paul, that's almost a thousand workers who'd get a month's salary plus a month's pay for each year served—if we lay them off one day earlier. A decent severance package. That one day'll make a huge difference to those folks. Now they'll get a lousy two weeks."

"June first is the beginning of the quarter—"

"I won't do that. Sorry. Make it May thirtieth. And as for those employees whose stock options are underwater, we'll give 'em twelve months to exercise them. And I'm taking a voluntary pay cut myself—to a dollar. How about you, Paul?"

Camilletti smiled nervously. "You get a lot more stock options than I do."

"We're doing this once," Goddard said. "Doing it once and doing it right. I'm not slicing twice."

"Understood," Camilletti said.

"All right," Goddard said with a sigh. "As I'm always telling you, sometimes you just gotta get in the car, get with the program. But first I want to run this by the entire management team, conference in as many of them as we can get together. I also want to get on the horn to our investment bankers. If it flies, as I fear it will, I'll tape a Webcast announcement to the company," Goddard said, "and we'll release it tomorrow, after the close of trading. And make the public announcement at the same time. I don't want a word of this leaking out before then—it's demoralizing."

"If you'd prefer, I'll make the announcement," Camilletti said. "That way you keep your hands clean."

Goddard glared at Camilletti. "I'm not hanging this on you. I refuse. This is my decision—I get the credit, the glory, the magazine covers, and I get the blame too. It's only right."

"I only say it because you've made so many pronouncements in the past. You'll get skewered—"

Goddard shrugged, but he looked miserable. "Now I suppose they're all going to be calling me Chainsaw Goddard or something."

"I think 'Neutron Jock' has a better ring to it," I said, and for the first time, Goddard actually smiled.

45

I left Goddard's office feeling both relieved and weighted down.

I'd survived my first meeting with the guy, didn't make too big a fool of myself. But I was also in possession of a serious company secret, real inside information that was going to change a lot of people's lives.

Here's the thing: I'd made up my mind that I wasn't going to pass this on to Wyatt and company. It wasn't part of my assignment, wasn't in my job description. It had nothing to do with the skunkworks. I wasn't required to tell my handlers. They didn't know I knew, anyway. Let them find out about the Trion layoffs when everyone else did.

Preoccupied, I stepped off the elevator on the third floor of A Wing to grab a late lunch in the dining room when I saw a familiar face coming at me. A tall, skinny young guy, late twenties, bad haircut, called out, "Hey, Adam!" as he got into the elevator.

Even in that fraction of a second before I could put a name to the face, my stomach clenched. My animal hindbrain had sensed the danger before my cerebrum figured it out.

I nodded, kept on walking. My face was burning.

His name was Kevin Griffin, an affable if goofy-looking guy, and a decent basketball player. I used to shoot hoops with him at Wyatt Telecommunications. He was in sales in the Enterprise Division, in routers. I remembered him as very sharp, very ambitious behind that laid-back demeanor. He always beat his numbers, and he used to joke with me, in a good-natured sort of way, about my casual attitude toward work.

In other words, he knew who I really was.

"Adam!" he persisted. "Adam Cassidy! Hey, what are *you* doing here?"

I couldn't exactly ignore him anymore, so I turned back. He had one hand on the elevator doors to keep them from closing.

"Oh, hey, Kevin," I said. "You work here now?"

"Yeah, in sales." He seemed thrilled, like this was a high-school reunion or something. He lowered his voice. "Didn't they kick you out of Wyatt because of that party?" He made a sort of sniggering sound, not nasty or anything, just kind of conspiratorial.

"Nah," I said, faltering for a second, trying to sound lighthearted and amused. "It was all a big misunderstanding."

"Yeah," he said dubiously. "Where're you working here?"

"Same old same old," I said. "Hey, nice to see you, guy. Sorry, I've got to run."

He looked back at me curiously as the elevator doors closed.

This was not good.

PART FIVE

BLOWN

Blown: Exposure of personnel, installation (such as a safe house) or other elements of a clandestine activity or organization. A blown agent is one whose identity is known to the opposition.

—*Spy Book: The Encyclopedia of Espionage*

46

I was screwed.

Kevin Griffin knew I wasn't on the Lucid project back at Wyatt, knew I wasn't any superstar either. He knew the real story. He was probably already back at his cubicle looking me up on the Trion intranet, amazed to see me listed as executive assistant to the president and CEO. How long would it be before he started talking, telling stories, asking around? Five minutes? Five *seconds?*

How the hell could this have happened, after all the careful planning, the laying of the groundwork by Wyatt's people? How could they have *let* Trion hire someone who could sabotage the whole scheme?

I looked around, dazed, at the cafeteria's deli counter. Suddenly I didn't have any appetite. I took a ham-and-cheese sandwich anyway, because I needed the protein, and a Diet Pepsi, and went back to my new office.

Jock Goddard was standing in the hall near my office talking to some other executive type. He caught my eye, held up an index finger to let me know he wanted to talk to me, so I stood there awkwardly at a distance while he finished his conversation.

After a couple of minutes Jock put a hand on the other man's shoulder, looking solemn, then led the way into my office.

"You," he said as he sat down in the visitor's chair. The only other place to sit was behind my desk, which felt all wrong—he was the goddamned

CEO!—but I had no choice. I sat down, smiled at him hesitantly, didn't know what to expect.

"I'd say you passed with flying colors," Goddard said. "Congratulations."

"Really? I thought I blew it," I said. "I didn't exactly feel comfortable taking someone else's side."

"That's why I hired you. Oh, not to take sides against me. But to speak truth to power, as it were."

"It wasn't truth," I said. "It was just one guy's opinion." Maybe that was going a little too far.

Goddard rubbed his eyes with a stubby hand. "The easiest thing in the world for a CEO—and the most dangerous—is to be out of touch. No one ever really wants to give me the unvarnished truth. They want to spin me. They've all got their own agenda. Do you like history?"

I'd never thought of history as something you could "like." I shrugged. "Some."

"During the Second World War, Winston Churchill set up an office outside of the chain of command whose job was to give him the straight, blunt truth. I think he called it the Statistical Office or something. Anyway, the point was, no one liked to give him bad news, but he knew he had to hear it or he couldn't do his job."

I nodded.

"You start a company, have fortune smile upon you a few times, and you can get to be almost a cult figure among folks who don't know any better," Goddard continued. "But I don't need my, er, ring kissed. I need candor. Now more than ever. There's an axiom in this business that technology companies inevitably outgrow their founders. Happened with Rod Canion at Compaq, Al Shugart at Seagate. Apple Computer even kicked out Steve Jobs, remember, until he came riding back in on his white horse and saved the place. Point is, there are no old, bold founders. My board has always had deep wells of faith in me, but I suspect those wells are starting to run dry."

"Why do you say that, sir?"

"The 'sir' stuff has got to stop," Goddard snapped. "The *Journal* piece was a shot across the bow. It wouldn't surprise me if it came from disgruntled board members, some of whom think it's time for me to step down, retire to my country house, and tinker with my cars full-time."

"You don't want to do that, do you?"

He scowled. "I'll do whatever's best for Trion. This damned company is my whole life. Anyway, cars are just a hobby—you do a hobby full-time and it's no fun anymore." He handed me a thick manila folder. "There's an Adobe PDF copy of this in your e-mail. Our strategic plan for the next eighteen months—new products, upgrades, the whole kit and caboodle. I want you to give me your blunt, unvarnished take—a presentation, whatever you want to call it, an overview, a helicopter ride."

"When would you like it?"

"Soon as you possibly can. And if there's any particular project you think you'd like to get involved in, as my emissary, be my guest. You'll see there are all kinds of interesting things in the pipeline. Some of which are quite closely held. My God, there's one thing in the works, codenamed Project AURORA, which may reverse our fortunes entirely."

"AURORA?" I said, swallowing hard. "I think you mentioned that in the meeting, right?"

"I've given it to Paul to manage. Truly mind-blowing stuff. A few kinks in the prototype that still need to be ironed out, but it's just about ready to be unveiled."

"Sounds intriguing," I said, trying to sound casual. "I'd love to help out on that."

"Oh, you will, no doubt about that. But all in good time. I don't want to distract you just yet from some of the housecleaning issues, because once you get caught up in AURORA . . . well, I don't want to send you in too many directions at once, spread you too thin." He stood up, clasped his hands together. "Now I've got to head over to the studio to tape the Webcast, which is *not* something I'm looking forward to, let me tell you."

I smiled sympathetically.

"Anyway," Goddard said, "sorry to plunge you in that way, but I have a feeling you're going to do just fine."

47

I arrived at Wyatt's house at the same time as Meacham, who made some crack about my Porsche. We were shown in to Wyatt's elaborate gym, in the basement level but, because of the landscaping, it wasn't below ground. Wyatt was lifting weights at a reclining bench—a hundred fifty pounds. He wore only a skimpy pair of gym shorts, no shirt, and looked more bulked-up than ever. This guy was Quadzilla.

He finished his set before he said a word, then got up and toweled himself off.

"So you get fired yet?" he said.

"Not yet."

"No, Goddard's got things on his mind. Like the fact that his company's falling apart." He looked at Meacham, and the two men chortled. "What'd Saint Augustine have to say about that?"

The question wasn't unexpected, but it came so abruptly I wasn't quite prepared. "Not that much," I said.

"Bullshit," Wyatt said, coming closer to me and staring, trying to intimidate me with his physical presence. Hot damp air rose from his body, smelling unpleasantly like ammonia: the odor of weight lifters who ingest too much protein.

"Not that much that I was around for," I amended. "I mean, I think the article really spooked them—there was a flurry of activity. Crazier than usual."

"What do you know about 'usual'?" said Meacham. "It's your first day on the seventh floor."

"Just my perception," I said lamely.

"How much of the article's true?" said Wyatt.

"You mean, you didn't plant it?" I said.

Wyatt gave me a look. "Are they going to miss the quarter or not?"

"I have no idea," I lied. "It's not like I was in Goddard's office all day." I don't know why I was so stubborn about not revealing the disastrous quarter numbers, or the news about the impending layoffs. Maybe I felt like I'd been entrusted with a secret by Goddard, and it would be wrong to break that confidence. Christ, I was a goddamned mole, a spy—where did I get off being so high and mighty? Why was I suddenly drawing lines: this much I'll tell you, this much I won't? When the news about the layoffs came out tomorrow, Wyatt would go medieval on me for holding back. He wouldn't believe I hadn't heard. So I fudged a little. "But there's something going on," I said. "Something big. Some kind of announcement coming."

I handed Wyatt a folder containing a copy of the strategic plan Goddard had given me to review.

"What's this?" Wyatt said. He set it down on the weight bench, pulled a tank top over his head, and then started leafing through the document.

"Trion's strategic plan for the next eighteen months. Including detailed descriptions of all the new products in the pipeline."

"Including AURORA?"

I shook my head. "Goddard did mention it, though."

"How?"

"He just said there was this big project codenamed AURORA that would turn the company around. Said he'd given it to Camilletti to run."

"Huh. Camilletti's in charge of all acquisitions, and my sources say Project AURORA was put together from a collection of companies Trion's secretly bought over the last few years. Did Goddard say what it was?"

"No."

"You didn't *ask*?"

"Of course I asked. I told him I'd be interested in taking part in something so significant."

Wyatt, paging through the strategic plan, was silent. His eyes were scanning the pages rapidly, excitedly.

Meanwhile, I handed Meacham a scrap of paper. "Jock's personal cell number."

"*Jock?*" said Meacham in disgust.

"Everyone calls him that. It doesn't mean we're asshole buddies. Anyway, this should help you trace a lot of his most important calls."

Meacham took it without thanks.

"One more thing," I said to Meacham as Wyatt continued reading, fascinated. "There's a problem."

Meacham stared at me. "Don't fuck with us."

"There's a new hire at Trion, a kid named Kevin Griffin, in Sales. They hired him away from you—from Wyatt."

"So?"

"We were sort of friends."

"*Friends?*"

"Sort of. We played hoops together."

"He knew you at the company?"

"Yep."

"Shit," Meacham said. "That *is* a problem."

Wyatt looked up from the document. "Nuke him," he said.

Meacham nodded.

"What does that mean?" I said.

"It means we'll take care of him," Meacham said.

"This is valuable information," Wyatt said at last. "Very, *very* useful. What does he want you to do with it?"

"He wants my overall take on the product portfolio. What's promising, what isn't, what might run into trouble. Whatever."

"That's not very specific."

"He told me he wants a helicopter ride over the terrain."

"Piloted by Adam Cassidy, marketing genius," Wyatt said, amused. "Well, get out a notepad and a pen and start taking notes. I'm going to make you a star."

48

I was up most of the night: unfortunately, I was starting to get used to this.

The odious Nick Wyatt had spent more than an hour giving me his whole take on the Trion product line, including all sorts of inside information, stuff very few other people would know. It was like getting Rommel's take on Montgomery. Obviously he knew a hell of a lot about the market, since he was one of Trion's principal competitors, and he had all sorts of valuable information, which he was willing to give up for the sole purpose of making Goddard impressed with me. His short-term strategic loss would be his long-term strategic gain.

I raced back to the Harbor Suites by midnight and got to work on PowerPoint, putting the slides together for my presentation to Goddard. To be honest, I was pretty amped up about it. I knew I couldn't coast; I had to keep performing at peak. As long as I had the benefit of inside information from Wyatt, I'd impress Goddard, but what would happen when I didn't? What if he asked my opinion on something, and I revealed my true, ignorant self? Then what?

When I couldn't work on the presentation anymore, I took a break and checked my personal e-mail on Yahoo and Hotmail and Hushmail. The usual junk-mail spam—"Viagra Online BUY IT HERE VIAGRA NO PRESCRIPTION" and "BEST XXX SITE!" and "Mortgage Approval!" Nothing more from "Arthur." Then I signed on to the Trion Web site.

One e-mail leaped out at me: It was from KGriffin@trionsystems.com. I clicked on it.

```
SUBJ: You
FROM: KGriffin
TO:   ACassidy

Dude! Great seeing you! Nice to see you looking so slick
& doing so well—way to go! Very impressed by your career
here. Is it something in the water? Give ME some!
I'm getting to know people around Trion & would love to
take you to lunch or whatever. Let me know!

Kev
```

I didn't reply—I had to figure out how to handle it. The guy had obviously looked me up, saw my new title, couldn't figure it out. Whether he wanted to get together out of curiosity, or to brownnose, this was big trouble. Meacham and Wyatt had said they'd "nuke" him, whatever that meant, but until they did whatever they were going to do, I'd have to be extra careful. Kevin Griffin was a loaded gun lying around, waiting to go off. I didn't want to go near it.

Then I signed off, and signed back on using Nora's user ID and password. It was two in the morning, and I figured she had to be offline. It would be a good time to try to get into her archived e-mail, go through it all, download anything that had to do with AURORA, if there was anything.

All I got was INVALID PASSWORD, PLEASE RE-ENTER.

I re-entered her password, this time more carefully, and got INVALID PASSWORD again. This time I was certain I hadn't made a mistake.

Her password had been changed.

Why?

When I finally crashed for the night, my mind was racing, running through all the possibilities as to why Nora had changed her password. Maybe the security guard, Luther, had come by one night when Nora happened to be staying a little later than usual, and he was expecting to see me, engage in a conversation about Mustangs or whatever, but he saw Nora instead. He might wonder what she was doing there in that office, might even—it wasn't totally unlikely—confront her. And then he'd give her a description and she'd figure it out; it wouldn't take her long at all.

But if that's what had happened, she wouldn't just change her password, would she? She'd do more than that. She'd want to know why I was in her office, when she hadn't given me permission to be there. Where that could lead, I didn't want to think about. . . .

Or maybe it was all innocent. Maybe she'd just changed her password routinely, the way every Trion employee was supposed to do every sixty days.

Probably that's all it was.

I didn't sleep well at all, and after a couple of hours of tossing and turning I decided to just get up, take a shower and get dressed, and head into work. My Goddard work was done; it was my *Wyatt* work, my espionage, that was way behind. If I got into work early enough, maybe I could try to find out something about AURORA.

I glanced in the mirror as I walked out. I looked—like shit.

"You up already?" Carlos the concierge said as my Porsche pulled up to the front curb. "Man, you can't keep hours like this, Mr. Cassidy. You get sick."

"Nah," I said. "Keeps me honest."

49

At a little after five in the morning the Trion garage was just about empty. It felt strange being there when it was all but deserted. The fluorescent lights buzzed and washed everything in a kind of greenish haze, and the place smelled of gasoline and motor oil and whatever else dripped from cars: brake fluid and coolant and probably spilled Mountain Dew. My footsteps echoed.

I took the back elevator to the seventh floor, which was also deserted, and walked down the dark executive corridor to my office, past Colvin's office, Camilletti's office, other offices of people I hadn't met yet, until I came to mine. All the offices were dark and closed; no one was in yet.

My office was all potential—not much more than a bare desk and chairs and a computer, a Trion-logo mousepad, a filing cabinet with nothing in it, a credenza with a couple of books. It looked like the office of an itinerant, a drifter, someone who could up and leave in the middle of the night. It was badly in need of some personality—framed photographs, some sporting-goods collectibles, something jokey and funny, something serious and inspirational. It needed an imprint. Maybe, once I caught up on my sleep, I'd do something about it.

I entered my password, logged in, checked my e-mail again. Sometime in the last few post-midnight hours a companywide e-mail had gone out to all Trion employees worldwide asking them to watch the company Web site later on today, at five o'clock Eastern Standard Time, for "an important announcement from CEO Augustine Goddard." That should set off the rumor mills.

The e-mails would be flying. I wondered how many people at the top—a group that now included me, bizarrely enough—knew the truth. Not many, I bet.

Goddard had mentioned that AURORA, the mind-blowing project he wouldn't talk about, was Paul Camilletti's turf. I wondered if there was anything in Camilletti's official bio that might shed some light on AURORA, so I entered his name in the company directory.

His photo was there, stern and forbidding and yet more handsome than in person. A thumbnail biography: born in Geneseo, New York, educated in public schools in upstate New York—translation, probably didn't grow up with money—Swarthmore, Harvard Business School, meteoric rise in some consumer-electronics company that was once a big rival to Trion but was later acquired by Trion. Senior VP at Trion for less than a year before being named CFO. A man on the move. I clicked on the hyperlinks for his reporting chain, and a little tree chart popped up, showing all the divisions and units that were under him.

One of the units was the Disruptive Technologies Research Unit, which reported directly to him. Alana Jennings was marketing director.

Paul Camilletti *directly oversaw* the AURORA project. Suddenly, he was very, very important.

I walked by his office, my heart hammering away, and saw, of course, no sign of him. Not at quarter after five in the morning. I also noticed that the cleaning crew had already been by: there was a fresh liner in his admin's trash can, you could see the undisturbed vacuuming lines on the carpet, and the place still smelled like cleaning fluid.

And there was no one in the corridor, likely no one on the entire floor.

I was about to cross a line, do something risky at a whole new level.

I wasn't worried so much about a security guard coming by. I'd say I was Camilletti's new assistant—what the hell did they know?

But what if Camilletti's admin came in really early, to get a jump on the day? Or, more likely, what if Camilletti *himself* wanted to get an early start? Given the big announcement, he might well have to start placing calls, writing e-mails, making faxes to Trion's European offices, which were six or seven hours ahead. At five-thirty in the morning, it was noon in Europe. Sure, he could e-mail from home, but I couldn't put it past him to get in to his office unusually early today.

So to break into his office today, I realized, was insanely risky.

But for some reason I decided to do it anyway.

50

Yet the key to Camilletti's office was nowhere to be found.

I checked all the usual places—every drawer in his admin's desk, inside the plants and paper-clip holder, even the filing cabinets. Her desk was open to the hallway, totally exposed, and I began to feel nervous poking around there, where I so clearly didn't belong. I looked behind the phone. Under the keyboard, under her computer. Was it hidden on the underside of the desk drawers? No. Underneath the desk? Also no. There was a small waiting-room area next to her desk—really just a couch, coffee table, and a couple of chairs. I looked around there, but nothing. There was no key.

So maybe it wasn't exactly unreasonable that the company's chief financial officer might actually take a security precaution or two, make it hard for someone to break into his office. You had to admire that, right?

After a nerve-wracking ten minutes of looking everywhere, I decided it wasn't meant to be, when suddenly I remembered an odd little detail about my own new office. Like all the offices on the executive floor, it was equipped with a motion detector, which is not as high-security as it sounds. It's actually a common safety feature in the higher-end offices—a way to make sure that no one ever gets locked inside his own office. As long as there's motion inside an office, the doors won't lock. (More proof that the offices on the seventh floor really were a little more equal.)

If I moved quickly I could take advantage of this. . . .

The door to Camilletti's office was solid mahogany, highly polished, heavy. There was no gap between the door and the deep pile carpet; I couldn't even slide a piece of paper under it. That would make things a bit more complicated—but not impossible.

I needed a chair to stand on, not his admin's chair, which rolled on casters and wouldn't be steady. I found a ladderback chair in the sitting area and brought it next to the glass wall of Camilletti's office. Then I went back to the sitting area. Fanned out on the coffee table were all of the usual magazines and newspapers—the *Financial Times, Institutional Investor, CFO, Forbes, Fortune, Business 2.0, Barron's. . . .*

Barron's. Yes. That would do. It was the size and shape and heft of a tabloid newspaper. I grabbed it, then—looking around once again to make sure I wasn't caught doing something I couldn't even *begin* to explain—I climbed up on the chair and pushed up one of the square acoustic ceiling panels.

I reached up into the empty space above the suspended ceiling, into that dark dusty place choked with wires and cables and stuff, felt for the next ceiling panel, the one directly over Camilletti's office, and lifted that one too, propped it up on the metal grid thing.

Taking the *Barron's*, I reached over, lowered it slowly, waving it around. I lowered it as far as I could reach, waved it around some more—but nothing happened. Maybe the motion detectors didn't reach high enough. Finally I stood up on tiptoe, crooked my elbow as sharply as I could, and managed to lower the newspaper another foot or so, waving it around wildly until I really began to strain some muscles.

And I heard a click.

A faint, unmistakable click.

Pulling the *Barron's* back through, I put the acoustic ceiling panel back, sat it snugly in place. Then I got down from the chair, moved it back where it belonged.

And tried Camilletti's doorknob.

The door came open.

In my workbag I'd brought a couple of tools, including a Mag-Lite flashlight. I immediately drew the Venetian blinds, closed the door, then switched on the powerful beam.

Camilletti's office was as devoid of personality as everyone else's—the generic collection of framed family photos, the plaques and awards, the same old lineup of business books they all pretended to read. Actually, this office was pretty disappointing. This wasn't a corner office, didn't have floor-to-ceiling windows like at Wyatt Telecomm. There was no view at all. I wondered whether Camilletti disliked having important guests visit such a humble office. This might be Goddard's style, but it sure didn't seem to be Camilletti's. Cheapskate or no, he seemed grandiose. I'd heard that there was a fancy visitors' reception suite on the penthouse of the executive building, A Wing, but no one I knew had ever seen it. Maybe that's where Camilletti received bigwigs.

His computer had been left on, but when I clicked the space bar on the modernistic black keyboard, and the monitor lit up, I could see the ENTER PASSWORD screen, the cursor blinking. Without his password, of course, I couldn't get into his computer files.

If he'd written down his password somewhere, I sure as hell couldn't find it—in drawers, under the keyboard, taped to the back of the big flat-panel monitor. Nowhere. Just for kicks I entered his user name (PCamilletti@trion-systems.com) and then the same password, PCamilletti.

Nope. He was more cautious than that, and after a few attempts I gave up.

I'd have to get his password the old-fashioned way: by stealth. I figured he probably wouldn't notice if I swapped out the cable between his keyboard and CPU with a Keyghost. So I did.

I admit I was even more nervous being inside Camilletti's office than I'd been inside Nora's. You'd think by now I'd be an old pro about breaking into offices, but I wasn't, and there was a vibe in Camilletti's office that scared the shit out of me. The guy himself was terrifying, and the consequences of being caught didn't bear thinking about. Plus I had to assume that the security precautions in the executive-level offices were more elaborate than in the rest of Trion. They *had* to be. Sure, I'd been trained to defeat most standard security measures. But there were always invisible detection systems that didn't set off any alarm bells or lights. That possibility scared me most of all.

I looked around, groping for inspiration. For some reason the office seemed somehow neater, more spacious than others I'd been in at Trion. Then I realized why: there were no filing cabinets in here. *That's* why it seemed so uncluttered. Well, so where *were* all his files?

When I finally figured out where they had to be, I felt like an idiot. Of course. They weren't in here, because there wasn't any room, and they weren't in his admin's area, because that was too open to the public, not secure enough.

They had to be in the back room. Like Goddard, every top-level Trion executive had a double office, a back conference room the same size as the front. That was the way Trion got around the equality-of-office-space problem. Hey, everyone's office is the same size; the top guys just get *two* of them.

The door to the conference room was unlocked. I shined the Mag-Lite around the room, saw a small copying machine, noticed that each wall was lined with mahogany file cabinets. In the middle was a round table, like Goddard's but smaller. Each drawer was meticulously labeled in what looked like an architect's hand. Most of them seemed to contain financial and accounting records, which probably had good stuff in them if only I knew where to look.

But when I saw the drawers labeled TRION CORPORATE DEVELOPMENT, I lost all interest in anything else. Corporate development is just a biz buzzword for mergers and acquisitions. Trion was known for gobbling up startups or small and midsize companies. More in the go-go years of the late nineteen-nineties than now, but they still acquired several companies a year. I guessed that the files were here because Camilletti oversaw acquisitions, focusing mainly on cost issues, how good an investment, all that.

And if Wyatt was right that Project AURORA was made up of a bunch of companies Trion had secretly acquired, then the solution to the mystery of AURORA had to be here.

These cabinets were unlocked, too, another stroke of luck. I guess the idea was that if you couldn't get into Camilletti's back office, you weren't going to even get near the file cabinets, so to lock them would be a pointless annoyance.

There were a bunch of files here, on companies Trion had either acquired outright or bought a chunk of or looked at closely and decided not to get involved. Some of the company names I recognized, but most I didn't. I dipped into a folder on each company to try to figure out what it did. This was pretty slow work, and I didn't even know what I was looking for, really. How the hell was I supposed to know if some small startup was part of

AURORA, when I didn't even know what AURORA *was?* It seemed totally impossible.

But then my problems were solved.

One of the corporate development drawers was labeled PROJECT AURORA.

And there it was. Simple as that.

51

Breathing shallowly, I pulled the drawer open. I half expected the drawer to be empty, like the AURORA files in HR. But it wasn't. It was jam-packed with folders, all color-coded in some way I didn't understand, each stamped TRION CONFIDENTIAL. This was clearly the good stuff.

From what I could tell, these files were on several small startups—two in Silicon Valley, California, and another couple in Cambridge, Massachusetts—that had recently been acquired by Trion in conditions of strictest secrecy. "Stealth mode," the files said.

I knew this was something big, something important, and my pulse really started pounding. Each *page* was stamped SECRET or CONFIDENTIAL. Even in these top-secret files kept in the CFO's locked office, the language was obscure, veiled. There were sentences, phrases, like "Recommend acquire soonest" and "Must be kept below the radar."

So the secret of AURORA was here.

I didn't really get it, much as I pored over the files. One company seemed to have developed a way to combine electronic and optical components in one integrated circuit. I didn't know what this meant. A note said that the company had solved the problem of "the low yield of the wafers."

Another company had figured out a way to mass-produce photonic circuits. Okay, but what did that *mean?* A couple more were software firms, and I had no idea what they did.

One company called Delphos Inc.—this one actually seemed interesting—had come up with a process for refining and manufacturing some chemical compound called indium phosphide, made of "binary crystals from metallic and nonmetallic elements," whatever that meant. This stuff had "unique optical absorption and transmission properties," its disclosure statement said. Apparently it was used for building a certain kind of laser. From what I could tell, Delphos Inc. had effectively cornered the market on indium phosphide. I was sure that better minds than mine could figure out what massive quantities of indium phosphide were good for. I mean, how many lasers could anyone need?

But here was the interesting part: the Delphos file was stamped ACQUISITION PENDING. So Trion was in negotiations to buy the company. The file was thick with financials, which were just a blur before my eyes. There was a document of ten or twelve pages, a term sheet for the acquisition of Delphos by Trion. The bottom line seemed to be that Trion was offering *five hundred million dollars* to buy the company. It looked like the company's officers, a bunch of research scientists from Palo Alto, as well as a venture-capital firm based in London that owned most of the company, had agreed to the terms. Yeah, half a billion dollars sure can grease the skids. They were just dotting the *i*'s. An announcement was tentatively scheduled for a week from now.

But how was I supposed to copy these files? It would take forever—hours of standing at a copy machine. By now it was six o'clock in the morning, and if Jock Goddard got in at seven-thirty, you'd better believe Paul Camilletti got in before that. So I really had to get the hell out of here. I didn't have *time* to make copies.

I couldn't think of any other way but to take them. Maybe move some files from somewhere else to fill up the empty space, and then . . .

And then raise all kinds of alarms the second Camilletti or his assistant tried to access the AURORA files.

No. Bad idea.

Instead, I took a key page or two from each of the eight company files, switched on the copying machine, and photocopied them. In less than five minutes I replaced the pages into the file folders and put the copies into my bag.

I was done, and it was time to get the hell out of here. Lifting a single slat in the front office window blinds, I peered out to make sure no one was coming.

By quarter after six in the morning I was back in my own office. For the rest of the day I was going to have to carry around these top-secret AURORA files, but that was better than leaving them in a desk drawer and risk having Jocelyn discover them. I know it sounds paranoid, but I had to operate on the assumption that she might go through my desk drawers. Maybe she was "my" administrative assistant, but her paycheck came from Trion Systems, not me.

Exactly at seven, Jocelyn arrived. She stuck her head in my office, eyebrows up, and said, "Good morning," with a surprised, meaningful lilt.

"Morning, Jocelyn."

"You're here early."

"Yeah," I grunted.

Then she squinted at me. "You—you been here a while?"

I blew out a lungful of air. "You don't want to know," I said.

52

My big presentation to Goddard kept getting postponed and postponed. It was supposed to be at eight-thirty, but ten minutes before, I got an InstaMail message from Flo telling me that Jock's E-staff meeting was running over, let's make it nine. Then another instant message from Flo: the meeting shows no sign of breaking up, let's push it back to nine-thirty.

I figured all the top managers were duking it out over who'd get the brunt of the cuts. They were probably all in favor of layoffs, in some general sense, but not in their own division. Trion was no different from any other corporation: the more people under you on the org chart, the more power you had. Nobody wanted to lose bodies.

I was starving, so I scarfed down a protein bar. I was exhausted also, but too wired to do anything but work some more on my PowerPoint presentation, make it even slicker. I put in an animated fade between slides. I stuck in that stick-figure drawing of the head-scratching guy with the question mark over his head, just for comic relief. I kept paring down the text: I'd read somewhere about the Rule of Seven—no more than seven words per line and seven lines or bullets per page. Or was it the Rule of Five? You heard that, too. I figured Jock might be a little short of patience and attention, given what he was going through, so I kept making it shorter, punchier.

The more I waited, the more nervous I got, and the more minimalist my PowerPoint slides became. But the special effects grew cooler and cooler. I'd figured out how to make the bar graphs shrink and grow before your eyes. Goddard would be impressed.

Finally, at eleven-thirty I got a message from Flo saying I could head over to the Executive Briefing Center now, since the meeting was just wrapping up.

People were leaving as I got there. Some I recognized—Jim Colvin, the COO; Tom Lundgren; Jim Sperling, the head of HR; a couple of powerful-looking women. None of them looked very happy. Goddard was surrounded by a gaggle of people who were all taller than him. It hadn't really sunk in before how small the guy was. He also looked terrible—red-rimmed, bloodshot eyes, the pouches under his eyes even bigger than normal. Camilletti stood next to him, and they seemed to be arguing. I heard only snatches.

". . . Need to raise the metabolism of this place," Camilletti was saying.

". . . All kinds of resistance, demoralization," Goddard muttered.

"The best way to deal with resistance is with a bloody ax," said Camilletti.

"I usually prefer plain old persuasion," Goddard said wearily. The others standing in a circle around them were watching the two go at it.

"It's like Al Capone said, you get a lot more done with a kind word and a gun than with a kind word alone," said Camilletti. He smiled.

"I suppose next you're going to tell me you've got to break eggs to make an omelet."

"You're always one step ahead of me," Camilletti said, patting Goddard on the back as he walked off.

Meanwhile I busied myself hooking up my laptop to the projector built into the conference table. I pushed the button that lowered the blinds electrically.

Now it was just Goddard and me in the darkened room. "What do we have here—a matinee?"

"Sorry, just a slide show," I said.

"I'm not so sure it's a good idea to turn off the lights. I'm liable to fall fast asleep," said Goddard. "I was up most of the night, agonizing over all this bushwa. I consider these layoffs a personal failure."

"They're not," I said, then cringed inwardly. Who the hell was I to try to reassure the CEO? "Anyway," I added quickly, "I'll keep it brief."

I started with a very cool animated graphic of the Trion Maestro, all the pieces flying in from offscreen and fitting perfectly together. This was followed by the head-scratching guy with the question mark floating above his head.

I said, "The only thing more dangerous than being in today's consumer-electronics market is not to be in the market at all." Now we were in a Formula One–type racecar moving at warp speed. "Because if you're not driving the car, you're liable to get run over." Then a slide came up that said TRION CONSUMER ELECTRONICS—THE GOOD, THE BAD, AND THE UGLY.

"Adam."

I turned around. "Sir?"

"What the hell is this?"

Sweat broke out at the back of my neck. "That was just intro," I said. Obviously too much of it. "Now we get down to business."

"Did you tell Flo you were planning to do, what the hell is this called, Power—PowerPoint?"

"No. . . ."

He stood up, walked over to the light switch, and put the lights on. "She would have told you—I hate that crap."

My face burned. "I'm sorry, no one said anything."

"Good Lord, Adam, you're a smart, creative, original-thinking young man. You think I want you wasting your time trying to decide whether to go with Arial eighteen point or Times Roman twenty-four point, for God's sake? How about you just tell me what you think? I'm not a child. I don't need to be spoon-fed this darned cream of wheat."

"I'm sorry—" I began again.

"No, I'm sorry. I shouldn't have snapped at you. Low blood sugar, maybe. It's lunchtime, and I'm starved."

"I can go down and get us some sandwiches."

"I have a better idea," Goddard said.

53

Goddard's car was a perfectly restored 1949 Buick Roadmaster convertible, sort of a custardy ivory, beautifully streamlined, with a chrome grille that looked like a crocodile's mouth. It had whitewall tires and a magnificent red leather interior and it gleamed like something you'd see in a movie. He powered down the cloth top before we emerged from the garage into the sunshine.

"This thing really moves," I said, surprised, as we accelerated onto the highway.

"Three-twenty cubic inch, straight eight," Goddard said.

"Man, it's a beauty."

"I call it my Ship of Theseus."

"Huh," I said, chuckling like I knew what he was talking about.

"You should have seen it when I bought it—it was a real junk heap, my goodness. My wife thought I'd taken leave of my senses. I must have spent five years of weekends and evenings rebuilding this thing from the ground up—I mean, I replaced everything. Completely authentic, of course, but I don't think there's a single part left from the original car."

I smiled, leaned back. The car's leather was buttery-smooth and smelled pleasantly old. The sun was on my face, the wind rushing by. Here I was sitting in this beautiful old convertible with the chief executive officer of the company I was spying on—I couldn't decide if it felt great, like I'd reached the mountaintop, or creepy and sleazy and dishonest. Maybe both.

Goddard wasn't some deep-pockets collector like Wyatt, with his planes and boats and Bentleys. Or like Nora, with her Mustang, or any of the Goddard clones at Trion who bought collectible cars at auction. He was a genuine old-fashioned gearhead who really got engine grease on his fingers.

He said, "You ever read *Plutarch's Lives?*"

"I don't think I even finished *To Kill a Mockingbird*," I admitted.

"You don't know what the devil I'm talking about when I call this my Ship of Theseus, do you?"

"No, sir, I don't."

"Well, there's a famous riddle of identity the ancient Greeks loved to argue over. It first comes up in Plutarch. You may recognize the name Theseus, the great hero who slew the Minotaur in the Labyrinth."

"Sure." I remembered something about a labyrinth.

"The Athenians decided to preserve Theseus's ship as a monument. Over the years, of course, it began to decay, and they found themselves replacing each rotting timber with a new one, and then another, and another. Until every single plank on the ship had been replaced. And the question the Greeks asked—it was sort of a philosophers' conundrum—was: Is this really the Ship of Theseus anymore?"

"Or just an upgrade," I said.

But Goddard wasn't joking around. He seemed to be in a serious frame of mind. "I'll bet you know people who are just like that ship, don't you, Adam?" He glanced at me, then back at the road. "People who move up in life and start changing everything about themselves until you can't recognize the original anymore?"

My insides clutched. Jesus. We weren't talking Buicks anymore.

"You know, you go from wearing jeans and sneakers to wearing suits and fancy shoes. You become more refined, more socially adept, you've got more polished manners. You change the way you talk. You acquire new friends. You used to drink Budweiser, now you're sipping some first-growth Pauillac. You used to buy Big Macs at the drive-through, now you're ordering the . . . salt-crusted sea bass. The way you see things has changed, even the way you *think*." He was speaking with a terrifying intensity, staring at the highway, and when he turned to look at me from time to time his eyes flashed. "And at a certain point, Adam, you've got to ask yourself: are you the same person or not? Your costume has changed, your trappings have changed, you're driving a fancy car, you're living in a big fancy house, you go to fancy parties, you have fancy friends. But if you have *integrity*, you know deep down that you're the same ship you always were."

My stomach felt tied up in knots. He was talking about *me;* I felt this queasy sense of shame, embarrassment, as if I'd been caught doing something embarrassing. He saw right through me. Or did he? How much *did* he see? How much did he *know?*

"A man has to respect the person he's been. Your past—you can't be a captive to it, but you can't discard it, either. It's part of you."

I was trying to figure out how to respond when he announced breezily, "Well, here we are."

It was an old-fashioned, streamlined, stainless steel dining car from a passenger train, with a blue neon sign in script that said THE BLUE SPOON. Beneath that, red neon letters said AIR CONDITIONING. Another red neon sign said OPEN and BREAKFAST ALL DAY.

He parked the car and we got out.

"You've never been here before?"

"No, I haven't."

"Oh, you'll love it. It's the real thing. Not one of those phony retro-repro things." The door slammed with a satisfying thunk. "It hasn't changed since 1952."

We sat at a booth that was upholstered in red Naugahyde. The table was gray fake-marble Formica with a stainless steel edge, and there was a tabletop jukebox. There was a long counter with swiveling stools bolted to the floor, cakes and pies in glass domes. No 1950s memorabilia, fortunately; no Sha-Na-Na playing on the jukeboxes. There was a cigarette vending machine, the kind where you pull on the handles to make the pack drop down. They served breakfast all day (Country Breakfast—two eggs, home fries, sausage or bacon or ham, and hotcakes, for $4.85), but Goddard ordered a sloppy joe on a bun from a waitress who knew him, called him Jock. I ordered a cheeseburger and fries and a Diet Coke.

The food was a little greasy, but decent. I'd had better, though I made all the right ecstatic sounds. Next to me on the Naugahyde seat was my workbag with the pilfered files in it from Paul Camilletti's office. Just their presence made me nervous, as if they were emanating gamma waves through the leather.

"So let's hear your thoughts," Goddard said through a mouthful of food. "Don't tell me you can't think without a computer and an overhead projector."

I smiled, took a gulp of Coke. "Well, to begin with, I think we're shipping way too few of the large flat-screen TVs," I said.

"Too *few?* In *this* economy?"

"A buddy of mine works for Sony, and he tells me they're having serious problems. Basically, NEC, which makes the plasma display panels for Sony, is having some kind of production glitch. We've got a sizeable lead on them. Six to eight months easy."

He put down his sloppy joe and gave me his complete attention. "You trust this buddy of yours?"

"Totally."

"I won't make a major production decision on rumor."

"Can't blame you," I said. "Though the news'll be public in a week or so. But we might want to secure a deal with another OEM before the price on those plasma display panels jumps. And it sure will."

His eyebrows shot up.

"Also," I continued, "Guru looks huge to me."

He shook his head, turned his attention back to his sloppy joe. "Ah, well, we're not the only ones coming out with a hot new communicator. Nokia's planning to wipe the floor with us."

"Forget Nokia," I said. "That's all smoke and mirrors. Their device is so tangled up in turf battles—we won't see anything new from them for eighteen months or more, if they're lucky."

"And you know this—from this same buddy of yours? Or a different buddy?" He looked skeptical.

"Competitive intelligence," I lied. Nick Wyatt, where else? But he'd given me cover: "I can show you the report, if you want."

"Not now. You should know that Guru's run into a production problem so serious the thing might not even ship."

"What kind of problem?"

He sighed. "Too complicated to go into right now. Though you might want to start going to some of the Guru team meetings, see if you can help."

"Sure." I thought about volunteering again for AURORA, but decided against it—too suspicious.

"Oh, and listen. Saturday's my annual barbecue at the lake house. It's not the whole company, obviously—just seventy-five, a hundred people tops. In the old days we used to have everyone out to the lake, but we can't do that anymore. So we have some of the old-timers, the top officers and their spouses. Think you can spare some time away from your competitive intelligence?"

"Love to." I tried to act blasé, but this was a big deal. Goddard's barbecue was really the inner circle. Given how few got invited, the Goddard lake-house party was the subject of major one-upsmanship around the company, I'd heard: "Gosh, Fred, sorry, I can't make it Saturday, I've got a . . . sort of barbecue thing that day. You know."

"No salt-crusted sea bass or Pauillac, alas," Goddard said. "More like burgers, hot dogs, macaroni salad—nothing fancy. Bring your swim trunks. Now, on to more important matters. They have the best raisin pie here you've ever tasted. Their apple is great, too. It's all homemade. Though my favorite is the chocolate meringue pie." He caught the eye of the waitress, who'd been hovering nearby. "Debby," he said, "bring this young man a slice of the apple, and I'll have the usual."

He turned to me. "If you don't mind, don't tell your friends about this place. It'll be our little secret." He arched a brow. "You can keep a secret, can't you?"

54

I got back to Trion on a high, wired from my lunch with Goddard, and it wasn't the mediocre food. It wasn't even that my ideas flew so well. No, it was the plain fact that I'd had the big guy's undivided attention, maybe even admiration. Okay, maybe that was overstating it a little. He took me seriously. Nick Wyatt's contempt for me seemed bottomless. He made me feel like a squirrel. With Goddard I felt as if his decision to single me out as his executive assistant might actually have been justified, and it made me want to work my ass off for the guy. It was weird.

Camilletti was in his office, door closed, meeting with someone important-looking. I caught a glimpse of him through the window, leaning forward, intent. I wondered whether he'd type up notes on his meeting after his visitor left. Whatever he entered into his computer I'd soon have, passwords and all. Including anything on Project AURORA.

And then I felt my first real twinge of—of what? Of guilt, maybe. The legendary Jock Goddard, a truly decent human being, had just taken me out to his shitty little greasy-spoon diner and actually listened to my ideas (they weren't Wyatt's anymore, not in my mind), and here I was skulking around his executive suites and planting surveillance devices for the benefit of that sleazeball Nick Wyatt.

Something was seriously wrong with this picture.

Jocelyn looked up from whatever she was doing. "Good lunch?" she asked. No doubt the admin gossip network knew I'd just had lunch with the CEO.

I nodded. "Thanks. You?"

"Just a sandwich at my desk. Lots to do."

I was heading into my office when she said, "Oh, some guy stopped by to see you."

"He leave a name?"

"No. He said he was a friend of yours. Actually, he said he was a 'buddy' of yours. Blond hair, cute?"

"I think I know who you're talking about." What could Chad possibly want?

"He said you left something for him on your desk, but I wouldn't let him into your office—you never said anything about that. Hope that's okay. He seemed a little offended."

"That's great, Jocelyn. Thank you." Definitely Chad, but why was he trying to snoop around my office?

I logged into my computer, pulled up my e-mail. One item jumped out at me—a notice from Corporate Security sent to "Trion C-Level and Staff":

SECURITY ALERT

Late last week, following a fire in Trion's Department of Human Resources, a routine investigation uncovered the presence of an illegally planted surveillance device. Such a security breach in a sensitive area is, of course, of great concern to all of us at Trion. Therefore, Security has initiated a prophylactic sweep of all sensitive areas of the corporation, including offices and workstations, for any signs of intrusion or placement of devices. You will be contacted soon. We appreciate your cooperation in this vital security effort.

Sweat immediately broke out on my forehead, under my arms.

They'd found the device I'd stupidly planted during my aborted break-in at HR.

Oh, Christ. Now Security would be searching offices and computers in all the "sensitive" areas of the company, which for sure included the seventh floor.

And how long before they found the thing I'd attached to Camilletti's computer?

In fact—what if there were surveillance cameras in the hallway outside Camilletti's office that had recorded my break-in?

But something didn't seem right. How could Security have found the key logger?

No "routine investigation" would have uncovered the tricked-up cable. Some fact was missing; some link in the chain hadn't been made public.

I stepped out of my office and said to Jocelyn, "Hey, you see that e-mail from Security?"

"Mmm?" She looked up from her computer.

"Are we going to have to start locking everything up? I mean, what's the real story here?"

She shook her head, not very interested.

"I figured you might know someone in Security. No?"

"Honey," she said, "I know someone in just about every department in this company."

"Hmph," I said, shrugged, and went to the rest room.

When I came back, Jocelyn was talking into her telephone headset. She caught my eye, smiled and nodded as if she wanted to tell me something. "I think it's time for Greg to go bye-bye," she said into the phone. "Sweetie, I've got to go. Nice catching up with you."

She looked at me. "Typical Security nonsense," she said with a knowing scowl. "I'm telling you, they'd claim credit for the sun and the rain if they could get away with it. It's like I thought—they're taking credit for a piece of dumb luck. One of the computers down in HR wasn't working right after the fire, so they called in Tech Support, and one of the techs saw something funny attached to the keyboard or something, some kind of extra wiring, I don't know. Believe me, the guys in Security aren't the sharpest knives in the drawer."

"So this 'security breach' is bogus?"

"Well, my girlfriend Caitlin says they really did find some kind of spy thingy, but it's not like those Sherlock Holmeses in Security would've ever found it if they didn't catch a lucky break."

I snorted amusement, went back to my office. My insides had just turned to ice. At least my suspicions were correct—Security got "lucky"—but the bottom line was, they'd discovered the Keyghost. I'd have to get back into Camilletti's office as soon as possible and retrieve the little Keyghost cable before it was discovered.

On my computer screen an instant message box had popped up while I was gone.

```
To:   Adam Cassidy
From: ChadP
Yo Adam - I had a very interesting lunch
with an old friend of yours from WyattTel.
You might want to give me a call
- C
```

Now I felt like the walls were closing in. Trion Security was doing a sweep of the building—and then there was Chad.

Chad, whose tone was definitely threatening, as if he'd learned just what I didn't want him to learn. The "very interesting" part was bad, as was the "old friend" part, but worst of all was "You might want to give me a call," which seemed to say, I've got you now, asshole. He wasn't going to call; no, he wanted me to squirm, to sweat, to call him in a panic . . . and yet how could I not call him? Wouldn't I naturally call him out of simple curiosity about an "old friend"? I had to call.

But right now I really needed to work out. It wasn't as if I could exactly spare the time, but I needed a clear head to deal with the latest developments. On my way out of the office, Jocelyn said, "You wanted me to remind you about the Goddard Webcast at five o'clock."

"Oh, right. Thanks." I glanced at my watch. That was in twenty minutes. I didn't want to miss it, but I could watch it while I was working out, on the little monitors on the cardio equipment. Kill two birds and all that.

Then I remembered my workbag and its radioactive contents. It was just sitting on the floor of my office next to my desk, unlocked. Anyone could open it and see the documents I'd stolen from Camilletti's office. Now what? Lock them in one of my desk drawers? But Jocelyn had a key to my desk. In fact, there wasn't a place I could lock it where she couldn't get in if she wanted.

Returning quickly to my office, I sat down at my desk, retrieved the Camilletti documents from my briefcase, put them in a manila folder, and took them with me to the gym. I'd have to carry these damned files around with me until I got home, when I could secure-fax them, and then destroy them. I didn't tell Jocelyn where I was off to, and since she had access to my MeetingMaker, she knew I had no meeting scheduled.

But she was too polite to ask where I was going.

55

At a few minutes before five, the company gym still hadn't gotten crowded. I grabbed an elliptical trainer and plugged in the headphones. While I warmed up, I surfed the cable channels—MSNBC, CSPAN, CNN, CNBC—and caught up on the market close. Both the NASDAQ and the Dow were down: another lousy day. Right at five I switched to the Trion channel, which normally broadcast tedious stuff like presentations, Trion ads, whatever.

The Trion logo came up, then a freeze-frame of Goddard in the Trion studio—wearing a dark blue open-necked shirt, his normally unruly fringe of white hair neatly combed. The background was black with blue dots and looked sort of like Larry King's set on CNN except for the Trion logo prominently positioned over Goddard's right shoulder. I found myself actually getting kind of nervous, but why? This wasn't live, he'd taped it yesterday, and I knew exactly what he was going to say. But I wanted him to do it well. I wanted him to make a case for the layoffs that was persuasive and powerful, because I knew that a lot of people around the company would be pissed off.

I didn't have to worry. He was not only good, he was amazing. In the whole of the five-minute speech there wasn't a phony note. He opened simply: "Hello, I'm Augustine Goddard, president and chief executive officer of Trion Systems, and today I have the unpleasant job of delivering some difficult news." He talked about the industry, about Trion's recent problems. He said, "I'm not going to mince words. I'm not going to call these layoffs 'involuntary attrition' or 'voluntary termination.' " He said, "In our business, no one likes to admit when things aren't going well, when the leadership of a company has misjudged, goofed, made mistakes. Well, I'm here to tell you that we've goofed. We've made mistakes. As the CEO of the company, *I've* made mistakes." He said, "I consider the loss of valuable employees, members of our family, to be a sign of grievous failure." He said, "Layoffs are like a terrible flesh wound—they hurt the entire body." You wanted to give the guy a hug and tell him it's okay, it's not your fault, we forgive you. He said, "I want to assure you that I take full responsibility for this setback, and I will do everything in my power to put this company back on a strong footing." He said that sometimes he thought of the company as one big dogsled, but he was only the lead dog, not the guy on the sled with the whip. He said he'd been opposed to layoffs for years, as everyone knew, but, well, sometimes you have to make the hard decision, just get in the car. He pledged that his management team was going to take good care of every single person affected by the layoffs; he said that he believed the severance packages they were offering were the best in the industry—and the very least they could do to help out loyal employees. He ended by talking about how Trion was founded, how industry veterans had predicted its demise time and time again, yet it had emerged from every crisis stronger than ever. By the time he was done I had tears in my eyes and I'd forgotten all about moving my feet. I was standing there on the elliptical trainer watching the tiny screen like a zombie. I heard loud voices nearby, looked around and saw knots of people gathered, talking animatedly, looking stunned. Then I pulled off the headphones and went back to my workout as the place started filling up.

A few minutes later someone got on the machine next to mine, a woman in Lycra exercise togs, a great butt. She plugged her headphones into the monitor, fooled with it for a while, and then tapped me on the shoulder. "Do you have any volume on your set?" she asked. I recognized the voice even before I saw Alana's face. Her eyes widened. "What are *you* doing here?" she said, part shocked, part accusing.

"Oh, my God," I said. I was truly startled; I didn't need to fake it. "I work here."

"You do? So do I. This is so *amazing*."

"Wow."

"You didn't tell me you—well, then again, I didn't ask, did I?"

"This is incredible," I said. Now I was faking it, and maybe not enthusiastically enough. She'd caught me off guard, even though I knew this might happen, and ironically I was too rattled to sound plausibly surprised.

"What a coincidence," she said. "Unbelievable."

56

"How long—how long have you worked here?" she said, getting down off the machine. I couldn't quite read her expression. She seemed sort of dryly amused.

"I just started. Like a couple of weeks ago. How about you?"

"Years—five years. Where do you work?"

I didn't think my stomach could sink any lower, but it did. "Uh, I was hired by Consumer Products Division—new products marketing?"

"You're *kidding*." She stared in amazement.

"Don't tell me you're in the same division as me or something. That I'd *know*—I'd have seen you."

"I used to be."

"*Used* to—? Where are you now?"

"I do marketing for something called Disruptive Technologies," she said reluctantly.

"Really? Cool. What's that?"

"It's boring," she said, but she didn't sound convincing. "Complicated, sort of speculative stuff."

"Hmm." I didn't want to seem too interested. "You catch Goddard's speech?"

She nodded. "Pretty heavy. I had no idea we were in such bad shape. I mean, *layoffs*—you sort of figure layoffs are for everyone else, not for Trion."

"How do you think he did?" I wanted to prepare her for the inevitable moment when she looked me up on the intranet and discovered what I really did now. At least later I'd be able to say I wasn't really holding back; I was sort of polling on my boss's behalf—as if I had anything to do with Goddard's speech.

"I was shocked, of course. But it made sense, the way he presented it. Of course, that's easy for me to say, since I probably have some job security. You, on the other hand, as a recent hire—"

"I should be okay, but who knows." I really wanted to get off the subject of what exactly I did. "He was pretty blunt."

"That's his way. The guy's great."

"He's a natural." I paused. "Hey, I'm sorry about the way our date ended."

"Sorry? Nothing to be sorry about." Her voice softened. "How is he, your dad?" I'd left her a voice message in the morning just to say that Dad had made it.

"Hanging in there. In the hospital he has a fresh cast of characters to bully and intimidate, so he has a whole new reason for living."

She smiled politely, not wanting to laugh at the expense of a dying man.

"But if you're up for it, I'd love to have another chance."

"I'd like that too." She got back on the machine and started moving her feet as she punched numbers into the console. "You still have my number?" Then she smiled, genuinely, and her face was transformed. She was beautiful. Really amazing. "What am I saying? You can look me up on the Trion Web site."

Even after seven o'clock Camilletti was still in his office. Obviously it was a busy time, but I wanted the guy to just go home so I could get into his office before Security did. I also wanted to get home and get some sleep, because I was crashing and burning.

I was trying to figure out how I could get Camilletti on my "buddy list" without his permission so I could know when he was online and when he'd signed off, when suddenly an instant-message box from Chad popped up on my computer screen.

```
ChadP: You never call, you never write.☹
Don't tell me you're too important now for
your old friends?
```

I wrote: **Sorry, Chad, it's been crazy.**

There was a pause of about half a minute, then he came back:

You probably knew about these layoffs in advance, huh? Lucky for you you're immune.

I wasn't sure how to answer, so for a minute or two I didn't, and then the phone rang. Jocelyn had gone home, so the calls were routed right to me. The caller ID came up on the screen, but it was a name I didn't recognize. I picked it up. "Cassidy."

"I know *that*," came Chad's voice, heavy with sarcasm. "I just didn't know if you were at home or in your office. I should have figured an ambitious guy like you gets in early and stays late, just like all the self-help books tell you to do."

"How're you doing, Chad?"

"I'm filled with admiration, Adam. For you. More than ever, in fact."

"That's nice."

"Especially after my lunch with your old friend Kevin Griffin."

"Actually, I barely knew the guy."

"Not exactly what he said. You know, it's interesting—he was less than impressed with your track record at Wyatt. He said you were a big party-hearty dude."

"When I was young and irresponsible, I was young and irresponsible," I said, doing my best George Bush the Younger.

"He also had no recollection of your being on the Lucid."

"He's in—what, in *sales*, isn't he?" I said, figuring that if I was going to imply that Kevin was out of the loop it was at least better to be subtle.

"He *was*. Today was his last day. In case you didn't hear."

"Didn't work out?" There was a little tremor in my voice, which I disguised by clearing my throat, then coughing.

"Three whole days at Trion. Then Security got a call from someone at Wyatt saying that poor Kevin had a nasty habit of cheating on his T&E

expense sheets. They had the evidence and everything, faxed it right over. Thought Trion should know. Of course, Trion dropped him like a hot potato. He denied it up and down, but you know how these things work—it's not exactly a court of law, right?"

"Jesus," I said. "Unbelievable. I had no idea."

"No idea they were going to make this call?"

"No idea about Kevin. I mean, like I said, I hardly knew him at all, but he seemed nice enough. Man. Well, I guess you can't do that kind of stuff too often and hope to get away with it."

He laughed so loud I had to pull my ear away from the receiver. "Oh, that's good. You're really good, big guy." He laughed some more, a big hearty laugh, as if I were the best stand-up act he'd ever seen. "You are so right. You can't do that kind of stuff too often and hope to get away with it." Then he hung up.

Five minutes earlier I'd wanted to lean back in my chair and doze off, but now I couldn't, I was way too freaked out. My mouth was dry, so I went to the break room and got an Aquafina. I took the long way, past Camilletti's office. He was gone, his office was dark, but his admin was still there. When I came by half an hour later, both of them were gone.

It was a little after eight. I got into Camilletti's office quickly and easily this time, now that I had the technique down. No one seemed to be around. I pulled the blinds closed, retrieved the little Keyghost cable, and lifted one slat to look around. I didn't see anyone, although I suppose I really wasn't as careful as I should have been. I raised the blinds and then opened the door slowly, looking first right, then left.

Standing against the wall of Camilletti's reception area, his arms folded, was a stocky man in a Hawaiian shirt and horn-rimmed glasses.

Noah Mordden.

He had a peculiar smile on his face. "Cassidy," he said. "Our thirty-four-pin Phinneas Finn."

"Oh, hi, Noah," I said. Panic flooded my body, but I kept my expression blasé. I had no idea what he was talking about, except that I figured it was probably some kind of obscure literary dig. "What are you up to?"

"I could ask you the same thing."

"Come by to visit?"

"I must have gone to the wrong office. I went to the one that said 'Adam Cassidy' on it. Silly me."

"They've got me working for everyone here," I said. It was the best I could think of, and it sucked. Did I really think he'd believe I was *supposed* to be in Camilletti's office? At eight o'clock at night? Mordden was too smart, and too suspicious, for that.

"You have many masters," he said. "You must lose track of whom you really work for."

My smile was tight. Inside I was dying. He knew. He'd seen me in Nora's office, now in Camilletti's office, and he *knew*.

It was over. Mordden had found me out. So now what? Who would he tell? Once Camilletti learned I'd been in his office, he'd fire me in an instant, and Goddard wouldn't stand in his way.

"Noah," I said. I took a deep breath, but my mind stayed blank.

"I've been meaning to compliment you on your attire," he said. "You're looking particularly upwardly mobile these days."

"Thanks. I guess."

"The black knit shirt and the tweed jacket—very Goddard. You're looking more and more like our fearless leader. A faster, sleeker Beta version. With lots of new features that don't quite work yet." He smiled. "I notice you have a new Porsche."

"Yeah."

"It's hard to escape the car culture in this place, isn't it? But as you speed along the highway of life, Adam, you might pause and consider. When everything's coming your way, maybe you're driving in the wrong lane."

"I'll keep that in mind."

"Interesting news about the layoffs."

"Well, you're safe, though."

"Is that a question or a proposition?" Something about me seemed to amuse him. "Never mind. I have kryptonite."

"What does that mean?"

"Let's just say I wasn't named Distinguished Engineer simply because of my distinguished career."

"What kind of kryptonite are we talking about? Gold? Green? Red?"

"At last a subject you know something about. But if I showed it to you, Cassidy, it would lose its potency, wouldn't it?"

"Would it?"

"Just cover your trail and watch your back, Cassidy," he said, and he disappeared down the hall.

PART SIX

DEAD DROP

Dead Drop: Drop; hiding place. Tradecraft jargon for a concealed physical location used as a communications cutout between an agent and a courier, case officer or another agent in an agent operation or network.

—*The International Dictionary of Intelligence*

57

An early night for me—I got home by nine-thirty, a nervous wreck, needing three days of uninterrupted sleep. Driving away from Trion, I kept replaying that scene with Mordden in my head, trying to figure it all out. I wondered whether he was planning to tell someone, to turn me in. And if not, why not? Would he hold it over my head somehow? I didn't know how to handle it; that was the worst part.

And I found myself fantasizing about my great new bed with the Dux mattress and how I was going to collapse onto it the second I got home. What had my life come to? I was fantasizing about sleep. Pathetic.

Anyway, I couldn't go right to sleep, because I still had work to do. I had to get those Camilletti files out of my hot little hands and over to Meacham and Wyatt. I didn't want to keep these documents around a minute longer than I had to.

So I used the scanner Meacham had provided me, turned them into PDF documents, encrypted them, and secure–e-mailed them through the anonymizer service.

Once I'd done that, I got out the Keyghost manual, hooked it up to my computer, and started downloading. When I opened the first document, I felt a spasm of irritation—it was a solid block of gibberish. Obviously I'd screwed this up. I looked at it more closely and saw that there actually was a pattern here; maybe I hadn't botched it after all. I could make out Camilletti's name, a series of numbers and letters, and then whole sentences.

Pages and pages of text. Everything the guy had tapped out on his computer that day, and there was a lot.

First things first: I'd captured his password. Six numbers, ending in 82—maybe it was the birth date of one of his kids. Or the date of his marriage. Something like that.

But far more interesting were all the e-mails. Lots of them, full of confidential information about the company, about the acquisition of a company he was overseeing. That company, Delphos, I'd seen in his files. The one that they were preparing to pay a shitload of money in cash and stock for.

There was an exchange of e-mails, marked TRION CONFIDENTIAL, about a secret new method of inventory control they'd put in place a few months ago to combat forgery and piracy, particularly in Asia. Some part of every Trion device, whether it was a phone or a handheld or a medical scanner, was now laser-etched with the Trion logo and a serial number. These micromachined identification marks could only be seen under a microscope: They couldn't be faked, and they proved that the thing was actually made by Trion.

There was a lot of information about chip-fabrication manufacturers in Singapore that Trion had either acquired or had invested heavily in. Interesting—Trion was going into the chip-making business, or at least buying up a stake in it.

I felt weird reading all this stuff. It was like going through someone's diary. I also felt really guilty—not because of any loyalty to Camilletti, obviously, but because of Goddard. I could almost see Goddard's gnomelike head floating in a bubble in the air, disapprovingly watching me go through Camilletti's e-mails and correspondence and notes to himself. Maybe it was because I was so wiped out, but I felt lousy about what I was doing. It sounds strange, I know—it was okay to steal stuff about the AURORA project and pass it to Wyatt, but giving them stuff I hadn't been assigned to get felt like an outright betrayal of my new employers.

The letters WSJ jumped out at me. They had to stand for the *Wall Street Journal*. I wanted to see what his reaction to the *Journal* piece was, so I zoomed in on the string of words, and I almost fell out of my seat.

From what I could tell, Camilletti used a number of different e-mail accounts outside of Trion—Hotmail, Yahoo, and some local Internet-access company. These other ones seemed to be for personal business, like dealing with his stockbroker, notes to his brother and sister and father, stuff like that.

But it was the Hotmail e-mails that grabbed my attention. One of them was addressed to BulkeleyW@WSJ.com. It said:

```
Bill—
Shit has hit the fan around here. Will be lot of pressure
on you to give up your source—hang tough. Call me at home
tonite 9:30.
—Paul
```

So there it was. Paul Camilletti was—he *had* to be—the leaker. He was the guy who had fed the damaging information on Trion, on Goddard, to the *Journal*.

Now it all made a creepy kind of sense. Camilletti was helping the *Wall Street Journal* wreak serious damage on Jock Goddard, portraying the old man as out of it, over-the-hill. Goddard had to go. Trion's board of directors, as well as every analyst and investment banker, would see this in the pages of the *Journal*. And who would the board appoint to take Goddard's place?

It was obvious, wasn't it?

Exhausted though I was, it took me a long time, tossing and turning, before I finally fell asleep. And my sleep was fitful, tormented. I kept thinking of little round-shouldered old Augustine Goddard at his sad little diner chowing down on pie, or looking haggard and beaten as his E-staff filed past him out of the conference room. I dreamed of Wyatt and Meacham, bullying me, threatening me with all their talk of prison time; in my dreams I confronted them, told them off, went off on them, really lost it. I dreamed of breaking into Camilletti's office and being caught by Chad and Nora together.

And when my alarm clock finally went off at six in the morning and I raised my throbbing head off the pillow, I knew I had to tell Goddard about Camilletti.

And then I realized I was stuck. How the hell could I tell Goddard about Camilletti when I'd gotten my evidence by breaking into Camilletti's office?

Now what?

58

The fact that Cutthroat Camilletti—the jerk who pretended to be so pissed off about the *Wall Street Journal* piece—was actually behind it really chafed my ass. The guy was more than an asshole: he was disloyal to Goddard.

Maybe it was a relief to actually have a moral conviction about something after weeks of being a low-down lying scumbag. Maybe feeling so protective of Goddard made me feel a little better about myself. Maybe by being pissed off about Camilletti's disloyalty I could conveniently ignore my own. Or maybe I was just grateful to Goddard for singling me out, recognizing me as somehow special, better than everyone else. It's hard to know how much of my anger toward Camilletti was really selfless. At times I was struck with this terrible knife-jab of anguish that I really wasn't any better than Camilletti. I mean, there I was at Trion, a fraud who pretended he could walk on water, when all the time I was breaking into offices and stealing documents and trying to rip the heart out of Jock Goddard's corporation while I rode around in his antique Buick. . . .

It was all too much. These four-in-the-morning flop-sweat sessions were wearing me down. They were hazardous to my mental health. Better for me not to think, to operate on cruise control.

So maybe I really did have all the conscience of a boa constrictor. I still wanted to catch that bastard Paul Camilletti.

At least *I* didn't have any choice about what I was doing. I'd been cornered into it. Whereas Camilletti's treachery was of a whole different order. He was actively plotting against Goddard, the guy who brought him into the company, put his trust in him. And who knew what else Camilletti was doing?

Goddard needed to know. But I had to have cover—a plausible way I might have found out that didn't involve breaking into Camilletti's office.

All the way into work, while I enjoyed the jet-engine thrust and roar of the Porsche, my mind was working on solving this problem, and by the time I got to my office, I had a decent idea.

Working in the office of the CEO gave me serious clout. If I called someone I didn't know and identified myself as just plain-vanilla Adam Cassidy, the odds were I wouldn't get my call returned. But Adam Cassidy, "calling from the CEO's office" or "Jock Goddard's office"—as if I were sitting in the office next to the old guy and not a hundred feet down the hall—got all his calls returned, at lightning speed.

So when I called Trion's Information Technology department and told them that "we" wanted copies of all archived e-mails to and from the office of the chief financial officer in the last thirty days, I got instant cooperation. I didn't want to point a finger at Camilletti, so I made it appear that Goddard was concerned about leaks from the CFO's *office*.

One intriguing thing I'd learned was that Camilletti made a habit of deleting copies of certain sensitive e-mails, whether he sent them or received them. Obviously he didn't want to have those e-mails stored on his computer. He must have known, since he was a sharp guy, that copies of all e-mails were stored somewhere in the company's data banks. That's why he preferred to use outside e-mail for some of the more sensitive correspondence—including the *Wall Street Journal*. I wondered whether he knew that Trion's computers captured *all* e-mail that went through the company's fiber-optic cables, whether Yahoo or Hotmail or anything else.

My new friend in IT, who seemed to think he was doing a personal favor for Goddard himself, also got me the phone records of all calls in and out of the CFO's office. No problem, he said. The company obviously didn't tape conversations, but of course they kept track of all phone numbers out and in; that was standard corporate practice. He could even get me copies of anyone's voice mails, he said. But that might take some time.

The results came back within an hour. It was all there. Camilletti had received a number of calls from the *Journal* guy in the last ten days. But far more incriminatingly, he'd placed a bunch of calls to the guy. One or two he might be able to explain away as an attempt to return the reporter's calls—even though he'd insisted he never talked to the guy.

But twelve calls, some of them lasting five, seven minutes? That didn't look good.

And then came copies of the e-mails. "From now on," Camilletti wrote, "call me only on my home number. Do not repeat do NOT call me at Trion anymore. E-mails should go only to this Hotmail address."

Explain *that* away, Cutthroat.

Man, I could barely wait to show my little dossier to Goddard, but he was in meeting after meeting from midmorning to late afternoon—meetings, I noted, that he hadn't asked me to.

It wasn't until I saw Camilletti coming out of Goddard's office that I had my chance.

59

Camilletti saw me as he walked away but didn't seem to notice me; I could have been a piece of office furniture. Goddard caught my eye and his brows shot up questioningly. Flo began talking to him, and I did the index-finger-in-the-air thing that Goddard always did, indicating I just needed a minute of his time. He did a quick signal to Flo, then beckoned me in.

"How'd I do?" he asked.

"Excuse me?"

"My little speech to the company."

He actually cared about what *I* thought? "You were terrific," I said.

He smiled, looked relieved. "I always credit my old college drama coach. Helped me enormously in my career, interviews, public speaking, all that. You ever do any acting, Adam?"

My face went hot. *Yeah, like everyday.* Jesus, what was he hinting at? "No, actually."

"Really puts you at ease. Oh, heavens, not that I'm Cicero or anything, but . . . anyway, you had something on your mind?"

"It's about that *Wall Street Journal* article," I said.

"Okay . . . ?" he said, puzzled.

"I've discovered who the leaker was."

He looked at me as if he didn't understand, so I went on: "Remember, we thought it had to be someone inside the company who was leaking information to the *Journal* report—"

"Yes, yes," he said impatiently.

"It's—well, it's Paul. Camilletti."

"What are you talking about?"

"I know it's hard to believe. But it's all here, and it's pretty unambiguous." I slid the printouts across his desk. "Check out the e-mail on top."

He took his reading glasses from the chain around his neck and put them on. Scowling, he inspected the papers. When he looked up his face was dark. "Where's this from?"

I smiled. "IT." I fudged just a bit and said, "I asked IT for phone records of all calls from anyone at Trion to the *Wall Street Journal*. Then when I saw all those calls from Paul's phone, I thought it might be an admin or something, so I requested copies of his e-mails."

Goddard didn't look at all happy, which was understandable. In fact, he looked fairly upset, so I added, "I'm sorry. I know this must come as a shock." The cliché just came barreling out of my mouth. "I don't really understand it, myself."

"Well, I hope you're pleased with yourself," Goddard said.

I shook my head. "Pleased? No, I just want to get to the bottom of—"

"Because I'm disgusted," he said. His voice shook. "What the hell do you think you're doing? What do you think this is, the goddamned *Nixon White House?*" Now he was almost shouting, and spittle flew from his mouth.

The room collapsed around me: it was just me and him, across a four-foot expanse of desk. Blood roared in my ears. I was too stunned to say anything.

"Invading people's privacy, digging up dirt, getting private phone records and private e-mails and for all I know steaming open envelopes! I find that kind of underhandedness reprehensible, and I don't ever want you doing that again. Now get the hell out of here."

I got up unsteadily, light-headed, shocked. At the doorway I stopped, turned back. "I want to apologize," I said hoarsely. "I thought I was helping out. I'll—I'll go clear out my office."

"Oh, for Christ's sake, sit back down." The storm seemed to have passed. "You don't have *time* to clear out your office. I've got far too much for you to do." His voice was now gentler. "I understand you were trying to protect me. I get it, Adam, and I appreciate it. And I won't deny I'm flabbergasted about

Paul. But there's a right way and a wrong way to do things, and I prefer the right way. You start monitoring e-mails and phone records and then you find yourself tapping phones, and next thing you know you've got yourself a police state, not a corporation. And a company can't function that way. I don't know how they did things at Wyatt, but we don't do 'em that way here."

I nodded. "I understand. I'm sorry."

He put up his palms. "It never happened. Forget about it. And I'll tell you something else—at the end of the day, no company ever failed because one of its executives mouthed off to the press. For whatever unfathomable reason. Now, I'll figure out some way of handling it. My way."

He pressed his palms together as if signifying the talk was over. "I don't need any kind of unpleasantness right now. We've got something far more important going on. Now, I'm going to need your input on a matter of the utmost secrecy." He settled himself behind his desk, put on his reading glasses, and took out his worn little black leather address book. He looked at me sternly over his reading glasses. "Don't ever tell anyone that the founder and chief executive officer of Trion Systems can't remember his own computer passwords. And *certainly* don't tell anyone about the specific type of handheld device I use to store them." Looking closely at the little black book, he tapped at his keyboard.

In a minute his printer hummed to life and spit out a few pages. He reached over, removed the pages, and handed them to me. "We're in the final stages of a major, major acquisition," he said. "Probably the most costly acquisition in Trion history. But it's probably also going to be the best investment we've ever made. I can't give you the details just yet, but assuming Paul's negotiations continue successfully, we should have a deal ready to announce by the end of next week."

I nodded.

"I want everything to go perfectly smoothly. These are the basic specs on the new company—number of employees, space requirements, and so on. It's going to be integrated into Trion immediately, and located right here in this building. Obviously that means that something here has to go. Some existing division's going to have to be moved out of headquarters and onto our Yarborough campus, or Research Triangle. I need you to figure out which division, or divisions, can be moved with the least disruption, to make room for . . . for the new acquisition. Okay? Look over these pages, and when you're done, please shred them. And let me know your thoughts as soon as possible."

"Okay."

"Adam, I know I'm dumping a whole lot on you, but it can't be helped. I need you to call it as you see it. I'm counting on your strategic savvy." He reached over and gave me a reassuring shoulder squeeze. "And your honesty."

60

Jocelyn, thank God, seemed to be taking more and more coffee- and little-girls'-room breaks the longer she worked for me. The next time she left her desk, I took the papers on Delphos that Goddard had given me—I knew it had to be Delphos, even though the company's name wasn't anywhere on the sheets—and made a quick photocopy at the machine behind her desk. Then I slipped the copies into a manila envelope.

I fired off an e-mail to "Arthur" telling him, in coded language, that I had some new stuff to pass on—that I wanted to "return" the "clothing" I'd bought online.

Sending an e-mail from work was, I knew, a risk. Even using Hushmail, which encrypted it. But I was short on time. I didn't want to have to wait until I got home, then maybe have to go back out. . . .

Meacham's reply came back almost instantly. He told me not to send the item to the post-office box but the street address instead. Translation: he didn't want me to scan the documents and e-mail them, he wanted to see the actual hard copies, though he didn't say why. Did he want to make sure they were originals? Did that mean they didn't trust me?

He also wanted them immediately, and for some reason he didn't want to set up a face-to-face. Why? I wondered. Was he nervous about my being tailed or something? Whatever his logic, he wanted me to leave the documents for him using one of the dead drops we'd worked out weeks before.

At a little after six, I left work, drove over to a McDonald's about two miles from Trion headquarters. The men's room here was small, one-guy-at-a-time, and you could lock the door. I locked it, found the paper towel dispenser and popped it open, put the rolled-up manila envelope inside and closed the dispenser. Until the paper towel roll needed changing, no one would look inside—except Meacham.

On the way out I bought a Quarter Pounder—not that I wanted one, but for cover, like I'd been taught. About a mile down the road was a 7-Eleven with a low concrete wall around the parking lot in front. I parked in the lot, went in and bought a Diet Pepsi, then drank as much of it as I could. The rest I poured down a drain in the parking lot. I put a lead fishing weight inside the can from the stash in my glove compartment, placed the empty can on the top of the concrete wall.

The Pepsi can was a signal to Meacham, who drove by this 7-Eleven regularly, that I'd loaded dead drop number three, the McDonald's. This simple bit of spy tradecraft would enable Meacham to pick up the documents without being seen with me.

The handover went smoothly, as far as I could tell. I had no reason to think otherwise.

Okay, so what I was doing made me feel sleazy. But at the same time, I couldn't help feeling a little proud: I was getting good at this spy stuff.

61

By the time I got home there was an e-mail on my Hushmail account from "Arthur." Meacham wanted me to drive to a restaurant in the middle of nowhere, more than half an hour away, immediately. Obviously they considered this urgent.

The place turned out to be a lavish restaurant-spa, a famous foodie mecca called the Auberge. The lobby's walls were decorated with articles about the place in *Gourmet* and magazines like that.

I could see why Wyatt wanted to meet me here, and it wasn't just the food. The restaurant was set up for maximum discretion—for private meetings, for extramarital affairs, whatever. In addition to the main dining room, there were these small, separate alcoves for private dining, which you could enter and leave directly from the parking lot without having to go through the main part of the restaurant. It reminded me of a high-class motel.

Wyatt was sitting at a table in a private alcove with Judith Bolton. Judith was cordial, and even Wyatt seemed a little less hostile than usual. Maybe that was because I'd been so successful in getting him what he wanted. Maybe he was on his second glass of wine, or maybe it was Judith, who seemed to exert a mysterious sway over him. I was pretty sure there was nothing going on between Judith and Wyatt, at least based on their body language. But they were obviously close, and he deferred to her in a way he didn't defer to anyone else.

A waiter brought me a glass of sauvignon blanc. Wyatt told him to leave, come back in fifteen minutes when he was ready to order. Now we were alone in here: me, Wyatt, and Judith Bolton.

"Adam," said Wyatt as he gnawed on a piece of focaccia, "those files you got from the CFO's office—they were very helpful."

"Good," I said. Now I was Adam? And an actual compliment? It gave me the heebie-jeebies.

"Especially that term sheet on this company Delphos," he went on. "Obviously it's a linchpin, a crucial acquisition for Trion. No wonder they're willing to pay five hundred million bucks in stock for it. Anyway, that finally solved the mystery. That put the last piece of the puzzle into place. We've figured out AURORA."

I gave him a blank look, like I really didn't care, and nodded.

"This whole business was worth it, worth every penny," he said. "The enormous trouble we went to to get you inside Trion, the training, the security measures. The expense, the huge risks—they were *all worth it*." He tipped his wineglass toward Judith, who smiled proudly. "I owe you big-time," he said to her.

I thought: And what am I, chopped liver?

"Now, I want you to listen to me very closely," Wyatt said. "Because the stakes are immense, and I want you to understand the urgency. Trion Systems appears to have developed the most important technological breakthrough since the integrated circuit. They've solved a problem that a lot of us have been working on for decades. They've just changed history."

"Are you sure you want to be telling me this?"

"Oh, I want you taking notes. You're a smart boy. Pay close attention. The age of the silicon chip is over. Somehow Trion's managed to develop an optical chip."

"So?"

He stared at me with boundless contempt. Judith spoke earnestly, quickly, as if to cover over my gaffe. "Intel's spent billions trying to crack this without success. The Pentagon's been working on it for over a decade. They know it'll revolutionize their aircraft and missile navigation systems, so they'll pay almost anything to get their hands on a working optical chip."

"The opto-chip," Wyatt said, "handles optical signals—light—instead of electronic ones, using a substance called indium phosphide."

I remember reading something about indium phosphide in Camilletti's files. "That's the stuff that's used for building lasers."

"Trion's cornered the market on the shit. That was the tip-off. They need indium phosphide for the semiconductor in the chip—it can handle much higher data-transfer speeds than gallium arsenide."

"You've lost me," I said. "What's so special about it?"

"The opto-chip has a modulator capable of switching signals at a hundred gigabytes a second."

I blinked. This was all Urdu to me. Judith was watching him, rapt. I wondered if she got this.

"It's the goddamned fucking *Holy Grail*. Let me put it to you in simple terms. A *single particle* of opto-chip one-*hundredth* the diameter of a human hair will now be able to handle all of a corporation's telephone, computer, satellite, and television traffic at once. Or maybe you can wrap your mind around this, guy: with the optical chip, you can download a two-hour movie in digital format in *one-twentieth of a second*, you get it? This is a fucking quantum leap in the industry, in computers and handhelds and satellites and cable TV transmission, you name it. The opto-chip's going to enable things like this"—he held up his Wyatt Lucid handheld—"to receive flicker-free TV images. It is so vastly superior to any existing technology—it's capable of higher speeds, requiring far lower voltage, lower signal loss, lower heat levels. . . . It's amazing. It's the real deal."

"Excellent," I said quietly. The import of what I'd done was beginning to sink in, and now I felt like a damned traitor to Trion—Jock Goddard's own Benedict Arnold. I had just given the hideous Nick Wyatt the most valuable, paradigm-shifting technology since color TV or whatever. "I'm glad I could be of service."

"I want every fucking last spec," Wyatt said. "I want their prototype. I want the patent applications, the lab notes, everything they've got."

"I don't know how much more I can get," I said. "I mean, short of breaking into the fifth floor—"

"Oh, that too, guy. That too. I've put you in the fucking catbird seat. You're working directly for Goddard, you're one of his chief lieutenants, you've got access to just about anything you want to get."

"It's not that simple. You know that."

"You're in a unique position of trust, Adam," put in Judith. "You can gain access to a whole range of projects."

Wyatt interrupted: "I don't want you holding back a single fucking thing."

"I'm not holding back—"

"The layoffs came as a surprise to you, is that it?"

"I told you there was some kind of big announcement coming. I really didn't know anything more than that at the time."

" 'At the time,' " he repeated nastily. "You knew about the layoffs before CNN did, asshole. Where was *that* intelligence? I have to watch CNBC to find out about the layoffs at Trion when I've got a mole in the fucking *CEO's* office?"

"I didn't—"

"You put a bug in the CFO's office. What happened with that?" His overly tanned face was darker than usual, his eyes bloodshot. I could feel the spray of his spittle.

"I had to pull it."

"*Pull* it?" he said in disbelief. "Why?"

"Corporate Security found the thing I put in the HR department, and they've started searching everywhere, so I had to be careful. I could have jeopardized everything."

"How long was the bug in the CFO's office before you pulled it?" he shot back.

"Not much longer than a day."

"A day would get you a shitload."

"No, it—well, the thing must have malfunctioned," I lied. "I don't know what happened."

Frankly, I wasn't sure why I was holding back. I guess it was the fact that the bug revealed that Camilletti had been the one who'd leaked to the *Wall Street Journal*, and I didn't want Wyatt knowing all of Goddard's private business. I hadn't really thought it through.

"Malfunctioned? Somehow I'm dubious. I want that bug in Arnie Meacham's hand by the end of the day tomorrow for his techs to examine.

And believe me, those guys can tell right away if you've tampered with it. Or if you never put it in the CFO's office in the first place. And if you're lying to me, you fuck, you're *dead*."

"Adam," said Judith, "it's crucial that we're totally open and honest with each other. Don't withhold. Far too many things can go wrong. You're not able to see the big picture."

I shook my head. "I don't *have* it. I had to get rid of it."

"Get *rid* of it?" Wyatt said.

"I was—I was in a tight spot, the security guys were searching offices, and I figured I'd better take the thing out and throw it in a Dumpster a couple of blocks away. I didn't want to blow the whole operation over a single busted bug."

He stared at me for a few seconds. "Don't ever hold anything back from us, do you understand? *Ever*. Now, listen up. We've got excellent sources telling us that Goddard's people are putting on a major press conference at Trion headquarters in two weeks. Some major press conference, some big news. The e-mail traffic you handed me suggests they're on the verge of going public with this optical chip."

"They're not going to announce it if they haven't locked down all the patents, right?" I said. I'd done a little late-night Internet research myself. "I'm sure you've had your minions checking all Trion filings at the U.S. Patent Office."

"Attending law school in your spare time?" Wyatt said with a thin smile. "You file with the Patent Office at the last possible second, asshole, to avoid premature disclosure or infringement. They won't file until just before the announcement. Until then, the intellectual property is kept a trade secret. Which means, until it's filed—which may be any time in the next two weeks—it's open season on the design specs. The clock's ticking. I don't want you to sleep, to rest for a goddamned minute until you have every last fucking detail on the optical chip, are we clear?"

I nodded sullenly.

"Now, if you'll excuse us, we'd like to order dinner." I got up from the table and went out to use the men's room before I drove off. As I came out of the private dining room, a guy walking past glanced at me.

I panicked.

I spun around and went back through the private room to the parking lot.

I wasn't one hundred percent sure at the time, but the guy in the hall looked a whole lot like Paul Camilletti.

62

There were people in my office.

When I got into work next morning, I saw them from a distance—two men, one young, one older—and I froze. It was seven-thirty in the morning, and for some reason Jocelyn wasn't at her desk. In an instant my mind ran through a menu of possibilities, one worse than the next: Security had somehow found something in my office. Or I'd been fired and they were clearing out my desk. Or I was being arrested.

Approaching my office, I tried to hide my nervousness. I said jovially, as if these were buddies of mine who'd dropped by for a visit, "What's going on?"

The older one was taking notes on a clipboard, and the younger one was now bent over my computer. The older one, gray hair and walrus mustache, rimless glasses, said, "Security, sir. Your secretary, Miss Chang, let us in."

"What's up?"

"We're doing an inspection of all the offices on the seventh floor, sir. I don't know if you got the notice about the security violation in Human Resources."

Was that all this was about? I was relieved. But only for a few seconds. What if they'd found something in my desk? Had I left any of my spycraft equipment locked in any of the desk or file cabinet drawers? I made it a habit never to leave anything there. But what if I'd slipped? I was stretched so thin I could easily have left something there by mistake.

"Great," I said. "I'm glad you're here. You haven't found anything, have you?"

There was a moment of silence. The younger one looked up from my computer and didn't reply. The older one said, "Not yet, sir, no."

"I wasn't thinking *I* was a target, necessarily," I added. "Gosh, I'm not that important. I mean anything on this floor, in any of the big guys' offices?"

"We're not supposed to discuss that, but no, sir, we haven't found anything. Doesn't mean we won't, though."

"My computer check out okay?" I addressed the young guy.

"No devices or anything like that have turned up so far," he replied. "But we're going to have to run some diagnostics on it. Can you log in for us?"

"Sure." I hadn't sent any incriminating e-mails from this computer, had I?

Well, yes, I had. I'd e-mailed Meacham on my Hushmail account. But even if the message hadn't been encrypted, it wouldn't have told them anything. I was sure I hadn't saved any files on my computer I wasn't supposed to have. That I was sure of. I stepped over behind my desk and typed in my password. Both security guys tactfully looked away until I was logged in.

"Who has access to your office?" the older man asked.

"Just me. And Jocelyn."

"And the cleaning crew," he persisted.

"I guess so, but I never see them."

"You've never seen them?" he repeated skeptically. "But you work late hours, right?"

"They work even later hours."

"What about interoffice mail? Any delivery person ever come in here when you're out, that you know of?"

I shook my head. "All that stuff goes to Jocelyn's desk. They never deliver to me directly."

"Has anyone from IT ever serviced your computer or phone?"

"Not that I know of."

The younger guy asked, "Gotten any strange e-mails?"

"Strange . . . ?"

"From people you don't know, with attachments or whatever."

"Not that I can recall."

"But you use other e-mail services, right? I mean, other than Trion."

"Sure."

"Ever accessed them from this computer?"

"Yeah, I suppose I have."

"And on any of those e-mail accounts did you ever get any funny-looking e-mail?"

"Well, I get spam all the time, like everyone else. You know, Viagra or 'Add Three Inches' or the ones about farm girls." Neither one of them seemed to have a sense of humor. "But I just delete all those."

"This'll just be five or ten minutes, sir," the younger one said, inserting a disk into my CD-ROM drive. "Maybe you can get a cup of coffee or something."

Actually, I had a meeting, so I left the security guys in my office, not feeling so good about it, and headed over to Plymouth, one of the smaller conference rooms.

I didn't like the fact that they'd asked about outside e-mail accounts. That was bad. In fact, it scared the shit out of me. What if they decided to dig up all my e-mails? I'd seen how easy it was to do. What if they found out I'd ordered copies of Camilletti's e-mail traffic? Would that make me a suspect somehow?

As I passed Goddard's office, I saw that both he and Flo were gone—Jock to the meeting, I knew. Then I passed Jocelyn carrying a mug of coffee. Printed on it was GONE OUT OF MY MIND—BACK IN FIVE MINUTES.

"Are those security goons still at my desk?" she asked.

"They're in my office now," I said and kept going.

She gave me a little wave.

63

Goddard and Camilletti were seated around a small round table along with the COO, Jim Colvin, and another Jim, the director of Human Resources, Jim Sperling, plus a couple of women I didn't recognize. Sperling, a black man with a close-cropped beard and oversize wire-rim glasses, was talking about "targets of opportunity," by which I assume he meant staff they could lop off. Jim Sperling didn't do the Jock Goddard mock turtleneck thing, but he was close enough—a sports-jacket-and-dark-polo-shirt. Only Jim Colvin wore a conventional business suit and tie.

Sperling's young blond assistant slid me some papers listing departments and individual poor suckers that were candidates for the axe. I scanned it quickly, saw that the Maestro team wasn't on there. So I'd saved their jobs after all.

Then I noticed a roster of New Product Marketing names, among them Phil Bohjalian. The old-timer was going to get laid off. Neither Chad nor Nora was on the list, but Phil had been targeted. By Nora, it had to be. Each VP and director had been asked to stack-rank their subordinates and lose at least one out of ten. Nora had obviously singled out Phil for execution.

This seemed to be more or less a rubber-stamp session. Sperling was presenting the list, making a "business case" for those "positions" he wanted to eliminate, and there was little discussion. Goddard looked glum; Camilletti looked intent, even a little jazzed.

When Sperling got to New Product Marketing, Goddard turned to me, silently soliciting my opinion. "Can I say something?" I put in.

"Uh, sure," said Sperling.

"There's a name on here, Phil Bohjalian. He's been with the company something like twenty, twenty-one years."

"He's also ranked lowest," said Camilletti. I wondered whether Goddard had said anything to him about the *Wall Street Journal* leak. I couldn't tell from Camilletti's manner, since he was no more, or less, abrasive to me than usual. "Plus given his tenure with the company, his benefits cost us an arm and a leg."

"Well, I'd question his ranking," I said. "I'm familiar with his work, and I think his numbers may be more of a matter of interpersonal style."

"Style," said Camilletti.

"Nora Sommers doesn't like his personality." Granted, Phil wasn't exactly a buddy of mine, but he couldn't do me any harm, and I felt bad for the guy.

"Well, if this is just about a personality clash, that's an abuse of the ranking system," said Jim Sperling. "Are you telling me Nora Sommers is abusing the system?"

I saw clearly where this could go. I could save Phil Bohjalian's job and jettison Nora, all at the same time. It was hugely tempting to just speak up and slash Nora's throat. No one in this room particularly cared one way or another. The word would go down to Tom Lundgren, who wasn't likely to battle to save her. In fact, if Goddard hadn't plucked me out of Nora's clutches, it would surely have been my name on the list, not Phil's.

Goddard was watching me keenly, as was Sperling. The others around the table were taking notes.

"No," I said at last. "I don't think she's abusing the system. It's just a chemistry thing. I think both of them pull their weight."

"Fine," Sperling said. "Can we move on?"

"Look," said Camilletti, "we're cutting four thousand employees. We can't possibly go over them one by one."

I nodded. "Of course."

"Adam," Goddard said. "Do me a favor. I gave Flo the morning off—would you mind getting my, uh, handheld from my office? Seem to have forgotten it." His eyes seemed to twinkle. He meant his little black datebook, and I guess the joke was for my enjoyment.

"Sure," I said, and I swallowed hard. "Be right back."

Goddard's office door was closed but unlocked. The little black book was on his bare, neat desk, next to his computer.

I sat down at his desk chair and looked around at his stuff, the framed photographs of his white-haired, grandmotherly-looking wife, Margaret; a picture of his lake house. No pictures of his son, Elijah, I noticed: probably too painful a reminder.

I was alone in Jock Goddard's office, and Flo had the morning off. How long could I stay here without Goddard becoming suspicious? Was there time to try to get into his computer? What if Flo showed up while I was there . . . ?

No. Insanely risky. This was the CEO's office, and people were probably coming by here all the time. And I couldn't risk taking more than two or three minutes on this errand: Goddard would wonder where I'd been. Maybe I took a quick pee break before I got his book: that might explain five minutes, no more.

But I'd probably never have this opportunity again.

Quickly I flipped the worn little book open and saw phone numbers, pencil scrawlings on calendar entries . . . and on the page inside the back cover was printed, in a neat hand, "GODDARD" and below that "62858."

It had to be his password.

Above those five numbers, crossed out, was "JUN2858." I looked at the two series of numbers and figured out that they were both dates, and they were both the *same* date: June 28, 1958. Obviously a date of some importance to Goddard. I didn't know what. Maybe his wedding date. And both variants were obviously passwords.

I grabbed a pen and a scrap of paper and copied down the ID and password.

But why not copy the whole book? There might well be other important information here.

Closing Goddard's office door behind me, I went up to the photocopier behind Flo's desk.

"You trying to do my job, Adam?" came Flo's voice.

I whipped around, saw Flo carrying a Saks Fifth Avenue bag. She was staring at me with a fierce expression.

"Morning, Flo," I said offhandedly. "No, fear not. I was just getting something for Jock."

"That's good. Because I've been here longer, and I'd hate to have to pull rank on you." Her stare softened, and a sweet smile broke out on her face.

64

As the meeting broke up, Goddard sidled up to me and put his arm around my shoulder. "I like what you did in here," he said in a low voice.

"What do you mean?"

We walked down the hall to his office. "I'm referring to your restraint in the case of Nora Sommers. I know how you feel about her. I know how she feels about *you*. It would have been the easiest thing in the world for you to get rid of her. And frankly, I wouldn't have put up much of a struggle."

I felt a little uncomfortable about Goddard's affection, but I smiled, ducked my head. "It seemed like the right thing to do," I said.

" 'They that have power to hurt and will do none,' " Goddard said, " 'They rightly do inherit heaven's graces.' Shakespeare. In modern English: When you have the power to screw people over and you don't—well, that's when you get to show who you really are."

"I suppose."

"And who's that older fellow whose job you saved?"

"Just a guy in marketing."

"Buddy of yours?"

"No. I don't think he particularly likes me either. I just think he's a loyal employee."

"Good for you." Goddard squeezed my shoulder, hard. He led me to his office, stopped for a moment before Flo's desk. "Morning, sweetheart," he said. "I want to see the confirmation dress."

Flo beamed, opened the Saks bag, pulled out a small white silk girl's dress, and held it up proudly.

"Marvelous," he said. "Just marvelous."

Then we went into his office and he closed the door.

"I haven't said a word to Paul yet," Goddard said, settling behind his desk, "and I haven't decided whether I will. You haven't told anyone else, right? About the *Journal* business?"

"Right."

"Keep it that way. Look, Paul and I have some differences of opinion, and maybe this was his way of lighting a fire under me. Maybe he thought he was helping the company. I just don't know." A long sigh. "If I do raise it with him—well, I don't want word of it getting around. I don't want any unpleasantness. We have far, far more important things going on these days."

"Okay."

He gave me a sidelong glance. "I've never been out to the Auberge, but I hear it's terrific. What'd you think?"

I felt a lurch in my gut. My face grew hot. That *had* been Camilletti there last night, of all the lousy luck.

"I just—I only had a glass of wine, actually."

"You'll never guess who happened to be having dinner there the same night," Goddard said. His expression was unreadable. "Nicholas Wyatt."

Camilletti had obviously done some asking around. To even try to deny that I was with Wyatt would be suicide. "Oh, that," I said, trying to sound weary. "Ever since I took the job at Trion, Wyatt's been after me for—"

"Oh, is that right?" Goddard interrupted. "So of course you had no choice but to accept his invitation to dinner, hmm?"

"No, sir, it's not like that," I said, swallowing hard.

"Just because you change jobs doesn't mean you give up your old friends, I suppose," he said.

I shook my head, frowned. My face felt like it was getting as red as Nora's. "It's not a matter of friendship, actually—"

"Oh, I know how it goes," Goddard said. "The other guy guilts you into taking a meeting with him, just for old times' sake, and you don't want to be rude to him, and then he lays it on nice and thick. . . ."

"You know I had no intention of—"

"Of course not, of course not," Goddard muttered. "You're not that kind of person. Please. I *know* people. Like to think that's one of my strengths."

When I got back to my office, I sat down at my desk, shaken.

The fact that Camilletti had reported to Goddard that he'd seen me at the Auberge at the same time as Wyatt meant that Camilletti, at least, was suspicious of my motives. He must have thought that I was, at the very least, allowing myself to be wooed, courted, by my old boss. But being Camilletti, he probably had darker thoughts than that.

This was a fucking disaster. I wondered, too, whether Goddard really did think the whole thing was innocent. "I *know* people," he'd said. Was he that naïve? I didn't know what to think. But it was clear that I was going to have to watch my ass very carefully from now on.

I took a deep breath, pressed my fingertips hard against my closed eyes. No matter what, I still had to keep plugging away.

After a few minutes, I did a quick search on the Trion Web site and found the name of the guy in charge of the Trion Legal Department's Intellectual Property Division. He was Bob Frankenheimer, fifty-four, been with Trion for eight years. Before that he'd been general counsel at Oracle, and before that he was at Wilson, Sonsini, a big Silicon Valley law firm. From his photo he looked seriously overweight, with dark curly hair, a five o'clock shadow, thick glasses. Looked like your quintessential nerd.

I called him from my desk, because I wanted him to see my caller ID, see I was calling from the office of the CEO. He answered his own phone, with a surprisingly mellow voice, like a late-night radio DJ on a soft rock station.

"Mr. Frankenheimer, this is Adam Cassidy in the CEO's office."

"What can I do for you?" he said, sounding genuinely cooperative.

"We'd like to review all the patent applications for department three twenty-two."

It was bold, and definitely risky. What if he happened to mention it to Goddard? That would be just about impossible to explain.

A long pause. "The AURORA project."

"Right," I said casually. "I know we're supposed to have all the copies on file here, but I've just spent the last two hours looking all over the place, and I just can't find them, and Jock's really in a snit about this." I lowered my voice. "I'm new here—I just started—and I don't want to fuck this up."

Another pause. Frankenheimer's voice suddenly seemed cooler, less cooperative, like I'd pressed the wrong button. "Why are you calling me?"

I didn't know what he meant, but it was clear I'd just stepped in it. "Because I figure you're the one guy who can save my job," I said with a little mordant chuckle.

"You think I have copies here?" he said tightly.

"Well, do you know where the copies of the filings are, then?"

"Mr. Cassidy, I've got a team of six top-notch intellectual-property attorneys here in house who can handle just about anything that's thrown at them. But the AURORA filings? Oh, no. Those have to be handled by outside counsel. Why? Allegedly for reasons of 'corporate security.' " His voice got steadily louder, and he sounded really pissed off. " 'Corporate security.' Because presumably outside counsel practice better security than Trion's own people. So I ask you: What kind of message is that supposed to send?" He wasn't sounding so mellow anymore.

"That's not right," I said. "So who *is* handling the filings?"

Frankenheimer exhaled. He was a bitter, angry man, a prime heart-attack candidate. "I wish I could tell you. But obviously we can't be trusted with that information either. What's that our culture badges say, 'Open Communication'? I love that. I think I'm going to have that printed on our T-shirts for the Corporate Games."

When I hung up, I passed by Camilletti's office on the way to the men's room, and then I did a double take.

Sitting in Paul Camilletti's office, a grave look on his face, was my old buddy.

Chad Pierson.

I quickened my stride, not wanting to be seen by either of them through the glass walls of Camilletti's office. Though *why* I didn't want to be seen, I had no idea. I was running on instinct by now.

Jesus, did Chad even *know* Camilletti? He'd never said he did, and given

Chad's modest and unassuming demeanor, it seemed just the sort of thing he'd have gloated about to me. I couldn't think of any legitimate—or at least innocent—reason why the two of them might be talking. And it sure as hell wasn't social: Camilletti wouldn't waste his time on a worm like Chad.

The only plausible explanation was the one I most dreaded: that Chad had taken his suspicions about me right to the top, or as close to the top as he could get. But why Camilletti?

No doubt Chad had it in for me, and once he'd heard about a new hire from Wyatt Telecom, he'd probably flushed Kevin Griffin out in an effort to gather dirt on me. And he'd got lucky.

But had he really?

I mean, how much did Kevin Griffin really know about me? He knew rumors, gossip; he might claim to know something about my past history at Wyatt. Yet here was a guy whose own reputation was in question. Whatever Wyatt Security had told Trion, clearly the folks at Trion believed it—or they wouldn't have gotten rid of him so fast.

So would Camilletti really believe secondhand accusations coming from a questionable source, a possible sleazebag, like Kevin Griffin?

On the other hand . . . now that he'd seen me out at dinner with Wyatt, in a secluded restaurant, maybe he would.

My stomach was starting to ache. I wondered if I was getting an ulcer.

Even if I was, that would be the least of my problems.

65

The next day, Saturday, was Goddard's barbecue. It took me an hour and a half to get to Goddard's lake house, a lot of it on narrow back roads. On the way I called Dad from my cell, which was a mistake. I talked a little to Antwoine, and then Dad got on, huffing and puffing, his usual charming self, and demanded I come over now.

"Can't, Dad," I said. "I've got a business thing I have to do." I didn't want to say I had to go to a barbecue at the CEO's country house. My mind spun through Dad's possible responses and hit overload. There was his corrupt-CEO rant, the Adam-as-pathetic-brownnoser rant, the you-don't-know-who-you-are rant, the rich-people-rub-your-face-in-their-wealth rant, the whassa-matter-you-don't-want-to-spend-time-with-your-dying-father rant. . . .

"You need something?" I added, knowing he'd never admit he needed anything.

"I don't need anything," he said testily. "Not if you're too busy."

"Let me come by tomorrow morning, okay?"

Dad was silent, letting me know I'd pissed him off, and then put Antwoine on the phone. The old man was back to being his usual asshole self.

I ended the call when I reached the house. The place was marked with a simple wooden sign on a post, just GODDARD and a number. Then a long, rutted dirt path through dense woods that suddenly broadened out into a big circular drive crunchy with crushed clamshells. A kid in a green shirt was serving temporary valet duty. Reluctantly I handed him the keys to the Porsche.

The house was a sprawling, gray-shingled, comfortable-looking place that looked like it had been built in the late nineteenth century or so. It was set on a bluff overlooking the lake, with four fat stone chimneys and ivy climbing on the shingles. In front was a huge, rolling lawn that smelled like it had just been mowed and, here and there, massive old oak trees and gnarled pines.

Twenty or thirty people were standing around on the lawn in shorts and T-shirts, holding drinks. A bunch of kids were running back and forth, shouting and tossing balls, playing games. A pretty blond girl was sitting at a card table in front of the veranda. She smiled and found my name tag and handed it to me.

The main action seemed to be on the other side of the house, the back lawn that sloped gently down to a wooden dock on the water. There the crowd was thicker. I looked around for a familiar face, didn't see anyone. A stout woman of about sixty in a burgundy caftan, with a very wrinkled face and snow-white hair, came up to me.

"You look lost," she said kindly. Her voice was deep and hoarse, and her face was as weathered and picturesque as the house.

I knew right away she had to be Goddard's wife. She was every bit as homely as advertised. Mordden was right: she really did look kind of like a shar-pei puppy.

"I'm Margaret Goddard. And you must be Adam."

I extended my hand, flattered that she'd somehow recognized me until I remembered that my name was on the front of my shirt. "Nice to meet you, Mrs. Goddard," I said.

She didn't correct me, tell me to call her Margaret. "Jock's told me quite a bit about you." She held on to my hand for a long time and nodded, her small brown eyes widening. She looked impressed, unless I was imagining it. She drew closer. "My husband's a cynical old codger, and he's not easily impressed. So you *must* be good."

A screened-in porch wrapped around the back of the house. I passed a couple of large black Cajun grills with plumes of smoke rising from the glowing charcoal. A couple of girls in white uniforms were tending sizzling burgers and steaks and chicken. A long bar had been set up nearby, covered in a white linen tablecloth, where a couple of college-age guys were pouring mixed drinks and soft drinks and beers into clear plastic cups. At another table a guy was opening oysters and laying them out on a bed of ice.

As I approached the veranda, I began to recognize people, most of them fairly high-ranking Trion executives and spouses and kids. Nancy Schwartz, senior vice president of the Business Solutions Unit, a small, dark-haired, worried-looking woman wearing a Day-Glo orange Trion T-shirt from last year's Corporate Games, was playing a game of croquet with Rick Durant, the chief marketing officer, tall and slim and tanned with blow-dried black hair. They both looked gloomy. Goddard's admin, Flo, in a silk Hawaiian muumuu, floral and dramatic, was swanning around as if she were the real hostess.

Then I caught sight of Alana, long legs tan against white shorts. She saw me at the same instant, and her eyes seemed to light up. She looked surprised. She gave me a quick furtive wave and a smile, and she turned away. I had no idea what that was supposed to mean, if anything. Maybe she wanted to be discreet about our relationship, the old don't-fish-off-the-company-pier thing.

I passed my old boss, Tom Lundgren, who was dressed in one of those hideous golf shirts with gray and bright pink stripes. He was clutching a bottle of water and nervously stripping off the label in a long perfect ribbon as he listened with a fixed grin to an attractive black woman who was probably Audrey Bethune, a vice president and the head of the Guru team. Standing slightly behind him was a woman I took to be Lundgren's wife, dressed in an identical golfing outfit, her face almost as red and chafed as his. A gangly little boy was grabbing at her elbow and pleading about something in a squeaky voice.

Fifty feet away or so, Goddard was laughing with a small knot of guys who looked familiar. He was drinking from a bottle of beer and wearing a blue button-down shirt rolled up at the sleeves, a pair of neatly creased, cuffed khakis, a navy-blue cloth belt with whales on it, and battered brown moccasins. The ultimate prepster country baron. A little girl ran up to him, and he leaned over and magically extracted a coin from her ear. She squealed in surprise. He handed her the coin, and she ran off, shrieking with excitement.

He said something else, and his audience laughed as if he were Jay Leno and Eddie Murphy and Rodney Dangerfield all rolled into one. To one side of him was Paul Camilletti, in neatly pressed, faded jeans and a white button-down shirt, also with the sleeves rolled up. *He'd* gotten the appropriate-dress memo, even if I hadn't—I had on a pair of khaki shorts and a polo shirt.

Facing him was Jim Colvin, the COO, his sandpiper legs pasty-white under plain gray Bermuda shorts. A real fashion show this was. Goddard looked up, caught my eye, and beckoned me over.

As I started toward him, someone came out of nowhere and clutched my arm. Nora Sommers, in a pink knit shirt with the collar standing up and oversized khaki shorts, looked thrilled to see me. "Adam!" she exclaimed. "How nice to see you here! Isn't this a *marvelous* place?"

I nodded, smiled politely. "Is your daughter here?"

She looked suddenly uncomfortable. "Megan's going through a difficult stage, poor thing. She never wants to spend time with me." Funny, I thought, I'm going through the exact same stage. "She'd rather ride horses with her father than waste an afternoon with her mother and her mother's boring work friends."

I nodded. "Excuse me—"

"Have you had a chance to see Jock's car collection? It's in the garage over there." She pointed toward a barnlike building a few hundred feet across the lawn. "You *have* to see the cars. They're *glorious!*"

"I will, thanks," I said, and took a step toward Goddard's little gang.

Nora's clutch on my arm tightened. "Adam, I've been meaning to tell you, I am *so* happy for your success. It really says something about Jock that he was willing to take a chance on you, doesn't it? Place his confidence in you? I'm just so *happy* for you!" I thanked her warmly and extricated my arm from her claw.

I reached Goddard and stood politely off to one side until he saw me and waved me over. He introduced me to Stuart Lurie, the exec in charge of Enterprise Solutions, who said, "How's it going, guy?" and gave me a soul clasp. He was a very good-looking guy of around forty, prematurely bald and shaved short on the sides so it all looked sort of deliberate and cool.

"Adam's the future of Trion," Goddard said.

"Well, hey, nice to meet the future!" said Lurie with just the slightest hint of sarcasm. "You're not going to pull a coin from *his* ear, Jock, are you?"

"No need to," Jock said. "Adam's always pulling rabbits out of hats, right, Adam?" Goddard put his arm around my shoulder, an awkward gesture since I was so much taller than him. "Come with me," he said quietly.

He guided me toward the screened porch. "In a little while I'm going to be doing my traditional little ceremony," he said as we climbed the wooden steps. I held the screen door open for him. "I give out little gifts, silly little things—gag gifts, really." I smiled, wondering why he was telling me this.

We passed through the screened porch, with its old wicker furniture, into a mudroom and then into the main part of the house. The floors were old wide-board pine, and they squeaked as we walked over them. The walls were all painted creamy white, and everything seemed bright and cheery and homey. It had that indescribable old-house smell. Everything seemed comfortable and lived-in and real. This was the house of a rich man with no pretensions, I thought. We went down a wide hallway past a sitting room with a big stone fireplace, then turned a corner into a narrow hall with a tile floor. Trophies and stuff were on shelves on either side of the hall. Then we entered a small book-lined room with a long library table in the center, a computer and printer on it and several huge cardboard boxes. This was obviously Goddard's study.

"The old bursitis is acting up," he apologized, indicating the big cartons on the library table, which were heaped with what looked like wrapped gifts. "You're a strapping young man. If you wouldn't mind carrying these out to where the podium's set up, near the bar. . . ."

"Not at all," I said, disappointed, but not showing it. I lifted one of the enormous boxes, which was not only heavy but unwieldy, unevenly weighted and so bulky that I could barely see in front of me as I walked.

"I'll guide you out of here," Goddard said. I followed him into the narrow corridor. The box scraped against the shelves on both sides, and I had to turn it sort of sideways and up to maneuver it through. I could feel the box nudge something. There was a loud crash, the sound of glass shattering.

"Oh, shit," I blurted out.

I twisted the box so I could see what had just happened. I stared: I must have knocked one of the trophies off a shelf. It lay in a dozen golden shards all over the tile floor. It was the kind of trophy that looked like solid gold but was actually some kind of gilt-painted ceramic or something.

"Oh, God, I'm sorry," I said, setting down the box and crouching down to pick up the pieces. I'd been so careful with the box, but somehow I must have knocked against it, I didn't know how.

Goddard glanced around and he turned white. "Forget it," he said in a strained voice.

I collected as many of the shards as I could. It was—it had been—a golden statuette of a running football player. There was a fragment of a helmet, a fist, a little football. The base was wood with a brass plaque that said 1995 CHAMPIONS—LAKEWOOD SCHOOL—ELIJAH GODDARD—QUARTERBACK.

Elijah Goddard, according to Judith Bolton, was Goddard's dead son.

"Jock," I said, "I'm so sorry." One of the jagged pieces sliced painfully into my palm.

"I said, forget about it," Goddard said, his voice steely. "It's nothing. Now come on, let's get going."

I didn't know what to do, I felt so shitty about destroying this artifact of his dead son. I wanted to clean the mess up, but I also didn't want to piss him off further. So much for all the goodwill I'd built up with the old guy. The cut in my palm was now oozing blood.

"Mrs. Walsh will clean this up," he said, a hard edge to his voice. "Come on, please take these gifts outside." He went down the hall and disappeared somewhere. Meanwhile, I lifted the box and carried it, with extreme caution, down the narrow corridor and then out of the house. I left a smeary handprint of blood on the cardboard.

When I returned for the second box, I saw Goddard sitting in a chair in a corner of his study. He was hunched over, his head in shadow, and he was holding the wooden trophy base in both hands. I hesitated, not sure what I should do, whether I should get out of here, leave him alone, or whether I should keep moving the boxes and pretend I didn't see him.

"He was a sweet kid," Goddard suddenly said, so quietly that at first I thought I'd imagined it. I stopped moving. His voice was low and hoarse and faint, not much louder than a whisper. "An athlete, tall and broad in the chest, like you. And he had a . . . gift for happiness. When he walked into a room, you just felt the mood lifting. He made people feel good. He was beautiful, and he was kind, and there was this—this *spark* in his eyes." He slowly raised his head and stared into the middle distance. "Even when he was a baby, he almost never cried or fussed or . . ."

Goddard's voice trailed off, and I stood there in the middle of the room, frozen in place, just listening. I'd balled up a napkin in my hand to soak up the blood, and I could feel it getting wet. "You would have liked him," Goddard said. He was looking toward me but somehow not *at* me, as if he were seeing his son where I was standing. "It's true. You boys would have been friends."

"I'm sorry I never met him."

"Everybody loved him. This was a kid who was put on the earth to make everybody happy—he had a spark, he had the best sm—" His voice cracked. "The best—smile. . . ." Goddard lowered his head, and his shoulders shook. After a minute he said, "One day I got a call at the office from Margaret. She was screaming. . . . She'd found him in his bedroom. I drove home, I couldn't think straight. . . . Elijah had dropped out of Haverford his junior year—really, they kicked him out, his grades had gone to shit, he stopped going to classes. But I couldn't get him to talk about it. I had a good idea he was on drugs, of course, and I tried to talk to him, but it was like talking to a stone wall. He moved back in, spent most of his time in his room or going out with kids I didn't know. Later I heard from one of his friends that he'd gotten into heroin at the beginning of junior year. This wasn't some juvenile delinquent, this was a gifted, sweet-natured fellow, a good kid. . . . But at some point he started . . . what's the expression, shooting up? And it changed him. The light in his eyes was gone. He started to lie all the time. It was as if he was trying to erase everything he was. Do you know what I mean?" Goddard looked up again. Tears were now running down his face.

I nodded.

A few slow seconds ticked by before he went on. "He was searching for something, I guess. He needed something the world couldn't give him. Or maybe he cared too much, and he decided he needed to kill that part of him." His voice thickened again. "And then the rest of him."

"Jock," I began, wanting him to stop.

"The medical examiner ruled it an overdose. He said there was no question it was deliberate, that Elijah knew what he was doing." He covered his eyes with a pudgy hand. "You ask yourself, what should I have done differently? How did I screw him up? I even threatened to have him arrested once. We tried to get him to go into rehab. I was on the verge of packing him off there, *making* him go, but I never got the chance. And I asked myself over and over again: Was I too hard on him, too stern? Or not hard enough? Was I too involved in my own work?—I think I was. I was far too driven in those days. I was too goddamned busy building Trion to be a real father to him."

Now he looked directly at me, and I could see the anguish in his eyes. It felt like a dagger in my gut. My own eyes got moist.

"You go off to work and you build your little kingdom," he said, "and you lose track of what matters." He blinked hard. "I don't want you to lose track, Adam. Not ever."

Goddard looked smaller, and wizened, and a hundred years old. "He was lying on his bed covered in drool and piss like an infant, and I cradled him in my arms just like he was a baby. Do you know what it's like seeing your child in a coffin?" he whispered. I felt goose bumps, and I had to look away from him. "I thought I'd never go back to work. I thought I'd never get over it. Margaret says I never have. For almost two months I stayed home. I couldn't figure out the reason I was alive anymore. Something like this happens and you—you question the value of everything."

He seemed to remember he had a handkerchief in his pocket, and he pulled it out, mopped his face. "Ah, look at me," he said with a deep sigh, and unexpectedly he sort of chuckled. "Look at the old fool. When I was your age I imagined that when I got to be as old as I am now I'd have discovered the meaning of life." He smiled sadly. "And I'm no closer now to knowing the meaning of life than I ever was. Oh, I know what it's *not* about. By process of elimination. I had to lose a son to learn that. You get your big house and your fancy car, and maybe they put you on the cover of *Fortune* magazine, and you think you've got it all figured out, right? Until God sends you a little telegram saying, 'Oh, forgot to mention, none of that means a thing. And everyone you love on this earth—they're really just on loan, you see. And you'd better love 'em while you can.' " A tear rolled slowly down his cheek. "To this day I ask myself, did I ever know Elijah? Maybe not. I thought I did. I do know I loved him, more than I ever thought I could love someone. But did I really *know* my boy? I couldn't tell you." He shook his head slowly, and I could see him begin to take hold of himself. "Your dad's goddamned lucky, whoever he is, so goddamned lucky, and he'll never know it. He's got a son like you, a son who's still with him. I know he's got to be proud of you."

"I'm not so sure of that," I said softly.

"Oh, I am," Goddard said. "Because I know *I'd* be."

PART SEVEN

CONTROL

Control: Power exerted over an agent or double agent to prevent his defection or redoubling (so-called "tripling").

—*The International Dictionary of Intelligence*

66

The next morning I checked my e-mail at home and found a message from "Arthur":

> `Boss very impressed by your presentation & wants to see more right away.`

I stared at it for a minute, and I decided not to reply.

A little while later I showed up, unannounced, at my dad's apartment, with a box of Krispy Kreme donuts. I parked in a space right in front of his triple-decker. I knew Dad spent all his time staring out the window, when he wasn't watching TV. He didn't miss anything that was going on outside.

I'd just come from the car wash, and the Porsche was a gleaming hunk of obsidian, a thing of beauty. I was stoked. Dad hadn't seen it yet. His "loser" son, a loser no more, was arriving in style—in a chariot of 450 horsepower.

My father was stationed in his usual spot in front of the TV, watching some kind of low-rent investigative show about corporate scandals. Antwoine was sitting next to him in the less comfortable chair, reading one of those color supermarket tabloids that all look alike; I think it was the *Star*.

Dad glanced up, saw the donut carton I was waving at him, and he shook his head. "Nah," he said.

"I'm pretty sure there's a chocolate frosted in here. Your favorite."

"I can't eat that shit anymore. Mandingo here's got a gun to my head. Why don't you offer him one?"

Antwoine shook his head too. "No thanks, I'm trying to lose a few pounds. You're the devil."

"What is this, Jenny Craig headquarters?" I set down the box of donuts on the maple-veneer coffee table next to Antwoine. Dad still hadn't said anything about the car, but I figured he'd probably been too absorbed in his TV show. Plus his vision wasn't all that great.

"Soon as you leave this guy's going to start crackin' the whip, making me do laps around the room," Dad said.

"He doesn't stop, does he?" I said to Dad.

Dad's face was more amused than angry. "Whatever floats his boat," he said. "Though nothing seems to get him off like keeping me off my smokes."

The tension between the two of them seemed to have ebbed into some kind of a resigned stalemate. "Hey, you look a lot better, Dad," I lied.

"Bullshit," he said, his eyes riveted on the pseudo-investigative TV story. "You still working at that new place?"

"Yeah," I said. I smiled bashfully, figured it was time to tell him the big news. "In fact— "

"Let me tell you something," he said, finally turning his gaze away from the TV and giving me a rheumy stare. He pointed back at the TV without looking at it. "These S.O.B.s—these bastards—they'll cheat you out of every last fucking nickel if you let them."

"Who, the corporations?"

"The corporations, the CEOs, with their stock options and their big fat pensions and their sweetheart deals. They're all out for themselves, every last one of them, and don't you forget it."

I looked down at the carpet. "Well," I said quietly, "not all of them."

"Oh, don't kid yourself."

"Listen to your father," Antwoine said, not looking up from the *Star*. There almost seemed to be a little affection in his voice. "The man's a fount of wisdom."

"Actually, Dad, I happen to know a little something about CEOs. I just got a huge promotion—I was just made executive assistant to the CEO of Trion."

There was just silence. I thought he hadn't been listening. He was staring at the TV. I thought that might have sounded a little arrogant, so I softened it a bit: "It's really a big deal, Dad."

More silence.

I was about to repeat it when he said, "Executive assistant? What's that, like a secretary?"

"No, no. It's, like, high-level stuff. Brainstorming and everything."

"So what exactly do you do all day?"

The guy had emphysema, but he knew just how to take the wind out of me. "Never mind, Dad," I said. "I'm sorry I brought it up." I was, too. Why the hell did I care what he thought?

"No, really. I'm curious what you did to get that slick new set of wheels out there."

So he had noticed, after all. I smiled. "Pretty nice, huh?"

"How much that vehicle cost you?"

"Well, actually—"

"Per month, I'm talking." He took a long suck of oxygen.

"Nothing."

"Nothing," he repeated, as if he didn't get it.

"Nada. Trion covers the lease totally. It's a perk of my new job."

He breathed in again. "A perk."

"Same with my new apartment."

"You moved?"

"I thought I told you. Two thousand square feet in that new Harbor Suites building. And Trion pays for it."

Another intake of breath. "You proud?" he said.

I was stunned. I'd never heard him say that word before, I didn't think. "Yeah," I said, blushing.

"Proud of the fact that they own you now?"

I should have seen the razor blade in the apple. "Nobody owns me, Dad," I said curtly. "I believe it's called 'making it.' Look it up. You'll find it in the thesaurus next to 'life at the top,' 'executive suite,' and 'high net-worth individuals.' " I couldn't believe what was coming out of my mouth. And all this time I'd been railing about being a monkey on a stick. Now I was actually boasting about the bling bling. *See what you made me do?*

Antwoine put down his newspaper and excused himself, tactfully, pretending to do something in the kitchen.

Dad laughed harshly, turned to look at me. "So lemme get this straight." He sucked in some more oxygen. "You don't own the car *or* the apartment, that right? You call that a perk?" A breath. "I'll tell you what that means. Everything they give you they can take away, and they will, too. You drive a goddamn company car, you live in company housing, you wear a company uniform, and none of it's yours. Your whole life ain't yours."

I bit my lip. It wasn't going to do me any good to let loose. The old guy was dying, I told myself for the millionth time. He's on steroids. He's an unhappy, caustic guy. But it just came out: "You know, Dad, some fathers would actually be proud of their son's success, you know?"

He sucked in, his tiny eyes glittering. "Success, that what you call it, huh? See, Adam, you remind me of your mother more and more."

"Oh, yeah?" I told myself: keep it in, keep the anger in check, don't lose it, or else he's won.

"That's right. You look like her. Got the same social-type personality—everyone liked her, she fit in anywhere, she coulda married a richer guy, she coulda done a lot better. And don't think she didn't let me know it. All those parent nights at Bartholomew Browning, you could see her getting all friendly with those rich bastards, getting all dressed up, practically pushing her tits in their faces. Think I didn't notice?"

"Oh, that's good, Dad. That's real good. Too bad I'm not more like *you*, you know?"

He just looked at me.

"You know—bitter, nasty. Pissed off at the world. You want me to grow up to be just like you, that it?"

He puffed, his face growing redder.

I kept going. My heart was going a hundred beats a minute, my voice growing louder and louder, and I was almost shouting. "When I was broke and partying all the time you considered me a fuckup. Okay, so now I'm a success by just about anyone's definition, and you've got nothing but contempt. Maybe there's a reason you can't be proud of me no matter what I do, Dad."

He glared and puffed, said, "Oh yeah?"

"Look at you. Look at your life." There was like this runaway freight train inside me, unstoppable, out of control. "You're always saying the world's divided up into winners and losers. So let me ask you something, Dad. What are you, Dad? What are you?"

He sucked in oxygen, his eyes bloodshot and looking like they were going to pop out of his head. He seemed to be muttering to himself. I heard "Goddamn" and "fuck" and "shit."

"Yeah, Dad," I said, turning away from him. "I want to be just like you." I headed for the door in a slipstream of my own pent-up anger. The words were out and couldn't be unsaid, and I felt more miserable than ever. I left his apartment before I could wreak any more destruction. The last thing I saw, my parting image of the guy, was his big red face, puffing and muttering, his eyes glassy and staring in disbelief or fury or pain, I didn't know which.

67

"So you really work for Jock Goddard himself, huh?" Alana said. "God, I hope I didn't ever say anything negative to you about Goddard. Did I?"

We were riding the elevator up to my apartment. She'd stopped at her own place after work to change, and she looked great—black boat-neck top, black leggings, chunky black shoes. She also had on that same delicious floral scent she wore on our last date. Her black hair was long and glossy, and it contrasted nicely with her brilliant blue eyes.

"Yeah, you really trashed him, which I immediately reported."

She smiled, a glint of perfect teeth. "This elevator is about the same size as my apartment."

I knew that wasn't true, but I laughed anyway. "The elevator really is bigger than my last place," I said. When I'd mentioned that I'd just moved into the Harbor Suites she said she'd heard about the condos there and seemed intrigued, so I'd invited her to stop by to check it out. We could have dinner at the hotel restaurant downstairs, where I hadn't had a chance to eat.

"Boy, quite the view," she said as soon as she entered the apartment. An Alanis Morissette CD was playing softly. "This is fantastic." She looked around, saw the plastic wrap still on one of the couches and a chair, said archly, "So when do you move in?"

"As soon as I have a spare hour or two. Can I get you a drink?"

"Hmm. Sure, that would be nice."

"Cosmopolitan? I also do a terrific gin-and-tonic."

"Gin-and-tonic sounds perfect, thanks. So you've just started working for him, right?"

She'd looked me up, of course. I went over to the newly stocked liquor cabinet, in the alcove next to the kitchen, and reached for a bottle of Tanqueray Malacca gin.

"Just this week." She followed me into the kitchen. I grabbed a handful of limes from the almost-empty refrigerator and began cutting them in half.

"But you've been at Trion for like a month." She cocked her head to one side, trying to make sense of my sudden promotion. "Nice kitchen. Do you cook?"

"The appliances are just for show," I said. I began pressing the lime halves into the electric juicer. "Anyway, right, I was hired into new-products marketing, but then Goddard was sort of involved in a project I was working on, and I guess he liked my approach, my ideas, whatever."

"Talk about a lucky break," she said, raising her voice above the electric whine of the juicer.

I shrugged. "We'll see if it's lucky." I filled two French bistro–style tumblers with ice, a shot of gin, a good splash of cold tonic water from the refrigerator, and a healthy helping of lime juice. I handed her her drink.

"So Tom Lundgren must have hired you for Nora Sommers's team. Hey, this is delicious. All that lime makes a difference."

"Thank you. That's right, Tom Lundgren hired me," I said, pretending to be surprised she knew.

"Do you know you were hired to fill my position?"

"What do you mean?"

"The position that opened up when I was moved to AURORA."

"Is that right?" I looked amazed.

She nodded. "Unbelievable."

"Wow, small world. But what's 'Aurora'?"

"Oh, I figured you knew." She glanced at me over the rim of her glass, a look that seemed just a bit too casual.

I shook my head innocently. "No . . . ?"

"I figured you probably looked me up too. I got assigned to marketing for the Disruptive Technologies group."

"That's called AURORA?"

"No, AURORA's the specific project I'm assigned to." She hesitated a second. "I guess I thought that working for Goddard you'd sort of have your fingers into everything."

A tactical slip on my part. I wanted her to think we could talk freely about whatever she did. "Theoretically I have access to everything. But I'm still figuring out where the copying machine is."

She nodded. "You like Goddard?"

What was I going to say, no? "He's an impressive guy."

"At his barbecue you two seemed to be pretty close. I saw he called you over to meet his buddies, and you were like carrying things for him and all that."

"Yeah, real close," I said, sarcastic. "I'm his gofer. I'm his muscle. You enjoy the barbecue?"

"It was a little strange, hanging with all the powers, but after a couple of beers it got easier. That was my first time there." Because she'd been assigned to his pet project, AURORA, I thought. But I wanted to be subtle about it, so I let it drop for the time being. "Let me call down to the restaurant and have them get our table ready."

"You know, I thought Trion wasn't really hiring from outside," she said, looking over the menu. "They must have really wanted you, to bend the rules like that."

"I think they thought they were stealing me away. I was nothing special." We'd switched from gin-and-tonics to Sancerre, which I'd ordered because I saw from her liquor bills that that was her favorite wine. She looked surprised and pleased when I'd asked for it. It was a reaction I was getting used to.

"I doubt that," she said. "What'd you do at Wyatt?"

I gave her the job-interview version I'd memorized, but that wasn't enough for her. She wanted details about the Lucid project. "I'm really not supposed to talk about what I did at Wyatt, if you don't mind," I said. I tried not to sound too priggish about it.

She looked embarrassed. "Oh, God, sure, I totally understand," she said.

The waiter appeared. "Are you ready to order?"

Alana said, "You go first," and studied the menu some more while I ordered the paella.

"I was thinking of getting that," she said. Okay, so she wasn't a vegetarian.

"We're allowed to get the same thing, you know," I said.

"I'll have the paella, too," she told the waiter. "But if there's any meat in it, like sausage, can you leave it out?"

"Of course," the waiter said, making a note.

"I love paella," she said. "I almost never have fish or seafood at home. This is a treat."

"Wanna stick with the Sancerre?" I said to her.

"Sure."

As the waiter turned to go, I suddenly remembered Alana was allergic to shrimp and said, "Wait a second, is there shrimp in the paella?"

"Uh, yes, there is," said the waiter.

"That could be a problem," I said.

Alana stared at me. "How did you know . . . ?" she began, her eyes narrowing.

There was this long, long moment of excruciating tension while I wracked my brain. I couldn't believe I'd screwed up like this. I swallowed hard, and the blood drained from my face. Finally I said, "You mean, you're allergic to it, too?"

A pause. "I am. Sorry. How funny." The cloud of suspicion seemed to have lifted. We both switched to the seared scallops.

"Anyway," I said, "enough talking about me. I want to hear about AURORA."

"Well, it's supposed to be kept under wraps," she apologized.

I grinned at her.

"No, this isn't tit-for-tat, I swear," she protested. "Really!"

"Okay," I said skeptically. "But now that you've aroused my curiosity, are you really going to make me poke around and find out on my own?"

"It's not *that* interesting."

"I don't believe it. Can't you at least give me the thumbnail?"

She looked skyward, heaved a sigh. "Well, it's like this. You ever hear of the Haloid Company?"

"No," I said slowly.

"Of course not. No reason you should have heard of it. But the Haloid Company was this small photographic-paper company that, in the late nineteen-forties, bought the rights to this new technology that had been turned down by all the big companies—IBM, RCA, GE. The invention was something called xerography, okay? So in ten, fifteen years the Haloid Company became the Xerox Corporation, and it went from a small family-run company to a gigantic corporation. All because they took a chance on a technology that no one else was interested in."

"Okay."

"Or the way the Galvin Manufacturing Corporation in Chicago, which made Motorola brand car radios, eventually got into semiconductors and cell phones. Or a small oil exploration company called Geophysical Service started branching out and getting into transistors and then the integrated circuit and became Texas Instruments. So you get my point. The history of technology is filled with examples of companies that transformed themselves by grabbing hold of the right technology at the right time, and leaving their competitors in the dust. That's what Jock Goddard is trying to do with AURORA. He thinks AURORA is going to change the world, and the face of American business, the way transistors or semiconductors or photocopying technology once did."

"Disruptive technology."

"Exactly."

"But the *Wall Street Journal* seems to think Jock's washed up."

"We both know better than that. He's just way ahead of the curve. Look at the history of the company. There were three or four points when everyone thought Trion was on the ropes, on the verge of bankruptcy, and then all of a sudden it surprised everyone and came back stronger than ever."

"You think this is one of those turning points, huh?"

"When AURORA's ready to announce, he'll announce it. And then let's see what the *Wall Street Journal* says. AURORA makes all these latest problems practically irrelevant."

"Amazing." I peered into my wineglass and said oh-so-casually, "So what's the technology?"

She smiled, shook her head. "I probably shouldn't have said even this much." Tilting her head to one side she said playfully, "Are you doing some sort of security check on me?"

68

I knew from the moment she said she wanted to eat at the restaurant at the Harbor Suites that we'd sleep together that night. I've had dates with women where an erotic charge came from "will she or won't she?" This was different, of course, but the charge was even stronger. It was there all along, that invisible line that we both knew we were going to cross, the line that separated us from friends and something more intimate; the question was when, and how, we were going to cross it, who'd make the first move, what crossing it would feel like. We came back up to my apartment after dinner, both a little unsteady from too much white wine and G & Ts. I had my arm around her narrow waist. I wanted to feel the soft skin on her tummy, underneath her breasts, on her upper buttocks. I wanted to see her most private areas. I wanted to witness the moment when the hard shell around Alana, the impossibly beautiful, sophisticated woman cracked; when she shuddered, gave way, when those clear blue eyes became lost in pleasure.

We sort of careened around the apartment, enjoying the views of the water, and I made us both martinis, which we definitely didn't need. She said, "I can't believe I have to go to Palo Alto tomorrow morning."

"What's up in Palo Alto?"

She shook her head. "Nothing interesting." She had her arm around my waist too, but she accidentally-on-purpose let her hand slip down to my butt, squeezing rhythmically, and she made a joke about whether I'd finished unpacking the bed.

The next minute I had my lips on hers, my groping fingertips gently stroking her tits, and she snaked a very warm hand down to my groin. Both of us were quickly aroused, and we stumbled over to the couch, the one that didn't have plastic wrap still on it. We kissed and ground our hips together. She moaned. She fished me greedily out of my pants. She was wearing a white silk teddy under her black shirt. Her breasts were ample, round, perfect.

She came loudly, with surprising abandon.

I knocked over my martini glass. We made our way down the long corridor to my bedroom and did it again, this time more slowly.

"Alana," I said when we were snuggling.

"Hmm?"

"Alana," I repeated. "That means 'beautiful' in Gaelic or something, right?"

"Celtic, I think." She was scratching my chest. I was stroking one of her breasts.

"Alana, I have to confess something."

She groaned. "You're married."

"No—"

She turned to me, a flash of annoyance in her eyes. "You're involved with someone."

"No, definitely not. I have to confess—I hate Ani DiFranco."

"But didn't you—you quoted her. . . ." She looked puzzled.

"I had an old girlfriend who used to listen to her a lot, and now it's got bad associations."

"So why do you have one of her CDs out?"

She'd seen the damned thing next to the CD player. "I was trying to make myself like her."

"Why?"

"For you."

She thought for a moment, furrowed her dark brow. "You don't have to like everything I like. I don't like Porsches."

"You don't?" I turned to her, surprised.

"They're dicks on wheels."

"That's true."

"Maybe some guys need that, but you definitely don't."

"No one 'needs' a Porsche. I just thought it was cool."

"I'm surprised you didn't get a red one."

"Nah. Red's cop bait—cops see red Porsches and they switch on their radar."

"Did your dad have a Porsche? My dad had one." She rolled her eyes. "Ridiculous. Like, his male-menopause, midlife-crisis car."

"Actually, for most of my childhood we didn't even *have* a car."

"You didn't have a *car*?"

"We took public transportation."

"Oh." Now she looked uncomfortable. After a minute she said, "So all this must be pretty heady stuff." She waved her hand around to indicate the apartment and everything.

"Yeah."

"Hmm."

Another minute went by. "Can I visit you at work some time?" I said.

"You can't. Access to the fifth floor is pretty restricted. Anyway, I think it's better if people at work don't know, don't you agree?"

"Yeah, you're right."

I was surprised when she curled up next to me and drifted off to sleep: I thought she was going to take right off, go home, wake up in her own bed, but she seemed to want to spend the night.

The bedside clock said three thirty-five when I got up. She remained asleep, buzzing softly. I walked across the carpet and noiselessly closed the bedroom door behind me.

I signed on to my e-mail and saw the usual assortment of spam and junk, some work stuff that didn't look urgent, and one on Hushmail from "Arthur" whose subject line said, "re: consumer devices." Meacham sounded royally pissed off:

```
Boss extremely disappointed by your failure to reply.
Wants additional presentation materials by 6 pm tomorrow
or deal is endangered.
```

I hit "reply" and typed, "unable to locate additional materials, sorry" and signed it "Donnie." Then I read through it and deleted my message. Nope. I wasn't going to reply at all. That was simpler. I'd done enough for them.

I noticed that Alana's little square black handbag was still on the granite bar where she'd left it. She hadn't brought her computer or her workbag, since she'd stopped at home to change.

In her handbag were her badge, a lipstick, some breath mints, a key ring, and her Trion Maestro. The keys were probably for her apartment and car and maybe her home mailbox and such. The Maestro likely held phone numbers and addresses, but also specific datebook appointments. That could be very useful to Wyatt and Meacham.

But was I still working for them?

Maybe not.

What would happen if I just quit? I'd upheld my side of the bargain, got them just about everything they wanted on AURORA—well, most of it, anyway. Odds were they'd calculate that it wasn't worth hassling me further. It wasn't in their interests to blow my cover, not so long as I could potentially be useful to them. And they weren't going to feed the FBI an anonymous tip, because that would just lead the authorities back to them.

What could they do to me?

Then I realized: I'd already quit working for them. I'd made the decision that afternoon in the study at Jock Goddard's lake house. I wasn't going to keep betraying the guy. Meacham and Wyatt could go screw themselves.

It would have been really easy at that moment for me to slip Alana's handheld into the recharging cradle attached to my desktop computer and hot-link it. Sure, there was a risk of her getting up, since she was in a strange bed, finding me gone, and wandering around the apartment to see where I'd gone. In which case she might see me downloading the contents of her Maestro to my computer. Maybe she wouldn't notice. But she was smart and quick, and she was likely to figure out the truth.

And no matter how fast I thought, no matter how cleverly I handled it, she'd know what I was up to. And I'd be caught, and the relationship would be over, and all of a sudden that mattered to me. I was smitten with Alana, and after only a couple of dates and one night together. I was just beginning to discover her earthy, expansive, sort of wild side. I loved her loopy, unrestrained laugh, her boldness, her dry sense of humor. I didn't want to lose her because of something the loathsome Nick Wyatt was forcing me to do.

Already I'd handed over to Wyatt all kinds of valuable information on the AURORA project. I'd done my job. I was finished with those assholes.

And I couldn't stop seeing Jock Goddard hunched over in that dark corner of his study, his shoulders shaking. That moment of revelation. The trust he'd put in me. And I was going to violate that trust for Nick Fucking Wyatt?

No, I didn't think so. Not anymore.

So I put Alana's Maestro back into her pocketbook. I poured myself a glass of cold water from the drinking-water dispenser on the Sub Zero door, gulped it down, and climbed back into my warm bed with Alana. She muttered something in her sleep, and I snuggled right up next to her and, for the first time in weeks, actually felt good about myself.

69

Goddard was scurrying down the hall to the Executive Briefing Center, and I struggled to keep up with him without breaking into a run. Man, the old guy moved fast, like a tortoise on methamphetamine. "This darned meeting is going to be a circus," he muttered. "I called the Guru team here for a status update as soon as I heard they're going to slip their Christmas ship date. They know I'm royally pissed off, and they're going to be pirouetting like a troupe of Russian ballerinas doing the 'Dance of the Sugar Plum Fairies.' You're going to see a side of me here that's not so attractive."

I didn't say anything—what could I say? I'd seen his flashes of anger, and they didn't even compare to what I'd seen in the only other CEO I'd ever met. Next to Nick Wyatt he was Mister Rogers. And in fact I was still shaken, moved by that intimate little scene in his lake house study—I'd never really seen another human being lay himself so bare. Until that moment there'd been a part of me that was sort of baffled as to why Goddard had singled me out, why he'd been drawn to me. Now I got it, and it rocked my world. I didn't just want to impress the old man anymore, I wanted his approval, maybe something deeper.

Why, I agonized, did Goddard have to fuck it all up by being such a decent guy? It was unpleasant enough working for Nick Wyatt without this complication. Now I was working against the dad I never had, and it was messing with my head.

"Guru's prime is a very smart young woman named Audrey Bethune, a real comer," Goddard muttered. "But this disaster may derail her career. I really have no patience for screwups on this scale." As we approached the room, he slowed. "Now, if you have any thoughts, don't hesitate to speak. But be warned—this is a high-powered and very opinionated group, and they're not going to show you any deference just because I brung you to the dance."

The Guru team was assembled around the big conference table, waiting nervously. They looked up as we entered. Some of them smiled, said, "Hi, Jock," or "Hello, Mr. Goddard." They looked like scared rabbits. I remembered sitting around that table not so long ago. There were a few puzzled glances at me, some whispers. Goddard sat down at the head of the table. Next to him was a black woman in her late thirties, the same woman I'd seen talking to Tom Lundgren and his wife at the barbecue. He patted the table next to him to tell me to sit by his side. My cell phone had been vibrating in my pocket for the last ten minutes, so I furtively fished it out and glanced at the caller ID screen. A bunch of calls from a number I didn't recognize. I switched the phone off.

"Afternoon," Goddard said. "This is my assistant, Adam Cassidy." A number of polite smiles, and then I saw that one of the faces belonged to my old friend Nora Sommers. Shit, she was on Guru, too? She wore a black-and-white striped suit and she had her power makeup on. She caught my eye, beamed like I was some long-lost childhood playmate. I smiled back politely, savoring the moment.

Audrey Bethune, the program manager, was beautifully dressed in a navy suit with a white blouse and small gold stud earrings. She had dark skin and wore her hair in a perfectly coifed and shellacked bubble. I'd done some quick background research on her and knew that she came from an upper-middle-class family. Her father was a doctor, as was her grandfather, and she'd spent every summer at the family compound in Oak Bluffs on Martha's Vineyard. She smiled at me, revealing a gap between her front teeth. She reached behind Jock's back to shake my hand. Her palm was dry and cool. I was impressed. Her career was on the line.

Guru—the project was code-named TSUNAMI—was a supercharged handheld digital assistant, really killer technology and Trion's only convergence device. It was a PDA, a communicator, a mobile phone. It had the power of a laptop in an eight-ounce package. It did e-mail, instant messages, spreadsheets, had a full HTML Internet browser and a great TFT active-matrix color screen.

Goddard cleared his throat. "So I understand we have a little challenge," he said.

"That's one way of putting it, Jock," Audrey said smoothly. "Yesterday we got the results of the in-house audit, which indicated that we've got a faulty component. The LCD is totally dead."

"Ah hah," Goddard said with what I knew was forced calm. "Bad LCD, is it?"

Audrey shook her head. "Apparently the LCD *driver* is defective."

"In every single one?" asked Goddard.

"That's right."

"A quarter of a million units have a bad LCD driver," Goddard said. "I see. The ship date is in—what is it, now?—three weeks. Hmm. Now, as I recall—and correct me if I'm wrong—your plan was to ship these before the end of the quarter, thus bolstering earnings for the third quarter and giving us all thirteen weeks of the Christmas quarter to rake in some badly needed revenue."

She nodded.

"Audrey, I believe we agreed that Guru is the division's big kahuna. And as we all know, Trion is experiencing some difficulties in the market. Which means that it's all the more crucial that Guru ship on schedule." I noticed that Goddard was speaking in an overly deliberate manner, and I knew he was trying to hold back his great annoyance.

The chief marketing officer, the slick-looking Rick Durant, put in mournfully, "This is a huge embarrassment. We've already launched a huge teaser campaign, placed ads all over the place. 'The digital assistant for the next generation.' " He rolled his eyes.

"Yeah," muttered Goddard. "And it sounds like it won't *ship* until the next generation." He turned to the lead engineer, Eddie Cabral, a round-faced, swarthy guy with a dated flattop. "Is it a problem with the mask?"

"I wish," Cabral replied. "No, the whole damned chip is going to have to be respun, sir."

"The contract manufacturer's in Malaysia?" said Goddard.

"We've always had good luck with them," said Cabral. "The tolerances and quality have always been pretty good. But this is a complicated ASIC. It's got to drive our own, proprietary Trion LCD screen, and the cookies just aren't coming out of the oven right— "

"What about replacing the LCD?" Goddard interrupted.

"No, sir," said Cabral. "Not without retooling the whole casing, which is another six months easy."

I suddenly sat up. The buzzwords jumped out at me. *ASIC . . . proprietary Trion LCD . . .*

"That's the nature of ASICs," Goddard said. "There are always some cookies that get burnt. What's the yield like, forty, fifty percent?"

Cabral looked miserable. "Zero. Some kind of assembly-line flaw."

Goddard tightened his mouth. He looked like he was about to lose it. "How long will it take to respin the ASIC?"

Cabral hesitated. "Three months. If we're lucky."

"If we're *lucky*," Goddard repeated. "Yep, if we're *lucky*." His voice was getting steadily louder. "Three months puts the ship date into December. That won't work at all, will it?"

"No, sir," said Cabral.

I tapped Goddard on the arm, but he ignored me. "Mexico can't manufacture this for us quicker?"

The head of manufacturing, a woman named Kathy Gornick, said, "Maybe a week or two faster, which won't help us at all. And then the quality will be substandard at best."

"This is a goddamned mess," Goddard said. I'd never really heard him curse before.

I picked up a product spec sheet, then tapped Goddard's arm again. "Will you please excuse me for a moment?" I said.

I rushed out of the room, stepped into the lounge area, flipped open my phone.

Noah Mordden wasn't at his desk, so I tried his cell phone, and he answered on the first ring: "What?"

"It's me, Adam."

"I answered the phone, didn't I?"

"You know that ugly doll you've got in your office? The one that says 'Eat my shorts, Goddard'?"

"Love Me Lucille. You can't have her. Buy your own."

"Doesn't it have an LCD screen on its stomach?"

"What are you up to, Cassidy?"

"Listen, I need to ask you about the LCD driver. The ASIC."

When I returned to the conference room a few minutes later, the head of engineering and the head of manufacturing were engaged in a heated debate about whether another LCD screen could be squeezed into the tiny Guru case. I sat down quietly and waited for a break in the argument. Finally I got my chance.

"Excuse me," I said, but no one paid any attention.

"You see," Eddie Cabral was saying, "this is *exactly* why we have to postpone the launch."

"Well, we can't *afford* to slip the launch of Guru," Goddard shot back.

I cleared my throat. "Excuse me for a second."

"Adam," said Goddard.

"I know this is going to sound crazy," I said, "but remember that robotic doll Love Me Lucille?"

"What are we doing," grumbled Rick Durant, "taking a swim in Lake Fuckup? Don't remind me. We shipped half a million of those hideous dolls and got 'em all back."

"Right," I said. "That's why we have three hundred thousand ASICs, custom-fabricated for the proprietary Trion LCD, sitting in a warehouse in Van Nuys."

A few chuckles, some outright guffaws. One of the engineers said to another, loud enough for everyone to hear, "Does he know about connectors?"

Someone else said, "That's hilarious."

Nora looked at me, wincing with fake sympathy, and shrugged.

Eddie Cabral said, "I wish it were that easy, uh, Adam. But ASICs aren't interchangeable. They've got to be pin-compatible."

I nodded. "Lucille's ASIC is an SOLC-68 pin array. Isn't that the same pin layout that's in the Guru?"

Goddard stared at me.

There was another beat of silence, and the rustling of papers.

"SOLC-68 pin," said one of the engineers. "Yeah, that should work."

Goddard looked around the room, then slapped the table. "All right, then," he said. "What are we waiting for?"

Nora beamed moistly at me and gave me the thumbs-up.

On the way back to my office I pulled out my cell phone again. Five messages, all from the same number, and one marked "Private." I dialed my voice mail and heard Meacham's unmistakable smarmy voice. "This is Arthur. I have not heard from you in over three days. This is not acceptable. E-mail me by noon today or face the consequences."

I felt a jolt. The fact that he'd actually *called* me, which was a security risk no matter how the call was routed, showed how serious he was.

He was right: I had been out of touch. But I had no plans to get back in touch. Sorry, buddy.

The next one was Antwoine, his voice high and strained. "Adam, you need to get over to the hospital," he said in his first message. The second, the third, the fourth, the fifth—they were all Antwoine. His tone was increasingly desperate. "Adam, where the hell are you? Come *on*, man. Get over here *now*."

I stopped by Goddard's office—he was still schmoozing with some of the Guru team—and said to Flo, "Can you tell Jock I've got an emergency? It's my dad."

70

I knew what it was even before I got there, of course, but I still drove like a lunatic. Every red light, every left-turning vehicle, every twenty-miles-an-hour-while-school-is-in-session sign—everything was conspiring to delay me, keep me from getting to the hospital to see Dad before he died.

I parked illegally because I couldn't take the time to cruise the hospital parking garage for a space, and I ran into the emergency room entrance, banging the doors open the way the EMTs did when they were pushing a gurney, and rushed up to the triage desk. The sullen attendant was on the phone, talking and laughing, obviously a personal call.

"Frank Cassidy?" I said.

She gave me a look and kept chattering.

"Francis Cassidy!" I shouted. "Where is he?"

Resentfully she put down the phone and glanced at her computer screen. "Room three."

I raced through the waiting area, pulled open the heavy double doors into the ward, and saw Antwoine sitting on a chair next to a green curtain. When he saw me he just looked blank, didn't say anything, and I could see that his eyes were bloodshot. Then he shook his head slowly as I approached and said, "I'm sorry, Adam."

I yanked the curtain open and there was my dad sitting up in the bed, his eyes open, and I thought, *You see, you're wrong, Antwoine, he's still with us, the bastard,* until it sank in that the skin of his face was the wrong color, with sort of a yellow waxy tinge to it, and his mouth was open, that was the horrible thing. For some reason that was what I fixated on; his mouth was open in a way it never is when you're alive, frozen in an agonized gasp, a last desperate breath, furious, almost a snarl.

"Oh, no," I moaned.

Antwoine was standing behind me with his hand on my shoulder. "They pronounced him ten minutes ago."

I touched Dad's face, his waxy cheek, and it was cool. Not cold, not warm. A few degrees cooler than it should be, a temperature you never feel in the living. The skin felt like modeling clay, inanimate.

My breath left me. I couldn't breathe; I felt like I was in a vacuum. The lights seemed to flicker. Suddenly I cried out, "Dad. No."

I stared at Dad through blurry tear-filled eyes, touched his forehead, his cheek, the coarse red skin of his nose with little black hairs coming out of the pores, and I leaned over and kissed his angry face. For years I'd kissed Dad's forehead, or the side of his face, and he'd barely respond, but I was always sure I could see a tiny glint of secret pleasure in his eyes. Now he really wasn't responding, of course, and it turned me numb.

"I wanted you to have a chance to say good-bye to him," Antwoine said. I could hear his voice, feel the rumble, but I couldn't turn around and look. "He went into that respirtary distress again and this time I didn't even waste time arguing with him, I just called the ambulance. He was really gasping bad. They said he had pneumonia, probably had it for a while. They kept arguing about whether to put the tube in him but they never had the chance. I kept calling and calling."

"I know," I said.

"There was some time . . . I wanted you to say good-bye to him."

"I know. It's okay." I swallowed. I didn't want to look at Antwoine, didn't want to see his face, because it sounded like he was crying, and I couldn't deal with that. And I didn't want him to see me crying, which I knew was stupid. I mean, if you don't cry when your father dies, something's wrong with you. "Did he . . . say anything?"

"He was mostly cursing."

"I mean, did he—"

"No," Antwoine said, really slowly. "He didn't ask after you. But you know, he wasn't really saying anything, he—"

"I know." I wanted him to stop now.

"He was mostly cursing the doctors, and me. . . ."

"Yeah," I said, staring at Dad's face. "Not surprised." His forehead was all wrinkled, furrowed angrily, frozen that way. I reached up and touched the wrinkles, tried to smooth them out but I couldn't. "Dad," I said. "I'm sorry."

I don't know what I meant by that. What was I sorry for? It was long past time for him to die, and he was better off dead than living in a state of constant agony.

The curtain on the other side of the bed pulled back. A dark-skinned guy in scrubs with a stethoscope. I recognized him as Dr. Patel, from the last time.

"Adam," he said. "I'm so sorry." He looked genuinely sad.

I nodded.

"He developed full-blown pneumonia," Dr. Patel said. "It must have been underlying for a while, although in his last hospitalization his white count didn't show anything abnormal."

"Sure," I said.

"It was too much for him, in his condition. Finally, he had an MI, before we could even decide whether to intubate him. His body couldn't tolerate the assault."

I nodded again. I didn't want the details; what was the point?

"It's really for the best. He could have been on a vent for months. You wouldn't have wanted that."

"I know. Thanks. I know you did everything you could."

"There's just—just him, is that right? He was your only surviving parent? You have no brothers or sisters?"

"Right."

"You two must have been very close."

Really? I thought. And you know this . . . how? Is that your professional medical opinion? But I just nodded.

"Adam, do you have any particular funeral home you'd like us to call?"

I tried to remember the name of the funeral home from when Mom died. After a few seconds it came to me.

"Let us know if there's anything we can do for you," Dr. Patel said.

I looked at Dad's body, at his curled fists, his furious expression, his staring beady eyes, his gaping mouth. Then I looked up at Dr. Patel and said, "Do you think you could close his eyes?"

71

The guys from the funeral home came within an hour and zipped his body up in a body bag and took it away on a stretcher. They were a couple of pleasant, thickset guys with short haircuts, and both of them said, "I'm sorry for your loss." I called the funeral-home director from my cell and numbly talked through what would happen next. He too said, "I'm sorry for your loss." He wanted to know if there would be any elderly relatives coming from out of town, when I wanted to schedule the funeral, whether my father worshipped at a particular church where I'd like to have the service. He asked if there was a family burial plot. I told him where my mom was buried, that I was pretty sure Dad had bought two plots, one for Mom and one for him. He said he'd check with the cemetery. He asked when I wanted to come in and make the final arrangements.

I sat down in the ER waiting area and called my office. Jocelyn had already heard there was some emergency with my father, and she said, "How's your dad?"

"He just passed," I said. That was the way my dad talked: people "passed," they didn't die.

"Oh," Jocelyn gasped. "Adam, I'm sorry."

I asked her to cancel my appointments for the next couple of days, then asked her to connect me with Goddard. Flo picked up and said, "Hey there. The boss is out of the office—he's about to fly to Tokyo tonight." In a hushed voice, she asked, "How's your father?"

"He just passed." I went on quickly, "Obviously I'm going to be out of it for a couple of days and I wanted you to give Jock my apologies in advance—"

"Of *course*," she said. "Of *course*. My condolences. I'm sure he'll check in before he gets on the plane, but I know he'll understand, don't worry about it."

Antwoine came into the waiting area, looking out of place, lost. "What do you want me to do now?" he asked gently.

"Nothing, Antwoine," I said.

He hesitated. "You want me to clear my stuff out?"

"No, come on. You take your time."

"It's just that this came on suddenlike, and I don't have any other place—"

"Stay in the apartment as long as you want," I said.

He shifted his weight from one foot to the other. "You know, he did talk about you," he said.

"Oh, sure," I said. He was obviously feeling guilty about telling me that Dad hadn't asked for me at the end. "I know that."

A low, mellow chuckle. "Not always the most positive shit, but I think that's how he showed his love, you know?"

"I know."

"He was a tough old bastard, your father."

"Yeah."

"It took us some time to kind of work things out, you know."

"He was pretty nasty to you."

"That was just his way, you know. I didn't let it get to me."

"You took care of him," I said. "That meant a lot to him even though he wasn't able to say it."

"I know, I know. Toward the end we kind of had a relationship."

"He liked you."

"I don't know about that, but we had a relationship."

"No, I think he liked you. I know he did."

He paused. "He was a good man, you know."

I didn't know what to say in response to that. "You were really great with him, Antwoine," I finally said. "I know that meant a lot to him."

It's funny: after that first time I broke out crying at my dad's hospital bed, something in me shut down. I didn't cry again, not for a long while. I felt like an arm that's gone to sleep, gone all limp and prickly after having been lain on all night.

On the drive out to the funeral home I called Alana at work and got her voice mail, a message saying she was "out of the office" but would be checking her messages frequently. I remembered she was in Palo Alto. I called her cell, and she answered on the first ring.

"This is Alana." I loved her voice: it was velvety smooth with a hint of huskiness.

"It's Adam."

"Hey, jerk."

"What'd I do?"

"Aren't you supposed to call a girl up the morning after you sleep with her, to make her feel less guilty about putting out?"

"God, Alana, I—"

"Some guys even send flowers," she went on, businesslike. "Not that this has ever happened to me personally, but I've read about it in *Cosmo*."

She was right, of course: I hadn't called her, which was truly rude. But what was I supposed to tell her, the truth? That I hadn't called her because I was frozen like some insect in amber and I didn't know what to do? That I couldn't believe how lucky I was to find a woman like her—she was an itch I couldn't stop scratching—and yet I felt like a complete and total evil fraud? Yeah, I thought, you've read in *Cosmo* about how men are users, baby, but you have no idea.

"How's Palo Alto?"

"Pretty, but you're not changing the subject so easily."

"Alana," I said, "listen. I wanted to tell you—I got some bad news. My dad just died."

"Oh, Adam. Oh, I'm so sorry. Oh God. I wish I were there."

"Me, too."

"What can I do?"

"Don't worry about it, nothing."

"Do you know . . . when the funeral's going to be?"

"Couple of days."

"I'll be out here till Thursday. Adam, I'm so sorry."

I called Seth next, who said pretty much the same thing: "Oh, man, buddy, I'm so sorry. What can I do?" People always say that, and it's nice, but you do begin to wonder, what is there to do, right? It wasn't like I wanted a casserole. I didn't know what I wanted.

"Nothing, really."

"Come on, I can get out of work at the law firm. No worries."

"No, it's okay, thanks, man."

"There going to be a funeral and everything?"

"Yeah, probably. I'll let you know."

"Take care, buddy, huh?"

Then the cell phone rang in my hand. Meacham didn't say hello or anything. His first words were, "Where the *fuck* have you been?"

"My father just died. About an hour ago."

A long silence. "Jesus," he said. Then he added stiffly, as if it were an afterthought: "Sorry to hear it."

"Yep," I said.

"Timing really sucks."

"Yep," I said, my anger flaring up. "I told him to wait." Then I pressed END.

72

The funeral-home director was the same guy who'd handled Mom's arrangements. He was a warm, amiable guy with hair a few shades too black and a large bristling mustache. His name was Frank—"just like your dad," he pointed out. He showed me into the funeral parlor, which looked like an underfurnished suburban house with oriental rugs and dark furniture, a couple of rooms off a central hallway. His office was small and dark, with a few old-fashioned steel file cabinets and some framed copies of paintings of boats and landscapes. There was nothing phony about the guy; he really seemed to connect with me. Frank talked a little about when his father died, six years ago, and how hard it was. He offered me a box of Kleenex, but I didn't need it. He took notes for the newspaper announcement—I wondered silently who would read it, who would really care—and we came up with the wording. I struggled to remember the name of Dad's older sister, who was dead, even the names of his parents, who I think I'd seen less than ten times in my life and just called "Grandma" and "Grandpa." Dad had had a strained relationship with his parents, so we barely saw them at all. I was a little fuzzy on Dad's long and complicated employment history, and I may have left out a school where he'd worked, but I got the important ones.

Frank asked about Dad's military record, and I only remembered that he'd done basic training in some army base and never went off anywhere to fight and he hated the army with a passion. He asked whether I wanted to have a flag on his coffin, which Dad was entitled to, as a veteran, but I said no, Dad wouldn't have wanted a flag on top of his coffin. He would have railed against it, would have said something like, "The fuck you think I am, John F. Kennedy lying in fucking state?" He asked whether I wanted to have the army play "Taps," which Dad was also entitled to, and he explained that these days there wasn't actually a bugler, they usually played a tape recording at the graveside. I said no, Dad wouldn't have wanted "Taps" either. I told him I wanted the funeral and everything as soon as he could possibly arrange it. I wanted to get it all over with.

Frank called the Catholic church where we had Mom's funeral and scheduled a funeral mass for two days off. There were no out-of-town relatives, as far as I knew; the only survivors were a couple of cousins and an aunt he never saw. There were a couple of guys who I guess could be considered friends of his, even though they hadn't talked for years; they all lived locally. He asked whether Dad had a suit I wanted him to be buried in. I said I thought he might, I'd check.

Then Frank took me downstairs to a suite of rooms where they had caskets on display. They all looked big and garish, just the sort of thing Dad would have made fun of. I remember him ranting once, around the time of Mom's death, about the funeral industry and how it was all a monumental rip-off, how they charged you ridiculously inflated prices for coffins that just got buried anyway, so what was the point, and how he'd heard they usually replaced the expensive coffins with cheap pine ones when you weren't looking. I knew that wasn't true—I'd seen Mom's coffin lowered into the ground with the dirt shoveled over it, and I didn't think any kind of scam was possible unless they came in the middle of the night and dug it up, which I doubted.

Because of this suspicion—that was his excuse, anyway—Dad had picked out one of the cheapest caskets for Mom, cheap pine stained to look like mahogany. "Believe me," he'd said to me in the funeral home when Mom died, when I was a slobbering mess, "your mother didn't believe in wasting money."

But I wasn't going to do that to him, even though he was dead and wouldn't know any different. I drove a Porsche, I lived in a huge apartment in Harbor Suites, and I could afford to buy a nice coffin for my father. With the money I was making from the job he kept ranting about. I picked out an elegant-looking mahogany one that had something called a "memory safe" in it, a drawer where you were supposed to put stuff that belonged to the deceased.

A couple of hours later I drove home and crawled into my never-made bed and fell asleep. Later in the day I drove over to Dad's apartment and went through his closet, which I could tell hadn't been opened in a long time, and found a cheap-looking blue suit, which I'd never seen him wear. There was a stripe of dust on each shoulder. I found a dress shirt, but couldn't find a tie—I don't think he ever wore a tie—so I decided to use one of my mine. I looked around the apartment for things I thought he'd want to be buried with. A pack of cigarettes, maybe.

I'd been afraid that going to the apartment would be hard, that I'd start crying again. But it just made me deeply sad to see what little the old guy had left behind—the faint cigarette stink, the wheelchair, the breathing tube, the Barcalounger. After an excruciating half hour of looking through his belongings I gave up and decided that I wouldn't put anything in the "memory safe." Leave it symbolically empty, why not.

When I got back home I picked out one of my least favorite ties, a blue-and-white rep tie that looked somber enough and I didn't mind losing. I didn't feel like driving back to the funeral home, so I brought it down to the concierge desk and asked to have it delivered.

The next day was the wake. I arrived at the funeral home about twenty minutes before it was to begin. The place was air-conditioned to almost frigid, and it smelled like air freshener. Frank asked if I wanted to "pay my respects" to Dad in private, and I said sure. He gestured toward one of the rooms off the central hall. When I entered the room and saw the open coffin I felt an electric jolt. Dad was lying there in the cheap blue suit and my striped blue tie, his hands crossed on his chest. I felt a swelling in my throat, but it subsided quickly, and I wasn't moved to cry, which was strange. I just felt hollow.

He didn't look at all real, but they never, ever do. Frank, or whoever had done the work, hadn't done a bad job—hadn't put on too much rouge or whatever—but he still looked like one of Madame Tussaud's wax museum displays, if one of the better ones. The spirit leaves the body and there's nothing a mortician can do to bring it back. His face was a fake-looking "flesh tone." There seemed to be subtle brown lipstick on his lips. He looked a little less enraged than he had at the hospital, but they still hadn't been able to make him look peaceful. I guess there was only so much they could do to smooth the furrow from his brow. His skin was cold now, and a lot waxier than it had felt in the hospital. I hesitated a moment before kissing his cheek; it felt strange, unnatural, unclean.

I stood there looking at this fleshy shell, this discarded husk, this pod that had once contained the mysterious and fearsome soul of my father. And I started talking to him, as I figure almost every son talks to his dead father. "Well, Dad," I said, "you're finally out of here. If there really is an afterlife, I hope you're happier there than you were here."

I felt sorry for him then, which was something I guess I was never quite able to feel when he was alive. I remembered a couple of times when he actually seemed to be happy, when I was a lot younger and he'd carry me around on his shoulders. A time when one of his teams had won a championship. The time he was hired by Bartholomew Browning. A few moments like that. But he rarely smiled, unless he was laughing his bitter laugh. Maybe he'd needed antidepressants, maybe that was his problem, but I doubted it. "I didn't understand you so well, Dad," I said. "But I really did try."

Hardly anyone showed up in the three-hour span of time. There were some buddies of mine from high school, a couple with their wives, and two college friends. Dad's elderly Aunt Irene came for a while and said, "Your father was very lucky to have you." She had a faint Irish brogue and wore overpowering old-lady perfume. Seth came early and stayed late, kept me company. He told Dad stories in an attempt to make me laugh, famous anecdotes about Dad's coaching days, tales that had become legend among my friends and at Bartholomew Browning. There was the time he took a marking pen and drew a line down the middle of a kid's face mask, a big lunk named Pelly, then all the way down his uniform to the kid's shoes, and along the grass in a straight line across the field, even though the pen didn't make a mark on the grass, and he said, "You run *this* way, Pelly, you get it? *This* is the way you run."

There was the time when he called time out and he went up to a football player named Steve and grabbed his face mask and said, "Are you stupid, Steve?" Then, without waiting for Steve to reply, he yanked the mask up and down, making Steve's head nod like a doll's. "Yes, I am, Coach," he said in a squeaky imitation of Steve's voice. The rest of the team thought it was funny, and most of them laughed. "Yes, I am stupid."

There was the day when he called time out during a hockey game and started yelling at a kid named Resnick for playing too rough. He grabbed Resnick's hockey stick and said, "Mr. Resnick, if I ever see you spear"—and he jabbed the stick into Resnick's stomach, which instantly made Resnick throw up—"or butt-end"—and he slammed him again in the stomach with the stick—"I will destroy you." And Resnick vomited blood, and then had the dry heaves. Nobody laughed.

"Yeah," I said. "He was a funny guy, wasn't he?" By now I wanted him to stop the stories, and fortunately he did.

At the funeral the next morning, Seth sat on one side of me in the pew, Antwoine on the other. The priest, a distinguished, silver-haired fellow who looked like a TV minister, was named Father Joseph Iannucci. Before the mass he took me aside and asked me a few questions about Dad—his "faith," what he was like, what he did for a living, did he have any hobbies, that sort of thing. I was pretty much stumped.

There were maybe twenty people in the church, some of them regular parishioners who'd come for the mass and didn't know Dad. The others were friends of mine from high school and college, a couple of friends from the neighborhood, an old lady who lived next door. There was one of Dad's "friends," some guy who'd been in Kiwanis with Dad years ago before Dad quit in a rage over something minor. He didn't even know Dad had been sick. There were a couple of elderly cousins I vaguely recognized.

Seth and I were pallbearers along with some other guys from the church and the funeral home. There were a bunch of flowers at the front of the church—I had no idea how they got there, whether someone sent them or they were provided by the funeral home.

The mass was one of those incredibly long services that involve a lot of getting up and sitting down and kneeling, probably so you don't fall asleep. I felt depleted, fogged in, still sort of shell-shocked. Father Iannucci called Dad "Francis" and several times said his full name, "Francis Xavier," as if that indicated that Dad was a devout Catholic instead of a faithless guy whose only connection to the Lord was in taking His name in vain. He said, "We are sad at Francis's parting, we grieve his passing, but we believe that he has gone to God, that he is in a better place, that he is sharing now in Jesus' resurrection by living a new life." He said, "Francis's death is not the end. We can still be united with him." He asked, "Why did Francis have to suffer so much in his last months?" and answered something about Jesus' suffering and said that "Jesus was not conquered or defeated by his suffering." I didn't quite follow what he was trying to say, but I wasn't really listening. I was zoning out.

When it was over, Seth gave me a hug, and then Antwoine gave me a crushing handshake and hug, and I was surprised to see a single tear rolling down the giant's face. I hadn't cried during the whole service; I hadn't cried at all the whole day. I felt anesthetized. Maybe I was past it.

Aunt Irene tottered up to me and held my hand in both of her soft age-spotted hands. Her bright red lipstick had been applied with a shaky hand. Her perfume was so strong I had to hold my breath. "Your father was a good man," she said. She seemed to read something in my face, some skepticism I hadn't meant to show, and she said, "He wasn't a comfortable man with his feelings, I know. He wasn't at ease expressing them. But I know he loved you."

Okay, if you insist, I thought, and I smiled and thanked her. Dad's Kiwanis friend, a hulking guy who was around Dad's age but looked twenty years younger, took my hand and said, "Sorry for your loss." Even Jonesie, the loading dock guy from Wyatt Telecom, showed up with his wife, Esther. They both said they were sorry for my loss.

I was leaving the church, about to get in the limousine to follow the hearse to the graveyard, when I saw a man sitting in the back row of the church. He'd come in some time after the mass had started, but I couldn't make out his face at such a distance, in the dark light of the church's interior.

The man turned around and caught my eye.

It was Goddard.

I couldn't believe it. Astonished, and moved, I walked up to him slowly. I smiled, thanked him for coming. He shook his head, waved away my thanks.

"I thought you were in Tokyo," I said.

"Oh, hell, it's not as if the Asia Pacific division hasn't kept me waiting time and time again."

"I don't . . ." I fumbled, incredulous. "You rescheduled your trip?"

"One of the very few things I've learned in life is the importance of getting your priorities straight."

For a moment I was speechless. "I'll be back in tomorrow," I said. "It might be on the later side, because I'll probably have some business to take care of—"

"No," he said. "Take your time. Go slow."

"I'll be fine, really."

"Be good to yourself, Adam. Somehow we'll manage without you for a little while."

"It's not like—not at all like your son, Jock. I mean, my dad was pretty sick with emphysema for a long time, and . . . it's really better this way. He wanted to go."

"I know the feeling," he said quietly.

"I mean, we weren't all that close, really." I looked around the dim church interior, the rows of wooden pews, the gold and crimson paint on the walls. A couple of my friends were standing near the door waiting to talk to me. "I probably shouldn't say it, especially in here, you know?" I smiled sadly. "But he was kind of a difficult guy, a tough old bird, which makes it easier, his passing. It's not like I'm totally devastated or anything."

"Oh, no, that makes it even harder, Adam. You'll see. When your feelings are that complicated."

I sighed. "I don't think my feelings for him are—were—all that complicated."

"It hits you later. The wasted opportunities. The things that could have been. But I want you to keep something in mind: Your dad was fortunate to have you."

"I don't think he considered himself—"

"Really. He was a lucky man, your father."

"I don't know about that," I said, and all of a sudden, without warning, the shut-off valve in me gave way, the dam broke, and the tears welled up. I flushed with shame as the tears started streaming down my face, and I blurted out, "I'm sorry, Jock."

He reached both of his hands up and placed them on my shoulders. "If you can't cry, you're not alive," Goddard said. His eyes were moist.

Now I was weeping like a baby, and I was mortified and somehow relieved at the same time. Goddard put his arms around me, clasped me in a big hug as I blubbered like an idiot.

"I want you to know something, son," he said, very quietly. "You're not alone."

73

The day after the funeral I returned to work. What was I going to do, mope around the apartment? I wasn't really depressed, though I felt raw, like a layer of skin had been peeled off. I needed to be around people. And maybe, now that Dad was dead, there'd be some comfort in being around Goddard, who was beginning to look like the closest thing I ever had to a father. Not to put myself on a shrink's couch or anything, but something changed, for me, after he showed up at the funeral. I wasn't conflicted or ambivalent anymore about my so-called real mission at Trion, the 'real reason' I was there—because that was no longer the real reason I was there.

At least by my reckoning, I'd done my service, paid my debt, and I deserved a clean slate. I wasn't working for Nick Wyatt any longer. I'd stopped returning Meacham's phone calls or e-mails. Once I even got a message, on my cell phone voice mail, from Judith Bolton. She didn't leave her name, but her voice was instantly recognizable. "Adam," she said, "I know you're going through such a difficult time. We all feel terrible about the death of your father, and please know you have our deepest condolences."

I could just imagine the strategy session with Judith and Meacham and Wyatt, all desperate and angry about their kite who'd slipped his string. Judith would say something about how they should go easy on the guy, he's just lost a parent, and Wyatt would say something foulmouthed and say he didn't give a shit, the clock was ticking, and Meacham would be trying to out-tough-guy his boss about how they were going to hold my feet to the fire and they were going to fuck me over; and then Judith would say no, we have to take a more sensitive approach, let me try to reach out to him. . . .

Her message went on, "But it's extremely important, even in this time of turmoil, for you to remain in constant contact. I want us all to keep everything positive and cordial, Adam, but I need you to make contact today."

I deleted her message as well as Meacham's. They would get the point. In time I'd send Meacham an e-mail officially severing the relationship, but for the time being I thought I'd just keep them dangling while the reality of the situation sank in. I wasn't Nick Wyatt's kite anymore.

I'd given them what they needed. They'd realize that it wasn't worth their while to hang tough.

They might threaten, but they couldn't force me to go on working for them. As long as I kept in mind that there really was nothing they could do, I could just walk away.

I just had to keep that in mind. I could just walk away.

74

My cell phone was ringing even before I pulled into the Trion garage the next morning. It was Flo.

"Jock wants to see you," she said, sounding urgent. "Right now."

Goddard was in his back room with Camilletti, Colvin, and Stuart Lurie, the senior VP for Corporate Development I'd met at Jock's barbecue.

Camilletti was talking as I entered.

". . . No, from what I hear the S.O.B. just flew into Palo Alto yesterday with a term sheet already drawn up. He had lunch with Hillman, the CEO, and by dinner they'd inked the deal. He matched our offer dollar for dollar—I mean, to the *penny*—but in cash!"

"How the *hell* could this happen!" Goddard exploded. I'd never seen him so angry. "Delphos signed a no-shop provision, for Christ's sake!"

"The no-shop's dated tomorrow—it hasn't been signed yet. That's why he flew out there so fast, so he could do the deal before we locked it in."

"Who are we talking about?" I asked softly, as I sat down.

"Nicholas Wyatt," Stuart Lurie said. "He just bought Delphos right out from under us for five hundred million in cash."

My stomach sank. I recognized the name Delphos but remembered I wasn't supposed to. *Wyatt bought Delphos?* I thought, astonished.

I turned to Goddard with a questioning look.

"That's the company we were in the process of acquiring—I told you about them," he said impatiently. "Our lawyers were just about finished drawing up the definitive purchase agreement. . . ." His voice trailed off, then grew louder. "I didn't even think Wyatt had that kind of cash on their balance sheet!"

"They had just under a billion in cash," said Jim Colvin. "Eight hundred million, actually. So five hundred million pretty much empties out the piggy bank, because they've got three billion dollars of debt, and the service on that debt's gotta be two hundred million a year easy."

Goddard smacked his hand down on the round table. "God*damn* it to hell!" he thundered. "What the hell *use* does Wyatt have for a company like Delphos? He doesn't have AURORA. . . . For Wyatt to put his own company on the line like that makes no goddamned sense at all unless he's just trying to screw us over."

"Which he just succeeded in doing," Camilletti said.

"For heaven's sake, without AURORA, Delphos is worthless!" Goddard said.

"Without Delphos, AURORA is fucked," said Camilletti.

"Maybe he knows about AURORA," said Colvin.

"Impossible!" said Goddard. "And even if he knows about it, he doesn't *have* it!"

"What if he does?" suggested Stuart Lurie.

There was a long silence.

Camilletti spoke slowly, intensely. "We're protecting AURORA with the exact same federal security regulations the Defense Department mandates for government contractors dealing in sensitive compartmented information." He stared fiercely at Goddard. "I'm talking firewalls, security clearances, network protection, multilevel secure access—every goddamned safeguard known to man. It's in the goddamned cone of silence. There's just no fucking way."

"Well," Goddard said, "Wyatt somehow found out the details of our negotiations—"

"Unless," Camilletti interrupted, "he had someone inside." An idea seemed to occur to him, and he looked at me. "You used to work for Wyatt, didn't you?"

I could feel the blood rushing to my head, and to mask it, I faked outrage "I used to work *at* Wyatt," I snapped at him.

"Are you in touch with him?" he asked, his eyes drilling into me.

"What are you trying to suggest?" I stood up.

"I'm asking you a simple yes-or-no question—are you in touch with Wyatt?" Camilletti shot back. "You had dinner with him at the Auberge not so long ago, correct?"

"Paul, that's enough," said Goddard. "Adam, you sit down this god-damned instant. Adam had no access whatsoever to AURORA. Or to the details of the Delphos negotiation. I believe today's the first time he's even heard the name of the company."

I nodded.

"Let's move on," Goddard said. He seemed to have cooled off a little. "Paul, I want you to talk to our lawyers, see what recourse we have. See if we can stop Wyatt. Now, AURORA's scheduled launch is in four days. As soon as the world knows what we've just done, there'll be a mad scramble to buy up materials and manufacturers up and down the whole damned supply chain. Either we delay the launch, or . . . I do *not* want to be part of that scramble. We're going to have to put our heads together and look around for some other comparable acquisition—"

"—*No one* has that technology but Delphos!" Camilletti said.

"We're all smart people," Goddard said. "There are always other possibilities." He put his hands on the arms of his chair and got to his feet. "You know, there's a story Ronald Reagan used to tell about the kid who found a huge pile of manure and said, 'There must be a pony around here somewhere.' " He laughed, and the others laughed as well, politely. They seemed to appreciate his feeble attempt to defuse the tension. "Let's all get to work. Find the pony."

75

I knew what had happened.

I thought things through as I drove home that night, and the more I did the angrier I got, and the angrier I got the faster and more erratically I drove.

If it weren't for the term sheet I'd gotten from Camilletti's files, Wyatt wouldn't have known about Delphos, the company Trion was about to buy. The more I reminded myself of this, the worse I felt.

Damn it, it was time to let Wyatt know it was over. I wasn't working for them anymore.

I unlocked my apartment door, switched on the lights, and headed right for the computer to send an e-mail.

But no.

Arnold Meacham was sitting at my computer, while a couple of tough-looking crew-cut guys were tearing the place apart. My stuff was everywhere. All my books had been taken off the shelves, my CD and DVD players had been taken apart, even the TV set. It looked like someone had gone on a rampage, throwing everything around, wrecking as much as possible, trying to cause maximum damage.

"What the fuck—?" I said.

Meacham looked up calmly from my computer screen. "Don't you *ever* fucking ignore me," he said.

I had to get the hell out of there. I spun around, bounded toward the door just as another of the crew-cut thugs slammed the door shut and stood in front of it, watching me warily.

There was no other exit, unless you counted the windows, a twenty-seven-story drop that didn't seem like a very good idea.

"What do you want?" I said to Meacham, looking from him to the door.

"You think you can *hide* shit from me?" Meacham said. "I don't think so. You don't have a safe-deposit box or a *cubbyhole* that's safe from us. I see you've been saving all my e-mails. I didn't know you cared."

"Of course I have," I said, indignant. "I keep backups of everything."

"That encryption program you're using for your notes of meetings with Wyatt and Judith and me—you know, that was cracked over a year ago. There's far stronger ones out there."

"Good to know, thanks," I said, heavy on the sarcasm. I tried to sound unfazed. "Now, why don't you and your boys get the hell out of here before I call the police."

Meacham snorted and made a hand signal that looked as if he was summoning me over.

"No." I shook my head. "I said, you and your buddies—"

There was a sudden movement I could see out of the corner of my eye, lightning-fast, and something slammed into the back of my head. I sagged to my knees, tasting blood. Everything was tinged dark red. I flung my hand out to grab my attacker, but while my hand was flailing in back of me, a foot slammed into my right kidney. A jagged bolt of pain shot up and down my torso, knocking me flat on the Persian rug.

"No," I gasped.

Another kick, this one to the back of my head, incredibly painful. Pinpoints of light sparkled before my eyes.

"Get 'em off me," I moaned. "Make your—buddy—stop. If I get too woozy, I might get talkative."

It was all I could think of. Meacham's accomplices probably didn't know much if anything of what Meacham and I were involved in. They were just muscle. Meacham wouldn't have told them, wouldn't have wanted them to know. Maybe they knew a little, just enough to know what to look for. But Meacham would want to keep them as much out of the loop as possible.

I cringed, braced myself for another kick to the back of my head, everything all white and sparkly, a metallic taste in my mouth. For a moment there was silence; it seemed that Meacham had signaled them to stop.

"What the hell do you want from me?" I asked.

"We're going for a drive," Meacham said.

76

Meacham and his goons hustled me out of my apartment, down the elevator to the garage, then out a service entrance to the street. I was scared out of my mind. A black Suburban with tinted windows was parked by the entrance. Meacham led the way, the three guys staying close to me, surrounding me, probably to make sure I didn't run, or try to jump Meacham, or anything. One of the guys was carrying my laptop; another had my desktop computer.

My head throbbed, and my lower back and chest were in agony. I must have looked like a mess, all bruised and beaten up.

"We're going for a drive" usually means, at least in Mafia movies, cement boots and a dunk in the East River. But if they'd wanted to kill me, why didn't they do it back in my apartment?

The thugs were ex-cops, I figured out after a while, employed by Wyatt Corporate Security. They seem to have been hired purely for their brute strength. They were blunt instruments.

One of the guys drove, and Meacham sat in the front seat, separated from me by a bulletproof glass enclosure, talking on a phone the whole way.

He'd done his job, apparently. He'd scared the shit out of me, and he and his guys had found the evidence I was keeping on Wyatt.

Forty-five minutes later, the Suburban pulled into Nick Wyatt's long stone driveway.

Two of the guys searched me for weapons or whatever, as if somehow between my apartment and here I could have picked up a Glock. They took my cell phone and shoved me into the house. I passed through the metal detector, which went off. They took my watch, belt, and keys.

Wyatt was sitting in front of a huge flat-panel TV in a spacious, sparely furnished room, watching CNBC with the sound muted, and talking on a cell phone. I glanced at myself in a mirror as I entered with my crew-cut escorts. I looked pretty bad.

We all stood there.

After a few minutes Wyatt ended his call, put the phone down, looked over at me. "Long time no see," he said.

"Yeah, well," I said.

"Look at you. Walk into a door? Fall down a flight of stairs?"

"Something like that."

"Sorry to hear about your dad. But Christ, breathing through a tube, oxygen tanks, all that shit—I mean, shoot me if I ever get like that."

"Be my pleasure," I murmured, but I don't think he heard me.

"Just as well he's dead, huh? Put him out of his fucking misery?"

I wanted to lunge at him, throttle him. "Thanks for your concern," I said.

"I want to thank *you*," he said, "for the information on Delphos."

"Sounds like you had to empty your piggy bank to buy it."

"Always gotta think three moves ahead. How do you think I got to where I am now? When we announce *we've* got the optical chip, our stock's gonna go into orbit."

"Nice," I said. "You've got it all figured out. You don't need me anymore."

"Oh, you're far from done, friend. Not until you get me the specs on the chip itself. And the prototype."

"No," I said, very quietly. "I'm done now."

"You think you're *done?* Man, are you hallucinating." He laughed.

I took a deep breath. I could feel my pulse throbbing at the base of my throat. My head ached. "The law's clear on this," I said, clearing my throat. I'd looked at a bunch of legal Web sites. "You're actually in a lot deeper than me, because you oversaw this whole scheme. I was just the pawn. You ran it."

"The *law,*" Wyatt said with an incredulous smile. "You're talking to me about the fucking *law? That's* why you've been saving up e-mails and memos and shit, trying to build a *legal* case against *me?* Oh, man, I almost feel sorry for you. I think you truly don't get it, do you? You think I'm going to let you walk away before you're finished?"

"You got all sorts of valuable intelligence from me," I said. "Your plan worked. It's over. From now on, you don't contact me anymore. End of transaction. As far as anyone's concerned, this never happened."

Sheer terror gave way to a kind of delirious confidence: I'd finally crossed the line. I'd jumped off the cliff and I was soaring in the air, and I was going to enjoy the ride until I hit ground.

"Think about it," I went on. "You've got a whole lot more to lose than I do. Your company. And your fortune. Me, I'm diddlyshit. I'm a small fish. No, I'm plankton."

His smile broadened. "What are you going to do, go to 'Jock' Goddard and tell him you're nothing but a shitty little snoop whose brilliant 'ideas' were spoon-fed him by his chief competitor? And then what do you think he's going to do? Thank you, take you to lunch at his little *diner* and toast you with a glass of Ovaltine? I don't think so."

I shook my head, my heart racing. "You really don't want Goddard to know how you learned all the details of their negotiations with Delphos."

"Or maybe you think you can go to the FBI, is that it? Tell them you were a spy-for-hire for Wyatt? Oh, they'll love that. You know how *understanding* the FBI can be, right? They will squeeze you like a fucking cockroach, and I will deny fucking *everything* and they'll have no choice but to believe me, and do you know why? Because you are a fucking little con man. You're on *record* as a hustler, my friend. I fired you from my company when you embezzled from me, and *everything's* documented."

"Then you're going to have a hard time explaining why everyone at Wyatt recommended me so enthusiastically."

"But no one did, get it? We'd never give a recommendation to a hustler like you. *You*, compulsive liar that you are, you counterfeited our letterhead to forge your own recommendations when you applied to Trion. Those letters didn't come from us. Paper analysis and forensic document examination will establish that without a doubt. You used a different computer printer, different ink cartridges. You forged signatures, you sick fuck." A pause. "You really think we weren't going to cover our asses?"

I tried to smile back, but I couldn't get the trembling muscles of my mouth to cooperate. "Sorry, that doesn't explain the phone calls from Wyatt executives to Trion," I said. "Anyway, Goddard'll see through it. He knows me."

Wyatt's laugh was more like a bark. "He *knows* you! That's a scream. Man, you really don't know who you're dealing with, do you? You are in so far over your fucking head. You think anyone's going to believe that our HR department called Trion with glowing recommendations, after we bounced you out on your ass? Well, do a little investigative work, dickwad, and you'll see that every single phone call from our HR department was rerouted. Phone records show they all came from your own apartment. You made all the HR calls yourself, asshole, impersonating your supervisors at Wyatt, making up all those enthusiastic recommendations. You're a sick fuck, man. You're pathological. You made up a whole fucking story about being some big honcho on the Lucid project, which is provably false. You see, asshole, my security people and theirs will get together and compare notes."

My head was spinning slowly, and I felt nauseated.

"And maybe you should check out that secret bank account you're so proud of—the one where you're so sure we've been depositing funds from some offshore account? Why don't you track down the real source of those funds?"

I stared at him.

"That money," Wyatt explained, "was routed directly from several discretionary accounts at Trion. With your goddamned digital fingerprints on it. You stole money from them, same way you stole from us." His eyes bulged. "Your fucking head is in a goddamned jaw trap, you pathetic sack of shit. Next time I see you, you'd better have all the technical specs for Jock Goddard's optical chip, or your life is fucking *over*. Now get the *fuck* out of my house."

PART EIGHT

BLACK BAG

Black Bag Job: Slang for surreptitious entry into an office or home to obtain files or materials illegally.

—*Spy Book: The Encyclopedia of Espionage*

77

"This better be important, buddy," Seth said. "It's like after midnight."

"This is. I promise."

"Yeah, you only call when you want something anymore. Or death of a parent, that kinda thing."

He was joking, and he wasn't. Truth is, he had a right to be pissed off at me. I hadn't exactly been in touch with him since I'd started at Trion. And he'd been there when Dad died, through the funeral. He'd been a much better friend than I'd been.

We met an hour later at an all-night Dunkin' Donuts near Seth's apartment. The place was almost deserted, except for a few bums. He was wearing his same old Diesel jeans and a Dr. Dre World Tour T-shirt.

He stared at me. "What the hell happened to you?"

I didn't keep any of the grisly details from him—what was the point anymore?

At first he thought I was making it up, but gradually he saw that I was telling the truth, and his expression changed from amused skepticism to horrified fascination to outright sympathy.

"Oh, man," he said when I'd wound up my story, "you are so lost."

I smiled sadly, nodded. "I'm screwed," I said.

"That's not what I mean." He sounded testy. "You fucking went along with this."

"I didn't 'go along with this.' "

"No, asshole. You fucking had a *choice.*"

"A choice?" I said. "Like what choice? Prison?"

"You took the deal they offered, man. They got your balls in a vise, and you caved."

"What other option did I have?"

"That's what lawyers are for, asshole. You could have told me, I could have gotten one of the guys I work for to help out."

"Help out *how?* I took the money in the first place."

"You could have brought in one of the lawyers at the firm, scare the shit out of them, threaten to go public."

I was silent for a moment. Somehow I doubted it really would have been that simple. "Yeah, well, it's too late for that now. Anyway, they would have denied everything. Even if one of your firm's lawyers agreed to represent me, Wyatt would have set the whole goddamned American Bar Association after me."

"Maybe. Or maybe he would have wanted the whole thing to stay quiet. You might have been able to make it go away."

"I don't think so."

"*I* see," Seth said, oozing sarcasm. "So instead, you bent over and took it. You went along with their illegal scheme, agreed to become a spy, pretty much guaranteed yourself a prison sentence—"

"What do you mean, 'guaranteed' myself a prison sentence?"

"—And then, just to feed your insane ambition, here you are, fucking over the one guy in corporate America who ever gave you a chance."

"Thanks," I said bitterly, knowing he was right.

"You pretty much deserve what you get."

"I appreciate the help and moral support, friend."

"Put it this way, Adam—I may be a pathetic loser in your eyes, but at least I came by my loserdom honestly. What are you? You're a total fraud. You're fucking *Rosie Ruiz.*"

"Huh?"

"She won the Boston Marathon like twenty years ago, set a women's record, remember? Barely broke a sweat. Turned out she'd jumped in half a mile from the finish line. Took the fucking *subway* to get there. That's you, man. The Rosie Ruiz of corporate America."

I sat there, my face growing redder and hotter, feeling more and more miserable. Finally I said, "Are you done yet?"

"For now, yeah."

"Good," I said. "Because I need your help."

78

I'd never been to the law firm where Seth worked, or pretended to work. It took up four floors in one of those downtown skyscrapers, and it had all the trappings people want in a high-end law firm—mahogany paneling, expensive Aubusson carpets, modern art on giant canvases, lots of glass.

He got us an appointment first thing in the morning with his boss, a senior partner named Howard Shapiro who specialized in criminal defense work and used to be a U.S. Attorney. Shapiro was a short, chubby guy, balding, round black glasses, a high voice and rapid-fire delivery, frenetic energy. He kept interrupting me, prodding me to get my story over with, looking at his watch. He took notes on a yellow pad. Once in a while he gave me wary, puzzled looks, as if he was trying to figure something out, but for the most part he didn't react. Seth, who was on good behavior, mostly sat there watching.

"Who beat you up?" Shapiro said.

"His security guys."

He made a note. "When you told him you were pulling out?"

"Before. I stopped returning their calls and e-mails."

"Teach you a lesson, huh?"

"I guess."

"Let me ask you something. Give me an honest answer. Say you get Wyatt what he wants, the chip or whatever it is. You don't think he'll leave you alone?"

"I doubt it."

"You think they're going to keep pushing you?"

"Probably."

"You're not afraid this whole thing might blow up in your face and you'll be left holding the bag?"

"I've thought about it. I know the folks at Trion are mighty pissed off their acquisition fell through. There'll probably be some sort of an investigation, and who knows what'll happen."

"Well, I got more bad news for you, Adam. I hate to tell you, but you're a tool."

Seth smiled.

"I know that."

"It means you have to strike first, or you're hosed."

"How?"

"Say this thing blows up and you're caught. Not unlikely. You throw yourself on the mercy of the court without cooperating, and you're going to go to jail, simple as that. Guarantee it."

I felt like I'd been punched in the stomach. Seth winced.

"Then I'd cooperate."

"Too late. No one's going to cut you any slack. Also, the only proof against Wyatt is *you*—but there'll be lots of proof against you, I bet."

"So what do you suggest?"

"Either they find you, or you find them. I've got a buddy in the U.S. Attorney's office, guy I trust. Wyatt's a big fish. You can serve him up on a silver platter. They'll be very interested."

"How do I know they won't arrest me, throw me in jail too?"

"I'll make a proffer. Call him up, tell him I've got something I think he might be interested in. I'll say, I'm not going to give you any names. If you're not going to work out a deal with my guy, you're not going to see him. You want to deal, you give him a queen for a day."

"What's a 'queen for a day'?"

"We go in, sit down with the prosecutor and an agent. Anything that's said in that meeting cannot be directly used against you."

I looked at Seth, raised my eyebrows, and turned back to Shapiro. "Are you saying I could get off?"

Shapiro shook his head. "With that little prank you pulled at Wyatt, the loading-dock guy's retirement party, we'll have to fashion a guilty plea to something. You're a dirty witness, the prosecutor's going to have to show you didn't get off scot-free. You won't get a total pass."

"More than a misdemeanor?"

"Could be probation, to probation and a felony, to a felony and six months."

"Prison," I said.

Shapiro nodded.

"If they're willing to deal," I said.

"Correct. Look, you're in a shitstorm of trouble, let's speak frankly. The Economic Espionage Act of 1996 made the theft of trade secrets a federal criminal offense. You could get ten years in prison."

"What about Wyatt?"

"If they catch him? Under the Federal Sentencing Guidelines, a judge has to take into account the defendant's role in the offense. If you're a ringleader, the offense level is increased by two levels."

"So they'll hit him harder."

"Right. Also, you didn't personally benefit materially from the espionage, right?"

"Right," I said. "I mean, I did get paid."

"You just got your Trion salary, which was for the work you did for Trion."

I hesitated. "Well, Wyatt's people continued to pay me, into a secret bank account."

Shapiro stared at me.

"That's bad, right?" I said.

"That's bad," he said.

"No wonder they agreed to it so easily," I groaned, more to myself than to him.

"Yeah," Shapiro said. "You put the hook in yourself. So, you want me to make the call or no?"

I looked at Seth, who nodded. There didn't seem to be any other choice.

"Why don't you guys wait outside," Shapiro said.

79

We sat in the waiting area outside his office, silent. My nerves were stretched to the breaking point. I called my office and asked Jocelyn to reschedule a couple of appointments.

Then I sat there for a few minutes, just thinking. "You know," I said, "the worst thing about it is, I gave Wyatt the keys so he could rob us blind. He's already derailed our big acquisition, and now he's going to fuck us over totally—and it's all my fault."

Seth stared at me for a long while. "Who's 'us'?"

"Trion."

He shook his head. "You're not Trion. You keep saying 'we' and 'us' when you talk about Trion."

"Slip of the tongue," I said.

"I don't think so. I want you to take a bar of whatever ten-dollar French-milled soap you use now and write on your bathroom mirror, 'I am not Trion, and Trion is not me.' "

"Enough," I said. "You're sounding like my dad now."

"Ever occur to you maybe your dad wasn't wrong about everything? Like a stopped clock's right twice a day, huh?"

"Fuck you."

Then the door opened and Howard Shapiro was standing there. "Sit down," he said.

I could tell from his face that things hadn't gone well. "What'd your buddy say?" I asked.

"My buddy got transferred to Main Justice. His replacement is a real prick."

"How bad?" I asked.

"He said, 'You know what, you take a plea and we'll see what happens.' "

"What's that supposed to mean?"

"It means you take a guilty plea in chambers, and no one will know about it."

"I don't get it."

"If you give him a great case, he's willing to write you a great Five-K. A Five-K is a letter the prosecutor writes to the judge asking him to depart from the sentencing guidelines."

"Does the judge have to do what the prosecutor wants?"

"Of course not. Also, there's no guarantee this prick will really write you a decent Five-K. Be honest, I don't trust him."

"What's his definition of a 'great case'?" asked Seth.

"He wants Adam to make an introduction of an undercover."

"An undercover *agent?*" I said. "That's *insane!* Wyatt'll never go for it. He won't meet with anyone but me. He's not an idiot."

"What about wearing a wire?" Seth asked. "Would he agree to that?"

"*I* won't agree to that," I said. "I get scanned for electronic devices every time I'm in Wyatt's presence. I'd get caught for sure."

"That's all right," said Shapiro. "Our friend in the U.S. attorney's office won't agree to it anyway. The only way he'll play ball is if you introduce an undercover."

"I won't do it," I said. "He'll never go for it. And what guarantee is there that I won't get jail time even if I do?"

"None," Shapiro admitted. "No federal prosecutor is going to give you a one-hundred-percent promise that a judge'll give you probation. The judge may not go for it. But whatever you decide, he's giving you seventy-two hours to make up your mind."

"Or what?"

"Or the chips fall where they may. He'll never give you queen for a day if you don't play by his rules. Look, they don't trust you. They don't think you can do this on your own. And face it, it's their ball."

"I don't need seventy-two hours," I said. "I've already decided. I'm not playing."

Shapiro looked at me strangely. "You're going to keep working for Wyatt."

"No," I said. "I'm going to handle this my own way."

Now Shapiro smiled. "How so?"

"I want to set my own terms."

"How so?" Shapiro said.

"Let's say I get some really concrete evidence against Wyatt," I said. "Serious, hard-core proof of his criminality. Could we take that directly to the FBI and make a better deal?"

"Theoretically, sure."

"Good," I said. "I think I want to do this myself. The only one who's going to get me out of this is me."

Seth half-smiled, reached out and put a hand on my shoulder. " 'Me' meaning 'me,' or 'me' meaning 'we'?"

80

I got an e-mail from Alana saying that she was back, her trip to Palo Alto had been cut short—she didn't explain, but I knew why—and she'd love to see me. I called her at home, and we talked a while about the funeral, and how I was doing, and all that. I told her I didn't much feel like talking about Dad, and then she said, "Are you aware you're in serious trouble with HR?"

My breath stopped. "Am I?"

"Oh, boy. Trion's Personnel Policy Manual expressly forbids workplace romances. Inappropriate sexual behavior in the workplace harms organizational effectiveness through its negative impact on participants and co-workers."

I let my breath out slowly. "You're not in my management chain. Anyway, I felt that we were organizationally quite effective. And I thought our sexual behavior was quite appropriate. We were practicing horizontal integration." She laughed, and I said, "I know that neither one of us has time, but don't you think we'll be better Trion employees if we take off a night? I mean really get out of town. Be spontaneous."

"That sounds intriguing," she said. "Yes, I think that could definitely boost productivity."

"Good. I booked a room for us tomorrow night."

"Where?"

"You'll see."

"Uh-uh. Tell me where," she said.

"Nope. It'll be a surprise. As our fearless leader likes to say, sometimes you just gotta get in the car."

She picked me up in her blue Mazda Miata convertible, drove us out to the country while I gave directions. In the silences I obsessed about what I was about to do. I was into her, and this was a problem. Here I was, using her to try to save my own skin. I was *so* going to hell.

The drive took forty-five minutes, on a stop-and-go road past a parade of identical shopping malls and gas stations and fast-food places, and then a narrow and very winding road through woods. At one point she peered at me, noticed the bruise around my eye, said, "What happened? You get into a fight?"

"Basketball," I said.

"I thought you weren't going to play with Chad anymore."

I smiled, didn't say anything.

Finally we came to a big, rambling country inn, white clapboard with dark green shutters. The air was cool and fragrant, and you could hear birds chirping, and no traffic.

"Hey," she said, removing her sunglasses. "Nice. This place is supposed to be excellent."

I nodded.

"You take all your girlfriends here?"

"Never been here before," I said. "I read about it, and it seemed like the perfect getaway." I put my arm around her narrow waist and gave her a kiss. "Let me get your bags."

"Just one," she said. "I travel light."

I took our bags up to the front door. Inside it smelled of wood fires and maple syrup. The couple who owned and ran the place greeted us like old friends.

Our room was sweet, very country-inn. There was an enormous four-poster bed with a canopy, braided throw rugs, chintz curtains. The bed faced a huge old brick fireplace that clearly got a lot of use. The furnishings were all antiques, the rickety kind that make me nervous. There was a captain's chest at the foot of the bed. The bathroom was enormous, with an old iron clawfoot tub in the middle of the room—the kind that looks great, but if you want to take a shower you have to stand in the tub with a little handheld shower thing and spray yourself the way you wash a dog, and try not to splash water all over the floor. The bathroom was connected to a little sitting area off the bedroom furnished with an oak desk and an old telephone on a rickety telephone table.

The bed squeaked and groaned, as we found out when we both plopped down on it after the innkeeper had left. "God, imagine what this bed has seen," I said.

"A lot of chintz," Alana said. "Reminds me of my grandmother's house."

"Is your grandmother's house as big as this place?"

She nodded once. "This is cozy. Great idea, Adam." She slipped a cool hand under my shirt, stroked my stomach, and then moved south. "What were you saying about horizontal integration?"

A roaring fire was going in the dining room when we came down for dinner. There were maybe ten or twelve other couples already seated at the tables, mostly older than us.

I ordered an expensive red Bordeaux, and I could hear Jock Goddard's words echoing in my head: *You used to drink Budweiser, now you're sipping some first-growth Pauillac.*

The service was slow—there seemed to be one waiter for the whole dining room, a Middle Eastern guy who barely spoke English—but it didn't bother me. We were both sort of blissed-out, floating on a postcoital high.

"I noticed you brought your computer," I said. "In the trunk of your car."

She grinned sheepishly. "I don't go anywhere without it."

"Are you sort of tethered to the office?" I asked. "Pager, cell phone, e-mail, all that?"

"Aren't you?"

"The good thing about having only one boss," I said, "is that it cuts down on some of that."

"Well, you're lucky. I've got six direct reports and a bunch of really arrogant engineers I have to deal with. Plus a huge deadline."

"What kind of deadline?"

She paused, but for just a moment. "The rollout's next week."

"You're shipping a product?"

She shook her head. "It's a demo—a big public announcement, demonstration of a working prototype of the thing we're developing. I mean, it's a really big deal. Goddard hasn't told you about it?"

"He might have, I don't know. He tells me about all kinds of stuff."

"Not the kind of thing you'd forget. Anyway, it's taking up all my time. A real time suck. Night and day."

"Not totally," I said. "You've had time for two dates with me, and you're taking tonight off."

"And I'll pay for it tomorrow and Sunday."

The overworked waiter finally showed up with a bottle of white wine. I pointed out his error, and he apologized profusely and went off to get the right one.

"Why *didn't* you want to talk to me at Goddard's barbecue?" I asked.

She looked at me incredulously, her sapphire-blue eyes wide. "I was serious about the HR manual, you know. I mean, workplace romances really are discouraged, so we've got to be discreet. People talk. People especially love gossiping about who's screwing who. And then if something happens . . ."

"Like a breakup or something."

"Whatever. Then it becomes awkward for everyone."

The conversation was starting to spin in the wrong direction. I tried to bring it back on course. "So I guess I can't just pop in on you one day at work. Show up on the fifth floor unannounced with a bouquet of lilies."

"I told you, they'd never let you in."

"I thought my badge lets me in anywhere in the building."

"Maybe most places, but not the fifth floor."

"Meaning *you* can get onto the executive floor, but I can't get onto yours?"

She shrugged.

"You have your badge with you?"

"They've trained me not to go to the bathroom without it." She pulled it out of her little black purse and flashed it at me. It was attached to a key ring with a bunch of other keys.

I grabbed it playfully. "Not as bad as a passport picture, but I wouldn't submit this head shot to a modeling agency," I said.

I inspected her badge. Hers had the same stuff on it as mine, the 3-D holograph Trion seal that changed color as light passed over it, the same pale blue background color with TRION SYSTEMS printed over and over on it in tiny white letters. The chief difference seemed to be that hers had a red-and-white stripe across the front.

"I'll show you mine if you show me yours," she said.

I took my badge out of my pocket and handed it to her. The basic difference was in the little transponder chip inside. The chip inside the badge was encoded with information that either opened a door lock or didn't. Her card got her into the fifth floor in addition to all the main entrances, the garage, and so on.

"You look like a scared rabbit here." She giggled.

"I think I felt that way on my first day."

"I didn't know employee numbers went this high."

The red-and-white stripe on her card had to be for quick visual identification. Meaning that there must be at least one additional checkpoint beyond waving the badge at the badge reader. Someone had to check you out as you entered. That made things a lot more difficult.

"When you leave to go down to lunch or up to the gym—must be a huge hassle."

She shrugged, uninterested. "It's not too bad. They get to know you."

Right, I thought. That's the problem. You can't get in the door unless the chip inside your proximity access badge has been coded right, and even once you're on the floor, you have to pass by a guard for facial confirmation. "At least they don't make you go through that biometric crap," I said. "We had to do that at Wyatt. You know—the fingerprint scan. A friend of mine at Intel even had to go through a retinal scan every day, and all of a sudden he started needing glasses." This was a total lie, but it got her attention. She looked at me with a curious grin, unsure whether I was joking.

"I'm kidding about the glasses part, but he was convinced all that scanning was going to ruin his eyesight."

"Well, there's this one inner area with biometrics, but only the engineers go in there. It's where they do work on the prototype. But I just have to deal with Barney or Chet, the poor security guards who have to sit in that little booth."

"It can't be as ridiculous as it was at Wyatt in the early stages of the Lucid," I said. "They made us go through this badge-exchange ritual where you had to hand your ID card to the guard, and then the guy gave you a *second* badge to wear on the floor." I was totally bullshitting, parroting back something Meacham had told me about. "So let's say you realize you left your car headlights on, or you forgot something in the trunk of your car, or you want to run down to the cafeteria to grab a bagel or something . . ."

She shook her head absently, snorted softly. She'd run out of what little interest she had in the intricacies of the badge-access system at work. I wanted to pump her for more information—like, do you have to hand your ID card to the guard, or do you just show it to them? If you had to hand the guard your card, the risk was a lot higher of the guard discovering a fake badge. Does the scrutiny get any more lax at night? Early in the morning?

"Hey," she said, "you haven't touched your wine. Don't you like it?"

I dipped a couple of fingertips into my glass of wine. "Delicious," I said.

This little act of stupid juvenile male goofiness made her laugh, loud and whooping, her eyes crinkling into slits. Some women—okay, most women—might have asked for the check at that point. Not Alana.

I was into her.

81

Both of us were stuffed from dinner, a little unsteady from too much wine. Actually, Alana seemed a little more toasted than me. She fell back on the creaky bed, her arms outstretched as if to embrace the whole room, the inn, the night, whatever. That was the moment for me to follow her onto the bed. But I couldn't, not yet.

"Hey, you want me to get your laptop from the car?"

She groaned. "Oh, I wish you hadn't mentioned it. You've been talking about work way too much."

"Why don't you just admit you're a workaholic, too, and be done with it?" I did my AA meeting riff: "Hi, my name is Alana, and I'm a workaholic. 'Hi, Alana!' "

She shook her head, rolled her eyes.

"The first step is always to admit you're powerless over your workaholism. Anyway, I left something in your car, so I'm going down there anyway." I held out my hand. "Keys?"

She was leaning back on the bed, looking too comfortable to move. "Mmph. Okay, sure," she said reluctantly. "Thanks." She rolled over to the edge of the bed, fished her car keys out of her purse, handed the key ring to me with a swanning, dramatic gesture. "Come back soon, huh?"

The parking area was dark and deserted by now. I looked back at the inn, about a hundred feet away, made sure our room didn't look over the parking lot. She couldn't see me.

I popped the trunk of her Miata and found her computer bag, a gray flannel-mohair-textured nylon satchel. I wasn't kidding: I had left something in here, a small knapsack. There was nothing else of particular interest in her trunk. I swung the satchel and knapsack onto my shoulder and got into her car.

I looked back toward the inn again. Nobody was coming.

Still, I kept the interior dome light off and let my eyes get used to the dark. I'd attract less attention this way.

I felt like a creep, but I had to be realistic about my situation. I really didn't have a choice. She was my best way into AURORA, and now I *had* to get inside. It was the only way I could save myself.

Quickly I unzipped the satchel, pulled out her laptop, and powered it on. The car's interior went blue from the computer screen. While I waited for it to boot up, I opened my knapsack and pulled out a blue plastic first aid kit.

Inside, instead of Band-Aids and such, were a few small plastic cases. Each contained a soft wax.

By the blue light I looked at the keys on her key ring. A few looked promising. Maybe one of them would open file cabinets on the AURORA project floor.

One by one, I pressed each key onto a rectangle of wax. I'd practiced this a few times with one of Meacham's guys, and I was glad I did; it took a while to get the hang of it. Now the password prompt on her screen was blinking at me.

Shit. Not everyone password-protected their laptops. Oh, well: at least this wasn't going to be a wasted errand. From the knapsack I pulled out the miniature pcProx reader that Meacham had given me and connected it to my handheld. I pressed the start button, then waved Alana's badge at it.

The little device had just captured the data on Alana's card and stored it on my handheld.

Maybe it was just as well that her laptop was password-protected. There was a limit to how much time I could spend out in the parking lot without her wondering where the hell I'd gone. Just before I shut down her computer, just for kicks, I decided to type in some of the usual-suspect passwords—her birth date, which I'd memorized; the first six digits of her employee number.

Nothing happened. I typed in ALANA, and the password prompt disappeared, and a plain screen came up.

Oh, man, that was easy. I was in.

Jesus. Now what? How much time could I risk spending on this? But how could I pass the opportunity up? It might never come again.

Alana was an extremely well-organized person. Her computer was set up in a clear, logical hierarchy. One directory was labeled AURORA.

It was all here. Well, maybe not all, but it was a gold mine of technical specs on the optical chip, marketing memos, copies of e-mails she'd sent and received, meeting schedules, staff rosters with access codes, even floor plans. . . .

There was so much that I didn't have time even to read through the file names. Her laptop had a CD drive; I had a little spindle of blank CDs in the knapsack. I grabbed one, popped it into her CD drive.

Even on a super-fast computer like Alana's, it took a good five minutes to copy all the AURORA files to a disk. That's how much there was.

"What took you so long?" she said poutily when I returned.

She was under the covers, her naked breasts visible, and she looked sleepy. A Stevie Wonder ballad—"Love's in Need of Love Today"—was playing softly on a little CD player she must have brought.

"I couldn't figure out which was your trunk key."

"A car guy like you? I thought you drove off and left me here."

"Do I *look* stupid?"

"Appearances can be deceiving," she said. "Come to bed."

"I'd never have figured you for a Stevie Wonder fan," I said. Truly, I would never have guessed, given her collection of angry women folk singers.

"You don't really know me yet," she replied.

"No, but give me a little time," I said. I know everything about you, I thought, yet I don't know anything. I'm not the only one keeping secrets. I put her laptop on the oak desk next to the bathroom. "There," I said, returning to the bedroom, taking off my clothes. "In case you're seized with some brilliant inspiration, some amazing brainstorm in the middle of the night."

Naked, I approached the bed. This beautiful naked woman was in bed, playing the role of seductress, when really I was the seducer. She had no idea what sort of game I was playing, and I felt a flush of shame mixed, oddly, with a tug of arousal. "Get up here," she said in a dramatic whisper, staring at me. "I just had a *brainstorm*."

We both got up after eight, unusually late for us hyper-driven type A workaholics—and fooled around in bed for a while before showering and going down to a country breakfast. I doubt people in the country actually eat this way, or they'd all weigh four hundred pounds: rashers of bacon (only at country bed-and-breakfasts does bacon come in "rashers"), mounds of grits, freshly baked hot blueberry muffins, eggs, French toast, coffee with real cream. . . . Alana really chowed down, which surprised me, for such a pencil-thin girl. I enjoyed watching her eat so ravenously. She was a woman of appetites, which I liked.

We went back up the room and fooled around some more, and hung out and talked. I made a point of not talking about security procedures or proximity badges. She wanted to talk about my dad's death and funeral, and even though the subject depressed me, I talked about it a little. Around eleven we reluctantly left, and the date was over.

I think we both wanted it to keep going, but we also needed to get home to our own nests for a while, get some work done, go back to the salt mines, make up for this delicious night away from work.

As we drove, I found myself grooving on the country road, the trees dappled with sunlight, the fact that I'd just spent the night with the coolest and most gorgeous and funniest and sexiest woman I'd ever met.

Man, what the hell was I doing?

82

By noon I was back in my apartment, and I immediately called Seth.

"I'm going to need some more cash, man," he said.

I'd already given him several thousand dollars, from my Wyatt-funded account, or wherever the money really came from. I was surprised he'd run through it already.

"I didn't want to fuck around, get cheap stuff," he said. "I got all professional equipment."

"I guess you had to," I said. "Even though it's one-time use."

"You want me to pick up uniforms?"

"Yeah."

"What about badges?"

"I'm working on that," I said.

"Aren't you nervous?"

I hesitated a moment, thought about lying just to bolster his courage, but I couldn't. "Totally," I said.

I didn't want to think about what might happen if things went wrong, though. Some prime real estate in my brain was now being colonized by worry, obsessively working through the plan I'd come up with after meeting with Seth's boss.

And yet there was another part of my brain that wanted to just escape into a daydream. I wanted to think about Alana. I thought about the irony of the whole situation—how this calculated scheme of seduction had led down this unexpected path, how I felt rewarded, wrongly, for my treachery.

I'd alternate between feeling crummy, guilty about what I was doing to her, and being overwhelmed by my attachment to her, something I really hadn't felt before. Little details kept popping into my mind: the way she brushed her teeth, scooping up water from the tap with a cupped hand instead of using a glass; the graceful hollow of her lower back swelling into the cleft of her butt, the incredibly sexy way she applied her lipstick. . . . I thought about her velvet-smooth voice, her crazy laugh, her sense of humor, her sweetness.

And I thought—this was by far the strangest thing—about our future together, a generally scary thought to a guy in his twenties, but somehow this wasn't at all scary. I didn't want to lose this woman. I felt like I'd stopped into a 7-Eleven to buy a six-pack of beer and a lottery ticket, and I'd won the lottery.

And because of that, I never wanted her to find out what I was really up to. That terrified me. That dark, awful thought kept popping up, interrupting my silly fantasy, like one of those kids' clown toys with the weighted bottom that always go *sproing* upright every time you bat them down.

A smudgy black-and-white image would be spliced into my gauzy color fantasy reel—a frame from a surveillance camera: me sitting in my car in the dark parking lot copying the contents of her laptop onto a CD, pressing her keys into the wax, copying her ID badge.

I'd bat back the evil clown doll and there we are on our wedding day, Alana walking down the aisle, gorgeous and demure, escorted by her father, a silver-haired, square-jawed guy in a morning suit.

The ceremony's performed by Jock Goddard as justice of the peace. Alana's family's all in attendance, her mother looking like Diane Keaton in *Father of the Bride*, her sister not as pretty as Alana but sweet, and they're all thrilled—this is a fantasy, remember—that she's marrying me.

Our first house together, a real house and not an apartment, like in an old leafy Midwestern town; I was imagining the great house Steve Martin's family lives in, in *Father of the Bride*. We're both rich high-powered corporate execs, after all. Somewhere in the background, Nina Simone is singing

"The Folks Who Live on the Hill." I'm hoisting Alana effortlessly over the threshold and she's laughing at how cornball and cliché I'm being, and then we boink in every room of the house to initiate the place, including the bathroom and the linen closet. We rent movies together while sitting in bed eating take-out Chinese food from the carton with wooden chopsticks, and every so often I sneak a look at her, and I can't believe I'm actually *married* to this unbelievable babe.

Meacham's goons had brought back my computers and such, which was fortunate, because I needed them.

I popped the CD into my computer with all the stuff I'd copied from Alana's laptop. A lot of it was e-mails concerning the vast marketing potential of AURORA. How Trion was poised to own the "space," as they say in techspeak. The huge increases in computing power it promised, how the AURORA chip really would change the world.

One of the more interesting documents was a schedule of the public demonstration of AURORA. It was to happen on Wednesday, four days from now, at the Visitors Center at Trion headquarters, a mammoth, modernistic auditorium. E-mail alerts, faxes, and phone calls were to go out only the day before to all the media. Obviously it was going to be an immense public event. I printed the schedule out.

But I was intrigued, most of all, by the floor plan and the security procedures that all AURORA team members were given.

Then I opened one of the pullout garbage drawers in the kitchen island. Wrapped in a trash bag were a few objects I'd stored in Zip-Loc bags. One was the Ani DiFranco CD I'd left around my apartment, expecting her to pick it up, as she did. The other was the wineglass she'd used here.

Meacham had given me a Sirchie fingerprint kit, containing little vials of latent print powder, transparent fingerprint lifting tape, and a fiberglass brush. Putting on a pair of latex gloves, I dusted both the CD and the wineglass with a little of the black graphite powder.

By far the best thumbprint was on the CD. I lifted that carefully on a strip of tape, put it in a sterile plastic case.

Then I composed an e-mail to Nick Wyatt.

It was addressed, of course, to "Arthur":

> Monday evening/Tuesday morning will complete assignment & obtain samples. Tuesday early morning will hand over at time and place you specify. Upon completion of assignment I will terminate all contact.

I wanted to strike the right note of resentfulness. I didn't want them to suspect anything.

But would Wyatt himself show up at the rendezvous?

I guess that was the big unanswered question. It wasn't crucial that Wyatt show up, though I sure wanted it to be him. There was no way to force Wyatt to be there himself. In fact, insisting on it would probably just warn him *not* to show. But by now I knew enough of Wyatt's psychology to be fairly confident that he wouldn't trust anyone else.

You see, I was going to give Nick Wyatt what he wanted.

I was going to give him the actual prototype of the AURORA chip, which I was going to steal, with Seth's help, from the secure fifth floor of D Wing.

I had to give him the real thing, the actual AURORA prototype. For a number of reasons it couldn't be faked. Wyatt, being an engineer, would probably know right away whether it was the genuine item or not.

But the main reason was, as I'd learned from Camilletti's e-mails and Alana's files, that for security reasons, the AURORA prototype had been inscribed with a micromachined identification mark, a serial number and the Trion logo, etched with a laser and visible only under a microscope.

That's why I wanted him to be in possession of the stolen chip. The real thing.

Because the moment Wyatt—or Meacham, if it had to be—took delivery of the pilfered chip, I had him. The FBI would be notified far enough in advance to coordinate a SWAT team, but they wouldn't know names or locations or anything until the very last minute. I was going to be in complete control of this.

Howard Shapiro, Seth's boss, had made the call for me. "Forget about dealing with the bureau chief in the U.S. Attorney's office," he said. "Something dicey like this, he's going to go to Washington, and that's going to take forever. Forget it. We go right to the FBI—they're the only ones who'll play the game at this level."

Without naming names, he struck a deal with the FBI. If everything came off successfully, and I delivered Nick Wyatt to them, I'd get probation, and nothing more.

Well, I was going to deliver Wyatt. But it was going to be my way.

83

I got into work early on Monday morning, wondering whether this was going to be my last day at Trion.

Of course, if everything went well, this would just be another day, a blip in a long and successful career.

But the chances that everything in this incredibly complicated scheme would go right were pretty small, and I knew it.

On Sunday, I'd cloned a couple of copies of Alana's proximity badge, using a little machine Meacham had given me called a ProxProgrammer and the data I'd captured from Alana's ID badge.

Also, I'd found among Alana's files a floor plan for the fifth floor of D Wing. Almost half the floor was marked with cross-hatching and labeled "Secure Facility C."

Secure Facility C was where the prototype was being tested.

Unfortunately, I had no idea what was *in* the secure facility, where in that area the prototype was kept. Once I got in, I'd have to wing it.

I drove by my dad's apartment to grab my industrial-strength work gloves, the ones I'd used when I worked as a window cleaner with Seth. I was sort of hoping to see Antwoine, but he must have gone out for a while. I got this funny feeling while I was there, like I was being watched, but I wrote it off as just your basic free-floating anxiety.

The rest of Sunday, I'd done a lot of research on the Trion Web site. It was amazing, really, how much information was available to Trion employees—

from floor plans to security badging procedures to even the inventory of security equipment installed on the fifth floor of D Wing. From Meacham I'd gotten the radio frequency the Trion security guards used for their two-way radios.

I didn't know everything I needed to know about the security procedures—far from it—but I did find out a few key things. They confirmed what Alana had told me over dinner at the country inn.

There were only two ways in or out of the fifth floor, both manned. You waved your badge at a card reader to get through the first set of doors, but then you had to show your face to a guard behind a bulletproof glass window, who compared your name and photograph to what he had on his computer screen, then buzzed you through to the main floor.

And even then, you weren't anywhere near Secure Facility C. You had to walk down corridors equipped with closed-circuit video cameras, then into another area set up with not only security cameras but motion detectors, before you came to the entrance to the secure area. That was unmanned, but in order to unlock the door you had to activate a biometric sensor.

So getting to the AURORA prototype was going to be grotesquely difficult, if not impossible. I wasn't even going to be able to get through the first, manned checkpoint. I couldn't use Alana's card, obviously—nobody would mistake me for her. But her card might be useful in other ways once I got onto the fifth floor.

The biometric sensor was even tougher. Trion was on the cutting edge of most technologies, and biometric recognition—fingerprint scanners, hand readers, automated facial-geometry identification, voice ID, iris scans, retina scans—was the next big thing in the security business. They all have their strengths and weaknesses, but finger scans are generally considered the best—reliable, not too fussy or tricky, not too high a rate of false rejections or false acceptances.

Mounted on the wall outside Secure Facility C was an Identix fingerprint scanner.

In the late afternoon, I placed a call, from my cell phone, to the assistant director of the security command center for D Wing.

"Hey, George," I said. "This is Ken Romero in Network Design and Ops, in the wiring group?" Ken Romero was a real name, a senior manager. Just in case George decided to look me up.

"What can I do for you?" the guy said. He sounded like he'd just found a turd in his Cracker Jack box.

"Just a courtesy call? Bob wanted me to give you guys a heads-up that we're going to be doing a fiber reroute and upgrade on D-Five early tomorrow morning."

"Uh huh." Like: why are you telling me?

"I don't know why they think they need laser-optimized fifty micron fiber or an Ultra Dense Blade Server, but hey, it's not coming out of my pocket, you know? I guess they've got some serious bandwidth-hog applications running up there, and—"

"What can I do for you, Mister—"

"Romero. Anyway, I guess the guys on the fifth floor didn't want any disruptions during the workday, so they put in a request to have it done early in the A.M. No big deal, but we wanted to keep you guys in the loop 'cause the work's going to set off proximity detectors and motion detectors and all that, like between four and six in the morning."

The assistant security chief actually sounded sort of relieved that he didn't have to *do* anything.

"You're talkin' the whole darned fifth floor? I can't shut off the whole darned fifth floor without—"

"No, no, no," I said. "We'll be lucky if my guys can get through two, maybe three wiring closets, the way they take coffee breaks. No, we're aiming for areas, lemme see, areas twenty-two A and B, I think? Just the internal sections. Anyway, your boards are probably going to light up like Christmas trees, probably going to drive you guys frickin' bonkers, but I wanted to give you a heads-up—"

George gave a heavy sigh. "If it's just twenty-two A and B, I suppose I can disable those. . . ."

"Whatever's convenient. I mean, we just don't want to drive you guys bonkers."

"I'll give you three hours if you need it."

"We shouldn't need three hours, but I guess better safe than sorry, you know? Anyways, appreciate your help."

84

Around seven that evening I checked out of the Trion building, as usual, and drove home. I got a fitful night's sleep.

Just before four in the morning, I drove back and parked on the street, not in the Trion garage, so there wouldn't be a record of my re-entering the building. Ten minutes later, a panel truck labeled J.J. RANKENBERG & CO—PROFESSIONAL WINDOW CLEANING TOOLS, EQUIPMENT, AND CHEMICALS SINCE 1963 pulled up. Seth was behind the wheel in a blue uniform with a J.J. Rankenberg patch on the left pocket.

"Howdy, cowboy," he said.

"J.J. himself let you have this?"

"The old man's dead," Seth said. He was smoking, which was how I could tell he was nervous. "I had to deal with Junior." He handed me a folded pair of blue overalls, and I slipped them over my chinos and polo shirt, not easy to do in the cab of the old Isuzu truck. It reeked of spilled gasoline.

"I thought Junior hates you."

Seth held up his left hand and rubbed his thumb and fingers together, meaning moolah. "Short-term lease, for a quickie job I got for my girlfriend's dad's company."

"You don't have a girlfriend."

"All he cared was, he doesn't have to report the income. Ready to rock 'n' roll, dude?"

"Press send, baby," I said. I pointed out the D Wing service entrance to the parking garage, and Seth drove down into it. The night attendant in the booth glanced at a sheet of paper, found the company name on the admit list.

Seth pulled the truck over to the lower-level loading dock and we took out the big nylon tote bags stuffed with gear, the Ettore professional squeegees and the big green buckets, the twelve-foot extension poles, the plastic gallon jugs filled with piss-yellow glass cleaner liquid, the ropes and hooks and Ski Genie and bosun chair and the Jumar ascenders. I'd forgotten how much miscellaneous *junk* the job required.

I hit the big round steel button next to the steel garage door, and a few seconds later the door began rolling open. A paunchy, pasty-faced security guard with a bristly mustache came out with a clipboard. "You guys need any help?" he asked, not meaning it.

"We're all set," I said. "If you can just show us to the freight elevator to the roof . . ."

"No problem," he said. He stood there with his clipboard—he didn't seem to be writing anything down on it, he just held it to let us know who was in charge—and watched us struggle with the equipment. "You guys can really clean windows when it's dark out?" he said as he walked us over to the elevator.

"At time-and-a-half, we clean 'em *better* when it's dark out," said Seth.

"I don't know why people get so uptight about us looking in their office windows when they're working," I said.

"Yeah, that's our main source of entertainment," Seth said. "Scare the shit out of people. Give the office workers a heart attack."

The guard laughed. "Just hit 'R,' " he said. "If the roof access door's locked, there should be a guy up there, I think it's Oscar."

"Cool," I said.

When we got to the roof, I remembered why I hated high-rise window cleaning. The Trion headquarters building was only eight stories high, no more than a hundred feet or so, but up there in the middle of the night it might as well have been the Empire State Building. The wind was whipping around, it was cold and clammy, and there was distant traffic noise, even at that time of night.

The security guard, Oscar Fernandez (according to his badge), was a short guy in a navy-blue security uniform with a two-way radio clipped to his belt squawking static and garbled voices. He met us at the freight elevator, shifting his weight awkwardly from foot to foot as we unloaded our stuff, and showed us to the roof-access stairs.

We followed him up the short flight of stairs. While he was unlocking the roof door, he said, "Yeah, I got the word you guys would be coming, but I was surprised, I didn't know you guys worked so early."

He didn't seem suspicious; he just seemed to be making conversation.

Seth repeated his line about time-and-a-half, and we replayed our bit about giving the office workers heart attacks, and he laughed too. He said he guessed it kind of made sense anyway that people didn't want us disrupting their work during normal working hours. We looked like legit window cleaners, we had all the right equipment and the uniforms, and who the hell else would be crazy enough to climb out on the roof of a tall building lugging all that junk?

"I've only been on nights a couple weeks anyway," he said. "You guys been up here before? You know your way around?"

We said we hadn't done Trion yet, and he showed us the basics—power outlets, water spigots, safety anchors. All newly constructed buildings these days are required to have rooftop safety anchors mounted every ten to fifteen feet apart, about six feet in from the edge of the building, strong enough to support five thousand pounds of weight. The anchors usually stick up like plumbing vent pipes, only with a U-bolt on top.

Oscar was a little too interested in how we rigged up our gear. He hung around, watching us fasten the locking steel carabiners. These were attached to half-inch orange-and-white kernmantle climbing rope and connected to the safety anchors.

"Neat," he said. "You guys probably climb mountains in your spare time, huh?"

Seth looked at me, then said, "You a security guard in your spare time?"

"Nah," he said, then he laughed. "I just mean you got to like climbing off tall places and stuff. That would scare the shit out of me."

"You get used to it," I said.

Each of us had two separate lines, one to climb down on, the other a back-up safety line with a rope grab, in case the first one broke. I wanted to do it right, and not just for appearance's sake. Neither one of us felt like getting killed by dropping off the Trion building. During those unpleasant couple of summers when we worked for the window cleaning company we kept hearing about how there was an industry average of ten fatalities a year, but they never told us if that was ten in the world or ten in the state or what, and we never asked.

I knew that what we were doing was dangerous. I just didn't know where the danger was going to come.

After another five minutes or so, Oscar finally got bored, mostly because we stopped talking to him, and he went back to his station.

The kernmantle rope attaches to a thing called a Sky Genie, a kind of long sheet-metal tube in which you wind the rope around a forged aluminum shank. The Sky Genie—gotta love the name—is a descent-control device that works by friction and pays out the rope slowly. These Sky Genies were scratched and looked like they'd been used. I held it up and said, "You couldn't buy us new ones?"

"Hey, they came with the truck, whaddaya want? What are you worried about? These babies'll support five thousand pounds. Then again, you look like you've put on a couple pounds the last few months."

"Fuck you."

"You have dinner? I hope not."

"This isn't funny. You ever look at the warning label on this?"

"I know, improper use can cause serious injury or even death. Don't pay attention to that. You're probably scared to remove mattress tags too."

"I like the slogan—'Sky Genie—Gets You Down.' "

Seth didn't laugh. "Eight stories is nothing, guy. You remember the time when we were doing the Civic—"

"Don't remind me," I interrupted. I didn't want to be a big pussy, but I wasn't into his black humor, not standing up there on the roof of the Trion building.

The Sky Genie got hooked up to a nylon safety harness attached to a waist belt and padded seat board. Everything in the window-cleaning business had names with the words "safety" or "fall-protection" in them, which just reminds you if anything goes even slightly wrong you're fucked.

The only thing we'd set up that was slightly out of the ordinary was a pair of Jumar Ascenders, which would enable us to climb back up the ropes. Most of the time when you're cleaning the windows on a high-rise you have no reason to go back up—you just work your way down until you're on the ground.

But this would be our means of escape.

Meanwhile, Seth mounted the electric winch to one of the roof anchors with a D-ring, then plugged it in. This was a hundred-and-fifteen-volt model with a pulley capable of lifting a thousand pounds. He connected it to each of our lines, making sure that there was enough play that it wouldn't stop us from climbing down.

I tugged on the rope, hard, to check that everything was locked in place, and we both walked over to the edge of the building and looked down. Then we looked at each other, and Seth smiled a what-the-fuck-are-we-doing smile.

"Are we having fun yet?" he said.

"Oh, yeah."

"You ready, buddy?"

"Yeah," I said. "Ready as Elliot Krause in the Port-O-San."

Neither one of us laughed. We climbed onto the guardrail slowly and then went over the side.

85

We only had to rappel down two stories, but it wasn't easy. We were both out of practice, we were lugging some heavy tools, and we had to be extremely careful not to swing too far to either side.

Mounted on the building's façade were closed-circuit TV surveillance cameras. I knew from the schematics exactly where they were mounted. I also knew the specs on the cameras, the size of the lenses, their focal range and all that.

In other words, I knew where the blind spots were.

And we were climbing down through one of them. I wasn't concerned about Building Security seeing us rappelling down the side of the building, since they were expecting window cleaners early in the morning. What I was concerned about was that, if anyone looked, they'd realize we weren't actually cleaning any windows. They'd see us lowering ourselves, slowly and steadily, to the fifth floor. They'd see that we weren't even positioning ourselves in front of a window, either.

We were dangling in front of a steel ventilation grate.

As long as we didn't swing too far to one side or the other, we'd be out of camera range. That was important.

Bracing our feet against a ledge, we got out our power tools and set to work on the hex bolts. They were securely fastened, through the steel and into concrete, and there were a lot of them. Seth and I labored in silence, the sweat pouring down our faces. It was possible that someone walking by, a security guard or whoever, might see us removing the bolts that held the vent grate in place and wonder what we were doing. Window cleaners worked with squeegees and buckets, not Milwaukee cordless impact wrenches.

But this time of the morning, there weren't many people walking by. Anyone who happened to look up would probably figure we were doing routine building maintenance.

Or so I hoped.

It took us a good fifteen minutes to loosen and remove each bolt. A few of them were rusted tight and needed a hit of WD-40.

Then, on a signal from me, Seth loosened the last bolt, and we both carefully lifted the grate away from the steel skin of the building. It was super heavy, a two-man job at least. We had to grip it by its sharp edges—luckily I'd brought gloves, a good pair for both of us—and angle it out so that it rested on the window ledge. Then Seth, grasping the grille for leverage, managed to swing his legs into the room. He dropped to the floor of the mechanical equipment room with a grunt.

"Your turn," he said. "Careful."

I grabbed an edge of the grate and swung my legs into the airshaft and dropped to the floor, looking around quickly.

The mechanical room was crowded with immense, roaring equipment, mostly dark, lit only by the distant spill from the floodlights mounted on the roof. There was all kinds of HVAC stuff in here—heat pumps, centrifugal fans, huge chillers and compressors, and other air filtration and air-conditioning equipment.

We stood there in our harnesses, still hooked up to the double ropes, which dangled through the ventilation shaft. Then we unsnapped the harness belts and let go.

Now the harnesses hung in midair. Obviously we couldn't just leave them out there, but we'd rigged them up to the electric winch up on the roof. Seth pulled out a little black remote-control garage-door opener and pressed the button. You could hear this whirring, grinding noise far off, and the harnesses and ropes began to rise slowly in the air, pulled by the electric winch.

"Hope we can get 'em back when we need 'em," Seth said, but I could barely hear him over the thundering white noise in the room.

I couldn't help thinking that this whole thing was little more than a game to Seth. If he was caught, no big deal. He'd be okay. I was the one who was in deep doodoo.

Now we pulled the grate in tight so that, from the outside, it looked like it was in place. Then I took an extra length of the kernmantle, ran it through the grips, then around a vertical pipe to tie the thing down.

The room had gone dark again, so I took out my Mag-Lite, switched it on. I walked over to the heavy-looking steel door and tried the lever.

It opened. I knew that the doors to mechanical rooms were required to be unlocked from the inside, to make sure no one got trapped, but it was still a relief to know we could get out of here.

In the meantime, Seth took out a pair of Motorola Talkabout walkie-talkies, handed me one, and then pulled out from his holster a compact black shortwave radio, a three-hundred-channel police scanner.

"You remember the security frequency? Something in the four hundreds UHF, wasn't it?"

I took a little spiral-bound notebook from my shirt pocket, read off the frequency number. He began to key it in, and I unfolded the floor map and studied my route.

I was even more nervous now than when I was climbing down the side of the building. We had a pretty solid plan, but too many things could go wrong.

For one, there might be people around, even this early. AURORA was Trion's top-priority program, with a big deadline a mere two days off. Engineers worked weird hours. Five in the morning, there probably wouldn't be anyone around, but you never knew. Better to stay in the window-washer uniform, carrying a bucket and a squeegee—cleaning people were all but invisible. Unlikely anyone would stop to ask what I was doing here.

But there was a gruesome possibility that I might run into someone who recognized me. Trion had tens of thousands of employees, and I'd met, I don't know, fifty of them, so the odds were in my favor I wouldn't see someone who knew me. Not at five in the morning. Still . . . So I'd brought along a yellow hard hat, even though window washers never actually wear them, jammed it down on my head, then put on a pair of safety glasses.

Once I was out of this dark little room, I'd have to walk several hundred feet of hallway with security cameras trained on me all the way. Sure, there were a couple of security guys in the command center in the basement, but they had to look at dozens of monitors, and they were probably also watching TV and drinking coffee and shooting the shit. I didn't think anyone would pay me much attention.

Until I reached Secure Facility C, where the security definitely got harsh.

"Got it," Seth said, staring at the police scanner's digital readout. "I just heard 'Trion Security' and something else Trion."

"Okay," I said. "Keep listening, and alert me if there's anything I should know."

"How long you gonna take, you think?"

I held my breath. "Could be ten minutes. Could be half an hour. Depends on how things go."

"Be careful, Cas."

I nodded.

"Wait, here you go." He'd spotted a big yellow wheeled cleaning bucket in the corner, rolled it over to me. "Take this."

"Good idea." I looked at my old buddy for a moment, wanting to say something like "Wish me luck," but then I decided that sounded too nervous and mushy. Instead, I gave him the thumbs-up, like I was cool about all this. "See you back here," I said.

"Hey, don't forget to turn your thingy on," he said, pointing to my Talkabout.

I shook my head at my own forgetfulness and smiled.

Opening the door slowly, I looked out, saw no one coming, stepped into the hall, and closed the door behind me.

86

Fifty feet up ahead, a security camera was mounted high on the wall, next to the ceiling, its tiny red light winking.

Wyatt said I was a good actor, and now I'd really need to be. I had to look casual, a little bored, busy, and most of all not nervous. That'd take some acting.

Keep watching the Weather Channel or whatever the hell is on now, I mentally willed whoever was in the command center. *Drink your coffee, eat your donuts. Talk basketball or football. Pay no attention to that man behind the curtain.*

My work boots squeaked softly as I walked down the carpeted hall, wheeling the cleaning bucket.

No one else around. That was a relief.

No, I thought, *it's actually better if there're other people walking by. Takes the focus off of you.*

Yeah, maybe. Take what you get. Just hope no one asks where I'm going.

I turned the corner into a large open cubicle-farm area. Except for a few emergency lights, it was dark.

Pushing the bucket through an aisle down the middle of the room, I could see even more security cameras. The signs in the cubicles, the weird unfunny posters, all indicated that engineers worked here. On a shelf above one of the cubicles was a Love Me Lucille doll, staring malevolently at me.

Just doin' my job, I reminded myself.

On the other side of this open area, I knew from the map, was a short corridor leading directly to the sealed-off half of the floor. A sign on the wall (SECURE FACILITY C—ADMITTANCE ONLY TO CLEARED PERSONNEL, and an arrow) confirmed it for me. I was almost there.

This was all going a lot more smoothly than I'd expected. Of course, there were motion detectors and cameras all around the entrance to the secure facility.

But if the call I'd made to Security the day before had worked, they'd have shut off the motion detectors.

Of course, I couldn't be sure of that. I'd know in a few seconds, when I got closer.

The cameras would almost certainly be on, but I had a plan for that.

Suddenly a loud noise jolted me, a high-pitched trill from my Talkabout.

"Jesus," I muttered, heart racing.

"Adam," came Seth's voice, flat and breathy.

I pressed the button on its side. "Yeah."

"We got a problem."

"What do you mean?"

"Get back here."

"Why?"

"Just get the fuck *back* here."

Oh, shit.

I spun around, left the cleaning bucket, started to run until I remembered I was being watched. I forced myself to slow down to a stroll. What the hell could have happened? Did the ropes give us away? Did the ventilation grate drop? Or did someone open the door to the mechanical room, find Seth?

The walk back took forever. An office door swung open just ahead, and a middle-aged guy came out. He was wearing brown double-knit polyester slacks and a short-sleeved yellow shirt, and he looked like an old-line mechanical engineer. Getting an extra-early start on the day, or maybe he'd been up all night. The guy glanced at me, then looked down at the carpet without saying anything.

I was a cleaning guy. I was invisible.

A couple dozen surveillance cameras had captured my image, but I wasn't going to attract anyone's attention. I was a cleaning guy, a maintenance guy. I was supposed to be here. No one would look twice.

Finally I reached the mechanical room. I stopped in front of the door, listening for voices, prepared to run if I had to, if someone was in there with Seth, even though I didn't want to leave him there. I could hear the faint squawk of the police scanner, that was all.

I pulled the door open. Seth was standing just on the other side of the door, the radio near his ear.

He looked panicked.

"We gotta get out of here," he whispered.

"What's—"

"The guy on the roof. On the seventh floor, I mean. The security guy who took us to the roof."

"What about him?"

"Must have come back out to the roof. Curious, whatever. Looked down, didn't see us. Saw the ropes and the harnesses, and no window cleaners, and he freaked. I don't know, maybe he got scared something happened to us, who knows."

"What?"

"*Listen!*"

There was squawking over the police scanner, a babble of voices. I heard a snatch: "Floor by floor, over!"

Then: "Bravo unit, come in."

"Bravo, over."

"Bravo, suspected illegal entry, D David wing. Looks like window cleaners—abandoned equipment on the roof, no sign of the workers. I want a floor-by-floor search of the whole building. This is a Code Two. Bravo, your men cover the first floor, over."

"Roger that."

I stared at Seth. "I think Code Two means urgent."

"They're searching the building," Seth whispered, his voice barely audible over the roar of the machinery. "We have to get the fuck *out* of here."

"How?" I hissed back. "We can't drop the ropes, even if they're still in place! And we sure as hell can't get out through the mantrap on *this* floor!"

"What the hell are we going to *do*?"

I inhaled deeply, exhaled, tried to think clearly. I wanted a cigarette. "All right. Find a computer, any computer. Log on to the Trion Web site. Look for the company security procedures page, see where the emergency points of egress are. I'm talking freight elevators, fire stairs, whatever. Any way we can get out, even if we have to jump."

"Me? So what are *you* going to do?"

"I'm going back out there."

"What? You're fucking *kidding* me. This building is crawling with security guards, you moron!"

"They don't know where we are. All they know is we're *somewhere* in this wing—and there's seven floors."

"Jesus, Adam!"

"I'll never get this chance again," I said, running toward the door. I waved my Motorola Talkabout at him. "Tell me when you find a way out. I'm going into Secure Facility C. I'm going to get what we came for."

87

Don't run.

I had to keep reminding myself. Stay calm. I walked down the hall, trying to look blasé when my head was about to explode. Don't look at the cameras.

I was halfway to the big open cubicle area when my walkie-talkie bleeped at me, two quick tones.

"Yeah?"

"Listen, man. It's asking me for an ID. The sign-on screen."

"Oh, shit, right, of course."

"Want me to sign on as you?"

"Oh *God* no. Use . . ." I whipped out the little spiral notebook. "Use CPierson." I spelled it out for him as I kept walking.

"Password? Got a password?"

"MJ twenty-three," I read off.

"MJ . . . ?"

"I assume it's for Michael Jordan."

"Oh, right. Twenty-three's Jordan's number. This guy some kind of amazing hoops player?"

Why was Seth blathering on? He must have been scared out of his mind.

"No," I said, distracted, as I entered the cubicle area. I took off the yellow hard hat and the safety glasses, since I no longer needed them, stowed them under a desk as I passed by. "Just arrogant, like Jordan. They both think they're the best. One of them's right."

"All right, I'm in," he said. "The Security page, you said?"

"Company security procedures. See what you can find out about the loading dock, whether we can get back down there using the freight elevator. That might be our best escape route. I gotta go."

"Hurry it up," he said.

Straight ahead of me was a gray-painted steel door with a small, diamond-shaped window reinforced with wire mesh. A sign on the door said AUTHORIZED PERSONNEL ONLY.

I approached the door slowly, at an angle, and looked through the window. On the other side was a small, industrial-looking waiting room, a concrete floor. I counted two CCTV cameras mounted high on the wall near the ceiling, their red lights blinking. They were on. I could also see the little white pods in each corner of the room: the passive infrared motion detectors.

No LED lights on the motion detectors, though. I couldn't be sure, but they seemed to be off. Maybe Security really had shut them down for a few hours.

In one hand I was holding a clipboard, trying to look official, like I was obeying printed instructions. With my other hand I tried the doorknob. It was locked. Mounted on the wall to the left of the door frame was a little gray proximity sensor, just like you saw all over the building. Would Alana's badge open it? I took out my copy of her badge, waved it at the sensor, willing the red light to turn green.

And I heard a voice.

"Hey! You!"

I turned slowly. A Trion security guard was running toward me, another guard lagging behind him.

"Freeze!" the first man shouted.

Oh, shit. My heart leaped in my chest.

Caught.

Now what, Adam?

I stared at the guards, my expression changing from startled to arrogant. I took a breath. In a quiet voice, I said, "You find him yet?"

"Huh?" said the first guard, slowing to a stop.

"Your goddamned intruder!" I said, my voice louder. "The alarm went off five fucking minutes ago, and you guys are still running around like idiots, scratching your asses!" *You can do this*, I told myself. *This is what you do*.

"Sir?" the second guard said. They both were frozen in place, looking at me, bewildered.

"You morons have any idea where the point of entry was?" I was shouting at them like a drill sergeant, tearing them new assholes. "You think we could have made it any easier for you guys? For Christ's sake, you do an exterior perimeter check, that's the first thing you do. Page twenty-three of the goddamned manual! You do that, and you'd find a ventilation grille dislodged."

"Ventilation grille?" said the first one.

"Are we going to have to spray-paint the trail in fucking Day-Glo colors? Should we have given you guys engraved invitations to a Bendix surprise security audit? We've run this drill in three area buildings in the past week, and you guys are the worst bunch of amateurs I've seen." I took the clipboard and the attached pen and began writing. "Okay, I want names and I want badge numbers. You!" The two guards had begun to retreat, backing up slowly. "Get the fuck back here! You think Corporate Security's all about the Krispy Kremes? Heads are going to roll, I promise you that, when we file our report."

"McNamara," the second guard said reluctantly.

"Valenti," said the first.

I jotted down their names. "Badge numbers? Aw, Christ, look—one of you get this goddamned door open, and then both of you, get the hell out of here."

The first one approached the card reader, waved his badge at it. There was a click and the light turned green.

I shook my head in disgust as I pulled the door open. The two guards turned and began loping back down the hall. I heard the first one say to the other sullenly, "I'm going to check with Dispatch right now. I don't like this."

My heart was hammering so loud it had to be audible. I'd bullshitted my way out of that, but I knew all I'd done was to buy a couple of minutes. The guards would radio in to their dispatch and find out the truth immediately—there was no "surprise security audit" going on. Then they'd be back with a vengeance.

I watched the motion detector, mounted high on the wall in this small lobby area, waiting to see whether a light would flash on, but it didn't.

When the motion detectors were on, they triggered the cameras, shifted them in the direction of any moving object.

But the motion detectors were off. That meant the cameras were fixed, couldn't move.

It's funny, Meacham and his guy had trained me to beat security systems that were more sophisticated than this. Maybe Meacham was right—forget about the movies, in reality corporate security always tends to be sort of primitive.

Now I could enter the little lobby area without being seen by the cameras, which were pointed at the door that opened directly into Secure Facility C. I took a few tentative steps into the room, flattening my back against the wall. I sidled slowly over to one of the cameras from behind. I was in the camera's blind spot, I knew. It couldn't see me.

And then the Talkabout bleeped to life.

"*Get the hell out!*" Seth's voice screeched. "Everyone's been ordered to the fifth floor, I just heard it!"

"I—I can't, I'm almost there!" I shouted back.

"*Move it!* Jesus, get the hell out of there!"

"No—I can't! Not yet!"

"Cassidy—"

"Seth, listen to me. You've got to get the hell out of here—stairs, freight elevator, whatever. Wait for me in the truck outside."

"Cassidy—"

"Go!" I shouted, and I clicked off.

A blast of sound jolted me—a throaty mechanical *hoo-ah* blaring from an alarm horn somewhere very close.

Now what? I *couldn't* stop here, just feet from the entrance to the AURORA Project! Not this close!

I had to keep going.

The alarm went on, *hoo-ah, hoo-ah*, deafeningly loud, like an air-raid siren.

I pulled the spray can out of my overalls—a can of Pam spray, that aerosol cooking oil—then leaped up at the camera and sprayed the lens. I could see an oil slick on the glass eyeball. Done.

The siren blared.

Now the camera was blind, its optics defeated—but not in a way that would necessarily attract attention. Anyone watching the monitor would see the image suddenly go blurry. Maybe they'd blame the network wiring upgrade they'd been warned about. The blurred-out image probably wouldn't draw much attention in a bank of TV monitors. That was the idea, anyway.

But now that careful planning seemed almost pointless, because they were coming, I could hear them. The same guards I'd just bamboozled? Different ones? I had no idea, of course, but they were coming.

There were footsteps, shouts, but they sounded far away, just background chatter against the ear-splitting siren.

Maybe I could still make it.

If I hurried. Once I was inside the AURORA laboratory, they probably couldn't come after me, or at least not easily. Not unless they had some kind of override, which seemed unlikely.

They might not even know I was in there.

That is, if I could get in.

Now I circled the room, keeping out of camera range until I reached the other camera. Standing in its blind spot, I leaped up, sprayed the oil, hit the lens dead on.

Now Security couldn't see me through the monitors, couldn't see what I was about to try.

I was almost in. Another few seconds—I hoped—and I'd be inside AURORA.

Getting out was another matter. I knew there was a freight elevator there, which couldn't be accessed from outside. Would Alana's badge activate it? I sure hoped so. It was my only shot.

Damn, I could barely think straight, with that siren blasting, and the voices getting louder, the footsteps closer. My mind raced crazily. Would the security guards even know of the *existence* of AURORA? How closely held was the secret? If they didn't know about AURORA, they might not be able to figure out where I was headed. Maybe they were just running through the corridors of each floor in some wild, uncoordinated search for the second intruder.

Mounted on the wall to the immediate left of a shiny steel door was a small beige box: an Identix fingerprint scanner.

From the front pocket of my overalls I pulled the clear plastic case. Then, with trembling fingers, I removed the strip of tape with Alana's thumbprint on it, its whorls captured in traces of graphite powder.

I pressed the tape gently on the scanner, right where you'd normally put your thumb, and waited for the LED to change from red to green.

And nothing happened.

No, please, God, I thought desperately, my brain scrambled by terror, and by the unbearably loud *hoo-ah* of the alarm. *Make it work. Please, God.*

The light stayed red, stubbornly red.

Nothing was happening.

Meacham had given me a long session on how to defeat biometric scanners, and I'd practiced countless times until I thought I'd gotten it down. Some fingerprint readers were harder to beat than others, depending on what technology they used. This was one of the most common types, with an optical sensor inside it. And what I'd just done was supposed to work ninety percent of the time. Ninety percent of the time this goddamned trick *worked!*

Of course, there's the other ten percent, I thought, as I heard footsteps thunder nearer. They were close, now, that much I knew. Maybe a few yards away, in the cubicle farm.

Shit, it *wasn't* working!

What were the other tricks they'd taught me?

Something about a plastic bag full of water . . . but I didn't have anything like a plastic bag with me. . . . What *was* it? Old fingerprints remained on the surface of the sensor like handprints on a mirror, the oily residue of people who'd been admitted. The old fingerprints could be re-activated with moisture. . . .

Yes, it sounds wacky, but no crazier than using a piece of tape with a lifted print on it. I leaned over, cupped my hands over the little sensor, *breathed* on it. My breath hit the glass, condensed at once. It disappeared in a second, but it was long enough—

A beep, sounding almost like a chirp. A happy sound.

A green light on the box went on.

I'd passed. The moisture from my breath had activated an old fingerprint.

I'd fooled the sensor.

The shiny steel door to Secure Facility C slid slowly open on tracks just as the other door behind me opened and I heard, "Stop right there!"

And: "Stay right there!"

I stared at the huge open space that was Secure Facility C, and I couldn't believe what I was seeing. My eyes couldn't make sense of it.

I must have made a mistake.

This couldn't be the right place.

I was looking at the area marked Secure Facility C. I was expecting laboratory equipment and banks of electron microscopes, clean rooms, supercomputers and coils of fiber-optic cable. . . .

Instead, what I saw was naked steel girders, bare unpainted concrete floors, plaster dust and construction debris.

An immense, gutted space.

There was *nothing* here.

Where was the AURORA Project? I was in the right place, but there was nothing here.

And then a thought came to me which made the floor beneath my feet buckle and sway: *Was there in fact no AURORA Project after all?*

"Don't move a fucking *muscle!*" someone shouted from behind me.

I obeyed.

I didn't turn around to face the guards. I froze.

I couldn't move if I wanted to anyway.

88

Slack-jawed, dizzy, I turned slowly and saw a cluster of guards, five or six of them, among them a couple of familiar faces. Two of them were the guys I'd scared off, and they were back, furious.

The security guard, the black guy who'd caught me in Nora's office—what was his name, again? The guy with the Mustang? He was pointing a pistol at me. "Mister—Mister *Sommers?*" he gasped.

Next to him, in jeans and a T-shirt that looked like they'd been thrown on moments ago, his blond hair a tousled mess, was Chad. He was holding his cell phone. I knew at once why he was here: he must have tried to sign on, found that he was *already* signed on, and so he made a call. . . .

"That's Cassidy. Call Goddard!" Chad bellowed at the guard. "Call the goddamned *CEO!*"

"No, man, that's not the way we do it," the guard said, staring, his gun still aimed at me. "Step *back,*" he shouted. A couple of other guards were fanning out to either side. He said to Chad, "You don't call the CEO, man. You call the security director. Then we wait for the cops. That's my orders."

"Call the fucking CEO!" Chad screamed, waving his cell phone. "I've got Goddard's home number. I don't *care* what time it is. I want Goddard to know what his goddamned executive assistant, this fucking *hustler*, did!" He pressed a couple of buttons on the phone, put it to his ear.

"You asshole," he said to me. "You are so fucked."

It took a long time before anyone answered. "Mr. Goddard," Chad said in a low, deferential voice. "I'm sorry to call so early in the morning, but this is extremely important. My name is Chad Pierson, and I work at Trion." He spoke a few minutes more, and slowly his malevolent grin began to fade.

"Yes, sir," he said.

He thrust the phone at me, looking deflated. "He says he wants to talk to you."

PART NINE

ACTIVE MEASURES

Active Measures: Russian term for intelligence operations that will affect another nation's policies or actions. These can be either covert or open and can include a wide variety of activities, including assassination.

—*Spy Book: The Encyclopedia of Espionage*

89

It was close to six in the morning when the security guards put me in a locked conference room on the fifth floor—no windows, only one door. The table was littered with scrawl-covered notepads, empty Snapple bottles. There was an overhead projector, a whiteboard that hadn't been erased, and, fortunately, a computer.

I wasn't a prisoner, exactly. I was being "detained." It was made clear to me that if I didn't cooperate, I'd be turned right over to the police, and that didn't seem to be a very good idea.

And Goddard—sounding weirdly calm—had told me that he wanted to speak with me when he got in. He didn't want to hear anything else, which was good, because I didn't know what to say.

Later I learned that Seth had just made it out of the building, though without the truck. I tried e-mailing Jock. I still didn't know how I could explain myself, so I just wrote:

```
Jock—
Need to talk. I want to explain.
Adam
```

But there was no reply.

I remembered, suddenly, that I still had my cell phone with me—I'd tucked it into one of my pockets, and they hadn't found it. I switched it on.

There were five messages, but before I could check my voice mail, the phone rang.

"Yeah," I said.

"Adam. Oh, shit, man." It was Antwoine. He sounded desperate, almost hysterical. "Oh, man. Oh, shit. I don't want to go back in. Shit, I don't want to go back inside."

"Antwoine, what are you talking about? Start from the beginning."

"These guys tried to break in your dad's apartment. They must've thought it was empty."

I felt a surge of irritation. Hadn't the neighborhood kids figured out yet that there was nothing in my dad's shithole apartment worth breaking in *for?*

"Jesus, are you okay?" I said.

"Oh, *I'm* okay. Two of 'em got away, but I grabbed the slower guy—oh, *shit!* Oh, man, I don't want to get in trouble now! You gotta help me."

This was a conversation I really didn't feel like having, not now. I could hear some kind of animal noise in the background, some sort of moaning or scuffling or something. "Calm down, man," I said. "Take a deep breath and sit down."

"I'm sittin' on the motherfucker right now. What's freaking me out is this fucker says he knows you."

"*Knows* me?" Suddenly I got a funny feeling. "Describe the guy, could you?"

"I don't know, he's a white guy—"

"His face, I mean."

Antwoine sounded sheepish. "Right now? Kinda red and mushy. My bad. I think I broke his nose."

I sighed. "Oh, Jesus, Antwoine, ask him what his name is."

Antwoine put down the phone. I heard the low rumble of Antwoine's voice, followed immediately by a yelp. Antwoine came back on. "He says his name is Meacham."

I flashed on an image of Arnold Meacham, broken and bleeding, lying on my dad's kitchen floor under three hundred pounds of Antwoine Leonard, and I felt a brief, blessed spasm of pleasure. Maybe I *had* been watched when I'd dropped by my dad's apartment. Maybe Meacham and his goons figured I'd hidden something there.

"Oh, I wouldn't worry about it," I said. "I promise you that asshole's not going to cause you any more trouble." If I were Meacham, I thought, I'd go into the witness protection program.

Antwoine now sounded relieved. "Look, I'm really sorry about this, man."

"Sorry? Hey, don't apologize. Believe me, that's the first piece of good news I've heard in a long time."

And it would probably be the last.

I figured I had a few hours to kill before Goddard would show up, and I couldn't just sit there anguishing over what I'd done, or what would be done to me. So I did what I always do to pass the time: I went on the Internet.

That was how I began to put some things together.

The door to the conference room opened. It was one of the security guards from before.

"Mr. Goddard's downstairs at the press conference," the guard said. He was tall, around forty, wore wire-rim glasses. His blue Trion uniform fit badly. "He said you should go down to the Visitors Center."

I nodded.

The main lobby of Building A was hectic with people, loud voices, photographers and reporters swarming all over the place. I stepped out of the elevator into the chaos, feeling disoriented. I couldn't really make out what anyone was saying in the hubbub; it was all background noise to me. One of the doors that led to the huge futuristic auditorium kept opening and closing. I caught glimpses of a giant image of Jock Goddard projected on a screen, heard his amplified voice.

I elbowed my way through the crowd. I thought I heard someone call my name, but I kept going, moving slowly, zombielike.

The auditorium's floor sloped down to a glittering pod of a stage, where Goddard was standing in a spotlight, wearing his black mock turtleneck and brown tweed jacket. He looked like a professor of classics at a small New England college, except for the orange TV makeup on his face. Behind him was a huge screen on which his talking head was projected five or six feet high.

The place was packed with journalists, glaringly bright with TV camera lights.

". . . This acquisition," he was saying, "will double the size of our sales force, and it will double and in some sectors even triple our market penetration." I didn't know what he was talking about. I stood in the back of the theater, listening.

"By bringing together two great companies, we're creating one world-class technology leader. Trion Systems is now without question one of the world's leading consumer electronics companies.

"And I'd like to make one more announcement," Goddard went on. He gave a twinkle-eyed pixie smile. "I've always believed in the importance of giving back. So this morning Trion is pleased to announce the establishment of an exciting new charitable foundation. Beginning with seed money of five million dollars, this new foundation hopes, over the course of the next several years, to put a computer into thousands of public schools in America, in school districts that don't have the resources to provide computers for their students. We think this is the best way to bridge the digital divide. This is a venture that's long been in the works at Trion. We call it the AURORA Project—for Aurora, the Greek goddess of the dawn. We believe the AURORA Project will welcome the dawn of a bright new future for all of us in this great country."

There was a smattering of polite applause.

"Finally, let me extend a warm welcome to the nearly thirty thousand talented and hardworking employees of Wyatt Telecommunications to the Trion family. Thank you very much." Goddard bowed his head slightly and stepped off the stage. More applause, which gradually swelled into an enthusiastic ovation.

The giant projection of Jock Goddard's face dissolved into a TV news broadcast—CNBC's morning financial program, *Squawk Box*.

On half the screen, Maria Bartiromo was broadcasting from the floor of the New York Stock Exchange. On the other half of the screen was the Trion logo and a graph of its share price over the last few minutes—a line that went straight up.

"—as trading in Trion Systems hit record volume," she was saying. "Trion shares have already almost doubled and show no sign of slowing down, after the announcement before the bell this morning by Trion founder and chief executive officer Augustine Goddard that it's acquiring one of its main competitors, the troubled Wyatt Telecommunications."

I felt a tap on my shoulder. It was Flo, elegant, a grave expression on her face. She was wearing a wireless headset. "Adam, can you please come to the Penthouse Executive Reception Suite? Jock wants to see you."

I nodded but kept watching. I wasn't really able to think clearly.

Now the picture on the big screen showed Nick Wyatt being hustled out of Wyatt headquarters by a couple of guards. The wide-angle shot took in the building's reflecting glass, the emerald turf outside, grazing flocks of journalists. You could tell that he was both furious and humiliated as he did the perp walk.

"Wyatt Telecommunications was a debt-plagued company, nearly three billion dollars in debt, when the stunning news leaked out late yesterday that the company's flamboyant founder, Nicholas Wyatt, had signed a secret and unauthorized agreement, without the vote or even the knowledge of his board of directors, to acquire a small California-based startup called Delphos, a tiny company without any revenue, for five hundred million dollars in cash," Maria Bartiromo was saying.

The camera zoomed in closer on the man. Tall and burly, hair gleaming like black enamel, coppery tan. Nick Wyatt in the flesh. The camera moved in even closer. His formfitting dove-gray silk shirt was dappled with flop sweat. He was being trundled into a town car. He had this "What the fuck did they do to me?" expression on his face. I knew the feeling.

"That left Wyatt without enough to cover its debt payments. The company's board met yesterday afternoon and announced the firing of Mr. Wyatt for gross violations of corporate governance, just moments before bondholders forced the sale of the company to Trion Systems at a fire-sale price of ten cents on the dollar. Mr. Wyatt was unavailable for comment, but a spokesman said he was resigning to spend more time with his family. Nick Wyatt is unmarried and has no children. David?"

Another tap on my shoulder. "I'm sorry, Adam, but he wants to see you right now," Flo said.

91

On the way up to the penthouse the elevator stopped at the cafeteria, and a man in an Aloha shirt with a ponytail got in.

"Cassidy," Mordden said. He was clutching a cinnamon-swirl bun and a cup of coffee, and he didn't seem surprised to see me. "The Sammy Glick of the microchip. Word has it that Icarus's wings have melted."

I nodded.

He bowed his head. "It's true what they say. Experience is something you don't get until just after you need it."

"Yep."

He pressed a button and was silent while the doors closed and the cabin ascended. It was just me and him. "I see you're going up to the penthouse. The Executive Reception Suite. I take it you're not receiving dignitaries or Japanese businessmen."

I just looked at him.

"Now perhaps you finally understand the truth about our fearless leader," he said.

"No, I don't think I do. As a matter of fact, I don't even understand *you*. For some reason, you're the one person here who has utter contempt for Goddard, everyone knows it. You're rich. You don't need to work. Yet you're still here."

He shrugged. "By my choice. I told you, I'm fireproof."

"What the hell does that mean, already? Look, you're never going to see my ass again. You can tell me now. I'm outta here. I'm fucking dead."

"Yes, roadkill is, I believe, the term of art around here." He blinked once. "I'll actually miss you. Millions wouldn't." He was making a joke out of it, but I knew he was trying to say something heartfelt. For whatever reason, he'd actually taken a liking to me. Or maybe it was just pity. With a guy like Mordden, it was hard to tell.

"Enough with the riddles," I said. "Will you please explain what the hell you're talking about?"

Mordden smirked, did a fairly passable imitation of Ernst Stavro Blofeld. "Since you're about to die, Mr. Bond—" He broke off. "Oh, I wish I could lay it all out for you. But I'd never violate the nondisclosure agreement I signed eighteen years ago."

"Mind putting it in terms my puny earthling mind can comprehend?"

The elevator stopped, the doors opened, and Mordden got out. He put his hand on one of the doors to hold it open. "That nondisclosure agreement is now worth about ten million dollars to me in Trion stock. Perhaps twice that, at today's share price. It certainly wouldn't be in my interest to jeopardize that arrangement by breaking my contractually obligated silence."

"What sort of NDA?"

"As I said, I surely don't wish to jeopardize my lucrative arrangement with Augustine Goddard by telling you that the famous Goddard modem was invented not by Jock Goddard, a rather mediocre engineer if brilliant corporate gamesman, but by yours truly. Why would I want to jeopardize ten million dollars by revealing that the technological breakthrough that transformed this company into a powerhouse of the communications revolution was the brainchild not of the corporate gamesman but of one of his earliest hires, a lowly engineer? Goddard could have had it for free, as my corporate contract stipulated, but he wanted sole credit. That was worth a good deal of money to him. Why should I want to reveal such a thing and thereby tarnish the legend, the sterling reputation of, what was it *Newsweek* once called him, 'Corporate America's Senior Statesman'? Certainly it would not be politic of me to point out the hollowness of Jock Goddard's whole Will Rogers shtick, that down-to-earth cornpone cracker-barrel image that cloaks such ruthlessness. For heaven's sake, that would be like telling you there's no

Santa Claus. Why would I want to disillusion you—and risk my financial bounty?"

"You're telling me the truth?" was all I could think to say.

"I'm not telling you anything," Mordden said. "It wouldn't be in my interest. Adieu, Cassidy."

92

I'd never seen anything like the penthouse of Trion Building A.

It didn't look at all like the rest of Trion—no choked offices or cluttered cubicles, no industrial-gray wall-to-wall carpeting or fluorescent lights.

Instead, it was a huge open space with floor-to-ceiling windows through which the sunlight sparkled. The floors were black granite, oriental rugs here and there, the walls some kind of gleaming tropical wood. The space was broken up by banks of ivy, clusters of designer-looking chairs and sofas, and right in the center of the room, a giant freestanding waterfall—the water rushed from some unseen fountain over rugged pinkish stones.

The Executive Reception Suite. For receiving important visitors: cabinet secretaries, senators and congressmen, CEOs, heads of state. I'd never seen it before, and I didn't know anyone who had, and no wonder. It didn't look very Trion. Not very democratic. It was dramatic, intimidating, grandiose.

A small round dining table was being set in the area between the indoor waterfall and a fireplace with roaring gas flames on ceramic logs. Two young Latinos, a man and a woman in maroon uniforms, were speaking quietly in Spanish as they put out silver coffee- and teapots, baskets of pastries, pitchers of orange juice. Three place settings.

Baffled, I looked around, but there was no one else. No one waiting for me. All of a sudden there was a *bing*, and a small set of brushed-steel elevator doors on the other side of the room slid open.

Jock Goddard and Paul Camilletti.

They were laughing loudly, both of them giddy, high as kites. Goddard caught a glimpse of me, stopped midlaugh, and said, "Well, there he is. You'll excuse us, Paul—*you* understand."

Camilletti smiled, patted Goddard's shoulder and remained in the elevator as the old man emerged, the doors closing behind him. Goddard strode across the big open space almost at a trot.

"Walk with me to the john, will you?" he said to me. "Gotta wash off this damned makeup."

Silently, I followed him over to a glossy black door that was marked with little silver male-and-female silhouettes. The lights went on as we entered. It was a spacious, sleek rest room, all glass and black marble.

Goddard looked at himself in the mirror. Somehow he seemed a little taller. Maybe it was his posture: he wasn't quite as hunched as usual.

"Christ, I look like fucking Liberace," he said as he worked up soapsuds in his hands and began splashing his face. "You've never been up here, have you?"

I shook my head, watching him in the mirror as he ducked his head down toward the basin and then up again. I felt a strange tangle of emotions—fear, anger, shock—that was so complex that I didn't know what to feel.

"Well, you know the business world," he went on. He seemed almost apologetic. "The importance of theatrics—pageantry, pomp and circumstance, all that crap. I could hardly meet the president of Russia or the crown prince of Saudi Arabia in my shabby little cubbyhole downstairs."

"Congratulations," I said softly. "It's been a big morning."

He toweled off his face. "More theatrics," he said dismissively.

"You knew Wyatt would buy Delphos, no matter what it cost," I said. "Even if it meant going broke."

"He couldn't resist," Goddard said. He tossed the towel, now stained orange-brown, onto the marble counter.

"No," I said. I became aware of my heartbeat starting to accelerate. "Not so long as he believed you were about to announce this big exciting breakthrough on the optical chip. But there never was an optical chip, was there?"

Goddard grinned his little pixie smile. He turned, and I followed him out of the rest room. I kept going: "That's why there were no patents filed, no HR files. . . ."

"The optical chip," he said, almost lunging across the oriental rugs toward the dining table, "exists only in the fevered minds and blotched notebooks of a handful of third-raters at a tiny, doomed company in Palo Alto. Chasing a fantasy, which may or may not happen in your lifetime. Certainly not in mine." He sat at the table, gestured to the place next to his.

I sat, and the two uniformed attendants, who'd been standing against the bank of ivy at a discreet distance, came forward, poured us each coffee. I was more than frightened and angry and confused; I was deeply exhausted.

"They may be third-raters," I said, "but you bought their company more than three years ago."

It was, I admit, an educated guess—the lead investor in Delphos was, according to the filings I'd come across on the Internet, a venture capital fund based in London whose money was channeled through a Cayman Islands investment vehicle. Which indicated that Delphos was actually owned, at a remove of about five shell companies and fronts, by a major player.

"You're a smart fellow," Goddard said, grabbing a sweet roll and tucking into it greedily. "The true ownership chain is pretty damned hard to unwind. Help yourself to a pastry, Adam. These raspberry-and-cream-cheese things are *killer*."

Now I understood why Paul Camilletti, a man who crossed every T and dotted every I, had conveniently "forgotten" to sign the no-shop clause on the term sheet. Once Wyatt saw that, he knew he had less than twenty-four hours to "steal" the company away from Trion—no time to get board approval, even if his board would have approved it. Which they probably wouldn't have anyway.

I noticed the unoccupied third place setting, and I wondered who the other guest would be. I had no appetite, didn't feel like drinking coffee. "But the only way to make Wyatt swallow the hook," I said, "was to have it come from a spy he thought he'd planted." My voice was trembling, and now I was feeling anger most of all.

"Nick Wyatt's a very suspicious man," Goddard said. "I understand him—I'm the same way. He's sorta like the CIA—they never believe a single damned scrap of intel unless they've gotten it by subterfuge."

I took a sip of ice water, which was so cold it made my throat ache. The only sound in this vast space was the splashing and burbling of the waterfall. The bright light hurt my eyes. It felt cheery in here, weirdly so. The waitress approached with a crystal pitcher of water to refill my glass, but Goddard waved a hand. "*Muchos gracias*. You two can be excused, I think we're all set here. Could you ask our other guest to join us, please?"

"It's not the first time you've done this, is it?" I said. Who was it who'd told me that whenever Trion was on the brink of failure, a competitor of theirs always made some disastrous miscalculation, and Trion came back stronger than ever?

Goddard gave me a sidelong glance. "Practice makes perfect."

My head swam. It was Paul Camilletti's resume and bio that gave it away. Goddard had hired him away from a company called Celadon Data, which was at the time the biggest threat to Trion's existence. Soon after, Celadon made a legendary technological gaffe—a Betamax-over-VHS kind of misstep—and went Chapter Eleven just before Trion scooped them up.

"Before me, there was Camilletti," I said.

"And others before him." Goddard took a swig of coffee. "No, you weren't the first. But I'd say you were the best."

The compliment stung. "I don't understand how you convinced Wyatt the mole idea could work," I said.

Goddard glanced up as the elevator opened, the same one he'd come up on.

Judith Bolton. My breath stopped.

She was wearing a navy suit and white blouse and looked very crisp and corporate. Her lips and fingernails were coral. She came up to Goddard, gave him a quick kiss on the lips. Then she reached over to me, clasped my hand in both of hers. They gave off a faint herbal scent and felt cold.

She sat down on Goddard's other side, unfolded a linen napkin on her lap.

"Adam's curious how you convinced Wyatt," Goddard said.

"Oh, I didn't have to twist Nick's arm, exactly," she said with a throaty laugh.

"You're far more subtle than that," Goddard said.

I stared at Judith. "Why me?" I said finally.

"I'm surprised you ask," she said. "Look at what you've done. You're a natural."

"That and the fact that you had me by the balls because of the money."

"Plenty of people in corporations color outside the lines, Adam," she said, leaning in toward me. "We had lots of choices. But you stood out from the crowd. You were far and away the most qualified. A pitch-perfect gift of blarney, plus father issues."

Anger welled up inside me until I couldn't sit there anymore listening. I rose, stood over Goddard, said: "Let me ask you something. What do you think Elijah would think of you now?"

Goddard looked at me blankly.

"Elijah," I repeated. "Your son."

"Oh, gosh, right, Elijah," Goddard said, his puzzlement slowly turning to wry amusement. "That. Right. Well, that was Judith's inspiration." He chuckled.

The room seemed to be spinning slowly and getting brighter, more washed out. Goddard peered at me with twinkling eyes.

"Adam," Judith said, all concern and empathy. "Sit down, please."

I just stood staring.

"We were concerned," she said, "that you might start to get suspicious if it all seemed to come too easily. You're an extremely bright, intuitive young man. Everything had to make sense, or it would start to unravel. We couldn't risk that."

I flashed on Goddard's lake-house study, the trophies that I now knew were fakes. Goddard's sleight-of-hand talent, the way the trophy somehow got knocked to the floor. . . .

"Oh, *you* know," Goddard said, "the old man's got a soft spot for me, I remind him of his dead son, all that bullshit? Makes sense, right?"

"Can't leave these things to chance," I said hollowly.

"Precisely," said Goddard.

"Very, very few people could have done what you did," Judith said. She smiled. "Most wouldn't have been able to endure the doubleness, straddle the line the way you did. You're a remarkable person, I hope you know that. That's why we singled you out in the first place. And you more than proved us right."

"I don't believe this," I whispered. My legs felt wobbly, my feet unsteady. I had to get the hell out of there. "I don't fucking believe this."

"Adam, I know how difficult this must be for you," Judith said gently.

My head was throbbing like an open wound. "I'll go clear out my office."

"You'll do no such thing," Goddard cried out. "You're not resigning. I won't allow it. Clever young fellows like you are all too rare. I *need* you on the seventh floor."

A shaft of sunlight blinded me; I couldn't see their faces.

"And you'd trust me?" I said bitterly, shifting to one side to get the sun out of my face.

Goddard exhaled. "Corporate espionage, my boy, is as American as apple pie and Chevrolet. For fuck's sake, how do you think America became an economic superpower? Back in 1811, a Yankee named Francis Lowell Cabot sailed to Great Britain and stole England's most precious secret—the Cartright loom, cornerstone of the whole damned textile industry. Brought the goddamn Industrial Revolution to America, turned us into a colossus. All thanks to one single act of industrial espionage."

I turned away, stepped across the granite floor. The rubber soles of my work boots squeaked. "I'm done being jerked around," I said.

"Adam," Goddard said. "You're sounding like an embittered loser. Like your father was. And I know you're not—you're a *winner*, Adam. You're brilliant. You have what it takes."

I smiled, then laughed quietly. "Meaning I'm a lying scumbag, basically. A bullshitter. A world-class liar."

"Believe me, you didn't do anything that isn't done every day in corporations the world over. Look, you've got a copy of Sun Tzu in your office—have you read it? All warfare is based on deception, he says. And business is war, everyone knows that. *Business, at the highest levels, is deception.* No one's going to admit that publicly, but it's the truth." His voice softened. "The game is the same everywhere. You just play it better than anyone else. No, you're not a liar, Adam. You're a goddamned master strategist."

I rolled my eyes, shook my head in disgust, turned back toward the elevator.

Very quietly, Goddard said: "Do you know how much money Paul Camilletti made last year?"

Without looking back, I said: "Twenty-eight million."

"You could be making that in a few years. You're worth it to me, Adam. You're tough-minded and resourceful, you're fucking brilliant."

I snorted softly, but I don't think he heard it.

"Did I ever tell you how grateful I am that you saved our bacon on the Guru project? That and a dozen other things. Let me be specific about my gratitude. I'm giving you a raise—to a million a year. With stock options thrown in, given the way our stock's started to move, you could pull in a neat five or six million next year. Double that the year after. You'll be a fucking multimillionaire."

I froze in my tracks. I didn't know what to do, how to react. If I turned around, they'd think I was accepting. If I kept on walking, they'd think I was saying no.

"This is the solid-gold inner circle," Judith said. "You're being offered something anyone would kill for. But remember: it's not being given to you—you've *earned* it. You were *meant* for this line of work. You're as good at this as anybody I've ever met. These last couple of months, you know what you've been selling? Not handheld communicators or cell phones or MP3 players, but *yourself*. You've been selling Adam Cassidy. And *we're buyers*."

"I'm not for sale," I heard myself say, and I was instantly embarrassed.

"Adam, turn around," Goddard said angrily. "Turn around, *now*."

I obeyed, my expression sullen.

"Are you clear on what happens if you walk away?"

I smiled. "Sure. You'll turn me in. To the cops, the FBI, or whatever."

"I'll do no such thing," Goddard said. "I don't want a goddamned word of this ever made public. But without your car, without your apartment, your salary—you'll have no assets. You'll have nothing. What kind of life is that for a talented fellow like you?"

They own you . . . You drive a company car, you live in company housing. . . . Your whole life ain't yours. . . . My dad, my stopped-clock father, was right.

Judith got up from the table, came over very close to me. "Adam, I understand what you're feeling," she said in a hush. Her eyes were moist. "You're hurt, you're angry. You feel betrayed, manipulated. You want to retreat into the comforting, secure, protective anger of a small child. It's totally understandable—we all feel that way sometimes. But now it's time to put away childish things. You see, you haven't fallen into something. You've *found* yourself. It's all good, Adam. It's all good."

Goddard was leaning back in his chair, arms folded. I could see shards of his face reflected in the silver coffeepot, the sugar bowl. He smiled benevolently. "Don't throw it all away, son. I know you'll do the right thing."

93

My Porsche, fittingly, had been towed away. I'd parked it illegally last night; what did I expect?

So I walked out of the Trion building and looked around for a cab, but none was anywhere to be found. I suppose I could have used a phone in the lobby to call for one, but I felt an overwhelming, almost physical need to get out of there. Carrying the white cardboard box filled with the few things from my office, I walked along the side of the highway.

A few minutes later a bright red car pulled over to the curb, slowed down next to me. It was an Austin Mini Cooper, about the size of a toaster oven. The passenger's side window rolled down, and I could smell Alana's lush floral scent wafting through the city air.

She called out to me. "Hey, do you like it? I just got it. Isn't it *fabulous?*"

I nodded and attempted a cryptic smile. "Red's cop bait," I said.

"I never go over the speed limit."

I just nodded.

She said, "Suppose you get down off your motorcycle and give me a ticket?"

I nodded, kept walking, unwilling to play.

She inched her car alongside me. "Hey, what happened to your Porsche?"

"Got towed."

"Yuck. Where're you going?"

"Home. Harbor Suites." Not home for long, I realized with a jolt. I didn't own it.

"Well, you're not *walking* all the way. Not with that *box*. Come on, get in, I'll give you a ride."

"No thanks."

She followed alongside, driving slowly on the shoulder of the road. "Oh, come on, Adam, don't be *mad*."

I stopped, went over to the car, set down my box, put my hands on the car's low roof. Don't be mad? All along I'd been torturing myself because I thought I was manipulating *her*, and she was just doing a goddamned job. "You—they told you to sleep with me, didn't they?"

"Adam," she said sensibly. "Get real. That wasn't part of the job description. That's just what HR calls a fringe benefit, right?" She laughed her swooping laugh, and it chilled me. "They just wanted me to guide you along, pass along leads, that sort of thing. But then you came after *me*. . . ."

"They just wanted you to guide me along," I echoed. "Oh, man. Oh, man. Makes me ill." I picked up the box and resumed walking.

"Adam, I was just doing what they *told* me to do. You of all people should understand that."

"Like we'll ever be able to trust each other? Even now—you're just doing what they want you to, aren't you?"

"Oh, please," said Alana. "Adam, darling. Don't be so goddamned paranoid."

"And I actually thought we had a nice relationship going," I said.

"It was fun. I had a *great* time."

"Did you."

"God, don't take it so seriously, Adam! It's just sex. *And* business. What's wrong with that? Trust me, I wasn't *faking* it!"

I kept walking, looking around for a cab, but there was nothing in sight. I didn't even know this part of town. I was lost.

"Come *on*, Adam," she said, inching the Mini along. "Get in the car."

I kept going.

"Oh, come on," she said, her voice like velvet, suggesting everything, promising nothing. "Will you just get in the *car*?"

ACKNOWLEDGMENTS

Roll the credits. They're woefully long, but this one's been in development and production a long time.

Researching my other novels has taken me around the world and into places like KGB headquarters in Moscow, but nothing prepared me for how strange and fascinating I'd find the world of the American high-tech corporation. No one opened more doors to me, or gave of his time more generously, than my old friend David Hsiao of Cisco Systems, where I was also helped immensely by Tom Fallon, Dixie Garr, Pete Long, Richard Henkus, Gene Choy, Katie Foster, Bill LePage, Armen Hovanessian, Sue Zanner, and Molly Tschang. At Apple Computer, Kate Lepow was enormously helpful. At Nortel, my friend Carter Kersh was a thoughtful (and witty) guide, arranging for me to meet his colleagues, including Martin McNarney, Alyene Mclennan, Matt Portoni, Raj Raman, Guyves Achtari, and Alison Steel. I also had some interesting conversations with Matt Zanner of Hewlett Packard, Ted Sprague of Ciena, Rich Wyckoff of Marimba, Rich Rothschild of Ariba, Bob Scordino of EMC, Adam Stein of Juniper Networks, and Colin Angle of iRobot.

Some very smart friends helped me dream up the financial shenanigans and stealth tactics in the background of the story. They included Roger McNamee, Jeff Bone, Glover Lawrence, and especially my friend Giles McNamee, who brainstormed with me in the spirit of a true unindicted co-conspirator. Nell Minow of The Corporate Library in Washington helped me understand boardroom politics and corporate governance.

In the area of corporate security and intelligence, I got some invaluable assistance from some of the greats in the field, including Leonard Fuld, Arthur Hulnick, George K. Campbell, Mark H. Beaudry, Dan Geer, and the corporate espionage expert Ira Winkler. The legal background of *Paranoia* benefited from the advice of my great friend Joe Teig; Jackie Nakamura of Day Casebeer Madrid & Batchelder (and thanks to Alex Beam for introducing us); and Robert Stein of Pryor Cashman Sherman & Flynn; as well as two of his colleagues, Jeffrey Johnson and particularly Jay Shapiro. Adam's expertise in cool new tech products came from Jim Mann of Compaq, the lead designer of the iPaq; Bert Keely of Microsoft; Henry Holtzman of MIT's Media Lab; Simson Garfinkel; Joel Evans of Geek.com; Wes Salmon of PDABuzz.com; and especially Greg Joswiak, Vice President of Hardware Product Marketing at Apple Computer.

Some of Adam's youthful exploits were inspired by the tales of Keith McGrath, Jim Galvin of the Boston Police, and Emily Bindinger. On Francis X. Cassidy's medical condition, I was helped by my brother, Dr. Jonathan Finder, and Karen Heraty, that angel of a nurse. Jack McGeorge of the Public Safety Group helped me, as always, with numerous technical details. My close friend Rick Weissbourd contributed in all sorts of ways. I've been fortunate to have the help of some excellent research assistants, including John H. Romero, Michael Lane, and the great Kevin Biehl. And my assistant, Rachel Pomerantz, is truly the best.

I'm awed by the enormous enthusiasm and support of the entire talented publishing team at St. Martin's Press, including John Sargent, Sally Richardson, Matthew Shear, and John Cunningham; in marketing, Matthew Baldacci, Jim DiMiero, and Nancy Trypuc; in publicity, John Murphy and Gregg Sullivan; Mike Storrings, Christina Harcar, Mary Beth Roche, Joe McNeely, Laura Wilson, Tom Siino, Tom Leigh, and Andy LeCount. To have a whole publishing house rooting for you is a rare thing in any writer's life, and I extend my deepest thanks to all of them.

Howie Sanders of the United Talent Agency has been an enthusiastic supporter of this book from the beginning. My literary agent, Molly Friedrich, is just all-round terrific: unswervingly loyal, smart, sage, and just really good people.

My brother, Henry Finder, the editorial director of *The New Yorker*, is a remarkable editor. Fortunately, he's my first reader and editor and collaborator as well; his contribution to this novel was truly immeasurable. And Keith Kahla, my editor at St. Martin's Press, is not only a marvelous editor but also a diplomat, a lobbyist, a tireless advocate, and a behind-the-scenes generalissimo with the patience of a saint. I'm grateful to him more than I can say, and certainly more than he'd allow me to say here.